THE CIRCUS TRAIN CONSPIRACY

THE CIRCUS TRAIN CONSPIRACY

EDWARD MARSTON

Allison & Busby Limited
12 Fitzroy Mews
London W1T 6DW
allisonandbusby.com

First published in Great Britain by Allison & Busby in 2017.
This paperback edition published by Allison & Busby in 2018.

A CIP catalogue record for this book is available from
the British Library.

10 9 8 7 6 5 4 3 2 1

ISBN 978-0-7490-2137-5

Typeset in 10.5/15 pt Adobe Garamond Pro by
Allison & Busby Ltd.

The paper used for this Allison & Busby publication
has been produced from trees that have been legally sourced
from well-managed and credibly certified forests.

Printed and bound by
CPI Group (UK) Ltd, Croydon, CR0 4YY

CHAPTER ONE

1860

During its stay in Carlisle, the circus had made a vast number of friends and many of them had turned up at the railway station to bid farewell to their visitors. The crowd consisted largely of cheering women, grateful for the thrilling entertainment they and their families had enjoyed, and tearful children, overwhelmed by a sense of loss and fearing that it might be an eternity before a circus of such size and quality visited the area again. While they were diverted by the sight of the animals being loaded – sometimes with great difficulty – into wagons, they were disappointed to see no sign of the clowns who'd brought so much merriment to Cumberland. Without realising it, however, they'd already rubbed shoulders with them on the platform as the men, without their make-up and garish costumes, boarded the train.

The noise was deafening. The hiss of steam, the slamming of carriage doors and the continuous hubbub of well-wishers were amplified by the cacophony set up by protesting horses and mutinous lions. When the whistle blew to signal departure, there was a scornful reply from Rosie the elephant, trumpeting her displeasure at being forced to leave the comfort of the compound they'd built for her. Waved off by the crowd, the first of the two trains pulled away with a rising chorus of dissent from the stock wagons. It was going to be an ear-splitting journey.

Mauro Moscardi, the owner of Moscardi's Magnificent Circus, sat back in a first-class compartment and pulled on a cigar. He was a short, portly, still handsome man of middle years with a swarthy complexion and a twirling moustache. When he was acting as ringmaster, he seemed to grow in stature and had a booming voice that could reach everyone in the audience, no matter how large it might be. Having been born and brought up in England, he could speak the language perfectly. Yet when he was among strangers, he preferred to use a bogus Italian accent supplemented by expressive gesticulations. Alone with his wife, no pretence was needed.

'I still can't get used to travelling by train,' he said, peevishly.

'Railways have been a blessing to us,' she argued. 'When your father was on tour with the circus, he was lucky if they made seven or eight miles a day. Bad weather slowed them down even more.'

'But he was carrying on a *tradition*, my love, and tradition is everything in the world of circus.'

'Would you rather ride to Newcastle in our caravan? It's about sixty miles away. This train will get us there by noon.'

'What's the rush? We're going through beautiful countryside. We'd enjoy it much more if we took our time.'

'And you'd never stop complaining how slowly we moved,' she said with a smile. 'You must learn to accept progress, Mauro.'

'Tradition is more important.'

'Your father would've loved railways – God rest his soul!'

But her husband was no longer listening because he'd just

glanced out of the window and been captivated by the glorious landscape on view. It was quite stunning. Anne gave his arm an affectionate squeeze. Now approaching fifty, she'd somehow preserved the startling prettiness that had caught his eye when he'd first seen her. She was a promising young acrobat in those days and the subject of constant male attention. To the consternation of her other suitors, Mauro Moscardi had wooed and won her with the promise that they would one day run the circus together. She had never, for a moment, regretted marrying him.

The only other occupant of the compartment was her dog, the Princess of Pomerania, a small poodle with eyes that sparkled with intelligence and with a fluffy white mane around her neck thrown into relief by the well-clipped body. Anne and the Princess were amongst the most popular performers. In a circus dominated by equestrian acts, they were also a welcome variation from the general fare. Nestling against her mistress, the dog gave an elaborate yawn before closing her eyes. While the animal was her most prized possession, Anne Moscardi was also travelling with her jewellery. It was locked away securely in the large strongbox standing on the floor. After a long and profitable visit to Carlisle, it also contained a substantial amount of money.

Moscardi eventually turned his head away from the window.

'Gianni is to blame,' he decided.

'Your brother is a genius.'

'We should never have let him go to America.'

'The month he spent there with a circus was a revelation,' she said. 'They not only travelled everywhere by train, they performed in a marquee that was easy to transport. Most of our rivals only visit towns that have a big hall or amphitheatre they can use, so there's a limit to the places where they can perform. Since we are now under canvas, Moscardi's Magnificent Circus can go *anywhere*. All we need is an open patch of land.'

'The marquee flaps in a high wind.'

'It's safe and secure.'

'I preferred the wooden structure we used to put up ourselves.'

'It had its virtues,' she conceded, 'but it took an age to erect. Also, it was too similar to the one used by Pablo Fanque's Circus and look what happened to that. The timber balcony collapsed during a performance in Leeds, killing his wife and causing serious injuries to hundreds of people.'

'That was a freak accident.'

'It was also a warning to others. Canvas is best, Mauro.'

'That's a matter of opinion,' he murmured.

'The marquee has brought us luck. Since we started using it, we've never had the slightest trouble.'

'Don't tempt Providence.'

'You always say that.'

'I can't help being superstitious, Anne. It's in my blood.'

She leant across to give him a peck on the cheek then turned her attention to the scenery outside. At their request, the hired train was travelling at a moderate pace out of consideration for their precious livestock. In earlier days, cattle, sheep, pigs and poultry were taken to market in open pens but roofs had now been added to many of the wagons. The circus horses therefore travelled in relative comfort, with straw at their feet and hay nets to keep them well fed during the journey. Locked in their cages, the lions were also under cover.

Rosie the elephant was the only animal in an open wagon. It was at the rear of the train next to the brake van. The sight of such a large and rare creature caused great interest in every station they passed through. Everyone on the platforms stared in wonder and waved. Labourers in the fields stopped to gape open-mouthed. At one point, when Rosie lifted her trunk and bellowed aloud, she frightened a herd of sheep so much that they scampered over the hillside to escape being trampled to death by the fearsome monster rolling towards them.

The train went on through open countryside filled with scenic delights. Fells, crags, streams, woodland, castles, churches, quaint cottages and sumptuous manor houses went past and the vestiges of Hadrian's Wall came frequently into view. One by one, stations of varying sizes popped up – Scotby, Wetheral, How Mill, Milton, Low Row, Rose Hill, Greenhead, Haltwhistle, Bardon Mill and Haydon Bridge where they crossed the South Tyne river. Moscardi and his wife were now in Northumberland.

Anne eventually broke the long silence.

'This is the way to travel,' she said, expansively. 'We don't have to ride along bad roads the way we used to and camp overnight like Gypsies. That's all in the past. We can travel in style now.'

'It's too expensive.'

'I think it's worth every penny.'

'Well, I don't.'

'Sit back and relax, Mauro. We worked hard in Carlisle. We're entitled to a rest and that's exactly what the railway gives us.' She spread her hands. 'This is sheer bliss to me.'

Anne spoke too soon. The moment the words left her mouth, there was an ominous screeching sound as the engine driver suddenly tried to slow the train down for an emergency stop. It juddered, swayed and sent up showers of sparks from the line. Fear spread like wildfire. Something was amiss. Driver and fireman were patently struggling to control the train. After another series of convulsions, there was an awesome thud as the locomotive hit an obstruction.

Mauro, his wife and the dog were thrown across the compartment.

* * *

9

Two timber sleepers wreaked havoc. Laid across the rails, they made the engine pitch off the line. Miraculously remaining upright, it continued on its way along a grass verge, its wheels digging deep into soft earth that helped it to slow more dramatically. Carriages and wagons were dragged along behind it, rocking precariously as they parted company with the rails yet somehow regaining enough balance to avoid being overturned. It was terrifying. People yelled out, animals became hysterical and, when it finally came to a halt against the trunk of a tree, the locomotive hissed angrily. Behind it, zigzagging its way along the grass, was the rolling stock, most of it perched at crazy angles. It was a scene of chaos.

Moscardi's Magnificent Circus had lost its magnificence.

CHAPTER TWO

Now that they had a young baby, days began even earlier at the Colbeck household and took on a very different form. In the past, Madeleine would have enjoyed a leisurely breakfast with her husband before spending the morning at her easel bringing a new painting to life. The arrival of Helen Rose Colbeck had changed everything. Her needs took priority and, though they had a nanny to help them, they had to cope with the largely unforeseen pressures of parenting. It was an education for both of them. When he left home that morning, therefore, Colbeck did so with mixed feelings, sad to leave his beautiful daughter yet embracing the sense of release. By the time he reached his office in Scotland Yard, domestic concerns had been put firmly aside. An article in the newspaper soon caught his attention and sent him straight into the superintendent's office.

'Good morning, sir,' he said, holding up his copy of *The Times*. 'Have you seen this item about a train crash?'

'I have, Inspector.'

'Then I hope you'll send me to Northumberland immediately.'

'I most certainly will not,' said Tallis, brusquely. 'We've had no request for your services from the railway company and – if you'd taken the trouble to read the article in its entirety – you'd have seen that nobody was actually killed and that the train itself was, by the grace of God, spared any irreparable damage.'

'Someone tried to destroy the circus,' argued Colbeck.

'It's a matter for the local constabulary.'

'They can't cope with something on this scale, Superintendent.'

'Then they will have to bring in help – but it will *not* come from here.'

His long years in the army had given Edward Tallis the habit of command and the ability to make firm decisions. It had also left him with an expectation of unquestioning obedience. Since the inspector was his most talented detective, he was loath to send him off to another part of the country when his skills were needed in the capital. And there was another reason why Tallis was unmoved by the disaster in Northumberland. He had a very low opinion of circuses. In his opinion, they consisted of lawless itinerants offering vulgar entertainment that included half-naked women indulging in all sorts of unseemly exercise. By its very nature, a circus contained and attracted some of the most disreputable elements in society and left audiences dangerously overexcited. Disorder and immorality trailed in its wake, much of it, he believed, because so many hot-blooded foreigners were employed in the sawdust ring. Tallis disliked foreigners. His hatred of Italians was particularly strong.

'I must ask you to think again, sir,' said Colbeck, politely.

'Then you are wasting your breath.'

'I did read the article in its entirety and I noticed something that you seem to have overlooked. The crash *did* result in deaths. One of the horses was so badly injured that it had to be shot.'

'That's neither here nor there.'

'It's of great significance to Mr Moscardi. He has just lost a highly expensive and well-trained Arab horse whose legs were broken when the train came off the line and tossed them around in their wagon. He loves his animals like children, sir.'

'So?'

'Someone was trying to destroy his livelihood. Doesn't that shock you? Had the rolling stock overturned, lives would have been lost and Moscardi's circus might never have survived.'

'Their continued existence is not something that troubles me, Inspector.'

'Then it should,' said Colbeck, sharply. 'Had that train been carrying an army battalion, you'd have dispatched me to Northumberland instantly.'

'Damn your impertinence, man!'

'The circus is in a crisis. It needs help.'

'You are leading a murder investigation here in London. Attend to it.'

'We've already identified the culprit, sir. The evidence against him is overwhelming. It's simply a case of tracking him down.'

'Then leave me in peace and find the man.'

'Inspector Vallence is more than capable of doing that,' said Colbeck. 'It would leave me free to catch the next train to Northumberland.'

'Don't you recognise an order when you hear it?' roared Tallis, rising to his feet and pointing a finger. 'I deploy my detectives in the way that I think fit. Unlike you, I don't regard the death of a circus horse as a reason to dispatch you and Sergeant Leeming northwards. Mr Moscardi must cope without you.'

There was a warning glare in his eye, signalling that the conversation was over. Heaving a sigh, Colbeck turned on his heel and left the room. For the time being, he accepted, he would be forced to remain in London.

His thoughts, however, were with the beleaguered circus.

They'd camped beside the railway line and spent a sleepless night nursing their bruises and wondering who had been responsible for causing the crash. Next morning, Moscardi and his wife had been joined in their caravan by Gianni, younger brother of Mauro. The three of them were assessing the damage.

'We've only had to put down one horse,' said Moscardi, 'but the rest of them are so shaken up that they'll be unable to perform for some time. It's the same with the other animals. Rosie is the worst. Elephants are sensitive creatures. It may take ages to settle her down. They're all so nervous.'

'I know how they feel,' said Anne, uneasily. 'We're on tenterhooks. As for Princess,' she went on, stroking the dog curled up in her lap, 'she won't let me out of her sight.'

'Someone is trying to wreck our circus, my love. From now on, we all have to watch each other's backs.'

'I've got a better idea,' said Gianni, eyes smouldering. 'We know who did this. It's the work of Greenwood's Circus. Why don't we find out where they are and wreak our revenge?'

'No,' said his brother, 'that's not the way to react.'

'You're growing soft in your old age, Mauro.'

'Don't you dare say that to me!'

'It's true,' insisted Gianni. 'When we had trouble from a rival circus in the past, Father would urge us to hit back at them at once. You were always ready to strike the first blow.'

'That was different. We were certain who the villains were.'

'It's the same this time – Greenwood's Circus.'

'The last we heard of them,' Anne reminded him, 'was that they were touring in the West Country. Why come all this way to cause us trouble?'

'It's more than trouble,' protested Gianni. 'They want to kill us off.'

'That's enough,' said Moscardi.

'Are we too cowardly to fight back?'

'Be quiet, Gianni!'

It was said with such force and authority that the younger man lapsed into silence. Gianni Moscardi was an impulsive character, always likely to explode in the face of what he considered an injustice. Now in his forties, he was a lithe man of medium height whose outstanding career as an acrobat had been cut short by a fall from a trapeze, obliging him to use a walking stick. He was still bristling with resentment at the fate that had befallen him.

His brother put a hand on Gianni's shoulder and looked into his eyes.

'We let the law take its course,' he asserted. 'We have no proof that someone from Greenwood's was involved. If they were, there'll be a prosecution. But ask yourself this, Gianni. How could Sam Greenwood and his men have possibly known that we'd be travelling by rail at precisely that time? We always keep our itinerary hidden from other circuses. They'd have no idea we'd be steaming through Haydon Bridge this morning.'

'We may not even have been the targets,' Anne interjected.

'Oh, I think that we were, my love. Someone was expecting us.'

'Someone from Sam Greenwood's circus,' said Gianni.

'No – you can forget about them.'

There was a sudden tension between the brothers. Anne sought to ease it.

'Instead of moaning,' she suggested, 'I think we should count our blessings. Only one train was involved. More than half our animals and our staff were due to be on the second train under Gianni's supervision. And – thank heaven – so were all of the children. They were unharmed because we split up into two groups.'

'That's a good point,' said Moscardi.

'Then here's another one. Nobody was killed. Most of us were bruised and a couple of people lost a little blood but we are otherwise intact. If that isn't a sign of God's mercy, I don't know what is. We live to fight another day.'

'And we *should* fight,' urged Gianni, 'with staves in our hands.'

'You can't fight an invisible enemy.'

'And we can't take the law into our hands,' added Moscardi. 'Let the police get on with their investigation. We've got more than enough to do. There are plans to be made, animals to be calmed down and a lot of frightened people to be reassured. Anne is right. We've had a lucky escape. If the train had been going at full pelt, there could have been a catastrophe.'

'That was Sam Greenwood's intention,' said Gianni, sourly.

'He may not be behind this, Gianni.'

'Then who is?'

Moscardi shrugged. 'Only time will tell.'

The circus had built its reputation on the quality of its artistes and the variety of its animals. Everyone had heard of Moscardi's horses, lions and celebrated elephant. To those who looked after the menagerie, however, there was an even more important member of it and that was Jacko, a much-loved capuchin monkey who was given licence to roam more freely than the other animals. Jacko was small, impish and unpredictable. A reliable performer

.in front of an audience, he was a free spirit when away from it and loved nothing more than causing trouble and playing tricks on everyone. As a rule, the monkey kept everyone laughing but his latest trick aroused no amusement. It provoked sadness and alarm. Jacko had disappeared.

'If this in another of his japes,' said Albert Stagg, ruefully, 'I'll starve the little devil for a whole week.'

'I'll just be glad to get him back,' said his companion.

'Where on earth can he *be*?'

'We'll find him sooner or later.'

'Alive or dead?'

'Hey,' said Brendan Mulryne, rounding on him. 'We'll have none of that kind of talk, if you don't mind. Jacko is fine. He just happens to have got lost, that's all. That crash scared the daylights out of him, Albert, and I'm not surprised. It did the same to me, so it did.'

They presented a complete contrast. Mulryne was a tall, muscular Irishman with enormous hands and a battered face that featured a broken nose, a scarred cheek and a thick lip. One of his ears was almost twice the size of its partner. Stagg, on the other hand, was a short, neat, skinny individual in his thirties with a bald head and protruding eyes. He looked after the monkey and performed with him. Having only been with the circus for a few months, Mulryne was simply searching for a missing animal. Stagg was looking for his best friend.

'He could be anywhere, Brendan,' he said.

'Keep shouting for him every few minutes.'

'My throat is already hoarse.'

'Ignore the pain. Jacko knows your voice. If he hears it, he'll come to you.'

'That's not what happened when we came off the line,'

recalled Stagg. 'Jacko jumped through the open window and ignored me altogether.'

'Thank heavens it was only a monkey who escaped,' said Mulryne. 'If it had been Rosie the elephant or some of the lions, we'd have a real problem.'

'Jacko is just as important to me as *any* of the animals.'

'I know that, but he's not as much of a danger to the public as a lion.'

'I won't rest till we find him.'

Stagg was desperately worried about the monkey. It was almost twenty-four hours since he'd disappeared. They'd searched until dark then started again at dawn. It was now almost noon and there was still no sign of Jacko. Hopelessly lost, the animal would be at the mercy of all sorts of predators. Where would he get food? How would he survive? They'd heard distant gunfire on more than one occasion. Had somebody shot him? The very thought made Stagg shudder.

When they came to a stretch of woodland, they decided to split up.

'Stay within earshot,' advised the Irishman.

'Jacko would be safer in here among the trees. He'd climb out of danger.'

Mulryne grinned. 'Well, don't ask me to climb up after him,' he said. 'You'll have to lure him down somehow.'

'When he hears my voice, he'll respond.'

'I hope you're right, Albert.'

Going in opposite directions, they began to pick their way through the woods. Each of them called for Jacko by name but there was no reply. Every now and then, Mulryne shouted to his friend and got an answering yell to confirm that they were still in touch with each other. As they pressed on, however, Stagg's voice became increasingly faint. Eventually, it disappeared altogether and Mulryne began to get worried. He stopped in a clearing, filled his lungs and bellowed.

'Can you hear me, Albert?'

There was no reply. Cupping his hands, he shouted even louder. 'Where are you?'

This time, there was an answer but it didn't come from Stagg. It was the distinctive squeal of a monkey and it made the Irishman's heart lift. He went off in the direction from which the sound came.

'Don't worry, Jacko,' he said. 'I'm coming.'

The squeals became more excited and acted as a guide. Trampling through the undergrowth, Mulryne rushed on with a sense of relief coursing through his body. The monkey was alive, after all. The search was over. When he got close to the area where the sound was coming from, however, he couldn't see the monkey. Instead, to his horror, he saw something that made his blood run cold. Having led a hard life, the Irishman was not easily shocked but this sight stopped him in his tracks.

Sticking out of the ground, a human hand was waving to him.

CHAPTER THREE

When the message came, Robert Colbeck and Victor Leeming were keeping a house in Wardour Street under surveillance. Since they believed their main suspect was inside, they'd placed men at the rear of the property to prevent an attempt at escape. They were discussing tactics as a uniformed policeman approached.

'The superintendent said I would find you here,' he said, handing a letter to Colbeck. 'It's urgent, sir.'

'Thank you, Constable,' said the other, opening the missive and reading it.

'Is there a reply?'

'I'll deliver it in person.'

'Very good, sir.'

'Come on, Victor,' said Colbeck. 'We're needed elsewhere.'

'But we may be in a position to make an arrest, sir,' complained Leeming.

'Someone else can have the pleasure of doing that.'

'We can't just walk away.'

'Yes, we can. Only one thing would make the superintendent pull us off this job and I fancy that I know what it is.'

Colbeck beckoned to one of the detective constables watching the house and gave him his orders. Confident that his men could handle the situation, he hailed a cab and asked the driver to take them to Scotland Yard. It was not long before he and the sergeant were standing side by side in front of the superintendent. Colbeck had a smile of anticipation but Leeming quailed inwardly. Though he was fearless when confronting violent criminals, he felt his legs turn to rubber whenever he faced Edward Tallis. The superintendent increased the sergeant's discomfort by keeping them waiting for a full minute. When he spoke, it was with obvious regret.

'I've received two telegraphs from Northumberland,' he said, grumpily. 'The first one is from the Newcastle and Carlisle Railway Company.'

'I had a feeling that they'd be in touch,' said Colbeck.

'Is it about this crash?' asked Leeming.

'Be quiet and listen,' said Tallis.

'Someone derailed a circus.'

'Close that irritating orifice known as your mouth.'

'The inspector has already shown me that article in the newspaper.'

'Silence!' Leeming winced and took a cautionary step backwards. 'There's been a development,' explained Tallis, 'and it's a disturbing one.'

'What's happened, sir?' asked Colbeck.

'The body of a woman has been found in a shallow grave not far from the scene. Foul play is evident. I've been asked to send you at the earliest possible opportunity.'

'Does the NCR believe there is a link between the crash and the murder?' asked Colbeck.

'There's no suggestion of that kind. They simply beg for assistance.'

'You said that there were *two* telegraphs.'

'Yes,' said Tallis, face darkening, 'and the second one is from a man whose vile name I hoped never to hear again.' He handed the paper to Colbeck. 'It looks as if Mulryne has ended up in a circus.'

'Would that be *Brendan* Mulryne?' asked Leeming, tentatively.

'It would, alas. Even when he wore a policeman's uniform, he was always something of a performing bear.'

'I liked him, sir. He was a good man to have beside you in a fight.'

'The trouble is that he always *started* the fight.'

Leeming turned to the inspector. 'What does he say?'

'He says very little,' replied Colbeck, 'but I'm just reading between the lines. Mulryne is pleading for us to head north. Strange things are happening up there.'

'When a circus comes to town,' said Tallis, 'there's always trouble.'

'In this case, they didn't even reach town, sir. Someone sought to stop them getting there in one piece. I'll be interested to find out why.' He handed the telegraph back to Tallis. 'It's lucky that Mulryne is involved. He'll be a great help. He's got a policeman's eye.'

'It was usually blackened from his latest brawl.'

'I always enjoyed being on duty with him,' said Leeming. 'I felt safe.'

'Nobody was safe when that mad Irishman was around. He broke every rule of policing. We did the people of London a great service when we dismissed him.'

Colbeck was about to point out that Mulryne had, in fact, been of considerable assistance to them in a private capacity but he decided against doing so. Tallis would never accept that Mulryne could be an asset to the Metropolitan Police Force. In any case, Colbeck had got what he wanted. The Railway Detective was at his best when dealing with crimes relating to the railway system that had spread so quickly and so haphazardly throughout the whole country. He was eager to get to the circus as soon as possible and to learn more about the crash and the mysterious death.

'We'll leave at once, sir,' said Colbeck. 'Inspector Vallence can take over our current investigation. Send him to Wardour Street.'

'But we did all the hard work,' moaned Leeming. 'Why should someone else have the credit of making the arrest? It's not fair.'

'It's an example of teamwork, Sergeant.'

'*We* should get the glory.'

'Don't be so selfish, man,' said Tallis. 'And let's have no more nonsense about glory. Your function is to solve major crimes, not to court approbation.'

Before he could speak again, the sergeant was hustled out of the office by Colbeck. Arguing with Tallis was pointless. It would only delay them and the inspector was anxious to be on their way.

As they walked down the corridor, Leeming asked a jolting question.

'What about your daughter, sir?'

'What about her?'

'Do you really want to go that far away from Helen?'

Colbeck came to an abrupt halt. He thought about the beautiful little girl who'd come into his life and given it a new direction. The child had been a blessing in every way and, since her birth, he'd been fortunate to be based entirely in London. For the first time, he was being torn away from her and it was going to be a painful experience. He tried to control an upsurge of regret.

'No, I don't,' he admitted, 'but duty comes first.'

From the moment when he heard that his daughter was pregnant, Caleb Andrews was convinced that he was about to have a grandson. So firm was his belief that he even named the child beforehand. When Madeleine gave birth to a daughter, therefore, he was at first upset but, the moment he set eyes on her, his disappointment was swiftly supplanted by joy. It was increased by the news that the parents had decided to name the baby after his late wife, Helen. Andrews had been profoundly moved. Every time he saw his granddaughter, he was reminded of his wife. As he looked at her now, sleeping contentedly in her crib, he chided himself for wanting to have a grandson instead.

Madeleine waited until he sat down again before she broke the news.

'Robert is going to be away for a while,' she said.

'A child needs its father close to her, Maddy.'

'That's the ideal situation, I agree, but it's not always possible when the father happens to be a famous detective. His work takes him everywhere.'

'And it's dangerous work at that,' said Andrews. 'I wonder if it isn't time for Robert to find a job with no risks that keeps him in London all the time.'

'You're a fine one to talk,' she said, laughing. 'When you were an engine driver all those years, you were always in danger and often hundreds of miles away.'

'That was different.'

'I don't agree.'

'I was tied hand and foot by the rules of employment.'

'And so is Robert. The main rule is crystal clear. If he's summoned by any railway company – regardless of where it is – then he simply has to go.'

'How much has he told you about this latest case?'

'Very little,' she replied. 'All that he had time to do was to dash off a quick note and have it delivered here by hand. He's off to Northumberland.'

He was appalled. 'You mean that he couldn't even come home to say a proper goodbye to you and the baby?'

'He and Victor Leeming had to catch a train from King's Cross. They're used to making sudden departures. That's why they always keep a change of clothing at Scotland Yard.' She saw the look of anguish on her father's face. 'Are you all right?'

'No,' he croaked, 'I feel sick to my stomach.'

'Can I get you something?' she asked with concern.

'This is not something that can be cured with a pill, Maddy. And I don't think an apology from your husband would make me feel any better.'

'I don't understand.'

'You just told me that he was travelling from King's Cross. That means he'll be on the Great Northern Railway.'

'Ah, I see,' she said, realisation dawning. 'You'd expect him to go to Euston.'

'A train from the LNWR would take him all the way to Carlisle.'

'Robert must have found a quicker route.'

'It's not a question of speed,' he wailed. 'It's a matter of loyalty.'

'You can't expect Robert to use only the London and North Western because you used to work for it. He always carries his Bradshaw with him and chooses the fastest train to get him where he wants to go. Besides, the LNWR only reaches certain parts of the country.'

'If he's going to Northumberland, he can change at Carlisle and pick up a train on the NCR. There's a regular service to Newcastle.'

'I'm sure that Robert has worked out his route very carefully.'

'He should have asked my advice.'

She suppressed a smile. 'I think he already knows what it would have been.'

'Well,' he said, shaking his head, 'I expected more of him than this. He can't be bothered to find time to see you before he goes, then he chooses the wrong train. I thought he'd be more caring as a father, I must say.'

'Nobody could be more considerate as a husband or as a father,' she said, firmly. 'Robert is the kindest man alive. When duty calls, however, he has to respond. He's gone to Northumberland because someone tried to wreck a train that was carrying a circus to Newcastle, and there's been a murder nearby.'

Andrews leapt to his feet. 'There'd be *another* murder if I caught the man who tried to wreck the train. They don't have a punishment strong enough for villains who do that sort of thing. I'm sorry for the circus,' he went on, 'but my sympathy goes to the engine driver and fireman. It must have been an ordeal for them.'

'Robert will send me more details in due course.'

'Well, be sure to pass them on to me, Maddy. Trains are a benefit to everyone, if they're allowed to be. They've changed this country out of all recognition. The trouble is,' he added, worriedly, 'that they're so easy to derail.'

'They call him the Railway Detective.'

'Why is that?'

'Inspector Colbeck got that name when he caught the men behind a train robbery. It was a difficult case,' recalled Mulryne, 'but he solved it in the end. He never gives up.'

'That's good to hear,' said Moscardi. 'I just hope that, when he catches the men behind the crash, he'll hand them over to me.'

'I'd like a crack at them first, Mr Moscardi. When our train came to a dead halt, I banged my head against the side of the compartment. I was holding Jacko at the time. He was so frightened that he hopped through the open window.'

'He's safely back with Albert now. Jacko is a survivor. One of the animals wasn't so lucky.'

'How will you replace that horse?'

'Buying a new one will be easy enough. Training him up to

the right standard is a different matter. It takes time and patience.'

'I know,' said Mulryne, appreciatively. 'You work wonders with them. And even when they're experienced performers, they rehearse day after day.'

'Practice makes perfect.'

The two men were standing beside the gaudy exterior of Moscardi's caravan. In the wake of the crash, constables had come from Hexham to support the railway policeman first to the scene. When the murder victim was discovered, however, it was deemed necessary to involve the Newcastle Constabulary and detectives had been duly dispatched. Not realising that the railway company had already done so, Mulryne had insisted that they should send for Colbeck and put his name on the telegraph because, he boasted, it would make all the difference.

'Thanks to you, Mulryne, the Railway Detective is coming.'

'He's an old friend, Mr Moscardi. We worked well together.'

'Why did you leave the police force?'

Mulryne chuckled. 'That's a long story.'

'Save it until this whole business has been sorted out.'

'Have you decided when we move on?'

'No,' said Moscardi, sadly. 'People involved in the crash are still jangled and so am I. We need time to get over it before we move on. The same goes for the animals, of course. They're all very restive.'

'Jacko won't sit still for a single minute.'

'He's like the rest of us – hurt and afraid.'

'I was hurt,' said Mulryne, straightening his shoulders, 'but I'm certainly not afraid. I want to help Inspector Colbeck catch whoever put those sleepers on the line. Then, of course, there's that poor woman we found.'

'God rest her soul!' said Moscardi. 'We're so worried about our own troubles that we're forgetting about her. If Jacko hadn't found the corpse for us, it might have lain undiscovered for ages. What sort of state would she be in by then?'

'I hate to think.'

'You said that she'd only been killed recently, didn't you?'

'That would be my guess,' replied Mulryne, 'and, I'm sorry to say, I've seen a lot of dead bodies in my time. The ones I hauled out of the Thames were the worst. They were hideously bloated. This woman was different. There was no sign of decomposition. She looked so normal. I've no idea how she died. There wasn't a mark of violence upon her.' He scratched his head. 'I'd love to know who she is and how she got there.'

Victor Leeming would never be reconciled to the notion of rail travel. In his opinion, trains were dirty, noisy, uncomfortable, unreliable and a potential source of danger. He was honest enough to admit that going to Northumberland by road would take vastly longer and would subject him to a very bumpy ride but he still preferred a stagecoach. For Colbeck, however, the railway was always a first choice. He was fascinated by the engineering involved and loved hurtling around the country in the course of his investigations. Since their compartment was almost full when they departed, they had little opportunity at first for private conversation. At a series of stops, they shed the other passengers one by one and eventually finished up alone. Colbeck was deep in thought. Leeming recognised the quiet smile on his lips.

'You're thinking about your daughter, aren't you, sir?'

'What?' said the other, jerked out of his reverie. 'Yes, I was, as a matter of fact. You're very perceptive, Victor.'

'I have children of my own, remember. I think of them all the time.'

'It's only natural.'

'I worry about them misbehaving when I'm not there.'

'Helen is far too young to misbehave but I daresay her turn

will come. However,' he went on, adjusting his position, 'we've indulged ourselves enough. The superintendent didn't send us to Northumberland to daydream about our children. We have a complex case ahead of us.'

'If only it wasn't so far away,' said Leeming.

'We go where we're needed, Victor.'

'That's the trouble.'

Adored by his wife, Leeming would never have been considered attractive by any other woman. He had a kind of unthreatening ugliness and looked wholly out of place in a top hat and frock coat. During his days in uniform, his stocky frame and readiness for action gained him great respect. As a detective, however, he seemed on first acquaintance to be out of his depth. There was an almost apologetic air about him as if he knew how unconvincing he must appear.

'I love circuses,' he said, fondly. 'Who would possibly want to harm one?'

'There's an obvious answer to that.'

'I can't see it.'

'I'm talking about another circus, Victor. There's a fierce rivalry between them. They're always trying to poach each other's artistes or steal each other's ideas.'

'But they wouldn't deliberately set out to destroy each other, would they?'

'It's a possibility we can't rule out.'

'Circuses are always full of such friendly people. There's such a welcoming atmosphere when you go to one. My boys laugh for days after they've seen clowns playing about. A circus makes them happy.'

'That's its intention and why it has a unique place in our culture. But not everyone shares our view of it, I'm afraid,' said Colbeck. 'The superintendent hates them and so do lots of other people.

Town councils in some places refuse to let a circus anywhere near them because they think it breeds mischief.'

'That's all part of the fun.'

'Fun worries some people, Victor. They fear that it can get out of hand. As for the present case,' he continued, 'we can only speculate. I've no doubt that Brendan Mulryne will have his theories and he won't need any encouragement to share them with us.'

Leeming grinned. 'No, he was never shy about thrusting himself forward.' He glanced through the window. 'We're going to spend an age on this train.'

'You'll get your reward when we reach our destination.'

'Why – have you been to Northumberland before?'

'Yes, I once took Madeleine to Wylam Colliery to see Puffing Billy, one of the very earliest locomotives.'

'That's not what *I'd* call a treat, sir.'

'The treat lies in the landscape,' said Colbeck. 'We're not just going to solve two heinous crimes. We're going to one of the most beautiful places in the whole of England.'

The man on the hill had no interest in the landscape. Concealed behind a bush, he used a telescope to look down on the encampment. To his dismay, the circus had a distressing air of normality about it. Hoping to see evidence of injury and widespread damage, he was instead gazing at acrobats practising their routines and animals being fed by their keepers. He could even hear the happy laughter of children carried on the wind. Only the sight of police uniforms hinted that something was amiss. Cursing his luck, he retracted the telescope, spat angrily on the ground and slunk away.

CHAPTER FOUR

It took several hours and two changes of train before Colbeck and Leeming finally got within a few miles of their destination. Having alighted at Fourstones railway station, they were driven in a dog cart by an old man whose beard was so dense and curly that words had difficulty finding a way through it. Because Leeming had his back to the driver, Colbeck, seated beside the old man, bore the brunt of his narrative. It was delivered in an almost impenetrable local dialect. Having spent his entire life in a sleepy little village where nothing untoward ever happened, the old man finally had a major incident to talk about and he freely embroidered the few facts he'd picked up into a vivid description of an event of epic proportions. His account was totally at variance with what the detectives had already learnt in Newcastle.

When they reached the circus, Colbeck expected to see the aftermath of a calamity, with dead bodies being carried out on stretchers and wounded animals being killed in relays. What he and Leeming actually found was a bustling camp in which the majority of people were far too busy to brood on the crash the previous day. Reacting quickly to the emergency, they lapsed comfortably back into their usual routine. The only real sign of unease was the sustained chorus of protest from the animals. Led by Rosie, it combined anger, confusion and fear.

Brendan Mulryne came forward eagerly to greet the newcomers.

'You're a sight for sore eyes, Inspector,' he said. 'And the same goes for you, Sergeant.'

Leeming was given an equally warm handshake. It was years since he'd seen the Irishman but the latter had changed very little in the interim. He had the same bristling energy and the same mischievous twinkle in his eye.

'What are you doing in a circus, Brendan?' he asked.

'Oh, I do just about everything.'

'Do you perform in the ring?'

'It's the one thing I don't do, Sergeant. They already have a Strong Man and there's not a tightrope thick enough to bear my weight. As for the trapeze, I've no head for heights.' He picked up their valises from the ground. 'But let me take you to Mr Moscardi. He's dying to meet you. And so is Inspector Lill.'

'Is he from the Newcastle Constabulary?'

'Yes – he was in charge here until you arrived.'

'What sort of man, is he?'

The Irishman snorted. 'He wouldn't last a fortnight in London.'

'Why is that?'

'You'll soon see.'

Mulryne set off and the others fell in beside him. Colbeck was curious.

'The telegraph said that you discovered the murder victim.'

'That's not strictly true. Jacko found her.'

32

'Then we'll need to speak to him.'

'All you'll get out of him is a few squeals, I'm afraid,' said Mulryne with a chuckle. 'Jacko is a monkey. He escaped during the crash and I went hunting for him with Albert, his keeper.'

'Where did you find him?'

'In the woods – it's not all that far away.'

'In that case,' said Colbeck, 'as soon as you've introduced us to Mr Moscardi, I want you to take Sergeant Leeming to the exact spot where the victim was buried.' He glanced upwards. 'Light will be fading soon. You might take a lantern.'

'There's something much more important to take than that.'

'What is it?' asked Leeming.

'Jacko.'

Mauro Moscardi was getting increasingly impatient. Seated in their caravan with his wife, he was firing questions at the man nominally leading the investigation and he was getting disappointing answers.

'Have you found any clues at all?'

'We believe so,' replied Lill, guardedly.

'What are they?'

'It's too soon to be certain that they are actually relevant.'

'You must have *some* idea who attacked my circus.'

'All I can offer you at the moment is a guess.'

'A guess!' exclaimed the Italian. 'What use is that, man?'

'I'm relying on intuition, sir.'

'And what does it tell you, Inspector?' asked Anne, calmly. 'I apologise for my husband. He doesn't mean to hector you like this. You must understand that this circus has been run by his family for the best part of eighty years. He will fight to the death to save it.'

'All I need to know,' said Moscardi, 'is who I'm fighting *against*.'

'Let the inspector speak, Mauro,' she advised, softly.

Cyrus Lill was a lanky man of middle years with a face that looked far too small for such a large head. Its most notable feature was the drooping moustache that hung beneath the snub nose and the watery eyes. He shrugged apologetically.

'We're doing our best, sir.'

Moscardi gave a dismissive gesture. 'Ha!'

'It's a complex investigation.'

'I just want a simple answer.'

'These things take time—'

He got no further. Someone rapped on the door and brought the interview to an end. Anne got up to see who the caller was. It was Mulryne's huge fist that had pounded on the door. When the three of them realised that the detectives had arrived from Scotland Yard, they climbed out of the caravan to give them an effusive welcome. Once introductions were over, Colbeck explained that he was sending Leeming to view the place where the victim had been found and to hear full details from Mulryne of the actual discovery. The two men set off.

Moscardi was hurt. 'The assault on my circus should come first,' he said, vehemently. 'Our whole future was at stake. Do you know what it's like to be in a train crash, Inspector Colbeck? We could all have been *killed*.'

'Thankfully,' said Colbeck, 'you were not. The victim, however, *was* killed.' He turned to Lill. 'Have you indentified her yet?'

'I'm afraid not,' replied Lill.

'Where was the body taken?'

'It's in Hexham.'

'I'll need to examine it.'

'And when you've done that,' said Moscardi, testily, 'will you get round to catching the fiend who did his best to destroy my circus?'

'That crime is at the forefront of my mind, sir,' said Colbeck.

'Inspector Lill was about to tell us who he suspects,' said Anne, giving the man his cue. 'He has a theory.'

'My brother thinks it was someone from Greenwood's Circus,' asserted Moscardi.

She put a hand on her husband's arm. 'Let the inspector speak.'

'Well,' said Lill, diffidently, 'it's early into the investigation and we are still gathering evidence but – if I had to hazard a guess – it would be that the crash was the work of some Gypsies. They've been around for a fortnight or more and caused all sorts of headaches for us before vanishing like a puff of smoke.'

'What motive would they have?' asked Colbeck.

'They love to cause trouble.'

'I wouldn't describe a train crash as mere trouble, Inspector Lill.'

'In my view, they're incorrigible and would stop at nothing.'

'Oh, I'd fancy they'd stop well short of inflicting damage on a circus. Gypsies and circus folk are kindred spirits, nomads who roam the country and who adapt to what they find in a particular place. Life is without frontiers to them. They relish freedom of movement.' He turned to Moscardi. 'Am I right, sir?'

'You are,' said the other. 'We were born to roam. As for Gypsies, they've never given us any trouble. I employ a couple of them. They're good men.'

'It was only a suggestion,' said Lill, defensively.

'I was against it at first but my brother's suggestion may be a better one, after all. The villain works for Sam Greenwood's Circus. He's sworn to put us out of business one day.'

Anne looked at Colbeck. 'What do you think, Inspector?'

'I have only one observation to make at this stage,' replied Colbeck after a moment's reflection. 'Before our train departed from Newcastle, I took the trouble to speak to the guard. He's been from Newcastle to Carlisle and back a number of times today and passed the scene of the crash on each occasion. He told me that your train was derailed by two sleepers laid across the line.'

'That's correct,' said Lill.

'I asked him where the sleepers would be stored and he told me.'

'What was your conclusion?'

'It's this,' said Colbeck, smoothly. 'I'm not going to waste precious time looking for Gypsies or tracking down a rival circus. The person who put those sleepers on the line was – or has recently been – employed by the NCR. Only someone with inside knowledge would have access to the train timetables and thus be aware of the likely time when the train would be passing a particular spot. And there's something else to consider. Who but a railwayman would know exactly where to find a couple of sleepers? That's my initial conclusion,' he went on, distributing a smile around the group. 'It should help to narrow the search a little.'

It had been a testing journey for Victor Leeming. Having spent so many long hours in a jolting train, he was delighted to have the opportunity to stretch his legs. The walk also gave him the chance to renew his acquaintance with Brendan Mulryne, a man with whom he'd once walked the beat in one of London's most dangerous districts. They had a lot of news to exchange but the presence of the monkey made any conversation almost impossible. Perched on the Irishman's shoulder, Jacko piped away continuously, making noises that ranged from a squeal of alarm to a soft kissing sound. Leeming was amused when the monkey kept snatching Mulryne's hat off before replacing it at a rakish angle but he didn't laugh when he became the animal's target. Without warning, Jacko suddenly hopped onto his back, snatched his top hat off and swung on the branch of a tree before depositing the hat out of reach of both men. When Leeming complained, the monkey shot up to the very top of the tree and emitted a mocking laugh. Leeming was furious.

'Do you know how much that hat cost?' he demanded.

'Don't shout at him, Sergeant. He's only having some fun.'

'Well, I'd rather he didn't do it at my expense.'

'He meant no harm,' said Mulryne, good-humouredly. 'I'll get your hat back, don't worry.' He clapped his hands. 'All right, Jacko. The game is over.' He patted his shoulder. 'Come back here.'

The monkey descended the tree at once and picked up the top hat on his way. Leaping on to Mulryne's shoulder, he knocked off his hat and replaced it with the one belonging to Leeming.

'Oh, it's far too good for me,' said Mulryne, whisking it off and handing it back to Leeming. 'Fetch *my* hat, Jacko.'

The monkey obeyed at once, retrieving it from the ground and putting it back on the Irishman's head. Afraid of losing it again, Leeming chose to keep his top hat in his hands. As they walked on, his friend recounted what had happened.

'We searched for Jacko, high and low – it was mostly high, actually, because he's at home in the trees, as you've just seen. He does things that the circus acrobats couldn't even try to do. Jacko's a delight to watch when he's showing off.'

'How did he lead you to the grave?'

'But he didn't. When I stumbled upon it with Albert, we didn't even know that Jacko was there. All I saw was this pale white hand sticking out of the earth and waving at me. Jesus! I almost filled my pants, so I did.'

'Was the woman still alive at that point?'

'No, but Jacko was. He decided to play a joke on us by digging up the hand and using it to wave. I didn't know whether to be grateful we'd found him or to strangle the little wretch.'

After another five minutes, they were close to the place where the discovery had been made. Mulryne had to check his bearings first. He looked around for guidance then spotted a tree stump.

'That's where we turned right,' he remembered, leading the way. 'It's not far. I hope we don't see another hand waving at us from the grave. My old heart couldn't stand that.'

After walking on slowly, they came to piles of loose earth around a shallow grave. The area had been roped off by the police. Jacko started screeching in alarm and hugged Mulryne for safety. Though the sky still had some brightness, trees were blocking out much of the light. Leeming therefore set his hat aside and lit the lantern he'd been carrying. He used it to illumine the whole area.

'You'll find nothing,' warned Mulryne. '*I* didn't and I searched for ages.'

'What condition was the woman in?'

'In the circumstances, she looked quite well. When the doctor examined her, he said she couldn't have been here for more than a day. Rigor mortis had set in, of course, but I'd have said she'd once been very pretty.'

'How old would she be?'

'She was older than you, perhaps, but not by many years.'

'Was there any sign of . . . interference?'

'No, I don't think so. She was fully clothed and there was no hint of a struggle. She looked almost peaceful. I began to wonder if she'd died of natural causes and been given a private burial.'

'If that had been the case, they'd surely have taken the trouble to dig a proper grave. It looks as if she was covered by less than six inches of earth.'

'That's what told me there'd been foul play.'

'Did the doctor confirm it?'

'Yes, Sergeant, he said that she'd been poisoned.'

'She was killed elsewhere,' observed Leeming, 'then brought to a place where she was highly unlikely to be discovered – by human beings, anyway. It was only a matter of time before animals found her and dug up the body.' He grimaced. 'I hate to think what would have happened to her then.'

'We saved her from that fate, thank God.'

'Her family will be eternally grateful to you.'

'It's Jacko who deserves the credit,' said Mulryne. 'He found the corpse and I found him, didn't I, Jacko?' He looked around but the monkey was nowhere to be seen. 'Where's he gone to now?'

There was a squeal of joy from the top of a nearby tree. They looked up to see the monkey waving something wildly in the air.

'That's my hat he's got up there!' wailed Leeming.

Whenever he went to investigate a serious crime associated with the railway, Colbeck found a recurring pattern of resistance. He and Leeming were resented by the local constabulary for taking over a case they felt they could solve, and disliked by railway policemen who hated to be reminded how limited their powers really were. This time it was different. Instead of meeting muted opposition, Colbeck found hero-worship. Cyrus Lill had followed the other man's career with a mixture of interest and awe. To him, it was an honour to work alongside the celebrated Railway Detective, albeit it in an inferior capacity.

'Are there any reports of missing persons?' asked Colbeck.

'There are a few,' replied Lill, 'but none of a woman fitting the description we've released to the newspapers. I've not just been in touch with police forces in Cumberland and Northumberland. I've sent telegraphs to neighbouring counties as well.'

'Excellent.'

'I reasoned that it's exactly what *you'd* have done, Inspector.'

'It is.'

'The victim might actually live hundreds of miles away.'

'That's true. Details of her discovery have already appeared in national newspapers. The net is being cast far and wide.'

'Without the crash, we might never have found her.'

'That was a fortunate coincidence,' said Colbeck. 'I'm deeply sorry for what happened to Moscardi's Magnificent Circus but one horrendous crime served to bring another to light. The sergeant and I won't leave until both have been solved.'

'You'll have our complete cooperation, sir.'

'Thank you, Inspector.'

'This is an opportunity I'll embrace to the full.'

There was an almost servile note in his voice and it troubled Colbeck. Adulation was gratifying but it was out of place in a murder investigation where cool heads and unremitting work were required. He began to fear that Lill's exaggerated respect for him might be as much of a handicap as the surly hostility he met from detectives in other constabularies. And yet the man had clearly been thorough. He'd conducted dozens of interviews and kept a record of them for Colbeck to see. Lill had also spoken to the engine driver and to the manager in Carlisle who'd arranged the two trains for the circus and fitted them into the timetable.

'My question was this,' explained Lill. 'What would the Railway Detective do in my position? I followed you in every way, sir. I've kept a scrapbook of your cases. I've learnt so much from studying your methods.'

'You ought to find your own way of working,' suggested Colbeck.

'Why do that when there's a better one available?'

'I can't claim that it's better in this case. To start with, I'm an outsider.'

'That hasn't held you back in the past.'

'You know this area, whereas I don't. That gives you an advantage.'

'When I'm standing next to you, I certainly don't feel it.'

They were close to the point where the crash had occurred. Since the train had left the line in its entirety, there had been only limited disruption to services. At the moment of impact, the sleepers had been knocked clear of the track. It had been a blessing to the NCR. Instead of having to cancel trains, they could concentrate on rescuing the stricken locomotive and rolling stock. The damage was mercifully restricted. Cranes were still working away and there were dozens of labourers at hand. It would be days before the site was cleared completely but something akin to normal service had been restored.

Colbeck looked meditatively up and down the line.

'They chose a good spot,' he said. 'It's fairly isolated and the engine driver wouldn't have seen the obstruction until he came around that bend.'

'Actually,' corrected Lill, 'the first thing he saw was a red flag, planted right on the curve. That's what the engine driver told me.'

'So he did have a warning.'

'Yes, sir.'

'It didn't come early enough. Even at the locomotive's reduced speed, there'd be no chance of stopping in time.'

'None at all, I'm afraid. One thing puzzles me.'

'What is it?'

'The nearest sleepers are stored half a mile away. How did they get here?'

'A horse and cart could have brought them.'

'Sleepers are heavy. Are we looking for one man or two?'

'That remains to be seen, Inspector, but a strong man could easily manoeuvre a couple of sleepers into position. The wonder is that he bothered to do so.'

Lill was surprised. 'What do you mean?'

'Well,' said Colbeck, thoughtfully, 'if his intention was to cause a major crash, he could have done it much more easily by using a pickaxe to lever some of the rails out of position. It was almost as if he *wanted* the locomotive to bounce off the sleepers at low speed and remain upright. He even provided a red flag to warn the driver to slow down.'

'That seems odd.'

'Had the accident happened a hundred yards farther back,' said Colbeck, pointing a finger, 'and had the rails been blocked there, then the train would've landed on that bank and been absolutely certain to overturn. In that event, lives would probably have been lost and many more passengers and animals would have been badly injured.'

'That never occurred to me,' admitted Lill.

'It's perplexing.'

'Are you claiming that the man we're after was . . . soft-hearted?'

'I don't see any evidence of a soft heart, Inspector Lill. What I see are the consequences of a despicable crime that's caused a lot of pain and inconvenience.'

'But you're right about the place he chose for those sleepers. Farther back down the line, they could have brought about a catastrophe.'

'What do you deduce from that?'

'The villain didn't do his job properly.'

'Oh, I think that he did,' said Colbeck. 'He picked a spot where the damage would be limited. In other words, he wasn't out to *destroy* the circus. He simply wished to stop it from reaching Newcastle.'

CHAPTER FIVE

During her confinement, Madeleine Colbeck had felt the absence of her mother most keenly. It was a time when she really needed the advice and reassurance of the person who'd brought her into the world and who therefore understood the mysteries of childbirth. Madeleine had an aunt who'd visited her regularly but could not offer anything like the same support. All that she and the older woman did was to have a version of the conversation they usually had, confined to questions about her father's health, her plans for a new painting and the details of her husband's latest case. Though she loved her aunt in spite of the woman's patent shortcomings, Madeleine drew far more strength from the visit of two people closer to her own age.

One of them was Victor Leeming's wife, Estelle, a mother of two sons and therefore able to talk with some authority about the problems of family life. She was a kind, considerate, down-to-earth woman with a pleasant manner and a quiet sense of humour that had often revived Madeleine during her darker moments. The friendship had grown out of the fact that their respective husbands worked together at Scotland Yard. Crime had produced Madeleine's other close friend as well. She'd met Lydia Quayle when Colbeck was investigating the murder of the latter's father in Derbyshire and the two women had been drawn together. In the weeks and months leading up to the birth of her daughter, Madeleine had come to rely more and more on Lydia's visits. Though she didn't realise it at the time, their friendship was having a significant impact on another relationship in Lydia's life.

On her visit that morning, Lydia hovered over the crib and beamed.

'She's the most beautiful baby in the world.'

'We think that,' said Madeleine, 'but we could be accused of prejudice.'

'I'd love to hold her again but I don't want to wake her up.'

'You won't have long to wait, Lydia, I promise you.'

'Good.' She sat beside Madeleine. 'But I came to see you as well as Helen. How are you? And how is Robert?'

'I'm fine, thank you, and so is my husband – but I'd rather he wasn't quite so far away at the moment.'

'Why – where is he?'

'He's somewhere in Northumberland. A train carrying a circus was derailed and the body of a woman was found in the vicinity. Robert didn't know if there was any connection between the two crimes.'

'It's such a pity he's so far away at a time like this.'

'I do feel that I've been deserted,' said Madeleine, sadly. 'Having him here in London for so many weeks was an absolute treat – for Robert as much as for me. I miss him already.'

'Then I'll have to call more often, if you can put up with me.'

'What a silly question! You're *always* welcome, Lydia.'

'Thank you – I love coming here.'

'So you should – you're an honorary aunt.'

Lydia laughed. She was about to reply when a maid came in with a fully laden tray. Madeleine took charge of pouring the tea. As she handed a cup to her visitor, she looked at her shrewdly.

'Is everything all right, Lydia?'

'Yes, yes, I'm in excellent health.'

'I wasn't asking about your health. You seem a trifle distracted, that's all. I noticed it when you first arrived. Has anything happened?'

There was a long pause during which Lydia went off into a world of her own and studied the carpet intently. When she looked up, she contrived a brave smile. Madeleine was worried.

'What's going on?' she asked.

'I can't burden you with my problems,' replied the other. 'In any case, they may turn out to be largely imaginary. I just want to enjoy your company.'

'I'd enjoy yours far more if I was in a position to help you.'

'I came as a friend – not as someone in search of help.'

'But you do *need* help, don't you?'

Lydia sighed. 'You're very perceptive.'

'That comes from living with a detective. Robert's taught me how to read people's faces and to look for certain signs.' She took Lydia's hand. 'I don't wish to pry. If it's a private matter, we'll talk about something else and I'll never pester you again with regard to . . . well, the way you're behaving.'

'Is it that obvious?'

'As a rule, you're always brimming with life when you come – but not today.'

'No,' confessed the other, 'it's true.'

Lydia took her hand away so that she could have a first sip of her tea. After pursing her lips for a moment, she reached a decision.

'I do need to talk to someone,' she conceded.

'Is it to do with your elder brother?'

'Thankfully, it's not. Now that everything is finally settled with regard to Mother's will, Stanley has gone very quiet. He's no longer a threat. I'm still in correspondence with Lucas, my younger brother, and he keeps me abreast of family matters.'

'I'm glad you still have a line of communication.'

'That's all it is, I'm afraid. My life is here now.'

She fell silent and Madeleine wanted to reach out and take her hand again. Not wishing to exert even the slightest pressure on her friend, she held back and waited for the words to come when Lydia was quite ready. Minutes drifted past. When she eventually spoke, the visitor blurted out the truth.

'I'm being followed by a man,' she said. 'He frightens me.'

'Do you know who he is?'

'No – and that's what's so unsettling. I never really have the chance to look at him properly. Whenever I try, he disappears.'

'Is it the man who once followed you here?'

'Oh, no, it's definitely not him. I was completely unaware of someone behind me on that occasion. Besides, he only followed me to find out where I was going so often. Once he had this address, he reported back to . . .' Lydia inhaled deeply. 'You know the rest.'

When they'd first met, Lydia had been living with Beatrice Myler, an older woman who'd become very possessive when Madeleine appeared on the scene. Her antagonism towards Lydia's new friend had been the catalyst that led to the departure from Beatrice's house. The older woman was so embittered at the loss of the person she loved that she hired someone to track Lydia's movements. When she learnt what Beatrice had done, Lydia was so hurt that she broke off the friendship completely.

'That was different,' she recalled. 'I didn't feel in any way threatened by that man. This time, I do.'

'Do you think he means to harm you?' asked Madeleine, anxiously.

'I don't know what he wants to do.'

'Can you describe him?'

'He's young, well dressed and . . . well, I suppose you'd say that he was quite handsome. That's all I've been able to deduce from the glimpses I've had of him.'

'Have you challenged him?'

'He doesn't stay long enough for me to do that, Madeleine.'

'What steps have you taken?'

'Well, I've moved to a different hotel in the hope that I can shake him off by doing so. But it's only a matter of weeks before I take possession of the house I'm buying. I hate the thought that he'll run me to earth there.'

'When did you last see him?'

'It was over a week ago. I usually walk here but, when he started following me, I began to take a cab.'

Madeline felt sympathy well up inside her. Her friend was obviously in distress. She tried to say something that had a degree of reassurance in it as well, she hoped, as a grain of truth.

'You're a very attractive woman, Lydia. Have you ever considered that he might simply be . . . an admirer?'

'If only he was,' said the other. 'I've coped with that situation more than once in the past. It's sometimes embarrassing but it's never disturbing. This man is no unwanted suitor. He's rather sinister, although, for the life of me, I can't understand why. What should I do, Madeleine?'

'In the first instance, you should confide in Robert. He'd soon solve the problem. Unfortunately,' added Madeleine, 'he's a very long way away.'

* * *

Mauro Moscardi had offered to find them accommodation somewhere in the camp but the detectives instead chose to spend the night at a public house in Fourstones. Though its comforts were few, Colbeck thought that it would be a better option than the circus where they'd have to endure the constant noise of the animals and the penetrating reek from their quarters. With all its faults, the Station Inn was nevertheless able to give them a room each, edible food and the privacy they needed to discuss the case. They were just finishing their breakfast when they had their first encounter with Tapper Darlow, a short, plump, lively old man with a ruddy face decorated by grey side whiskers. He took off his hat to reveal a gleaming bald pate.

'Heavens above!' he cried. 'What on earth are you doing in this place? I left word that you should stay at the White Hart in Hexham at the expense of the NCR. I'm the chairman of the company,' he continued, grandly. 'My name is Tapper Darlow and yours, I fancy, is Inspector Colbeck.'

'That's correct, Mr Darlow,' said Colbeck, getting up to shake his hand then indicating his companion. 'This is Sergeant Leeming.'

Leeming rose from the table in readiness for a handshake but all that he was given by the newcomer was a cursory inspection and a curt nod. Darlow's only interest was in the Railway Detective.

'You'd have been welcome to stay at my home,' he said, expansively, 'but I live north of Newcastle and I reasoned that you'd prefer to be closer to the scene of the crime. Hexham would have been ideal for you. It's a delightful old town filled to the brim with historic significance.'

'We came here as policemen, sir,' said Colbeck, 'not as antiquarians.'

'You came as our guests and should be treated accordingly.'

'This place suits us well enough,' said Leeming as he looked around. 'They sell good beer and a tasty meat pie.'

'It also has the advantage of being closer to where we need to be,' Colbeck pointed out. 'We're north of the river here. Had we stayed in Hexham, we'd have been further away and obliged to cross the river every time we wished to visit the circus.'

'I won't argue,' said Darlow, 'but don't blame me if the beds are too hard and you keep banging your heads on these low beams. Luckily, that's not a problem for someone like me,' he went on with a chortle. 'Being this short sometimes has its advantages.' He had a sudden fit of coughing. 'It's very musty in here. Do you mind if we all step outside?'

'Lead the way, sir,' invited Colbeck.

He and Leeming followed the old man out into the fresh air. They were greeted by bright sunshine and a bracing wind. Darlow looked at the nearby line.

'How much do you know about the NCR?' he asked.

'Next to nothing,' replied Leeming.

'I know something of its history,' said Colbeck. 'Like so many railway companies, it faced stiff opposition from local landowners. Having overcome the enemy, so to speak, it surged ahead and was completed, I believe, in 1839. Nine or ten years later, it was leased by George Hudson, the now deposed Railway King, on behalf of the York, Newcastle and Berwick Railway.'

'That was never a satisfactory arrangement,' explained Darlow, 'and we regained our independence very quickly. The company profited from astute management. We increased traffic markedly by offering reduced rates for people going to markets, wrestling matches, race meetings and so on. And we kept our potential passengers well informed with regular handbills.'

'How long have you been at the helm, Mr Darlow?'

'Oh, I only became chairman by default, as it were. My predecessor was taken ill and I was the only person foolish enough to put himself forward. Darlow is a name with some impact in this county,' he said, thrusting out his chest. 'Until a few years ago, I was one of the two Members of Parliament representing the good people of Newcastle. The borough has a population of almost seventy thousand, you know.'

'But most of them, I suspect, don't have a vote,' said Colbeck.

'Over five thousand of them do,' returned the other with a hint of annoyance. 'Suffice it to say that, when I felt it was time to retire, I suddenly found myself catapulted into the position I now hold. As for the company, I've been a major shareholder for many years and a champion of the NCR's independence.' He replaced his hat. 'That brings me to the crux of the matter. Having only arrived yesterday, you'll have had no time to formulate any theories about who was responsible for the train crash.'

'Our minds are also focused on the murder of an unknown woman.'

'That's as it should be, Inspector, but you'll understand why the railway accident weighs more heavily on my mind. Mr Moscardi's brother is convinced that it was the work of a rival circus.'

'Inspector Lill favours alternative villains.'

'Yes,' said Leeming. 'He's certain that Gypsies are responsible.'

Darlow brushed the suggestion aside, 'Then Lill is quite wrong.'

'Don't be too hard on him, sir,' said Colbeck. 'In all probability, Inspector Lill was one of the men who elected you to Parliament. And it was a logical supposition, after all. There *have* been Gypsies in the area, apparently, and they've caused mayhem.'

'This crime has a purely commercial basis.'

'You say that with real conviction, sir.'

'I meant every word,' said Darlow with sudden passion. 'The NCR has been fighting off repeated attempts by the North Eastern Railway to secure a leasing arrangement with us or –

ideal for them – a merger. In other words, they want to swallow us up wholesale and spit out the pips. Since we've refused to budge, they are starting to resort to more desperate measures.'

'That's a very serious allegation, sir.'

'It's one that I stand by, Inspector.'

'A railway company wouldn't stoop that low, surely?' said Leeming.

'The NER would.'

'I beg to differ, Mr Darlow,' said Colbeck. 'If they have designs on taking over the NCR, why try to destroy one of its locomotives and some of its rolling stock?'

'That's commercial folly,' said Leeming.

'It's a way of applying more pressure on us. I could be barking up the wrong tree altogether,' admitted Darlow, 'but I've been party to some abrasive negotiations with the NER. Ruthless men sat around that table. My belief is this. Since they can't achieve their objective by peaceful means, they're trying something else.'

'Leave it to Inspector Colbeck,' urged Mulryne.

'He knows nothing about circuses,' said Gianni Moscardi with contempt.

'He knows a lot about catching criminals.'

'We have to sort this out ourselves.'

'But we can't do that, Gianni.'

'We can do anything we want if we all pull together. That's why I organised those patrols last night. I put armed men all round the camp. *Nobody* could've got in.'

'Nobody *wanted* to get in.'

'We're being watched by people from Greenwood's Circus.'

'The only people watching us are children who are dying to catch a glimpse of Rosie or of the lions. It's always the same. Wherever we go, we get interlopers and they're usually harmless.'

'Not this time, Brendan.'

'I simply don't think we're in danger.'

'You've only been with us for a while. Most of us have spent our entire lives in a circus. It's made us wary. We know when we're under attack.'

'I think you should talk to the inspector.'

'I'll be too busy waiting for Sam Greenwood's thugs to turn up.' He pulled back his coat to reveal a long knife. 'That's why I'm carrying this.'

Gianna was not content to hand over the investigation to detectives from Scotland Yard. He was scornful of the praise heaped on them by Mulryne. It was not enough for him to catch the person or persons who'd derailed one of their trains. Gianni wanted to exact revenge. To that end, he'd assembled a group of the toughest men in the circus and placed them strategically around the camp at night. He was now ready to lead them in search of their enemy.

Fond though he was of the Italian, Mulryne disagreed with his tactics.

'You won't catch anyone with a gang of vigilantes.'

'Yes, we will – you watch.'

'But you don't know where to start.'

'Neither do your friends from London. We came close to having a disaster on our hands but all that those detectives can think about is that woman you stumbled on. Look around you,' he said with a gesture that took in the whole camp. 'Haven't you noticed how many people have got bandaging around their heads or an arm in a sling or cuts and bruises of some sort? Didn't you hear the shot when we had to kill one of our best horses?'

'Yes, of course I did,' said Mulryne.

'Then why didn't you tell Inspector Colbeck about the sheer

scale of the damage caused? Why did you lead the sergeant to view the grave where the corpse was found? We needed him here, searching for clues to do with the crash.'

'They won't let us down, Gianni, I promise you that.'

'Well, I'm not waiting around for them to realise that what happened to us is far more important than the murder of one person. Over forty people were in that train when it came off the rails.'

'I know,' said Mulryne, ruefully. 'I was one of them, so you don't need to tell me what a nasty experience it was. I've still got cuts and bruises as well.'

As he was speaking, people drifted up to them and took their place alongside Gianni. They were the vigilantes he'd recruited and they included Samson, the circus Strong Man, a massive individual in his forties with a muscular torso, a rough beard and hair that hung to his shoulders. Mulryne counted fifteen of them in all.

'We've come for our orders,' said Samson.

'Follow me,' said Gianni, walking away and beckoning them to follow.

Mulryne watched them go and shook his head in dismay. While he understood their anger, he regretted the way that they'd despaired of the police investigation before it had really got under way. The detectives had to be warned. Gianni and his men could pose a real problem in the future.

Colbeck had handled two cases simultaneously before but there had been discernible links between them. No such overlap existed here or, if it did, it had yet to come to light. It meant that he had competition for his attention. Should he concentrate on the derailment or did the murder have a stronger claim? Mauro Moscardi had complained so loudly that the plight of the circus was not at the heart of the investigation that it had taken hours for Colbeck to convince him otherwise. It was late when he and Leeming had finally left the camp and gone to the inn where they were staying. Since he'd had no time to view the body of the murder victim, he made it a priority for the next morning. Tapper Darlow was highly critical.

'What's the point of bothering with her when you don't even know who she is?' he asked.

'I might be able to pick up clues as to her identity, sir.'

'How can you do that from a body on a slab?'

'You'd be surprised what you can sometimes learn. I speak from personal experience. A severed head was once found in a hatbox on Crewe station. That was all that we had to guide us. It proved to be more than adequate. We identified the murder victim, uncovered the motive for the crime and arrested the killers. If we can learn so much from a head, think how much more we'll be able to deduce from a whole body.'

'I still think that the train crash should come first.'

'It's not being ignored. Sergeant Leeming is with the circus right now.'

'Sergeant Leeming is not *you*, Inspector. Going to Hexham to look at a corpse sends out the wrong signal to me and to Mr Moscardi.'

'Not so long ago,' Colbeck remembered, 'you were telling us what a beautiful old town Hexham was. Now you're trying to stop me going there.'

They were travelling together on a train they'd joined at Fourstones. Darlow spent the whole of the short journey arguing that his demands should be respected first. Though he was glad to get off alone at the next stop, Colbeck was wise enough to realise that Darlow could be an asset to them. For all his pomposity, he was clearly a man of political skills and had a detailed knowledge of the workings of the NCR. His claim that the derailment had been engineered by a rival company had failed to convince Colbeck, yet it had to be borne in mind. It would certainly not be the first time that an acquisitive company was ready to employ underhand means to achieve its ends. Some people were prepared to go to any lengths to achieve power and wealth.

Having consulted his copy of Bradshaw on his way north, Colbeck had already learnt that Hexham was a picturesque town of almost five thousand souls with a population chiefly engaged in leather, shoe, glove, hat and woollen manufacture. As he left the station, he had the impression of a contented community, living in pleasant surroundings and preserving its many links to the past. The address he'd been given was that of Dr Thomas Fereby, the man who'd been summoned to examine the body of the murder victim and who'd had it moved to his house. A tall, angular, owlish man of sixty, Fereby had had experience of working as a pathologist and was well respected in the area. When he welcomed his visitor, he gave Colbeck a clammy handshake that was redeemed by his warm smile.

'It's good to meet you, Inspector,' he said. 'Your reputation precedes you.'

'I'm told that people have the highest opinion of you as well, Doctor.'

'I do my best.'

'What have you discovered about the victim?'

'There's very little to report, I fear, but I've made some notes and you can take a copy away with you. As you may know, the cause of death was poison but I'm no toxicologist. The body is being moved to Newcastle today for a post-mortem. They'll bring in an expert to decide exactly what she died of.'

'Could you describe your reaction when you first saw the body?'

55

'I can do so in great detail.'

Fereby was a refreshing contrast to Tapper Darlow. Unlike the former, he had a soft voice and an easy manner. He recalled his surprise at being unable to determine the cause of death at first. The woman had been lying on her back and care had been taken to arrange her in a natural position. She had not simply been dumped into the cavity then hastily covered over.

'Whoever buried her, Inspector, took some trouble.'

'That's interesting.'

'There were very few effects – no reticule, no rings on either hand, no accessories of any kind. Her dress and underwear are all that remained.'

'What about shoes?'

'There were none.'

When he'd completed the list, he took Colbeck into his office and handed him a box that contained everything belonging to the woman. Examining the dress, the inspector saw that the label had been torn out. He felt the quality of the material.

'This was expensive,' he observed. 'She had taste.' He noticed two tiny holes on the front of the dress. 'She was wearing a brooch of some kind, I fancy.'

'It wasn't in the grave.'

'The killer may have stolen it along with any other jewellery.'

'And yet he laid her out so gently and caringly.' He looked at Colbeck. 'There is, of course, another explanation. She *was* wearing jewellery, after all.'

'I can see what you're hinting at, Doctor Fereby. You think that the person who discovered the body then robbed it of any valuables. Let me put your mind at rest on that score,' Colbeck went on. 'The man who actually found her – with, I gather, the assistance of a monkey – was a Brendan Mulryne who works for the circus.

Earlier in his career, he was a member of the Metropolitan Police Force. I can vouch for his character. He's no thief.'

'That's reassuring to hear, Inspector.'

'I can't speak for the monkey, however.'

They shared a laugh. Fereby then led him to the rear of the house and out into a stone-built annexe with a paved floor. There was a chill atmosphere. Herbs had been scattered to sweeten the smell of death. The woman lay on a table under a shroud. At the doctor's invitation, Colbeck pulled it back to reveal everything above the waist. He first looked at the hands, noting impressions that suggested rings had been worn on two fingers on each hand. The skin was pale and tiny blue veins could be seen beneath it, reaching out in all directions like a miniature river delta. What he was looking at was the face of an attractive woman in her forties who, judging by her coiffure, could afford a very good hairdresser. The face intrigued him.

'There's no sign of pain or suffering,' he said. 'I've seen people who've been given corrosive poisons and they die in agony with their teeth clenched and their faces crumpled up. If there is such a thing, this woman died from a benign poison.'

'Poisons that can kill are never benign, Inspector. My explanation would be that she was given it in small doses over a long period. The effect was cumulative.'

Fereby went on to talk of other cases of poisoning he'd seen in the course of his career and how the person administering the dose had clearly wanted their victim to writhe in torment before dying. That was clearly not the case here.

'There'll have to be an inquest,' said Colbeck.

'It's going to be a very short one. Since we don't know who she is or where she comes from, there'll be no family to call upon.'

'I'll find them somehow.'

'What about the killer?'

'He won't escape, I assure you.' He drew the shroud slowly across the body. 'At the moment, this lady is unidentified. Our first task is to put a name to her. When we've done that, we can go after the man who murdered her.'

It was just after noon when Lydia Quayle returned to the hotel. Situated in a quiet backstreet, it was smaller than the one where she had been living but it was clean and comfortable. More importantly, it was unknown to her stalker. She was glad that she'd finally confided in Madeleine Colbeck. Her friend had told her that a shared burden was lighter to bear and the truth of that was soon evident. When she left the house, she did so with a spring in her step. Lydia was so heartened by Madeleine's support that she found the courage to walk all the way back to the hotel. At no point did she feel that she was being watched or followed. When she entered the building, she had an overwhelming sensation of being safe.

Lydia went up to her room. After removing her hat and coat and hanging them up, she crossed to the window and looked out at the buildings opposite. They were reassuringly nondescript, reinforcing the belief that she'd found an anonymous haven. When her gaze travelled down to ground level, however, she was given an unexpected shock. He was there and he did not walk away this time. Standing on the pavement opposite, he was not only looking up at her, he was smiling in triumph.

She'd been found.

CHAPTER SIX

As soon as he arrived at the camp that morning, Victor Leeming
was pounced on by Cyrus Lill. When he'd first met the inspector,
he'd been less than impressed by him but ten minutes alone with
the man served to change his opinion radically. Lill produced two
sheets of paper from his pocket and held them out.

'What are they?' asked Leeming.

'Take them and you'll see.' He handed them over. 'Well?'

'They're lists of who exactly was on the two trains hired by the
circus,' said Leeming, admiring the neat handwriting. 'You've put
down everyone's name and occupation along with the number of
animals. You've even listed the items being carried by each of the
two trains.'

'That was what I found most revealing, Sergeant.'

'Why?'

'Look more carefully at what the second train was supposed
to bring.'

Leeming glanced at the relevant page. 'It's just a list of paraphernalia.'

'Yes, but it contains the marquee and all of the seating.'

'I don't follow,' confessed the other.

'Let me explain. It was not solely my idea. I'll be honest about that. Inspector Colbeck happened to say that it would be interesting to see in detail how the circus was divided between the two trains. I found out for him.'

'That was very good of you but I can't see what revelation it produced.'

'He went for the wrong target.'

'Who did?'

'The man who caused the derailment, of course,' said Lill. 'If he'd wanted to cripple the circus, he should have made the second train his target. It contained most of the animals and all of the main equipment needed to stage a performance. By destroying the marquee, he'd have made it impossible for Mauro's Magnificent Circus to carry on.'

'You have a point,' said Leeming, 'and it's an important one. But I'd still argue that he chose the right target.'

'What makes you think that?'

'The evidence is right here in this list of names. The first train was carrying Mr Moscardi and his wife as well as some of the senior members of the circus. Rosie the Elephant was also on board and she is one of the main attractions. If the man who put those sleepers on the line had managed to kill Moscardi and wound the elephant so badly that it had to be shot, he'd have brought the circus to its knees.'

'According to Inspector Colbeck, he didn't set out to kill anyone.'

'Yes, he mentioned his theory about that.'

'Didn't you agree with it?'

'I did and I didn't,' said Leeming. 'I'm keeping an open mind.'

'Well, I thought his reasoning was sound. It would have been relatively easy to inflict far more damage – especially if the second train had been derailed instead of the first.' He stretched out a hand towards the caravans and tents. 'This camp would have been like a field hospital. Lots of children would have been among the casualties and they'd have needed to shoot lots of badly injured animals.'

'That would have been a tragedy.'

'The circus would've been put out of business.'

Handing back the sheets of paper, Leeming took a moment to reflect on what he'd just been told. Lill had been busy and deserved praise for that. Care had clearly been taken in apportioning people and animals to the two trains. Mauro Moscardi had led the advance guard, leaving his brother in charge of a vulnerable cargo in the second train. There was a definite imbalance between the two groups.

Leeming frowned. 'How did the man behind the derailment know what each train would be carrying?' he asked.

'When they hired the transport, they would have requisitioned so many carriages and so many wagons. It would've been quite clear which train carried the marquee. Because it had all the equipment as well, the second train had far more wagons attached. If – as the inspector believes – we are hunting for someone inside the NCR, such a person would have ready access to details of the travel arrangements and realise which of the two trains would be the better target.'

'Yet he chose the other one.'

'That tells us everything.'

Lill spoke with such quiet enthusiasm that he sounded very

persuasive. Since the inspector's argument was rooted in a suggestion by Colbeck, it had to be taken seriously. Leeming accepted that the accident could have been much more serious. During a previous case, he'd seen what happened when gunpowder had been used to cause a rockfall that made an entire train leave the rails at speed and overturn. The driver, fireman and guard had been killed instantly, the locomotive had caught fire and the rolling stock had been comprehensively wrecked. Nothing like that had happened to the circus. To all intents and purposes, it was still in one piece.

'Something is missing,' said Leeming. 'It's asking too much to accept that one man was responsible for what happened. If he works for the NCR, he might have found out at what time the first train would depart and be able to work out its likely time of arrival at the place where he chose to derail it. But he'd need help and it wouldn't have come from another railwayman.'

'Where else would it come from?'

'It came from right here.'

'No,' said Lill. 'I won't believe that. Mr Moscardi prides himself on the fact that his circus is a big happy family.'

'That's how it may look on the surface,' said Leeming, 'but it's just not true. Somewhere in this camp, they have a spy.'

With a fight in the offing, a small crowd had gathered. They formed a semicircle around the two men. Their spokesman was Otto Hickstead, a big, hulking man who worked as a lion tamer. He waved a threatening fist at Karl Liebermann, a lithe young acrobat who always began his performance with a series of high-speed cartwheels around the perimeter of the ring. There was no room for such a display now. The hostile onlookers were pushing ever closer. The German was trapped. Hickstead flung his accusation at the acrobat.

'You were behind it, Liebermann.'

'No, I wasn't – I swear it.'

'Now I see why you changed trains. You were supposed to be on the first one but you made sure you missed that so you wouldn't be involved in the crash.'

'That's not true, Otto.'

'If it was left to me, I'd never have let you join this circus after you'd spent three years working for Sam Greenwood. It was a big mistake of Mr Moscardi to trust you.'

'I work hard for him because I'm very grateful.'

'You're still working hard for Greenwood as well, aren't you?'

'No – I give you my word.'

'What use is that?' roared Hickstead, advancing closer. 'You're a dirty, rotten, dishonest German and you're trying to destroy this circus.'

'I'd never do that – it's my livelihood.'

'You've got no livelihood here.'

'Throw him out, Otto,' urged a voice. 'Beat him up and throw him out.'

'No, no,' pleaded Liebermann, raising both palms as he backed away.

'Stand still and fight, you bastard,' yelled the lion tamer.

'I've got no quarrel with you, Otto. We used to be friends.'

'That was before I saw you in your true colours.'

Encouraged by the crowd, Hickstead leapt forward and swung a punch. It was easily dodged by the acrobat but he could not evade the next punch and the kick that followed it. Stung into action, he began to fight back but his blows had nothing like the sting of his opponent. He could only hurt Hickstead. The lion tamer was strong enough and angry enough to kill him. The two men flailed away. Liebermann put up a brave defence but he was no match for the bigger man. It was only a matter of time before he'd be felled to the ground but, fortunately for him, the fight was interrupted.

'What the hell is going on here?' demanded Mulryne, pushing his way through the crowd. 'Stop it, the pair of you!'

When they continued to trade blows, the Irishman stepped between them, grabbed each of them by the scruff of his neck and lifted them from the ground.

'If you really want a brawl,' he said, 'you can have one with me.' He flung them yards apart. 'This is a circus. We stick together, especially at a time like this.' He glared at Liebermann. 'Who started it?'

'I did,' shouted Hickstead. 'That lying turd is working for Sam Greenwood. I was just about to beat a confession out of him.'

'I belong *here* now,' affirmed the German. 'I love this circus. It's better in every way than the other one. I'd never harm it in any way.'

'I believe you, Karl,' said Mulryne. He turned to the others. 'The fun is over. You can all disappear. And I don't want any more fighting in this camp, do you understand? Mr Moscardi pays me to look after this circus. Go on – get out of my sight before I help you on your way.'

There was a lot of resentful muttering but nobody dared to challenge him. Faced with the Irishman, even Hillstead backed down. After looking sullenly at the acrobat, he led the others away. Mulryne patted Liebermann on the shoulder.

'Keep out of their way, Karl.'

'Thank you for coming when you did.'

'Somebody had to stop the fight.'

The acrobat nodded before moving away. Robert Colbeck had watched it all from the moment that Mulryne had arrived. He moved in with an approving smile.

'Well done – you've lost none of your skills.'

'That's right, Inspector. It was just like old times in London when I had to break up a tavern brawl. I always enjoyed cracking a few heads together.'

'What happened?'

'They needed someone to blame.'

'Why did they pick on that young man as the scapegoat?'

'Three reasons. The main one is that Karl used to belong to a circus owned by Sam Greenwood. He hates us. Karl came here because he was offered more money and a chance to perform in front of bigger audiences. The second reason is that he's a German. Some people don't like that.'

'I find that rather odd,' said Colbeck. 'This is a very cosmopolitan group of people. The owner is Italian and he employs artistes from every part of Europe.'

'Karl is the only German. He sticks out.'

'What's the third reason?'

'It's the one that really irks Otto Hickstead. He's the man who started the fight, by the way. Otto is good at his job. He can turn those snarling lions into harmless pets.' Mulryne grinned. 'I think they're frightened of him because he's so big and ugly. Karl, on the other hand, is young and handsome. When a performance comes to an end, there are no women waiting outside the marquee in the hope of meeting Otto. All they want to do is to get close to Karl.'

'That's understandable, I suppose.'

'It's bound to make Otto jealous.'

'Are you going to report the fight to Mr Moscardi?'

'No, I'd rather not.'

'Why is that?'

'To start with,' replied Mulryne, 'he already has enough on his plate. The last thing he needs to know is that there's trouble brewing among his performers. My job is to stamp out that kind of thing quickly so that Mr Moscardi doesn't even get to hear of it. What I will warn him about is his brother.'

'Oh,' said Colbeck, 'what's the reason for that?'

'Gianni Moscardi is seething with anger . . .'

Though he had to use a walking stick, Gianni could hobble along at a good speed. Once outside the camp, he divided up his men and sent them off in various directions. The two accompanying him picked their way east along the riverbank. One of them, a clown by profession, was in a serious mood for once.

'What do we do if we catch someone, Gianni?' he asked.

'We frighten the life out of him until he talks.'

'Are you sure that he'll be from Greenwood's circus?'

'Where else would he come from?' demanded Gianni, rounding on him. 'Use your head, Pepe. We only have one enemy bent on destroying us and that's what he ordered a henchman to do.'

'Won't he run off and report back to Sam Greenwood?'

'No, he'll stay here. When he derailed the train, he didn't cause anything like the damage he'd hoped. He'll be lurking nearby so that he can strike at us again. That's why we've got to be vigilant.'

'What if we do catch him and he won't talk?'

'Oh, he'll talk with my knife at his throat,' said Gianni, fingering his weapon. 'If he doesn't – I'll make it quite clear to him – we'll kill him there and then. I don't believe in mercy. We'll toss him into the river with heavy stones tied to him to hold him underwater. That threat will be enough to loosen his tongue.'

The clown was worried. 'Would you really *kill* him?'

'I would and I'd enjoy doing it.'

'But that would be murder, Gianni.'

'What do you think that villain was trying to do to us?'

'We ought to hand him over to that inspector.'

'Forget about Colbeck,' said Gianni, stopping to shake the man by the shoulders. 'He won't find the culprit.'

'Mulryne says he's a brilliant detective.'

'Then why isn't he out searching like we are? All he's done so far is to ask lots of questions then send his sergeant off to look into the murder of that woman Brendan found in the woods. Colbeck can't even be bothered to give us his full attention.'

'He'll certainly give it if you actually kill someone.'

'Only if he finds out and there's no chance of him doing that. Three of us will know what happened and we'll all keep our mouths shut.' He looked deep into Pepe's eyes then transferred his stare to the other man. 'We will, won't we?'

'Yes, Gianni,' said the others in unison.

'Then let's carry on with our hunt.'

Spreading out so that they could cover a wider area, they moved along and looked behind every bush, tree and possible hiding place they could find. Their search was short-lived. The rural serenity was suddenly shattered by the sound of a shotgun to the north of them. They could hear distant voices calling out.

'They've found him!' cried Gianni. 'Let's get over there quick.'

Leading the way, he skipped through the grass as fast as he could.

It was an hour before Lydia Quayle plucked up enough courage to look out of the window again, though she didn't stand directly in front of it this time. Edging slowly towards it, she held the curtain then peeped around it. She heaved a long sigh of relief. He was not there. The only person she could see on the pavement opposite was an old man, walking along with a dog on a leash. Lydia relaxed slightly. After a few minutes, she was emboldened enough to step in front of the window and be in full sight. There was still no danger down below. Her stalker had vanished.

As she thought about what had happened, she wondered if it had all been an illusion. Since the man had come unbidden into her life, she'd been prey to all kinds of fears. There were times when she imagined him to be following her, only to turn round and see that nobody was there. Was that what had happened to her an hour ago? Had he wormed his way so completely into her consciousness that she thought he was there when there was, in fact, no sign of him? Besides, if a man *had* been there in the street, it could have been someone else altogether. Unlike her stalker, he didn't disappear as soon as she looked at him. He held his ground and smiled. The man who followed her had never done that.

Lydia did her best to convince herself that it had been a case of mistaken identity. The man she'd seen had been a complete stranger who just happened to be down below in the street when she looked down. It was no use. No matter how much she longed for it to be someone else, she knew in her heart that it was not. The man with the broad smile was her stalker, confident enough to show himself properly and to communicate his feelings about her. How he could possibly have discovered her whereabouts she didn't know, but he'd done so somehow. Lydia had left her other hotel in order to escape him, taking a cab from the rank opposite the building. What if he'd simply waited at the rank and asked each driver in turn if he'd taken a young woman from one hotel to another? It was conceivable. Cab drivers would always yield up information if they were paid enough and, as she'd now seen, her stalker was patently a man of means. He was dressed in an almost dandyish way that reminded her of Colbeck. What he didn't have, it seemed, was Colbeck's impeccable manners and his ingrained respect for women.

It took her a few minutes to reach her decision. After packing some things into a valise, she took it downstairs and asked the porter to walk down to the main street to summon a cab. When it arrived, she was confident that it would not be so easily tracked down. It was one of a legion of cabs that cruised the capital in search of fares. If her stalker was watching – and she didn't get the uneasy feeling that he was – he wouldn't know from which rank it had come. Lydia had made a successful escape this time.

'I don't believe it!' yelled Mauro Moscardi. 'It doesn't make sense.'

'It's backed up by evidence,' said Colbeck.

'Yes,' added Lill, waving the two sheets of paper at him. 'Examine these and you'll see why the inspector and I are of one accord. The aim of the derailment was not to bring about a catastrophe.'

'That's nonsense!'

'We disagree.'

'My circus was attacked by someone bent on killing us off,' asserted Moscardi, 'and his paymaster may be Sam Greenwood.'

The three of them were in Moscardi's caravan and he was resisting all of the suggestions that the two men put to him. Having come round to his brother's conclusion, he was clinging to it. Alternative theories were simply swatted away like irritating flies.

Colbeck tried to reason with him.

'Have you ever encountered trouble before?' he asked.

'We do it all the time,' replied the Italian. 'Wherever we go, we become a target for thieves. In Carlisle, someone tried to steal one of our horses.'

'What happened to him?'

'Mulryne caught him and gave him the hiding of his life.'

'And was the horse thief working for this Mr Greenwood?'

'No,' admitted the other. 'He was just one of the usual rogues

69

we meet in every locality. Because we live in a camp, they think it will be easy to sneak in and rob us. They pay a high price for their mistake.'

'Were any of these people employed by Mr Greenwood?'

Moscardi shook his head. 'They were the sort of villains you meet anywhere.'

'In other words,' said Colbeck, 'you've never had a problem from a rival circus.'

'Oh, yes, we have. They're always trying to lure away some of our artistes. Every circus in this country covets our acrobats and equestrian acts. Our clowns are the finest in Europe. They're always a main target.'

'So you're not only competing with Greenwood's circus?'

'No – there are lots of others, some large, some very small.'

'Would any of them deliberately try to maim you?'

'They're too scared even to try. Sam Greenwood isn't – that's why I'm sure he's behind what happened to us.'

'In that case,' said Lill, 'you have a rotten apple in the camp. Sergeant Leeming and I are certain of it. You have a spy in your midst who feeds information to someone who wants to hurt you.'

'That's a lie!' exclaimed Moscardi, grabbing him by his cravat. 'Nobody would dare to betray *me*.' He pushed Lill backwards. 'Get out of here!'

'The inspector was making a reasonable assumption.' said Colbeck, stepping quickly between the two men to separate them. 'He didn't mean to insult you. In almost every bank robbery I've investigated, the burglar had inside help from someone who worked in the bank. It's one of the first things I expect to find.'

'This is not a bank,' said Moscardi, quivering with emotion. 'It's a family. Nobody would join us unless he was ready to put up with the hardship we're bound to meet along the way. That kind of thing bonds us together. If I was harbouring a traitor, I'd smell him out immediately.'

'Then I take back what I suggested,' said Lill, adjusting his cravat.

It took the detectives a few minutes to pacify the Italian. They talked about his visit to Newcastle and where he would perform once the circus got there. When they asked where the next venue would be, Moscardi refused to tell them.

'It is an article of faith with us that we never give away advance notice of our movements,' he said. 'When we plan our itinerary, we insist that the places we visit do not advertise our arrival until a week before we get there. It means that our rivals can't get there before us to steal our audience. No town needs two circuses.'

Colbeck smiled at Lill. 'No case needs two inspectors,' he said.

'I'd be happy with only one if he actually devoted himself to our plight instead of trying to solve a murder investigation at the same time.'

'You will not be neglected, Mr Moscardi.'

'Then why do I *feel* neglected?'

'Coming back to our argument . . .'

Ignoring the blank expression on Moscardi's face, Colbeck tried once again to persuade him that his circus had actually been spared any wholesale damage. Had someone set out to disable it completely, he would have picked on the second of the two trains. Unfolding a map, Colbeck indicated the exact spot where the first train had left the line. He then went on to point out various locations he'd marked where a derailed train would either have rolled down a hill or crashed through a bridge and ended up in the river.

'Think how much worse *those* situations would have been,' he urged. 'You were saved from obliteration.'

'We were attacked,' said Moscardi, vengefully. 'That's all I need to know. And the only person capable of doing that is the man I've told you about. The two of you can save yourself the trouble of playing around with these clever theories. They'll never convince me. If you want to solve this crime,' he went on, voice rising and face puce with anger, 'then go off and arrest the man behind it – Sam Greenwood.'

The last performance had gone badly. Nobody could dispute that. The people of Bristol had flocked to the amphitheatre with the highest expectations and been let down. There was a general lack of vitality and commitment. Even the clowns had been jaded. The worst moment was when someone lost her balance and fell from the tightrope. Landing awkwardly in the sawdust, she ricked her ankle and had to limp forlornly away. It was an image that summed up the whole evening.

The owner of the circus spared nobody. Having assembled the entire circus, the tall, red-faced big-bellied owner harangued them until they hung their heads in shame. They had to do better, he warned, or some of them would be dismissed. As he watched them slink out, he was in a vile mood. Suddenly, however, it changed. His wife came in with a newspaper that carried details of events in Northumberland. After reading of the troubles of Moscardi's Magnificent Circus, the man put back his head and roared with laughter.

Sam Greenwood had found something to cheer him up at last.

'When did this happen, Lydia?'

'The moment I got back to the hotel.'

'Did someone follow you?'

'I wasn't aware of it.'

'Then how did he know you were there?'

'I wish I knew,' said Lydia. 'When I got to my room, I looked out of the window and there he was, smiling up at me. It was almost as if he knew exactly which room I occupied.'

'How dreadful for you!' exclaimed Madeleine.

'I almost fainted with shock.'

'I don't blame you.'

Having taken the cab to her friend's house, Lydia Quayle poured out her woes. Her only hope, she admitted, was that the man in the street had not been her stalker, after all, but a stranger who happened to glance upwards at the very moment when she appeared in the window. As soon as she voiced the possibility, however, she realised how unlikely it was and so did Madeleine Colbeck.

'You have to face the truth, Lydia,' she said. 'For some reason, you've become the object of this man's unwanted attentions.'

'That's why I had to get away from that hotel. If he knows where I'm living, then I've no chance of evading him. I came here to ask you a big favour, Madeleine.'

'What is it?'

'May I spend tonight here, please?' asked Lydia with a note of desperation. 'At a time like this, I need to be with a friend.'

'Of course you can,' said Madeleine, giving her a warm hug. 'Stay as long as you like. It will be a pleasure to have you.'

CHAPTER SEVEN

Having a friend inside the circus was a tremendous help to the detectives. Instead of having to start from scratch and gather information assiduously, they had someone who could explain how it operated and what its constituent elements were. As well as performers, there were musicians, animal keepers, those in charge of distributing handbills and selling tickets, and a gang of sturdy men whose job was to erect and dismantle the marquee. They were also in charge of the seating and loaded everything when the circus was on the move. Where sheer strength was needed, Brendan Mulryne was always ready to lend a hand but his main function related to security. His task was to make sure that nobody infiltrated the camp in order to steal valuables, release animals or cause trouble by some other means.

The best way for the artistes to take their minds off the horror of the crash was to practise their routines. Those with only minor injuries made light of any discomfort and honed their performances.

Victor Leeming was mesmerised by a family of tumblers – a father and his three sons – who stood on each other's shoulders with the father supporting them. At a given signal, the human tower toppled forward in a controlled fall and each of them did a somersault in perfect time with the others. The synchronisation was so perfect that Leeming clapped his hands.

'Hey,' teased Mulryne, coming up behind him, 'if you want to watch them, you'll have to buy a ticket like everyone else.'

'They're wonderful,' said Leeming. 'I'm not sure that I could hold my sons on my shoulders like that and they're still quite young and light. We'd collapse in a heap.'

'Then you'd never get a job in a circus.'

'I don't think I'd want to.'

'It's a great life. You certainly get to see the country.'

'Working with Inspector Colbeck, I get to do that in any case. Frankly, I'd like to see a lot less of the country and a lot more of my family.'

'How is the investigation going?'

'It's too early to say, Brendan. Unfortunately, there are *two* major crimes to solve so we've had to divide our resources. Inspector Lill and I will be working on the derailment while Colbeck flits between the two cases. He says that it will be like keeping two balls in the air.'

Mulryne laughed. 'He ought to meet Serge Arnaud.'

'Who's that?'

'He's the best juggler in the world. He can keep six balls in the air and do the same trick with seven plates. His arms wheel around like a windmill in a gale.'

'Can he solve a murder and catch a man who derailed a train?'

'He's working on that trick.'

'The inspector will do both, I promise you. It's uncanny.'

75

'You know, there's something different about him. I can't put my finger on it but there's a change in his manner.'

'He's become a father since you last met him.'

'Good for him!' said Mulryne before lowering his voice. 'I probably did the same when I slipped back to Ireland last year to see friends.' Leeming was shocked. 'We all have to sew a few wild oats.'

'I believe in the sanctity of marriage.'

'Why – so do I. That's why I'd never touch another man's wife.'

'You're an old reprobate, Brendan!'

'Some women like that,' said Mulryne, chuckling. 'Did the inspector tell you what happened earlier on?'

'Yes, you had to break up a fight.'

'We came close to losing one of our best acrobats.'

'Is there much unrest in the camp?'

'People are bound to be suspicious of each other. If someone has worked for Sam Greenwood – as Karl once did – he's likely to get the blame for what happened. I just hope that you and the two inspectors catch the villain before we have any real upset here. The one fault with this circus is that we have too many hotheads in it.' He looked at the group of men walking towards them. 'Here's the worst of them – Gianni Moscardi. Beware a man with Mediterranean blood.'

'Those with *Irish* blood can be very impulsive at times,' said Leeming, producing a loud guffaw from his friend. 'Are these the vigilantes you warned the inspector about?'

'That's them.'

Leading the way, Gianni had the strut of a man who'd just achieved a success. Those around him also seemed happy with what they'd done. Mulryne took Leeming across to meet them and introduced him to Mauro's younger brother.

'It's good to meet you,' said the sergeant, good-naturedly. 'I'm told that you are trying to solve the crime before us.'

'Somebody has to,' replied Gianni. 'The difference is that when *we* start searching, we make progress right away.'

'What did you find?'

'This,' said the other, holding up a telescope.

'Where did you get it?'

'It was up on that hill,' explained Gianni, pointing in that direction. 'Henry has sharp eyes. He saw something glinting in the bushes and ran towards them. As soon as Henry did that, a man leapt out of the bushes and ran away.'

'But I hit him,' said Henry, a thickset young man with a shotgun. 'I got him in the hand and he dropped the telescope. He was watching the camp.'

'Why else would he do that if he wasn't the man we're after?' asked Gianni.

'There are all sorts of reasons,' suggested Leeming. 'If I saw someone running at me with a shotgun, I'd make myself scarce very quickly.'

'He ran away because he was guilty.'

'I agree with Gianni,' said Mulryne. 'It *has* to be our man.'

'He could equally well be a harmless birdwatcher,' argued Leeming. 'They always conceal themselves well so that the birds don't know they are there.'

'This man was there to spy on us,' insisted Gianni.

'Did you get a good look at him?'

'I wasn't actually there, Sergeant, but Henry and the others were.'

'Yes,' said Henry, 'I got within thirty yards of him but he was too fast for me. By the time I got to the top of the hill, he was riding off on the horse he'd tethered to a tree. He was going hell for leather.'

'I don't blame him,' said Leeming, taking out a notepad. 'I'd be grateful if you could give me a description of the man. If he *is* a criminal, he may well be known to the local police. That would save us a lot of time. The wounded hand is a valuable clue. It might be decisive.'

'We saw him first,' declared Gianni.

'Well done, Henry!' said Mulryne.

'We're much more likely to catch him than you and the inspector.'

'Leave it to us, Mr Moscardi,' said Leeming, reasonably. 'We have experience of dealing with dangerous men.'

'You're far too slow, Sergeant. All you've done since you got here is to take notes and go around in circles. Having started a search for the man, we actually found him. This telescope is evidence that he was watching us because he wants to attack us again.'

'You're making a very big assumption.'

'We shall see,' boasted Gianni. 'Unlike you, we're ready to die for our circus.' There was a murmur of agreement from the others. 'That's why we're ready to take the chances that you and Inspector Colbeck would never think of taking. One last thing,' he added, wagging a finger. 'If you do catch wind of him, leave him to us.' He slapped his chest. 'He's *ours*.'

Now that she'd shared her secret with one person, Lydia Quayle was ready to pass on her concerns to another. After bottling it up for so long, it was a relief to let the truth out. Caleb Andrews listened with growing alarm. It had taken him time to get to know and like Lydia. The clear differences in their background and education made them unlikely friends. While Andrews came from humble stock, Lydia belonged to a privileged family with considerable wealth. It had made him uncomfortable in her presence. When he saw her more often, however, and when he realised how important she'd become to his daughter, he gradually mellowed towards her. For her part, Lydia had grown fond of him. She felt no embarrassment when she recounted details of her predicament. Andrews responded with characteristic pugnacity.

'Next time he bothers you,' he said, bunching a fist, 'he'll have to deal with me. I'll soon send him on his way.'

'That's not the answer,' warned his daughter.

'Someone needs to frighten him off, Maddy.'

'Well, it won't be you. Be realistic, Father. He's young and you're old.'

'I'm not *that* old.'

'Madeleine is right,' said Lydia. 'I wasn't asking you to take up cudgels on my behalf. I simply need advice.'

'My advice is that I tackle him directly.'

'It's too dangerous, Mr Andrews.'

'I've been toughened by long years of hard work.'

'Then you've earned the right to enjoy some leisure,' said Madeleine, firmly. 'For the time being, Lydia will stay here. We have plenty of room and she'll be able to see the baby every day. What might be helpful is if you go back with her to the hotel so that she can pick up the rest of her things.'

'That *would* be a help,' said Lydia. 'I'd hate to go back there alone.'

'Then you can rely on me,' said Andrews.

'I'll leave that hotel altogether. In view of what happened, I wouldn't feel safe staying there any longer.'

'I'll stand guard.'

'You may be able to do that today,' said Madeleine, 'but you can't watch over Lydia twenty-four hours a day. Somehow we need to identify this man and find a way to get rid of him for good.'

'Bring in the police,' suggested Andrews. 'What's the point

of having a detective inspector in the family, if we can't call on someone at Scotland Yard?'

'I'm not happy with that idea,' said Lydia, shaking her head.

'Why not?'

'Well, it's not as if any real crime has been committed. The police have their hands full dealing with serious offences like murder, arson and forgery. I'd feel embarrassed going to them.'

'What happened to you,' said Madeleine, 'is a crime of sorts. It certainly ought to be. This man has caused you untold suffering. All that he's done so far is to follow you everywhere. There may be worse to come.'

'Go to the police, Maddy,' urged her father. 'Speak to Superintendent Tallis.'

'No, thank you.'

'But he *knows* you.'

'He knows *of* me,' she said, 'but he certainly doesn't approve. He believes that, in order to do their jobs properly, detectives should never marry. Women don't really exist in Superintendent Tallis's life. He's the last person on earth in whom Lydia should confide.'

'If she's afraid to do so,' volunteered Andrews, '*I* could speak to him instead.'

'You'd only be sent on your way with a flea in your ear. The superintendent wouldn't take the matter seriously. We should stay well clear of him.'

It was as well for Colbeck that he was well clear of Tallis at that moment. The older man was furious when he read the telegraph sent to him by the inspector. Terse and peremptory, it ordered him to find out the current location of Greenwood's Circus and to provide as much information about it as possible. No explanation was given for the demand. It made Tallis fume for minutes. He lit a cigar to calm himself down but the pounding inside his head continued. Colbeck was treating him like an inferior and Tallis would not put up with that. Since circuses were anathema to him, he had no intention of obeying the command in the telegraph. Instead, he scrunched it up and hurled it into the wastepaper basket.

Reaching for his pen, he dipped it into the inkwell and composed his reply.

Tapper Darlow had not been idle. When he returned to his office in Newcastle, he instituted a series of enquiries at once. Clerks were deputed to look into recent changes of staff in the NCR. What they discovered was conveyed to Colbeck by means of a telegraph. Three people had left the railway company in the last few months. Significantly, one of them had taken up a post with the NER. Colbeck showed the telegraph to Leeming.

'Do you detect the note of triumph, Victor?' he asked. 'Mr Darlow seems to think that he's solved the crime. All we have to do is to arrest this Geoffrey Enticott and the mystery surrounding the derailment will disappear.'

'If only it was as easy as that.'

'He implies that we needn't bother with the other two men who left the NCR. The fact that Enticott works for the North Eastern Railway is proof positive of guilt in his eyes. Mr Darlow is desperate for the villain to belong to the NER.'

'But according to the telegraph, he works as a manager for the company.'

'So?'

'How can he find the time to watch the camp through a telescope when he has full-time commitments to the NER? I'm allowing for the fact that the man found on that hill by Gianni Moscardi's gang *is* the person we're after.'

'I'd need more evidence before I accept that,' said Colbeck. 'As for Enticott, if he *was* engaged to do the NER's dirty business, he could easily hire someone to act on his behalf. I'll sound him out and, if he's not involved in any way, I'll look at the other two people mentioned by Mr Darlow.'

'I could do that for you, sir.'

'You'll be otherwise engaged.'

'Will I?'

'Yes, Victor. When I sent a request to Superintendent Tallis, I hoped at least for a modicum of cooperation.' He extracted a telegraph from his pocket and passed it over. 'This was his reply.'

Leeming read it aloud. 'How dare you!'

'It has his distinctive whiff, does it not?'

'He sounds as if he's offended.'

'Then the first thing you must do,' said Colbeck, 'is to exonerate me. Explain to the superintendent that abbreviation is at the heart of sending a telegraph. Because my words were kept to a bare minimum, he may have misunderstood the tone in which they were sent.'

'Wait a moment,' said Leeming. 'Did you say I have to *speak* to him?'

'Indeed, I did. You're going to London immediately.'

'Why?'

'I've mentioned the first thing for you to do. The second is to deliver a letter to Madeleine for me and – if you arrange to call the next day – bring one for me in return. Thirdly, you can spend the night at home and tell your children about some of the sights you've seen in the circus.'

'Thank you, sir. Estelle and the boys will be thrilled to see me.'

'Tomorrow morning, you find out where Greenwood's Circus happens to be and visit them. Since it was beneath the superintendent to gather information about them for me, you'll have to do it instead. You have no objection, I take it?'

'None at all,' said the other, beaming.

'Collect your things from the Station Inn and catch the first train to Carlisle.'

'Carlisle? Don't you mean Newcastle, sir?'

'You heard me aright the first time. We only came north up the eastern side of the country so that we could get a feel for the landscape of Northumberland. A train from Carlisle will take you all the way to Euston. Make sure that my father-in-law gets to hear about it,' said Colbeck, taking the telegraph from the sergeant's hand. 'He'll be appeased when he hears that you favoured his beloved LNWR.'

Because the two detectives had suddenly left the camp, it fell to Cyrus Lill to face the wrath of Mauro Moscardi and his brother.

'Where on earth have they gone?' demanded Moscardi.

'The inspector is on his way to Newcastle while the sergeant is heading south to London.'

'London!' echoed the other. 'We need him here.'

'No, we don't, Mauro,' said his brother. 'We don't need either of them.'

'With respect,' said Lill, 'I think that you do.'

'We've already found the man who derailed the train.'

'You found a man who aroused your suspicions but that's all you did. You have no proof that he was definitely the culprit.'

'Why else was he watching the camp?' asked Moscardi.

'Lots of people do that, sir. Circuses always arouse interest. Mulryne told me that he's had to send dozens of people on their way today. They'll do anything for a glimpse of the animals.'

'This man was not like that. He was in hiding and had a

telescope,' recalled Gianni. 'When he was approached, he took to his heels. If he had a good reason for being there, he'd have explained himself.'

'I agree,' conceded Lill. 'Thanks to one of your men, we have an excellent description of him. Sergeant Leeming has sent it to all the constabularies in the county. If he's from around here, we have a good chance of tracking him down.'

'I'm glad to hear that the sergeant has finally done something useful,' said Moscardi. 'I just wish that he hadn't fled back to London when we need him here.'

'He's pursuing a course of action suggested by you, sir.'

'Oh?'

'The inspector has sent him to find Greenwood's Circus.'

Moscardi was pleased. 'Someone has listened to us at last!'

'It's only right that we look closely at every suspect.'

'Sam Greenwood is not just a suspect,' said Gianni. 'He and my brother have waged a vendetta for many years. This is his latest attempt to cripple us.'

'As to that, sir, Sergeant Leeming will find out the truth.'

'Meanwhile, what is the inspector doing in Newcastle?'

'He's following another line of inquiry. Since he's certain that an employee of the NCR must be involved somehow, he's gone to interview someone who recently left the company and who now has loyalties elsewhere.'

When he reached Newcastle-on-Tyne, Colbeck had a stroke of good fortune. Since the man he was after had joined another company, it was likely that he'd moved south to its head office. In fact, however, he'd taken a week's leave to oversee the sale of his house in Northumberland. When he went to the address given to him by Darlow, therefore, Colbeck found that Geoffrey Enticott was actually there. The latter was of medium height but carried himself so well and with such confidence that he appeared taller. Enticott was excessively well groomed. Colbeck put him in his mid thirties. When he heard his visitor's name, the man recognised it at once.

'Well,' he said, appraising Colbeck, 'this *is* a surprise. I never thought to find the Railway Detective on my doorstep. Do please come in.'

Colbeck entered the house. Once pleasantries had been exchanged, Enticott explained why he happened to be there that day. When he heard the reason for Colbeck's visit, however, his manner changed abruptly. He became resentful.

'Are you telling me that I'm a suspect?'

'Not at all, sir,' said Colbeck. 'We just hope that you can help us with our enquiries. As a former employee of the NCR, you'll know the exact place where the train was derailed.'

'So will the thousands of people who go past it by train on a daily basis.'

'You were principally dealing with freight, I'm told.'

'Is there anything wrong with that?'

'You'd have been in charge of scheduling ballast trains and those carrying sleepers to any new sidings that were being built.'

'I did the job that I was asked, Inspector. Unlike you, I did so without having to upset people with insulting questions.'

'Can you account for your movements over the past two or three days?'

'I've been in negotiation with an estate agent.'

'That wouldn't have taken up all your time.'

'You'd be amazed how protracted such things are.'

'Let's go back two days,' said Colbeck. 'Were you here all day?'

'Indeed, I was, and my wife will testify to the fact. So will a number of other witnesses. If you're trying to place me near Fourstones, you're wasting your time.'

Colbeck smiled. 'I think that perhaps I am.'

When he arrived at the house, the first thing that Colbeck had looked at was the man's hands. There was no bandaging on either. Whoever had been hiding up on the hill with a telescope, it had not been Enticott. In any case, he was far too fastidious about his appearance to crouch in any bushes and risk scuffing his shoes or tearing part of his attire. Had he been involved in the derailment, he would have engaged an accomplice. Colbeck looked him up and down. Enticott was expressionless.

'Why did you leave the NCR?'

'I was offered a promotion with another company.'

'Did they approach you,' asked Colbeck, 'or were you already in their pay?'

'That question is *more* than insulting.'

'I only put it to you because of information I've received. It seems that you left the NCR after a row with the board of directors. You kept urging them to secure the company's future by merging with the NER.'

'That was a sound commercial judgement.'

'Mr Darlow doesn't think so.'

'Tapper Darlow is an old fool. The NCR will never flourish under him.'

'It will lose its identity if it's gobbled up by your company. Correct me if I'm wrong,' Colbeck went on, 'but the NER was the result of a merger between the York, Newcastle and Berwick, the York and North Midland and the Leeds Northern – including the Malton and Driffield Junction, I believe.'

Enticott gave him a grudging nod. 'You've done your homework well.'

'Meanwhile, you're having trouble with the NER on which, incidentally, I travelled to get here yesterday. It's formed an alliance with the West Hartlepool Railway, which is encroaching on your territory east and north of Leeds.'

'We can fight them off.'

'That's as maybe but it would be easier to do so if you'd taken over the WHR. Your company tried to do that earlier this year but the deal was stillborn, thanks to legal and financial difficulties.'

'Where is all this leading, Inspector?'

'I'm trying to emphasise that the NCR would be a much-needed prize for the NER. That's why you lobbied on its behalf, didn't you?'

'I was not employed by the NER at the time.'

'But you had a firm promise of employment, I daresay.'

Enticott faltered for a second then quickly recovered. 'If you intend to charge me with a crime,' he said, holding out his hands, 'please do so but you will end up with a very red face in court. Come on,' he continued, 'I'm waiting for the handcuffs.'

Since they were thrust under his nose, Colbeck had the opportunity to scrutinise both hands. Neither of them bore an injury but he had the feeling that, metaphorically speaking, he could see traces of blood on them.

'Thank you for your hospitality, Mr Enticott,' he said, moving to the door.

'Does that mean my name has been cleared?'

Colbeck turned back. 'It means that I'd like to have the address to which you're soon moving,' he said, quietly. 'I feel that we should keep in touch.'

He was pleased to see Enticott swallow hard.

Since the offer had been made, Lydia accepted it gratefully. She and Caleb Andrews hired a cab to take them back to her hotel.

Simply having a man beside her made her feel more secure and he was plainly enjoying his role as a bodyguard. While she went up to her room, Andrews hovered by the reception desk and admired the decorative objects on the stands and side tables. Lydia, meanwhile, tripped confidently up the stairs and used the key to let herself into the room. When she turned up the gaslight, she saw that someone had closed the curtains. In one way, she was sad to leave because it was a very comfortable room and the hotel served all her needs. But it was no longer a refuge from the stalker. She had to go.

Packing everything into the trunk took some time, especially as she folded each item with great care. Eventually, only one last dress was left and she went back to the wardrobe. When she opened the door, however, it was completely empty. The dress was not there. She could not believe that anyone from the hotel would dare to steal it. That left only one possibility and it shook her to the core.

He'd been in her room. He'd taken her dress.

Lydia began to shiver uncontrollably.

CHAPTER EIGHT

Since his first task was the least pleasurable, Victor Leeming decided to get it out of the way as quickly as possible. Even at that hour, he knew that Tallis would still be at Scotland Yard. The superintendent had no social life. His day began and ended with the problem of policing a city that was awash with criminal activity. Fighting off the familiar feeling of dread, the sergeant went straight to Tallis's office, gritted his teeth and tapped apologetically on the door. The barked reply from within was more of a warning to disappear than an invitation to enter. Leeming nevertheless turned the doorknob and went in.

'Ah,' said Tallis, 'you've come at last. I had a telegraph from Colbeck to warn me of your arrival. I'm told that an apology is forthcoming.'

'Yes, sir – I'm very sorry it took me so long to get here.'

'I don't want *your* apology, man. I want the one sent by the inspector.'

'Oh, of course,' said Leeming with a nervous laugh. 'I'd forgotten that. You misunderstood Inspector Colbeck's earlier telegraph. It was not meant to sound so abrupt. He was trying to use as few words as possible to speed things up. He sends his profound apologies, sir.'

'So I should think.'

'The inspector has also sent a report for you,' he went on, taking it from his pocket and handing it over. 'It explains why he's so eager to have information about the whereabouts of Greenwood's Circus.'

'I've never even heard of it.'

'I daresay that the circus has never heard of *you*, sir.'

What was intended as a droll remark came out as a waspish quip and earned him a look of thunder. Getting to his feet, Tallis snatched the report from his grasp. As the older man read it, Leeming stood there in silence and resolved to say as little as possible from that point on. That decision was soon revoked.

'Right,' said Tallis, briskly, 'I've heard what Colbeck has to say. Give me your version of events, Sergeant.'

'It's exactly the same as the one in your hand, sir.'

'Don't be so obtuse. The two of you are not joined at the hip. You've seen things that the inspector did not. While he was questioning Mr Moscardi, for instance, you were taken to the grave where the body was found. Describe the experience in detail.'

With Tallis looming over him, Leeming had difficult finding his voice.

'Well, sir,' he whispered, 'it all began with this monkey called Jacko . . .'

An hour after discovering the theft, Lydia was still inconsolable. Though she was now safely back at the Colbeck house, she remained visibly on edge. Seated beside her on the sofa, Madeleine was holding both of her hands.

'There's still a chance that someone from housekeeping took the dress.'

'They'd have no cause to do so, Madeleine.'

'Did you challenge the manager?'

'Of course,' said Lydia. 'He was upset that I should even make the suggestion. Every member of the housekeeping department was of good character, he insisted. In all the years he'd been there, they'd never had one complaint against them.'

'Well, I have a complaint to make,' said Andrews, butting in. 'I'd like to know why a respectable hotel like that allows a complete stranger into the room of one of the guests.'

'He swore that nobody sneaked past the receptionist. You heard him.'

'Then how did the stalker get into your room?'

'There is one explanation,' said Madeleine, pensively. 'He didn't sneak into the hotel at all. He was there as a guest.'

'That's right,' agreed Andrews. 'The cunning devil could have booked a room there for himself. What a clever girl you are, Maddy.'

'It's a horrible thought,' cried Lydia. 'If I'd stayed at the hotel tonight, I might have been sleeping under the same roof as him. And since he obviously has a way of getting into my room, he could let himself in when I was asleep and . . .'

She burst into tears. Madeleine wrapped her in both arms and rocked her gently to and fro. It was minutes before Lydia regained her composure. It was a mark of just how deep her anxiety was. When they'd first met, the feature that Madeleine had noticed about her was her equanimity. Even when talking about her murdered father, she'd somehow remained self-possessed. It was only when she decided to return to the family from which was estranged that she'd called on Madeleine for help. That iron self-control had now vanished completely. Lydia was scared.

Sitting up again, she plucked a handkerchief from her sleeve and dabbed at her eyes. Madeleine's suggestion had unnerved her. The stalker had dared to book a room in the same hotel. His intentions took on a more threatening appearance.

'There's no certainty that he did stay there,' said Andrews, trying to reassure her. 'If he did, then he gave himself away. His name will be in the register.'

'He may have given a false one,' Madeleine pointed out. 'In fact, I'm quite sure that he would. On the other hand, we can find out if a man who looked like the one Lydia saw through her window did take a room there. We shouldn't believe that's what happened until we have clear proof.'

'We don't need proof,' said Lydia, soulfully. 'He was there. I know it.'

Andrews suddenly leapt to his feet and waved his arms.

'Be quiet!' he hissed.

'What are you doing?' asked Madeleine.

'Somebody's out there. I can hear him.'

Creeping to the front window, he pulled back the curtain enough to allow him a glimpse of the pavement. The sound of approaching footsteps was quite clear now. It was all he needed to stir him into action. Rushing into the hall, he grabbed a walking stick from the stand and flung open the front door, raising the stick to strike. The figure in front of him stepped smartly backwards and held up both hands.

'Don't do it, Mr Andrews. It's me – Victor Leeming.'

'What the blazes are *you* doing here at this time of night?'

'I came to deliver a letter from Inspector Colbeck.'

'Is that you, Victor?' asked Madeleine, running to the door. 'Thank God you've come! We need your help so much.'

* * *

At the end of the day, Colbeck found himself sharing a drink at the Station Inn with Cyrus Lill. Now that the latter had started to treat him as a fellow human being rather than as some God-like creature, Lill was much more amenable company. They discussed the two crimes at length. When Colbeck had described his visit to Geoffrey Enticott, he produced the other names of former employees who'd left the NCR. One of them was new to Lill but he recognised the other at once.

'Jake Goodhart, eh?'

'Do you know him?'

'I did so when I was in uniform in Newcastle. I locked him up a few times.'

'What was his offence?'

'Drunkenness – he wasn't so much a bad man as a weak one. Goodhart could never stop after the first drink. He had to go on until he could hardly stand up. That's when he'd end up in a fight.'

'If he had a problem with alcohol, however did he get employment?'

'He always managed it somehow. When he's sober, he's intelligent and hard-working. And things got much better when he married. His wife ruled the roost and it did him the world of good.'

'Why did he leave the NCR?'

'He was dismissed for being asleep on duty. The head clerk at Newcastle Central caught him snoring away, apparently. He won't get a job with that company again.'

Colbeck sipped his drink. 'Would you say that he was a vengeful type?'

'He was in his younger days. I daresay he's calmed down a bit now.'

'Find out for me,' said Colbeck. 'He's probably still living at the address provided by Mr Darlow. I must say that he's been very diligent.'

'It's his watchword.'

'Was he a good Member of Parliament?'

'He was an active one, that's for sure. He was always protesting that London got priority over the rest of the country. MPs in the south didn't believe that anything of importance happened north of the River Thames and that's true. Tapper Darlow tried to bang the drum for us but I don't think he achieved much.' He emptied the remains of his beer in a gulp. 'Let's look at the other name.'

'Owen Probert.'

'I've never heard of him.'

'He wasn't a mere clerk like Goodhart. He reached management status. Given that he had such a good position with the NCR, I'm surprised that he resigned.'

'Do we know why he left?'

'That was one thing Mr Darlow wasn't able to find out.'

'Shall I question Probert as well?'

'No,' said Colbeck. 'I'll call on him. He lives in Hexham.'

'Then he's not very far from here,' said Lill, raising an eyebrow. 'That could turn out to be a coincidence, of course. Then again . . .'

The unexpected arrival of Victor Leeming was a blessing. He was both a friend of the family and an efficient guardian of the law. The fact that he was in the house with them acted as a reassurance to Lydia. She had fought shy of involving the police earlier on because she didn't think that her case merited their attention. Leeming soon changed her mind. Once he'd heard about her problems with a stalker, he promised instant action.

'No woman should have to put up with that kind of thing,' he said. 'I'll make it my business to find out who walks the beat in this part of Westminster. They'll be told to keep a close eye on this house and to look out for anyone lingering nearby. That message will go out to the night shift as well.'

'Thank you so much, Victor,' said Madeleine.

'It's the least I can do.'

'What about the hotel?' asked Andrews.

'I'll go there by cab at once,' promised Leeming. 'If the man Miss Quayle describes is there, I'll ask him to explain himself. When I joined the police force, I swore to protect the citizens of London. In my book, that includes protecting young women from being pursued against their will.'

'See if he has my dress,' said Lydia.

'It's the first thing I'll ask him. If he *did* steal it – and that sounds likely – then I have grounds for making an arrest. He'll spend the night behind bars.'

'I'll come with you,' offered Andrews.

'That won't be necessary.'

'What if he puts up a fight?'

'He'll live to regret it, Mr Andrews.'

'This is so kind of you, Sergeant,' said Lydia. 'I feel better already. I thought that if I moved to a different hotel, he'd be unable to find me and, in time, he'd lose interest. That was a vain hope.'

'The only way to stop him is to confront him. That's what I'll do.'

'Give him a punch on the nose from me,' said Andrews.

'Father!' chided his daughter.

'It's no more than he deserves, Maddy.'

'I just want him out of my life,' said Lydia, wearily. 'How will we know what happens at the hotel, Sergeant Leeming?'

'I'll make a point of calling first thing in the morning,' he replied. 'Apart from anything else,' he went on, turning to Madeleine, 'there may be a letter for me to collect.'

'There most certainly will be,' she confirmed.

'Then I'll be on my way. I've had a long train journey and an uncomfortable visit to Scotland Yard. When I've been to the hotel, I'd like to go home to my family.'

'Give our love to Estelle and the boys.'

'I will, don't worry. In the morning, I'll be back quite early. Inspector Colbeck said that I had to give the baby a kiss on his behalf. I'll save that treat for tomorrow.'

Thanking him once again, Madeleine saw him to the door and waved him off. When she returned to the drawing room, she saw a smile on Lydia's face. The gloom had finally been lifted.

'The nightmare is over,' said Madeleine, confidently. 'Victor will see to that.'

During the hours of darkness, the camp was patrolled by the men Gianni Moscardi had selected as guards. Brendan Mulryne also took it upon himself to mount a vigil in case there was further trouble. In the event, all that disturbed the night were the plaintive cries of some of the animals. When daylight came, there was a collective sigh of relief in the camp that there'd been no further trouble. Mulryne had just been feeding nuts to Jacko when he was approached by Mauro Moscardi.

'We're leaving today,' he announced.

'Have you hired two more trains?'

'One will be enough. It will carry the marquee, the seating and all of the equipment. Anything heavy will go by train but none of us will be aboard.'

Mulryne was taken aback. 'We're going to *walk* there?'

'It's the safest way to go.'

'But it must be over twenty miles.'

'We need the exercise,' said Moscardi. 'Also, it's *traditional*.'

'It will slow us right down, Mr Moscardi.'

'Not if we keep up a good pace. We'll be travelling light, unencumbered by any paraphernalia. That's what made my father move at a snail's pace. He had to carry *everything*. The circus stretched for hundreds of yards and took an age to move from place to place. We'll be much quicker.'

'I won't be sorry to leave this place,' said Mulryne. 'It has too many bad memories for us.' The monkey screeched. 'There you are – Jacko agrees with me.'

'Pass the word round, Mulryne. We leave in an hour.'

'Have you hired another train?'

'Yes,' said Moscardi. 'I did it without telling anybody but my wife and brother. It will arrive around mid morning. But I'm not risking anyone's life on the railway. Our caravans and wagons will get us there. The cavalcade will act as a good advertisement wherever we go.'

'Yes,' agreed Mulryne. 'I don't suppose they get to see an elephant walking past their houses every day.' Jacko screeched again. 'And they certainly won't have seen a capuchin monkey.' He fed the animal another nut. 'What about Inspector Colbeck?'

'What do you mean?'

'Have you told him what your plans are?'

'No, I haven't. He'll find out what they are soon enough.'

'You should've taken him into your confidence.'

'Don't tell me what I should and shouldn't do,' said Moscardi, sharply. 'It's your friend, the inspector, who needs to be pushed into action. He should have given us his full concentration. He should have kept the sergeant here instead of sending him off to London for some reason. He should have been out looking for the man who derailed our train instead of leaving it to Gianni and his men. He should have done all sorts of things that he didn't. That's why I've lost faith in him. We'll be on the move in an hour,' he continued. 'I'll wave goodbye to the inspector as we pass him.'

Colbeck was up early to catch a train to Hexham so that he could call on Owen Probert. Assuming that the man now had another job, he wanted to get to the house before Probert went off to work. When he arrived, the family was just finishing its breakfast. Colbeck explained why he was there and was shown into the front room of the cottage. Probert's wife and two children remained in the kitchen.

'What time do you have to leave, sir?' asked Colbeck.

'There's no hurry. I'm not due in Newcastle until eleven o'clock.'

'Is that where you're employed now?'

'It's where I hope to take up a new post,' said the other, choosing his words with care. 'The interview is today.'

'Is it with another railway company, by any chance?'

'No, Inspector, it's a position in management in the coal trade.'

'Nothing could be more appropriate in Newcastle-on-Tyne.'

Probert was a short, muscular Welshman in his thirties with a pleasing sing-song voice and thick, dark hair. His eyebrows were so prominent that they all but obscured the deep-set eyes. When Colbeck glanced at the man's hands, he saw no wound. Probert spoke with a mingled surprise and wariness.

'I'm not quite sure why you've come, Inspector,' he said.

'It's because you left your post with the NCR.'

'There's no law against that, is there?'

'None at all, sir,' said Colbeck. 'In a company as large as that, there's bound to be a turnover of staff. My particular interest is in those people who left recently. You're one of them.'

'What do you wish to know?'

'I'd like you to tell me why you parted company with the NCR.'

'That's my business.'

'I could always go to your superiors and ask them,' warned Colbeck. 'If you told me yourself, you'd be saving me the trouble. You obviously want to hide the reason you left. Does that mean you were dismissed?'

'No!' retorted Probert. 'I find that suggestion insulting.'

'Then I take it back willingly, sir.'

'As a matter of fact, I was offered inducements to stay with the NCR.'

'Yet you went ahead and resigned.'

'It was time for a change.'

'Then I think you're a brave man.'

'Why do you say that?'

'Well,' said Colbeck, watching him carefully, 'most people would never dare to leave one job unless they had another already lined up for them.'

'I told you. I have my interview today.'

'And are you confident that you'll be offered the post?'

Probert straightened his back. 'I'm very confident, Inspector.'

'Do you have no regrets about leaving the railway?'

'I have none whatsoever.'

'Can I hear a tinge of bitterness in your voice, Mr Probert?'

'That's for you to decide.'

'You are nothing, if not blunt,' observed Colbeck. 'I hope that you adopt a more friendly approach to those who interview you. Signs of disrespect will not be appreciated there.'

The Welshman remained silent. He was clearly unaware of Colbeck's reputation and seemed only interested in sending him on his way. Probert was beginning to exude a kind of mute antagonism. Colbeck leant in closer to him.

'What is your view of the derailment?' he asked.

'It was very unfortunate.'

'You've been to see the extent of the damage, I suppose.'

'No,' said the other. 'Why should I do that?'

'Having worked for the NCR for a number of years, I'd have thought you'd take some interest in what happened to it, Mr Probert. It's not as if you have a job at the moment. In your position, I'd have got across there at once.'

'You have your priorities – I have mine.'

'What about your children? Didn't they beg you to take them to have a look at the circus? That's what every other child in the area wanted to do.' The Welshman hunched his shoulders by way of reply. 'What did your work on the railway involve?'

'Does it matter, Inspector?'

'It might do. I can easily find out, if you can't remember what it was.'

'I dealt with timetabling.'

'Then that's even more reason for you to take an interest in what happened. A train was derailed, part of the track was ripped up and there was extensive damage to the locomotive and rolling stock. In the short term, that would have involved some emergency timetabling.'

'It did.'

'Wasn't that enough to arouse your interest?'

'I had other things to do, Inspector.'

Colbeck concealed his irritation behind a bland smile. He wondered why the Welshman was being so deliberately unhelpful. After chatting inconsequentially to him for a couple of minutes, he suddenly fired a crucial question at him.

'Have you ever met a man named Geoffrey Enticott?'

Caught off guard, Probert was momentarily lost for words.

'No, I haven't,' he said at length.

'That seems strange. You must have worked in the same building.'

'I had lots of colleagues, Inspector. I only knew a selection of them by name. I may have nodded to the man you just mentioned but I certainly never knew him.'

Colbeck rose to his feet. 'Thank you for your time, sir,' he said. 'With regard to your interview, I'd like to give you some advice.'

'What is it?'

'Don't tell such a palpable lie as the one you just told me. I've met

Mr Enticott. He's a striking individual. It's impossible to work in the same building as him without being very aware of his presence.' He put on his top hat. 'Good day to you, Mr Probert. You'll understand why I'm unable to wish you luck at your interview.'

True to his promise, Leeming was back at the house early that morning. Shown into the drawing room, the first thing he did was to cross to the crib and look down at the baby. Gurgling happily, she seemed to be giving him a toothless grin. He beamed back at her. Madeleine and Lydia had got to their feet the moment he walked in. They were desperate for news.

'Did you go to the hotel?' asked Lydia.

'Yes, I did.'

'Was he there?'

'No, Miss Quayle, he wasn't. But I think that he had been. A man who sounded very much like the one you told me about *did* take a room there. He left the hotel yesterday evening without any explanation.'

'What name did he give?' asked Madeleine.

'Mr Daniel Vance.'

'Is that name familiar to you, Lydia?'

'No, it isn't,' replied the other, face clouding. 'So I'm back where I started. I don't know his real name or why he's picking on me.'

'We know that he definitely booked into the same hotel as you,' said Leeming, 'and that shows how serious his pursuit of you is. In all probability, he stole a dress from your room. Since he met him face-to-face, the manager was able to give me a more detailed description than you. I've circulated it to the people who'll be on patrol in this district. If he turns up, their orders are to detain him.'

'Take heart, Lydia,' said Madeleine with a consoling arm around her. 'You have the Metropolitan Police on your side now.'

Lydia rallied slightly. 'Yes, I suppose that I do. I'm so grateful to you, Sergeant,' she said to Leeming. 'You've gone out of your way to help.'

'I'm sorry I couldn't bring more cheering news. However,' he said, 'I must go. I have to catch a train to Bristol. Is there anything for me to take with me?'

'Yes,' said Madeleine. 'It's on the hall table.'

When she saw Leeming out, she gave him a letter addressed to her husband.

'Tell him how much we all miss him.'

'I will, I promise.'

After closing the front door after him, Madeleine went back into the room. Lydia was seated on the sofa, gazing in front of her. She was totally unaware of her friend's reappearance.

'Are you all right, Lydia?'

'What?' She came out of her reverie. 'Oh, I'm sorry. I was miles away. It's that name – Daniel Vance.'

'What about it?'

'Perhaps I *have* heard it before. It's starting to ring a bell. It's a very faint bell, admittedly, but it's tinkling away at the back of my mind.'

When he got back to Fourstones, Colbeck picked up the trap he'd hired and drove towards the camp. As he got within sight of it, he was astonished to see frantic activity. Tents had been taken down, caravans and wagons had formed themselves into a line and everyone was milling round. Colbeck was shocked that he hadn't been forewarned about the departure. He cracked the whip and his horse broke into a canter. When he was close enough to pick out individuals, he saw Mulryne giving orders to the men who were piling the circus's marquee, scenery and heavy equipment beside the railway line. Evidently, it was going to be transported by rail while everything else went by road. In Colbeck's absence, Mauro Moscardi had been making major decisions.

Heaving on the reins, Colbeck pulled up beside the owner's flamboyant caravan. Anne Moscardi came out to greet him. She was shamefaced.

'I said that my husband should have consulted you first,' she began, 'but Mauro is given to rash judgements.'

'He has a perfect right to move the circus where and when he likes, Mrs Moscardi. I couldn't object to that. The courtesy of a warning is all I require.'

'You weren't here when he set everything in motion.'

'This decision wasn't made on the spur of the moment,' said Colbeck. 'A train must have been hired at least a day in advance. Mr Moscardi probably made all the arrangements yesterday. I could have been told at that stage what your husband had in mind.'

'Yes, you could,' she confessed.

'So why was I kept in the dark?'

'I can answer that,' said a booming voice behind him.

Colbeck turned to see Moscardi striding purposefully towards the trap.

'Good morning, sir.'

'We didn't inform you because you're not sufficiently committed to the search for the man who's caused us all this grief.'

'That's untrue. I've just come from speaking to a potential suspect.'

'Did you make an arrest?'

'No,' said Colbeck. 'As yet, I don't have any evidence.'

'That's because you haven't been looking hard enough. You claim that you're here to help us but your mind is on the killer of that woman.'

'I'm dealing with both crimes at once.'

'In other words,' said Moscardi, curling a lip, 'the most we can expect of you is a half-hearted investigation and that's not good enough for me. You don't even have someone to help you today. Where's Inspector Lill? Where's the sergeant?'

'The inspector is in Newcastle, looking for a man who was dismissed by the railway company and who might therefore have a reason to disrupt it in some way. In other words, he's another credible suspect.'

'What's his name?' asked Anne.

'Jake Goodhart.'

'Do you think he could be the villain?'

'Let me just say that he'll repay looking at.'

'You're just spitting in the wind,' said Moscardi. 'You know nothing for certain. It's all wild guesswork. We've told you who was responsible for the derailment.'

'And I listened to you,' said Colbeck, earnestly. 'It's why Sergeant Leeming is at present on his way to Bristol. That's where Sam Greenwood's Circus is at present. I learned that from a telegraph sent to me earlier. The sergeant has a few tart questions for him.' He was pleased to see the expressions of astonishment on the faces of Moscardi and his wife. 'Just because you can't see us working away in front of your eyes, sir, it doesn't mean that we're neglecting you. There are times when we have to be invisible. I'd urge you to remember that.'

With a flick of the reins, he brought the horse to life and drove off. To a great extent, the complex investigation relied on cooperation from the circus. Colbeck had just served notice that he intended to manage without it.

CHAPTER NINE

For once in his life, Leeming boarded a train with something akin to pleasure. It was taking him to Bristol, a city that held special memories for him and for Colbeck. They'd been in pursuit of two men who'd organised an audacious train robbery then fled to Bristol with the intention of making their escape by sea. By way of insurance against arrest, they'd taken a hostage with them by the name of Madeleine Andrews, the daughter of the driver of the train they'd stopped and robbed. In a dangerous situation, Colbeck and Leeming had acquitted themselves well, capturing the two villains and releasing the woman they'd abducted. It was an occasion when the sergeant had earned rare praise for his bravery from Tallis but the real beneficiary was Robert Colbeck. From the moment they rescued Madeleine, his relationship with her slowly developed into a close friendship that eventually blossomed into marriage.

Arriving at Temple Meads Station, Leeming didn't need to ask where the circus was performing. Garish posters greeted him the moment he alighted. Among the images on display was one of a shapely young woman in pink tights standing on one leg on the back of a white horse. It verged on indecency in his opinion and was certainly not the sort of thing he'd want his children to see in reality. Circus people, it seemed to him, were allowed to get away with things that would arouse a storm of protest in another context. He'd discovered that from his observation of Moscardi's Magnificent Circus. Watching some of the female artistes rehearsing their routines, he'd been close to blushing.

There was another reason for enjoying the trip to the West Country. He was on his own and relished the freedom. Had he been with Colbeck, he'd have had to listen to a lecture on the value of the Great Western Railway's broad gauge and stand quietly by as Colbeck listed the individual features of Brunel's famous station. While nobody admired the Railway Detective as much as he did, there were times when it was a relief to be operating in a solo capacity. Still feeling a glow after a night with his wife and family, he made his way to the cab rank. Leeming was buoyant. He'd been given the opportunity of meeting the man who'd been named as the architect of the derailment. The task of calling him to account had fallen to him.

When he reached the amphitheatre, he was told that Sam Greenwood was in the office that had been set aside for his use. Leeming already had some idea of what the man he was about to meet looked like because Greenwood's head had appeared on the circus posters. Wearing a top hat, he was baring his teeth in a manic grin. It was no longer in place. Shown into the office, the visitor found himself facing a man of middle years and generous proportions. Greenwood's red face was distorted by a dark scowl. Seated behind the desk, he'd been counting the takings from the performance on the previous evening. They were disappointing.

'Who are you?' he growled.

'I'm Sergeant Leeming from Scotland Yard.'

'We allow no discounts for policemen.'

'That's not why I'm here, Mr Greenwood.'

'Then you're an exception to the general rule. I've never met a city with so many scroungers. Everybody wants a free ticket. The Lord Mayor – believe it or not – asked for ten. The brazen cheek of it! We're supposed to let in ten civic worthies for nothing? How are we supposed to make a living? Doesn't he realise that circus folk need to be paid for their services? Entertainment of such quality doesn't come gratis.'

'I need to ask you some questions, sir.'

'They'll be asking for free rides on our horses next.'

'It concerns a rival of yours – Moscardi's Magnificent Circus.'

'Ha!' cried the other with a sneer of contempt. 'The only magnificent thing about Mauro Moscardi is the length of his cigar. I loathe the man.'

'I can't say that he speaks too kindly of you, sir.'

'So he's sent you here – is that it?'

'Not exactly, Mr Greenwood. I suppose the best way to describe it is that I'm acting on information supplied to me by Mr Moscardi. I could be here for some time.' Leeming indicated the chair in front of him. 'May I sit down, please?'

Lydia Quayle had made the mistake of thinking that all her troubles were over. After the assurances from Victor Leeming that he'd visit the hotel where she'd been staying and challenge her stalker, she'd slept soundly for the first time in weeks. When the sergeant came, she believed, he'd bring news of an arrest and would be able to return her silk dress to its rightful owner. The fact that he did neither of these things was devastating. Before Leeming got to the hotel, the man had left altogether and melted back into obscurity. Lydia was still under threat.

'Would you like a cup of tea?'

'No, thank you.'

'Can I tempt you into a walk, then?'

'I'm afraid to leave the house, Madeleine.'

'He wouldn't dare to approach you while I'm with you. In any case, he doesn't know that you're here. You mustn't let him dominate your life, Lydia.'

'If you were in my place, you'd realise that you couldn't help it.'

'Well,' said Madeleine, 'I can't claim that I've been in an identical position but I did once have the experience of being followed. I haven't told you before because it wasn't as serious as the situation you're in but . . . it's the reason my heart goes out to you. The worst thing is that you don't know who the man is.'

'That's right. It's unnerving.'

'Shall I tell you what happened to me?'

'Please do, Madeleine.'

'It was almost ten years ago . . .'

She went on to tell Lydia about a time when her life consisted very largely of looking after her father who'd been so shattered by the death of his wife that he needed constant support. Madeleine had provided it, acting more like a mother than a daughter. Keeping him afloat had been a burden for her. She'd had no social life at all. When she went shopping in the market one day, she was conscious that someone was watching her and she felt him dogging her footsteps on the way home.

'Did you actually *see* him?' asked Lydia.

'No, I didn't. I tried lots of times, but whenever I spun round, he wasn't there. If I *had* seen him, I'd have realised that there was nothing to worry about.'

'Why?'

'It was someone I knew, Lydia. He worked for the LNWR with my father. I liked Gideon but not in the way that he liked me. He was very possessive.'

'What happened?'

'Ironically, he may have saved my life. He just happened to be watching my house when two men knocked on the door, grabbed hold of me and bundled me into a cab. It was over in a flash.'

Lydia was aghast. 'Do you mean that you were kidnapped?'

'Yes, and it was terrifying.'

'What happened?'

'Because he'd witnessed it, Gideon was able to get word to Scotland Yard. That alerted Robert and – after a period of time I'd rather forget – he rescued me from a ship in Bristol. I was reminded of it all when Victor told me that he was going back there today.'

'Why have you never mentioned this before?'

'It turned out to have a happy ending – a very happy one, in fact,' she went on, crossing to the crib and bending over it to kiss the baby. 'It's how I met Robert and how, in due course, this little darling came into the world.'

'My story is different, Madeleine. I don't expect a happy ending at all.'

'Have you remembered where you heard the name of Daniel Vance before?'

'No – it's maddening.'

'It will come back in time, Lydia.'

'I don't believe it's *his* name. It's a false one he gave to the hotel. Sergeant Leeming agreed on that. This man worries me at a deep level,' she went on. 'He came into my hotel room and took something. Why on earth should he want my dress?'

* * *

Wearing only shirt and trousers, he was propped up on the bed as he gazed at the silk dress on the tailor's dummy. In his mind's eye, he could see Lydia and longed for the day when he'd share a bedroom with her in person. He got up, crossed the room and put his arms gently around the dummy. The feel of the silk was exquisite.

'You're *mine* now,' he purred. 'You're all mine . . .'

Though there were marked physical differences between them, Samuel Greenwood had the same character traits as Mauro Moscardi. Both were peppery, dogmatic and authoritarian. They had the battle-hardened look of men who'd survived in a highly precarious profession. Each of them was convinced of his own innate superiority. As he sat in front of the desk, Leeming was forced to hear a litany of Greenwood's triumphs as a circus owner. Only when he finally ran out of boasts did the sergeant have a proper chance to question him.

'Did you know that Mr Moscardi was in Northumberland?'

'Yes,' replied Greenwood. 'I saw mention of it in the newspaper.'

'I'm asking if you knew about it beforehand?'

'How could I?'

'Circuses have been known to spy on each other.'

'It's not as sinister as you make it sound, Sergeant. We all have scouts in search of new talent. Fresh blood is a necessary part of our existence. We have to inject it regularly to increase our appeal. A few years ago, Mauro sent a scout to watch us. Do you know the result?'

'No, I don't.'

'When he saw the report of our brilliant young acrobat, Karl Liebermann, he dangled more money in front of him than we could afford to pay and lured him away. That still hurts. I discovered Karl in Germany and brought him to England at my expense. I put time and effort into that lad. He was stolen by Mauro.'

'I'm sure you'd have done the same in his place.'

'No, I wouldn't – I have moral standards.'

'Have you had a scout watching his circus recently?'

'I don't need to do that. I know that he'll never be able to compare with us.'

'You're much smaller than he is.'

'But we have greater quality. That's what audiences appreciate. They want the very best and only Greenwood's Circus can provide it for them.'

'You can't provide Karl Liebermann.'

'He betrayed us. We're better off without him.'

'How did you react when you heard about the train crash?'

Greenwood beamed. 'I laughed for a long time.'

'That's rather cruel, sir.'

'I'm being honest. I detest Mauro and he hates me.'

'He thinks that you may have engineered the derailment.'

'Then he'd better watch that big Italian mouth of his,' said Greenwood, blustering. 'There's such a thing as slander.'

'It's only slander if it's untrue, sir.'

'Nobody is going to blacken my name. You can tell that to Mauro.' He regarded Leeming for a few seconds. 'Why are you here, Sergeant?'

'If someone makes an allegation, I'm bound to follow it up.'

'Mauro is a liar. Surely, you've realised that by now.'

'The inspector and I are in the process of eliminating possible suspects, sir. That's all you are. Given the long-standing feud between you and Mr Moscardi, we were bound to add your name to the list.'

'Then you can take it off again and get back to Northumberland. Hey,' he added, reaching for the newspaper on the desk. 'It isn't just the derailment you're investigating, is it? There's a mention in the report of a dead body that was found.' Opening the paper, he jabbed a finger at it. 'Yes, here's the article. It says that two detectives from Scotland Yard have been dispatched to investigate both cases. I'm sorry for the poor woman who was murdered but I'm delighted at what happened to Moscardi's Mouldy Old Circus. Tell that to Mauro. Say that when I first heard the news, I had a drink to celebrate.'

His derisive cackle filled the room.

Colbeck had left the circus with mixed feelings. He was annoyed that he'd been given no hint at all of its imminent departure but, at the same time, he was glad that it had recovered so quickly from the shock of the derailment. Having seen many passengers who'd been involved in rail accidents, he knew how long it took for their confidence to return. Circus people were obviously more resilient. They coveted an audience. The overpowering urge to perform enabled them to forget their aches and pains and soldier on. What concerned Colbeck most, however, was that they might be exposing themselves to further danger. As long as it was camped near the site of the crash, the circus was safe. It was well protected day and night. Once on the move, it was much more vulnerable.

Having returned to the Station Inn, Colbeck pored over his map of the county and searched for the most likely places of ambush. The man who'd brought about the derailment had not achieved his ambition. He'd only managed to inflict punishment on the circus whereas Colbeck believed the intention was to disable it enough to stop it in its tracks. Providence – divine or otherwise – had come to its aid. Though the train had left the rails, the locomotive and rolling stock had not overturned. Passengers and animals were badly shaken rather than seriously incapacitated. Colbeck was certain that their enemy had watched the derailment and would have been disappointed that the damage was so limited. If he wanted to prevent it from reaching Newcastle-on-Tyne, he would have to strike again.

Colbeck was still studying the map when Tapper Darlow came into the inn.

'I was hoping you'd still be here,' he said. 'Good morning to you.'

Colbeck looked up. 'Good morning, sir.'

'The stationmaster here just told me that he's expecting another circus train to go through in due course. I thought it would be a week at least before Mr Moscardi was able to get everyone on the move.'

'The train won't be carrying any people or animals. They'll be travelling by road. Only the circus's marquee, seating, equipment and baggage will go by rail. Without that to impede it, they'll be able to move much faster.'

He confided his fear that there might be a second attack and pointed to places on the map that he'd identified as possible sites for a trap of some sort. Darlow had little interest in the fate of the circus as it wended its way east. His overriding concern was for the NCR and he wanted to know if the inspector felt that the latest circus train was under threat.

'I think it's unlikely,' said Colbeck. 'The man will know that extra security arrangements have been put in place on the line itself. Railway policemen are on the alert now, and the staff at every station between here and Newcastle will be more vigilant. Longer stretches of the line will be patrolled.'

'That was done on my initiative.'

'You moved with commendable speed, Mr Darlow.'

'I wish that I could return the compliment,' said the other, meaningfully.

Stung by the comment, Colbeck defended his actions

robustly and explained how he'd deployed Victor Leeming. Darlow was critical.

'The sergeant is far more use to you here,' he said, irritably. 'He'll find nothing of value in Bristol. The man we're hunting has nothing whatsoever to do with this rival circus. He's being paid by the NER to disrupt our services.'

'We're still looking for evidence to support that theory.'

'Did you interview the former employees whose names I sent you?'

'I spoke to two of them in person,' answered Colbeck, 'and Inspector Lill will be talking to the third person this very morning.'

'In my opinion, Geoffrey Enticott is the most likely suspect.'

'I have my doubts about that, sir.'

'He actually works for the NER.'

'So do a large number of other people. Are they to be listed as suspects as well? Enticott is moving away from the area. He claims that making the arrangements to sell one house and buy another has taken up all his time.'

'What manner of man was he?'

'To be honest, I found him rather shifty but that's not proof he was implicated in any way. Besides, there was no injury to his hand.'

'What do you mean?'

Colbeck told him about the man caught watching the camp through a telescope and how he'd been injured when fleeing the scene and forced to drop the instrument. Darlow was worried. Hearing that someone was keeping the area under surveillance, he decided that the man had been planning a second strike at the NCR. That seemed crystal clear to him. Colbeck disagreed.

'The target was the circus, Mr Darlow, not your railway company.'

'The two are intertwined.'

'Had Mr Moscardi and his cavalcade been travelling by road, I believe they'd still have been attacked. Your railway would have been left unharmed.'

'I beg leave to question that judgement.'

'That's your prerogative, sir,' said Colbeck, easily. 'As for the second man whose name you kindly gave us, he also aroused my suspicion. Owen Probert was a little too sure of himself at first. When I mentioned Geoffrey Enticott, however, he pretended that he didn't know the man but it was a blatant lie.'

'My information was that he left the NCR without explaining why.'

'He's expecting a more lucrative post elsewhere.'

Darlow snapped his fingers. 'It's with the NER, I'll wager.'

'You're quite wrong. He's going to work in the coal industry. As a Welshman, he should be well suited to that. Probert justifies a second visit at some point. He was pointlessly evasive. Like Enticott, however, he had no bandaging on one hand.'

'So he was not the mystery man up on that hill?'

'It appears not.'

'What about this other fellow who left the NCR?'

'Inspector Lill will be able to tell us about him,' said Colbeck, producing a watch from his waistcoat pocket and flicking it open. 'My guess is that he should be talking to Jake Goodhart any time now.'

When the inspector eventually found him, Jake Goodhart was leaning against a wall opposite a pub in one of the more disreputable parts of the city. He was a hefty man in his forties with rounded shoulders and a face clearly showing he'd spent most of his working life outdoors. Goodhart wore rough garb and a flat cap that was set on the back of his head. A shock of greying hair sprouted from beneath it. He wore a pair of filthy mitts. Cyrus Lill recognised him at once.

'Hello, Jake,' he said, jocularly. 'It's been a long time since we last met.'

'Who the 'ell are ya, man?'

'Don't you remember me?'

Goodhart peered at him. 'No – what are ya? If it's the rent ya want, ya'll 'ave to wait a week or so.'

'I'm not a rent collector. You once knew me as Constable Lill.'

'Hadaway and pelt shite!'

'I'd have arrested you in the old days for saying that. And you wouldn't have been standing *opposite* a pub, as you are now. You'd have been inside, spoiling for a fight. You were a real worky-ticket in those days.'

Goodhart subjected him to a long stare then ran his eyes down Lill's frock coat.

'Where's ya uniform, then?'

'I'm a detective inspector now.'

'Ah liked ya best as a copper. Ya smacked me sneck and ah bloodied yer gob, so that makes us squitts.' He bared his blackened teeth in a grin.

For all the trouble Goodhart had given him, Lill quite liked the man. He was coarse, ugly and down to earth. When sober, as now, he could almost pass as a human being. Lill surmised that two things kept him from going into the Black Horse pub on the other side of the street. The first was his wife, a doughty woman by all accounts who'd only agreed to marry him on condition that he gave up drinking. The second reason was that Goodhart had no money. Dismissed without pay, he and his family would struggle until he found another job. If he couldn't afford to pay the rent, Goodhart might even be threatened with eviction.

'You lost your job, I'm told,' said Lill.

'Aye, man.'

'Why was that?'

'Nivvor ya mind.'

'I heard that you were caught napping. If they pay you as a porter, they expect to get so many hours work out of you. How did it make you feel towards the NCR? Were you angry with them?'

'Aye, man.'

'Would you like to hit back at them?'

'Oh, aye.'

'And how would you do that?'

Goodhart laughed. 'Ah'm no tellin' the polis.'

'Have you been anywhere near Fourstones recently?' The other man shook his head. 'What about Haydon Bridge?' There was a second negative reaction. 'How well do you know the countryside around there?'

'Very well, man. Ma wife's from 'Exh'm.'

A seraphic smile spread across his face and he went on to talk about the days when he courted her. He'd been employed by the NCR as a labourer at the time so had little money to spend. Long walks together in the country were real treats to Goodhart and his future wife. They cost nothing yet yielded immense pleasure. He admitted that getting married had changed his life in every way. He was too slow-witted for most jobs but he usually managed to hang on to the ones that he actually got. There was no more drinking and brawling. He was proud of the fact that he hadn't spent a night in a police cell for years. Jake Goodhart was an example of a man who been reborn and refashioned by a loving woman. Since the couple now had three children, there had to be a regular wage coming into the house. His wife took in washing and did other

117

chores for the neighbours but she earned a mere pittance. The loss of his job had hurt Goodhart deeply.

'All ah did was to close ma eyes for a minute, then ah'm oot. That's the bleedin' NCR for ya! Where am ah s'pposed to gan?'

Lill felt sympathy for him. Nothing that Goodhart had said convinced him that the man would be involved in derailing a train. His name could be crossed off the list of suspects. The inspector then thrust out a hand in farewell. Without thinking and without removing his mitt, Goodhart shook it by reflex, then let out a yelp of pain. He pulled his hand away and rubbed it gently.

'What's wrong?' asked Lill. 'Did I hurt you?'

'Ah've a nasty cut on ma hand, that's all.'

They were still at the inn when the message arrived. Since there was no telegraph station at Fourstones, it had been sent to Haydon Bridge. It was of sufficient importance to merit instant delivery. The stationmaster dispatched a local man in his dog cart, insisting that, however long it took him, he had to put the telegraph into Inspector Colbeck's hands. Since the Station Inn was his first port of call, he was able to follow orders without difficulty. Colbeck read the message with excitement.

'I have to go to Newcastle,' he said.

'What's happened?' asked Darlow.

'Someone has come forward to identify the murder victim.'

Leeming was conscientious. Having made the effort to go all the way to Bristol, he didn't wish to leave with nothing more than his chat with Samuel Greenwood to report. He therefore went out of his way to speak to as many members of the circus as he could. Without exception, they first looked over their shoulders to make sure that nobody was listening. While most of them claimed they had a good employer, Leeming sensed that they had reservations about Greenwood that they were too scared to admit. A few complained that they were poorly paid and badly treated at times. It was left to one of the clowns to be more explicit.

'Sam is a tyrant,' said the man. 'I hate working for him.'

'Why don't you leave?'

'It's not easy to join a bigger circus. Clowns are ten a penny. Circus owners can pick and choose. You have to have a very special talent to be in demand. If I could swing from a trapeze by one foot, I might have a chance. As it is, I'm stuck here.'

He was a short, moon-faced man in his thirties with a furrowed brow and dark, resentful eyes. Leeming was struck by the paradox of a man whose job was to make people laugh being so steeped in misery. During a performance, the clown explained, he spent most of his time walking around in circles on stilts.

'The thing is,' he went on, lowering his voice, 'that we wouldn't *dare* to look for a job with someone else. If we show any interest in another circus, Sam will throw us out straight away. Once we're here, we're trapped. Our only hope is that a different owner likes us enough to buy us out of this damn prison. That's what happened to Karl Liebermann. He was poached by Mauro Moscardi.' He gave a gesture of despair. 'That would never happen to me.'

'Does Mr Greenwood go in search of new performers?'

'He does it all the time. We're always threatened with being replaced. It's his favourite way of keeping us under his thumb.'

'What are the others?'

The man went on to give a long list of strategies used by the owner to keep his employees in subjection. Greenwood's approach differed sharply from that adopted by his great rival. Moscardi had created a family atmosphere in his circus. Once a member of it, people were nurtured and given constant encouragement.

Leeming saw that, in coming to Bristol, he'd exchanged a happy circus for one that was full of unresolved tensions. He probed for more detail.

'Has Mr Greenwood been away recently?'

'He disappeared for a day or two last week.'

'Did he go up north, by any chance?'

'No,' replied the other. 'He went to see his relations in Brighton.' Leeming was disappointed. 'It was Bevis who went north.'

'Who's Bevis?'

'He used to be our Strong Man but he's getting on and was fed up with doing the same old tricks. Mr Greenwood found him work as a scout. If he heard of anything interesting in another circus, he'd send Bevis off to bring back a full report of whoever it was. It had to be delivered by mouth, of course, because Bevis can't read or write.'

'Do you know exactly *where* he went recently?'

'He did tell me,' said the clown, face puckering. 'Now where was it?'

'Can you remember who he went to see?'

'Oh, yes, I know that – Moscardi's Magnificent Circus. And I seem to remember that he mentioned . . . Carlisle.'

'When did this man get back from there?'

'He hasn't come back yet,' said the other. 'As far as I know, Bevis is still up there doing whatever Mr Greenwood told him to do.'

CHAPTER TEN

Colbeck was forced to share a compartment with Tapper Darlow. Instead of being able to focus all his attention on the latest development in the murder investigation, he had to listen to the proud history of the NCR and the alleged skulduggery of rival rail companies. There was, however, a bonus from having him as a travelling companion. Having represented Newcastle in Parliament for so many years, the old man was a mine of information about the city. Colbeck encouraged him to talk about how it had grown to be such a major industrial centre. Reminiscing fondly about his city, Darlow gave him a real insight into its character and background. Colbeck was grateful. In providing so much pertinent detail, his companion was saving him the trouble of having to acquire it by other means.

'What about crime?' he asked.

'We have more than our fair share of that, Inspector.'

'How common is murder?'

'Thankfully, it's very uncommon. Parts of the city have a

reputation for violence. When it spills out, it leaves a lot of bloody noses and broken bones in its wake but, I'm pleased to say, very few dead bodies.'

'How efficient are the police?'

'There are not enough of them,' said Darlow. 'We need a bigger force that is more visible on the streets.'

'Police sometimes do their best work *invisibly*, sir.'

'I'll have to take your word for it, Inspector. With regard to your investigation so far, I've certainly seen no visible progress.'

'It has taken place, I assure you.'

'Show me the evidence.'

'In the fullness of time, I'll show you the culprit as well.'

'How can you do that if you get diverted by this other case?'

'Do you have any children?' enquired Colbeck.

'I have five, as a matter of fact – two sons and three daughters.'

'What age is the oldest of the daughters?'

'Olivia is in her late thirties.'

'Then she was probably born in the same decade as the murder victim. Suppose – for the sake of argument – that your daughter had been discovered in that shallow grave.'

'Heaven forbid!'

'How would you react?'

'I'd demand that a manhunt was launched immediately.'

'Would it take preference over an investigation into a train crash?'

'That's an unfair question, Inspector.'

'I think we both know the answer to it. Somewhere our anonymous victim has a family who'd grieve in the same way that *you* would in similar circumstances. Nothing compares with an unnatural death, Mr Darlow. It rips the heart out of a family. I'm very sorry for what happened to the NCR,' he continued. 'I have an attachment to railways that goes well beyond the sentimental.

Anyone who causes damage to them in any way should be dealt with mercilessly, in my view.'

'I'd have them burnt alive.'

'The law provides adequate punishment. My point is this,' said Colbeck. 'I am not abandoning one case in order to concentrate all my energies on another. Neither the circus nor the NCR will be ignored. Inspector Lill and Sergeant Leeming will take my place. Both are highly competent.'

'I sent for *you*, man!'

'And I was gratified that you did so.'

'Then stay and defend my railway. It may still be under threat.'

'I've told you before that that's not the case. Danger does still exist,' said Colbeck, 'but it hangs over Moscardi's Magnificent Circus.'

The decision to move provoked diverse opinions among them. Some people were glad to get away from the scene of the derailment, others would have preferred to stay there longer in order to recuperate and a third group wanted to cancel the visit to Newcastle entirely so that they could head south and leave the county altogether. Among those happy to move, there was a preference for going by rail but they were overruled. Mauro Moscardi had made the decision and everyone had to abide by it. His brother, Gianni, continued to bicker.

'We should have gone by train, Mauro. It's so much quicker.'

'It wasn't very quick last time. We came to a dead halt.'

'And we both know why,' said Gianni. 'But that won't happen again. The railway company is policing the line more carefully now.'

'We go by road, all the same.'

They were at the head of a long, winding procession that stretched for well over a hundred yards. Mauro was driving the horses that pulled his caravan and his brother was seated beside him.

'I never thought that you'd lose your nerve,' said Gianni, clicking his tongue.

'I've lost nothing!' retorted Mauro.

'You've always been a man of steel until now.'

'I still am, Gianni.'

'Then why have you been scared off the railway?'

'I'm not scared off. I'm considering people's feelings. They were frightened and upset by what happened. If we go to Newcastle in a more leisurely way, they'll have time to recover. And they'll also have the chance to appreciate this lovely countryside instead of racing through it in a train. This is what our parents always did, Gianni,' he stressed. 'This is circus life.'

'You should have come with me to America.'

'We know all about what you saw there.'

'They travel enormous distances by rail.'

'I'm happy to let them go on doing it.'

'We should *learn* from them, Mauro.'

'That's what we did,' said his brother. 'When you came back, brimming with all those ideas, we were happy to try some of them. Be patient, Gianni. When we move on from Newcastle, I promise you that we'll do so by train. Meanwhile, enjoy the wonderful sense of freedom from travelling under an open sky. Breathe in this cool, clear air.'

Gianni lapsed into silence. Across his knees was a shotgun and at his feet was the telescope dropped by the man who'd been seen on the hill. From time to time, he used it to scan the landscape. He was frustrated. Before they left the camp, Gianni and his men scoured the area around them in an ever-widening circle. They'd failed to find anything remotely suspicious. The man on the hill was long gone. Instead of being able to continue the search, Gianni was now committed to a long, slow trudge across Northumberland.

For someone who loved speed and adventure, it was an irritation.

'Why can't we go faster?' he asked.

'Think of the animals. They can't be rushed.'

'We'll take ages at this rate.'

'It's what we always used to do as children, Gianni, and we loved it.'

'That was then. We're adults now.'

'Then we should have learnt the value of pacing ourselves.'

He tried to put a brotherly arm around him but Gianni shrugged it away.

They were following a track that meandered gently along over bone-dry earth that was badly rutted in places. Caravans and wagons were treated to occasional lurches but the circus horses, walking in a group, had no difficulties with the surface. A copse lay ahead of the cavalcade. Moscardi led the way confidently into the trees. Overhanging branches blocked out the light temporarily but they soon emerged into sunshine once more.

They'd gone no more than forty yards when disaster struck again. As the horses entered the copse, the bushes on one side of them suddenly burst into fire. Flames crackled and a plume of smoke went up. In a matter of seconds, there was a real blaze. It all happened so quickly and unexpectedly that people cried out in alarm and the lions went berserk in their cages. Trunk in the air, the elephant trumpeted aloud and Jacko, the monkey, squealed in terror. Because they were closest to the fire and could feel its heat, the horses became frenzied. Neighing, kicking, pulling and bucking, they snapped the reins that held them together and fled out of the trees in a mad panic. There was simply no way of stopping them. Mauro Moscardi was distraught. Some of the finest Arab horses ever seen in England were now galloping away from him.

* * *

When he got to the main police station in Newcastle, the first person Colbeck saw was Cyrus Lill. Looking very much at ease, he was talking familiarly to the duty sergeant. As soon as he realised who'd just walked in, his tone altered in a flash. Lill became almost subservient, introducing him to the duty sergeant then gazing at him with something of the awe he'd displayed at their first meeting. Colbeck was embarrassed.

'You've heard the news, then,' said Lill.

'I was contacted by your superintendent.'

'I've just been told about it myself and I couldn't be more pleased. It could very well be the breakthrough we need.'

'Don't be too optimistic,' warned Colbeck. 'All we have is someone who *thinks* he knows who the victim might be. Before I celebrate, I want to know that a positive identification has been made.'

'Superintendent Finlan will be able to give us the details.'

'Then I look forward to meeting him.'

'I'll show you the way, Inspector . . .'

Lill took him through a door and down a corridor. Like most other police stations Colbeck had been in, the place was nondescript and purely functional with a pervasive air of bleakness. After tapping on a door, Lill opened it and conducted him into the superintendent's office. As introductions were made, Archibald Finlan rose to his feet but offered no handshake. Colbeck was relieved to find that the man had nothing of Lill's deference. If anything, the superintendent exuded the quiet hostility that Colbeck routinely found when called in to take over cases from a provincial constabulary.

'Thank you for sending me a telegraph, Superintendent,' said Colbeck.

'I'm glad that it reached you, Inspector. You are, by report, constantly on the move. I hoped you were still at that camp.'

'The camp no longer exists. Mr Moscardi decided to head for Newcastle by road. Even as we speak, he's on his way here.'

'Why not go by train?' asked Lill.

'His reluctance is understandable, I think.'

'Didn't they seek a police escort?'

'The circus believes it can look after itself. Besides, I don't think that you could spare the number required.'

'That's true,' confirmed Finlan. 'Our manpower is limited.'

Resuming his seat, he sifted through some papers on his desk. Colbeck saw no resemblance whatsoever between him and Tallis. Whereas the latter was stern and military, Finlan was soft-spoken and fairly relaxed. He was a tall, pale, skinny man with a gaunt face out of which dark green eyes bulged. His lips were unusually thin.

'First of all,' he said, handing some sheets of paper to Colbeck, 'you might care to see this. It's the post-mortem report.'

'Thank you, sir.' After reading it avidly, he looked back at Finlan. 'So she was killed by belladonna.'

'If administered in the right dose, it's fatal. We had a suicide recently where belladonna was involved.'

'But it's not the only poison used in this case. Apparently, there are traces of other elements in the compound. The killer knew how to contrive a quick death. That suggests he might conceivably have had some medical training.' He gave the report to Lill. 'Here you are, Inspector. It's a much more detailed analysis than Dr Fereby was able to give us.' His gaze shifted to the superintendent. 'What about the victim's identity?'

'Her name is Margaret Pulver,' said Finlan.

'Can we be certain of that?'

'I believe so. I'm told that the gentleman recognised her instantly when he visited the morgue.'

'Is he a family member or a friend?'

127

'He described himself as an acquaintance,' replied the other. 'His name is Donald Underhill and he's spending the night at the Grand Hotel.'

'That's more than I could afford to do,' said Lill.

'I'll get over there at once,' said Colbeck.

Before he could even move, however, there was a tap on the door and it opened to admit a uniformed constable with something in his hand.

'This telegraph has just arrived, Superintendent,' he said, handing it over.

When Finlan read it, his eyes threatened to pop out of their sockets.

'The circus has been attacked again,' he said.

The cavalcade had been sliced apart. One section of it was ahead of the copse and the other was well behind it. Those caught in the trees when the fire broke out had made a hasty exit from the area. A posse had been formed to search for the escaped horses and keepers were doing their best to calm the other animals. Most people had been stunned by the crisis but Mulryne's reaction was immediate. Leaping from the wagon on which he'd been travelling, he'd braved the flames as he went in search of the man who'd started the fire. He was much too late. Having caused mayhem, the culprit had disappeared in the confusion. Though others eventually joined the Irishman to comb the whole area, they could find nobody. It was small consolation to them that the fire didn't spread. Once the bushes had burnt to ashes, the blaze died out. Some of the trees were singed but none were in danger of being set alight. Evidently, the aim had been to disrupt the circus rather than destroy the copse.

Mauro Moscardi believed that his deadly rival had struck again and vowed to get retribution. For the moment, however, he had to soothe everyone, form them into two separate camps and organise armed guards to patrol them. His brother, Gianni, was leading the chase after the horses, animals that were quintessential members of the circus. Having already lost one of their number, Moscardi prayed that no others were so badly injured that they had to be put down. His wife worried for their future.

'A lot of our people will be afraid to move,' she said.

'They'll do what I tell them,' asserted her husband.

'No, they won't. Circus folk are superstitious by nature, as you well know. They'll think that we'll always be a target if we remain in this county. I've talked to some of them. They want to cut our losses and move south.'

'We have to honour our commitments, Anne.'

'Our major commitment is to the people and animals we employ.'

'I'll guarantee their safety.'

'How can you do that, Mauro? In view of what's happened, who will believe you? When we're on the move like this through open country, we'd need an army to escort us.'

'I'll send scouts ahead to make sure there's no danger.'

'We can't always sense danger,' she said, anxiously. 'When we drove through that copse, we had no idea that someone was lurking there to start that fire. He waited until the horses were within reach.'

'That's how we know Sam Greenwood is behind this,' he said, bitterly. 'He understands how important our equestrian acts are. Without them, we could only offer very meagre fare.'

Before his wife could reply to Moscardi, they were interrupted by Mulryne.

'I've examined those bushes,' he said. 'Something had been poured over them to make them catch fire so quickly. It was only a question of tossing a burning rag on to the bushes and they'd burst into flame. Inspector Colbeck needs to be told about all this.'

'You can forget about him,' said Moscardi, fiercely. 'We don't matter to the inspector. He's much more interested in a dead woman than he is in us. I have to be honest, Mulryne. He may be your friend but I think the Railway Detective has betrayed us.'

Confronted with the choice between the two cases, Colbeck now opted for the tribulations of the circus. The murder had to wait in the queue. Before he left the police station, he sent word to Donald Underhill that he would join him at the Grand Hotel later in the day. He and Lill then caught a train to Corbridge.

'It gives me no satisfaction to say this,' he confided, 'but I did warn Mr Darlow that the circus was far more likely to be attacked than his railway. Even he won't be able to blame *this* ambush on the NER.'

'It's a convenient whipping boy, sir. If he opens the curtains one morning and sees a raging blizzard outside, Mr Darlow will claim that the NER is responsible.'

'What's the likely outcome?'

'Oh, I think that a merger is inevitable one day. I've seen articles to that effect in the newspapers. Darlow will fight against it to his last breath but, once Parliament authorises it, he'll have to admit defeat.'

'But he has friends in Parliament, surely.'

'They'll do their best to delay things.'

'Politicians are masters of delaying tactics. But let's put the fate of the NCR aside for a moment,' suggested Colbeck. 'Tell me about Jake Goodhart.'

'I had a job finding him at first but I sniffed him out in the end.'

'Did he remember you?'

'Only when I prompted him,' said Lill. 'Most people I've arrested revile me. Goodhart didn't. He accepted that I had a job to do and that was that. We had some rare tussles in the past. He fought tooth and nail. I'm glad those days are over.'

'What did he have to say for himself?'

Lill consulted his notebook and gave a detailed account of the interview. He admitted that he couldn't see how Goodhart could possibly have been involved in the attack on the train and was ready to absolve him of any suspicion.

'Then he shook my hand,' he recalled.

'That's always a good sign in an offender.'

'He yelped as if I'd just driven a spike through his palm.'

'Was his hand bandaged?'

'I couldn't see because he was wearing gloves. What I do know is that he was carrying an injury. He said it was a nasty cut but it could just as easily have been a gunshot wound.'

'Did that make you change your mind about him?'

'It did, sir. There are three salient points to bear in mind. First, he lost his job. He blames the head porter for that and, by extension, the NCR itself. He loathes it. Second, he knows the countryside around Fourstones very well because he and his wife used to go on long walks there, before they were married. In other words, he'd have been aware of a remote place where a body could be buried without fear of discovery.'

'That's a telling point.'

'Third, he's desperately short of money and has a family to feed.'

'Will he find it easy to get another job?'

'No, he won't. It will take time. What little savings he has will soon disappear. Goodhart's children will starve. He'll do absolutely anything to get money.'

'Does that mean he'd readily break the law?'

'I'm certain of it, sir.'

Jake Goodhart always felt uncomfortable in the wealthier districts of the city. The streets were wide, the houses detached and there was a general cleanliness to which he was unaccustomed. Living in a terraced house with one room and a scullery downstairs, and two tiny bedrooms above it, he led a different kind of existence altogether. When he had a glimpse of how the middle classes lived, he was cowed by what were to him unattainable standards of luxury. Turning a corner, he crossed the street diagonally and stopped outside a house. After ringing the bell, he had to wait some time before the door was opened. Goodhart whisked off his hat and gave an ingratiating smile.

'It's me,' he said.

The other man looked up and down the street before issuing a command.

'You'd better come in,' said Geoffrey Enticott.

Caleb Andrews arrived at the house in the confident expectation that he'd hear of an arrest. Instead of that, he learnt that Victor Leeming's visit to the hotel on the previous night had been futile.

'So that dreadful man is still on the loose,' he moaned.

'I'm afraid so, Father.'

'What did Lydia have to say to that?'

'It came as a slap in the face to her.'

'Where is she now?'

'Lydia's up in her room,' said Madeleine. 'I've tried to coax her into taking a walk with me but she refuses to leave the house.'

They were in the nursery. When her father first arrived, Madeleine was studying her daughter intently as she attempted some portraiture. Holding out her sketch pad, she showed the result to Andrews and he pulled a face.

'That's nothing like her, Maddy.'

'I know. I'm hopeless at figurative art. All I can draw are steam locomotives.'

'They're much more important than faces.'

'You're the only person who thinks so. People will pay thousands of pounds to have their portrait painted. I can't command that sort of money for my work.'

'You will one day,' he said, patting her shoulder. 'I was pleased to hear that Victor had had the sense to travel on the LNWR, by the way. If he went to Bristol, he'll have done the same again. Remind me why he's going there?'

'Robert sent him to look at a circus.'

'Dear God!' exclaimed Andrews. 'He gets paid for doing *that*?'

'The man who owns it is a suspect in the investigation in Northumberland. Victor went to interview him.'

'Robert should have done that himself, Maddy. It would've given him the chance to see his wife and daughter, not to mention his father-in-law.'

'He knows best.'

'Not if he spurns the LNWR.' When the door opened behind him, he turned to see Lydia coming into the room. 'Good day to you!'

'Hello, Mr Andrews.'

'I know that you didn't want to go for a walk with Maddy but how would you feel about a stroll with a distinguished elderly gentleman?'

'That's an invitation I'll happily accept,' she said, smiling. 'I've just given myself a strict talking-to. Nobody should be allowed to make me go into hiding. I've a perfect right to walk the streets of London, if I wish.'

'It's wonderful to hear you say that, Lydia,' said Madeleine.

'It's exactly what *you'd* say and do.' She turned to the old man. 'I'm ready when you are, Mr Andrews.'

*   *   *

They left Corbridge Station in a hired trap and drove to the scene of the ambush. In the aftermath of the derailment, the circus population had quickly adapted to the situation. They'd refused to be downhearted. That spirit of resistance was not in evidence now. When Colbeck and Lill saw one of the camps set up near the copse, there was a lacklustre air about it. The armed guards might be alert but the rest of the people seemed to be slouching around in a fit of depression. The detectives felt sorry for them. One attack might be dismissed as an unfortunate hazard. The second one, though far less serious in some ways, was thoroughly demoralising.

Mulryne saw them coming and waved them to a halt. He gave them a brief but vivid description of what had happened. He'd been in the copse at the time of the fire and seen the horses being stampeded.

'I just hope they don't come to any harm,' he said. 'They're thoroughbreds and they've been trained to a standard that takes years to achieve. Thanks to a mass of burning bushes, all of that could vanish.'

'A burning bush is usually an omen,' remarked Colbeck, wryly. 'Remember your Bible?'

'I'm a God-fearing Catholic. I never forget it.'

'Nor did the man who started the blaze. He was sending a message.'

'Could you show us exactly where it happened?' asked Lill.

'Indeed, I could.'

'In that case,' said Colbeck, 'climb aboard and I'll drive you there.'

A few minutes later, the three of them got out of the trap and walked across to the charred remains of the bushes. Colbeck readily accepted the Irishman's claim that something had been poured over the foliage to accelerate the fire but he questioned the claim that a burning rag would have been used.

'He'd have had to stand too close in order to throw it,' he reasoned. 'Having set it alight, he'd have wanted a speedy escape route. That means he'd have been much further back, hidden behind the trees with a horse. Let's take a look.'

Picking his way through the undergrowth, Colbeck walked for well over twenty yards before he stopped beside an oak tree with a wide girth. Its lowest branches reached down to some thick bushes that masked a convenient hollow in the ground. He pointed it out to his companions.

'This is the kind of spot,' he decided. 'Crouched down here, he could have chosen his moment and lit a very long fuse that led to a rag soaked in oil. As soon as that was ignited, those bushes would burst into flame.'

'What a clever devil!' observed Lill.

'Are you referring to me or to him?' asked Colbeck.

'To both of you, I suppose.'

'Yours is a better explanation than mine, Inspector,' said Mulryne. 'Not that it will make much difference to Mr Moscardi. He doesn't care *how* the fire started. The only thing he thinks about is coping with the results.'

'What sort of mood is he in?'

'He's throbbing with anger.'

'What about everyone else?' said Colbeck. 'When you were camped near Fourstones, there was a lively atmosphere. Everybody caught up in the derailment was quick to recover. A pall of sadness is hanging over you now.'

'It's the same with both camps. People are losing hope.'

'Let's go and report to Mr Moscardi. What sort of a welcome can we expect?'

Mulryne grinned. 'Oh, he'll throw his arms around you and kiss you on both cheeks. Then again,' he added, 'he might refuse to speak a word to either of you.'

* * *

It was a short but enjoyable walk. Lydia Quayle looked straight ahead of her at all times so that she exhibited no fear or nervousness. Caleb Andrews, on the other hand, was keen to look in every direction. His neck twisted so quickly and at such acute angles that it was soon aching. Wherever he turned, he saw nobody watching them. What he did see were the two uniformed policemen on their beat. It was a reassuring sight for him and for Lydia.

'They'll never be far away from the house,' he said.

'I know and I'm very grateful.'

'How do you feel?'

'I'm just happy to be out in the fresh air again, Mr Andrews,' she replied. 'It's a tonic in itself.'

'I'd never call this *fresh* air but it's far better than what I had to breathe in on the footplate. Being an engine driver is a filthy job. I'd come home almost black sometimes.'

'Do you miss the railway?'

'No,' he said with a chuckle, 'but I bet that it misses me.'

When they returned finally to John Islip Street, he paused at the door and looked behind him. Lydia kept her gaze fixed on the house. She'd had the courage to defy the stalker and go for a walk. It was a minor triumph.

'All clear,' announced Andrews. 'There's nobody following us.'

'Thank you,' she said, squeezing his arm. 'You've been a great help. I might even take another walk later on.' Inhaling deeply, she drew herself up to her full height. 'I feel better now.'

It was no more than the detectives had expected. When they called on Moscardi, they had to withstand a long tirade before they could even get a word in. Shaking with fury, he raised his voice to full volume. He also included many words in Italian to add spice and colour. Having survived many such rants from Edward Tallis,

Colbeck bore up well. Lill was more sensitive and twitched at some of the accusations levelled at them.

'I'm sorry that you feel we deserted you, sir,' said Colbeck, 'but face the truth, if you will. Had the inspector and I been travelling with you, that fire would still have been set alight and your wonderful horses would still have been scattered over the countryside. How are they, by the way?'

'Most of them have been caught,' replied the other, sulkily.

'Had they come to any harm?'

'Luckily, they hadn't.'

'Then the attack failed in its purpose. That's worthy of celebration, surely?'

'I agree,' Lill chimed in.

'What is there to celebrate?' yelled Moscardi. 'My circus is falling to pieces. The men are fearful, the women are crying and the animals are turning on their keepers. Nobody wants to go on yet they're afraid to stay here. We're in purgatory, Inspector, and you're telling me to celebrate.'

'I was merely suggesting that you look at this in a different light,' said Colbeck. 'You came through it more or less intact. And you won't be caught unawares next time because you know another attack may be planned. One man caused that derailment. It's likely that he was also responsible for stampeding your horses. Are you really frightened of one man?'

'Of course, I'm not. What frightens me is the state my circus is now in. You can *feel* the dejection. We've always been able to solve any problems in the past but not this time. We've become victims. And all our troubles,' he went on, increasing the volume, 'can be laid at the door of Sam Greenwood. If you'd had the sense to listen to me and arrest him, today's attack would never have happened and we'd be singing all the way to Newcastle.'

'Sergeant Leeming will already have confronted Mr Greenwood. He's on his way back from Bristol with a full report.'

'I don't need any report about that black-hearted bastard. I know him of old.'

'If he *is* involved,' said Colbeck, 'I promise you that he'll answer for it.' He looked Moscardi in the eye. 'Let me say this to you. When we spoke this morning, you were so scornful of my abilities that I decided to let you manage without them. I can't operate successfully without the respect and cooperation of the victims I'm actually trying to help. Sadly, I'm getting neither of those things from you, Mr Moscardi.'

'You don't deserve either,' murmured the Italian.

'I'll pretend I didn't hear that. What I'm prepared to offer you is a bargain. I will do everything in my power to bring your enemy to justice. That doesn't mean I'll be here in person twenty-four hours a day but, when I'm absent, Inspector Lill or Sergeant Leeming will be here in my stead and they'll have policemen at their behest. In return,' continued Colbeck, meeting his glare without flinching, 'I expect you to show patience and understanding. You know how to run a circus better than anyone. I know how to catch villains.'

'It's true,' said Lill. 'The inspector has had an incomparable record of success.'

'Bear with me, Mr Moscardi. Let me do things *my* way and give me your full support. Is that too much to ask?'

CHAPTER ELEVEN

He'd been in such good spirits when he left Bristol that he was not daunted by the prospect of a long train journey north. Victor Leeming believed that he'd had a successful visit to Greenwood's circus. After a probing interview with its owner, he came away with the feeling that the man was more than capable of employing someone to inflict harm on a hated rival. The sergeant had also done some detective work among the circus artistes, getting honest answers to all the questions Colbeck had asked him to pose. When he heard that Greenwood had sent a man to keep an eye on Moscardi's Magnificent Circus, he was convinced that he'd identified the villain behind the derailment. All that he had to do on his return, Leeming thought, was to arrest someone named Bevis. The evidence against him was persuasive. As a former Strong Man, he'd have had no difficulty lifting a couple of sleepers. If he'd mingled with the circus employees, he might easily have overheard talk of the plan to travel to Newcastle by train. Bevis was the man on the hill, he concluded. When they caught him, they'd surely find that one of his hands had been bandaged.

Secure in the knowledge that he was returning with vital evidence, he let his thoughts turn to the murder investigation. They were still in the dark there. Unaware of the recent advance in the case, he believed that they didn't know who the victim was or exactly how she'd died. Anonymous corpses were a common sight to him. During his years in uniform, he'd come upon several victims of a harsh winter, miserable creatures who'd frozen to death in the streets or tossed themselves into the river in despair. When some excavation was taking place in London, he was on hand when three skeletons were unearthed. Each had appalling wounds to their skull and two of them had had an arm cut off. Their identities were never discovered. They were nameless victims of brutal murder. Leeming wondered if the woman in the shallow grave would join them in the catalogue of unsolved crimes.

Then he remembered that he was working with Robert Colbeck, a man who would never admit defeat in an investigation. Regardless of how long it took and how much hard work it demanded, Colbeck had a knack of digging up information about murder victims. When he and Leeming had found the body of a man whose face had been made unrecognisable by corrosive acid, Colbeck had identified him within days. He'd done the same with a headless woman fished out of the Thames. A surge of pride coursed through him. Nothing was beyond them. Leeming felt that he'd already met the man behind the conspiracy to ruin Moscardi's circus. It was more than likely that, during his absence, Colbeck had solved the murder as well. Both cases would have been brought to a satisfactory conclusion and the detectives could return to the bosom of their respective families. Instead of travelling in a train, Leeming was being swept along on a wave of optimism that was invigorating.

* * *

'Thank you so much for responding to our appeal,' said Colbeck. 'You've lifted a veil from the investigation.'

'When I saw the appeal,' admitted Underhill, 'I ignored it at first.'

'Why was that, sir?'

'Well, I thought, it couldn't possibly be Mrs Pulver. What could she be doing up there in Northumberland? And who could want to kill such a gentle soul as her? Margaret Pulver was a saint.'

'You speak as if you know her well.'

'Oh, no,' said Underhill, quickly. 'My wife and I only met her from time to time. But I heard about the kind things she did for other people. If anyone was in trouble, Mrs Pulver was always the first person to help and console them. Given her circumstances, I find that remarkable. After a shattering blow like the one she'd suffered, most people would tend to lock themselves away and mourn in private.'

Even though Underhill had provided vital information, Colbeck was not sure if he could bring himself to like the man. He was too sleek and self-assured. Now in his forties, he was a handsome individual with the kind of long, curly hair and moustache that would need constant attention. Underhill was a solicitor in Shrewsbury but the quality of his apparel and the note of superiority in his voice hinted at private wealth as well. As a rule, Colbeck liked solicitors. He talked their language. Before he'd joined the Metropolitan Police Force, he had been a rising young barrister and, as such, was constantly in touch with one firm of solicitors or another. He was grateful that Donald Underhill had not been among them.

'What exactly was this blow she suffered?' asked Colbeck.

'She lost her husband and two children. It was tragic.'

'When was this, Mr Underhill?'

'Oh, it must have been four or five years ago,' replied the other.

'Richard Pulver – he was her husband – had a passion for sailing. They had a cottage on the Welsh coast where they spent their holidays. Whenever it was possible, Richard would take his wife and the two boys out in his boat.'

'Was he a good sailor?'

'He was an excellent one, Inspector, but even his skills were unequal to the situation in which he found himself. They were caught in a squall near the Menai Straits and were blown miles off course. When the squall developed into a gale, they were done for. It was weeks before the bodies were found.'

'That must have been devastating for Mrs Pulver.'

'I made a point of speaking to the police sergeant who had to deliver the news to her. He told me that she fainted on the spot.'

'I've been in situations like that myself. It's always distressing.'

'Yet somehow she found the strength to go on alone. That was when I realised what an extraordinary woman she was. How many of us could withstand a loss like that and go on to craft a new and fulfilling life?'

'Very few, I should imagine,' said Colbeck. 'What did Mr Pulver do?'

'He was a man of independent means who liked to dabble in the property market. At least, that's how he described himself. My own view is that he was much more than a dabbler. His property empire extended to London. When he wasn't sailing his boat, he was often visiting the capital.'

'Where did they live?'

For a man who claimed to be a mere acquaintance of the family, Underhill knew a great deal about it. The Pulvers, he told Colbeck, lived in the manor house of a small village near Shrewsbury. Most of the three hundred acres attached to it were leased out to a tenant farmer. What intrigued Colbeck was the news that a branch railway line had been built across the outer edge of the estate.

'Such developments often meet with local opposition,' he said.

'Richard Pulver rode roughshod over that, Inspector.'

'That wouldn't have endeared him to the villagers.'

'I doubt very much if he cared about that at the time. It was only months after work began on the line that he was drowned with his two sons. Some ignorant people said he'd been rightly punished. I think it was simply appalling bad luck.'

The two men were seated either side of a low table in Underhill's hotel room. Colbeck had noted how large and well appointed it was. The solicitor was clearly a man who chose the best of everything. His manner had been gently modified. There'd been a whiff of condescension about him at first. When he realised how astute and well educated Colbeck was, he became more respectful. Most of the policemen with whom he usually dealt with as a solicitor had neither the money nor the good taste to dress in the same way as Colbeck. Underhill knew that he was dealing with someone out of the ordinary.

'I'm sorry you were put through the ordeal of visiting the morgue, sir,' said Colbeck. 'It can be a harrowing experience.'

'That's exactly what it was. All I saw was Mrs Pulver's face but I was keenly aware that the body beneath the shroud had been cut open during the post-mortem. Frankly, it made my stomach heave.'

'Are you absolutely certain that it was Margaret Pulver?'

'Yes, I am.'

'There must have been obvious changes in her appearance. Death often paints unkind portraits of its victims.'

'It wasn't just her face that I recognised, Inspector. Bizarrely, the thing that was still intact was her air of refinement. She was a true lady,' Underhill continued. 'Death couldn't obliterate that fact.'

'You talk about her with affection, Mr Underhill, yet you were not part of her social circle.' Colbeck watched him carefully. 'Why did you decide to come here in person instead of telling a family member of your suspicion that the body of a murder victim in Northumberland might be that of Margaret Pulver? Identification of a corpse is always more reliable if given by someone close to them. Why did *you* take it upon yourself to get in touch with us?'

Confronted by what was, in effect, an ultimatum, Mauro Moscardi had conceded that the circus did need the expertise of detectives from Scotland Yard. They could do things that he, realistically, could not. While Moscardi and his brother were tempted to go in search of Greenwood and beat a confession out of him, they were held back by a grudging respect for the law. If their rival was indeed behind the attacks on the circus, Colbeck and Leeming would amass the evidence necessary to prosecute him. Moscardi, meanwhile, had to decide on a strategy for protecting the circus from a further assault. When he'd first elected to travel by road, he'd hoped that, by pushing along at a reasonable speed, they might actually get close to Newcastle by the end of the day. That possibility had now disappeared. They would have to camp overnight somewhere and reach their destination some time on the following day.

When he discussed the matter with his wife and with Gianni, he also invited Mulryne to offer an opinion. Time and again in awkward situations, the Irishman had proved his worth. The four of them met outside Moscardi's caravan.

'I say that we move on,' declared Gianni. 'It was galling to watch the train with all our equipment on board shoot past us earlier on. It's already being unloaded at the park set aside for us. We should have been on that train.'

'It's too late to argue about that now,' said Moscardi.

'I think we should spend the night here,' said Anne, looking around. 'This is as good a place as any. We should bring everyone together into one large camp. It's what most people would want.'

'It's not a question of what *they* want,' said Gianni. 'We make the decisions and you all know what mine would be. While the rest of you stay on the road, I'll ride ahead with a scouting party to make sure there are no more nasty surprises waiting for us. Is it agreed?'

'No,' replied Moscardi. 'I'd like to hear what Mulryne has to say first.'

'Well,' said the Irishman, 'I have sympathy with both sides of the argument. If we press on, we show our determination; if we stay here, we please the majority of people. They're unsettled and it's easy to see why. My own view is that it's highly unlikely we'll be attacked again. Whoever set those bushes alight hoped to cause more chaos than he actually did. Yes, he frightened us. Yes, he scattered the horses far and wide. But that's all he did. We've recovered every animal and not one of them was harmed in any way.'

'Yes, they were,' contended Anne. 'They've been thoroughly disturbed. There's no way that any of those animals would be in a fit state to perform today.'

'We're not asking them to do that, Mrs Moscardi.'

'They need rest and a chance to recover. They won't get either if we set off once more. There's plenty of grazing here. My vote is that we stay.'

Moscardi looked around the faces. 'Gianni says we go and Anne urges us to camp here. Mulryne has tackled the main question. If we continue on our way, is there more danger ahead?'

'I doubt it very much,' said Mulryne.

'And if there is,' added Gianni, 'we meet it with every weapon we possess and shoot to kill. We were caught out in that copse. We'll be more wary from now on.'

'There's more protection this time. Inspector Lill has drafted in some extra men to guard us. The sight of those police uniforms will keep an attacker at bay. Why waste several hours of daylight by sitting on our hands?'

Gianni was firm. 'I agree with Brendan.'

'Well, I don't,' said Anne.

'I'm sorry, my love,' said her husband, 'but I think that we have to get back on the road. Whatever the obstacles in our way, we'll reach Newcastle somehow.'

'Inspector Colbeck would say the same,' confirmed Mulryne.

'Then why isn't he here to say it?'

'He explained that. He has to keep one eye on the other case.'

Colbeck remembered his sorrow when viewing the body of the nameless victim. She'd looked so defenceless and forlorn. Now that he'd heard who she was and what sort of life she'd lived, Margaret Pulver became a real human being. It had surprised him that nobody had reported her missing but Underhill had explained that. She shared the house with servants who were accustomed to seeing her go off to London on a fairly regular basis. They had no reason to believe that she might be the victim of foul play in Northumberland. As for her parents, they were in the Channel Islands.

'Margaret was born and brought up in Sark,' said Underhill.

'That's little more than a rock in the sea, isn't it?'

'I've never been there, Inspector. It's remote, that's all I know about it.'

'How did she meet her future husband?' asked Colbeck.

'He was sailing on his own among the islands. Richard told me that he moored the boat on the coast of Sark, pitched a tent and went off to sleep. Next morning, he felt a dog licking his face. Margaret was taking her spaniel for a walk.'

'That's hardly the most romantic way to meet one's future wife.'

'It obviously worked, Inspector. They were made for each other.'

Underhill's ability to supply such details made it clear that he not only knew more about the Pulvers than he claimed, but that he had an obvious fondness for the wife. It was that affection which prompted him to travel up to Newcastle and to pray that his journey was in vain. In the event, it was not and he was grieving.

'The whole village will miss her,' he prophesied. 'The news will spread horror as much as sadness. The vicar is going to be especially distressed.'

'Why is that, sir?'

'Margaret Pulver was a stalwart member of the local church. She not only took part in all its activities, she made generous donations to it. That's why the whole congregation loved her so much. She was, as I said before, a saint.'

'Even saints sometimes have a need for companionship,' said Colbeck. 'What you've described to me is a remarkable woman. She was kind, talented, beautiful and a pillar of the local community. Such a person must have attracted attention wherever she went.'

'If you're asking me if she had any suitors, the truthful answer is that I don't know of any. Mrs Pulver had had a very happy marriage. She probably felt that it could never be entirely replaced so didn't seek another husband.'

'You mentioned regular trips to London.'

'She inherited the property her husband had there. I assume that she kept in regular touch with the agent who handled the letting and,' said Underhill with a smile, 'she probably took advantage of such trips to do some shopping. Mrs Pulver was always immaculately dressed. Such a wardrobe couldn't be bought anywhere in Shropshire.'

'So what was she doing in this part of the world?'

'I haven't a clue, Inspector.'

'What about her husband's family? Do they live up here somewhere?'

'They're down in Falmouth, I believe.'

'So Mrs Pulver had no known connection with Northumberland?'

'I'm fairly certain of it.'

'Was she a secretive woman?'

'Quite the reverse,' replied Underhill. 'You couldn't meet a more open and approachable person. She inspired trust the moment you met her.'

The more he heard about her, the more interesting she became to Colbeck. His visit to the hotel had taught him two things. The first was that Underhill was lying about his relationship with the deceased. Instead of seeing her occasionally, he was the sort of man to go out of his way to contrive a meeting with her. The second thing was even more important. Colbeck was certain that Margaret Pulver had a secret life outside the confines of a Shropshire village. In order to solve her murder, he had to find out exactly what it was.

By the time he'd got to Birmingham, the wave of optimism had died down to a mere ripple. When his train stuttered to a halt in Crewe, the wave had spent its force and was no more than a wet patch. Leeming chided himself for being so naïve. Crimes were never solved so easily. Samuel Greenwood had talked openly about his feud with Moscardi and threatened to bring him and his circus crashing down, but he'd had the same animosity for years and taken no action to damage his rival. As for what had seemed like vital information about a former Strong Man, this now appeared to be less convincing. In fact, Leeming could see that it ought to be dismissed as circus tittle-tattle with no real basis in truth. Instead of being able to make a significant arrest, therefore, he'd have nothing whatsoever of moment to report. High hopes had turned to broken dreams. He felt as Moses might have done if he'd mislaid the Ten Commandments on his way down Mount Sinai.

Cold reality set in. Sad, weary and uncomfortable, he was travelling by a mode of transport he abhorred and still had hours of it to endure. He didn't relish the prospect of telling Colbeck that his mission had been a failure. Then he remembered the letter from Madeleine in his pocket. It would certainly earn him thanks for acting as an emissary. He was also bolstered by the thought that he'd been able to give some comfort to Lydia Quayle. While he hadn't managed to catch the man who'd been tormenting her, he'd ensured that, as long as she was staying at the Colbeck residence, policemen on that beat would pay particular attention to the house. He drew satisfaction from the memory of being able to help and reassure a troubled young woman.

'You're still doing it.'

'Am I?'

'You can't stop it, Madeleine.'

'I'm sorry.'

'Without even thinking, you keep glancing upwards.'

'I didn't mean to irritate you, Lydia.'

'It's not irritating, it's very touching. The baby is up in the nursery and she's fast asleep. You can actually afford to relax for a few hours. If she does wake up, the nanny will take care of her.'

'My family couldn't afford that sort of help. Whenever I cried, my mother was there to look after me.'

'I sometimes wish that I'd been in that situation,' said Lydia. 'I might have developed a real bond with my mother. Instead of that, I felt closer to Nanny Jenkins than to her. It's a terrible thing to say, but it's the truth.'

'I hope that never happens to Helen.'

'No, she's a very different kind of child. She knows who her mother is. When you pick her up, you always get a radiant smile. Nobody else manages that.'

Lydia was almost cheerful now. As a result of her walk with Caleb Andrews, she felt stronger, safer and less haunted. She was even talking about finding a new hotel to which she could move, though Madeleine had scotched that notion at once, insisting that she stayed much longer.

'How long will Robert be in Northumberland?'

'I wish I knew,' said Madeleine.

'He must hate being away from you and his daughter.'

'Investigations have to go at a steady pace, Lydia. That's why they take so much time as a rule.'

'You've shown the most amazing patience.'

'I try my best.'

Without warning, Lydia got up from the sofa and made a decision.

'I'm going for another walk.'

'That's a good idea. I'll come with you.'

'No, you stay where you are, Madeleine. Much as I'd love your company, I feel that I must go alone. It's an important step in rebuilding my confidence.'

Madeleine was dubious. 'Are you quite sure?'

'Your father made me feel so much better about myself.'

'I'll tell him that. He likes to be appreciated.' She got up. 'It's not healthy for me to sit here all day. I could really do with a walk.'

'Then we'll have a compromise,' decided Lydia. 'You can come with me part of the way, then I'll go on alone after that. Is that fair?'

'It's more than fair.' She glanced upwards and Lydia

laughed. 'Oh dear!' she exclaimed. 'I'm doing it again, aren't I?'

'The only way to stop you is to take you out of the house altogether.'

The main reason why Donald Underhill kept him there so long was that he wanted the pleasure of talking about Margaret Pulver. It seemed odd that the solicitor could derive so much satisfaction that way. When Colbeck had been called upon in the line of duty to console bereaved parents or family members, emotions often got the better of them and fond memories of the deceased gushed out inconsequentially. Underhill had too much self-control to do that. He wanted to reconstruct Margaret Pulver in his mind and used Colbeck as his audience because there was nobody else to whom he could talk in such an intimate way. The inspector heard things that, he suspected, would certainly be kept from Underhill's wife.

When he'd finished, the solicitor issued a surprise invitation.

'I don't suppose you'd like to join me for dinner, would you?'

'Thank you all the same,' said Colbeck, 'but I'm afraid not.'

'I promise not to ramble on about Mrs Pulver.'

'The answer is still the same, sir.'

'What a pity! You're far more intelligent than the average policeman. It's a privilege to talk with a man who knows so much about the law. I don't know anyone who'd give up his career as a barrister in favour of law enforcement.'

'It's a decision I've never regretted, sir.'

'I applaud you for that.'

'What time will you be leaving tomorrow?' asked Colbeck, ignoring the compliment. 'It may be that I need to speak to you again.'

'I'm at your service.'

'I won't hold you up unnecessarily. If I decide that we don't need to see each other again, I'll send word.'

'Thank you.'

Colbeck rose to his feet and exchanged a farewell handshake. He then let himself out and descended the winding staircase. Before he'd entered the room, all that he possessed was the name of the dead woman. She'd now been given a history by someone who admired her greatly. How far that admiration went was an open question. Underhill had asked to be informed of any developments in the case. It was an understandable request from a man who'd been able to identify the body of a friend. There was, thought Colbeck, another way of looking at it. Underhill wanted progress reports because he was more closely involved in Margaret Pulver's private life than he cared to admit.

Out of courtesy, Colbeck returned to the police station and gave a heavily edited account of what he'd learnt to Superintendent Finlan. Saying nothing about his suspicions of Underhill, he simply passed on details of the deceased. Finlan was appeased.

'Thank you for keeping me abreast of developments, Inspector.'

'It's only right, sir.'

'What do you propose to do next?'

'I may have to find time to visit Mrs Pulver's home. Apart from anything else, her servants will need to be questioned about her supposed whereabouts at the time of her death.'

'Does that mean you'll leave the circus entirely in the hands of Sergeant Leeming and Inspector Lill?'

'No, sir, it doesn't. In fact, I mean to return to it right now.'

'Then there's something you need to be told,' said Finlan, reaching for a piece of paper. 'Lill sent a telegraph to warn you that Mr Moscardi has set off again. Don't return to Corbridge. You should get off at Stocksfield Station. By the time you reach that, they should be somewhere in the vicinity.'

'Thank you for the advice, Superintendent.'

'We do have our uses,' said the other, complacently. 'We may be far away from London, but we know how to conserve police time.'

It was easier to announce their departure than to activate it. Moscardi had to use a mixture of persuasion and threat to get everyone into line. Ordinarily, his decisions were unquestioned but there were unusual circumstances this time. It was a full hour before the circus had formed into a single unit and set off. As promised, Gianni had gone ahead with a group of selected men, acting as scouts. He made great use of the telescope but saw nothing that constituted a threat. What helped to revive the jaded members of the cavalcade was the reception they were given in every village and hamlet they passed. Mothers and children came out to cheer and goggle. People still at work, opened windows and waved excitedly. The circus had an audience. It took their minds off any potential dangers ahead.

When they stopped beside a stream to water the horses and other livestock, Cyrus Lill drove the trap alongside Moscardi's caravan and climbed out. The Italian came across to him.

'Pressing on was a wise move, sir,' said Lill.

'You're one of the few people who thought that, Inspector. Most of them wanted to stay where we were.'

'Thankfully, there have been no incidents on the way.'

'I still get the feeling that we're being watched.'

'That's more than I do,' said Lill, 'and, even if it's true, we're under scrutiny from a distance. Nobody would dare to get close to us now. Your brother is acting as our advanced guard and there are too many shotguns visible among your artistes.'

153

'We're entitled to defend ourselves.'

'I'm sure that won't prove necessary.'

'No disrespect to you, but I'd like to have Inspector Colbeck with us as well. We have our differences but he talks sense.'

Lill laughed. 'Does that mean I *don't*, sir?'

'We're glad of all the help we can get. It was very foolish of me to think that we could look after ourselves. Now that we're prepared, we may be able to defend ourselves better but we couldn't root out the villain who's preying on us. Only someone like Inspector Colbeck can do that.'

'He'll be delighted to hear that you now recognise that.'

'Please pass on the information.'

'You'll be able to do that yourself, sir,' said Lill, gazing ahead. 'Unless I'm much mistaken, the Inspector is on his way to join us.'

A rider had just crested the hill and was cantering towards them. There was something about him that convinced Lill that it had to be Colbeck. Instead of coming by trap this time, he'd hired a horse and was clearly a more than competent rider. As Colbeck got closer, Moscardi was able to identify him and waved an arm in welcome. Colbeck was glad to see the Italian's change of heart. When he reined in his horse and dropped from the saddle, he smiled at the man.

'I'm glad to see that we're friends again, sir,' he said.

'Mr Moscardi made the same observation only minutes ago,' Lill told him. 'He now appreciates what you bring to the investigation.'

'When you are actually here, that is,' said Moscardi.

'Even when I'm not,' said Colbeck, 'you and your circus are never far from my mind. On the way from Newcastle, I've been thinking hard about this case and I come back to the conclusion that I reached at the very start. A railwayman is somehow involved.'

'Then he's in the pay of Sam Greenwood.'

'That seems more and more unlikely to me, sir. In fact, I'm beginning to regret that I sent Sergeant Leeming to speak to the man.'

'Why do you say that?' asked Lill.

'It's based on my observation of Mr Moscardi,' said Colbeck. 'He's one of a unique breed. Circus people are different to the rest of us. They don't seek the security of a house and a job that helps to pay the bills. Dedicated to their art, they brave all weathers as they seek new audiences. They're proud of their skills and they love their animals.'

'It's true,' conceded Moscardi. 'If we didn't love them, we couldn't put up with the bother and the expense of keeping them.'

'I know that you hate Mr Greenwood, and I accept that his circus can't compete with you in terms of size and quality, but he's cut from the same cloth as you. He's ready to cope with the many problems of touring from place to place.'

Moscardi tensed. 'You can't compare Greenwood to *me*.'

'Yes, I can, sir. He's a member of that unique breed I spoke about. Would someone who lives with circus people really want to harm some of them? Would someone who cares for animals, as he surely must do, devise a way to injure them? I don't believe it,' said Colbeck. 'Mr Greenwood might well want to cause you delays, or arrange for equipment to be stolen or even entice some of your artistes away, but I can't see him being party to a derailment that could have resulted in far more damage than it actually did.'

'That's a sound argument,' agreed Lill. 'I'd endorse it.'

'If we blame Mr Greenwood, we're going down a blind alley.'

'He's been threatening to obliterate us for years,' claimed Moscardi.

'Then why hasn't he done so?' asked Colbeck. 'More to the

point, why haven't you launched a direct attack on his circus? The answer is simple. At the end of the day, both of you respect the law too much. You also draw back from inflicting injuries on your own kind. That's why your vendetta with Mr Greenwood is almost exclusively a war of words.'

'It's not true. He has resorted to violence.'

'I can understand why you believe that, sir, but you are wrong.'

'We shall see.'

'Sergeant Leeming will help to clarify the situation. He'll have met Mr Greenwood and, at my suggestion, taken soundings from some of the artistes.'

'All that he'll learn is that Sam Greenwood is a born liar.'

'He's also a circus man at heart.'

'That's a crucial fact,' said Lill.

'It is in my opinion,' Colbeck went on. 'That's why I'm certain that we'll find your attacker is in some way connected to the Newcastle and Carlisle Railway.'

The door opened and Jake Goodhart stepped out into the street. As he put on his cap, he mumbled his thanks. Geoffrey Enticott was terse.

'Don't ever come to me again.'

CHAPTER TWELVE

It had been several weeks since Madeleine Colbeck had even been into her studio. As she showed Lydia Quayle into the room, she realised how much the arrival of the baby had changed her life and its regular patterns. Instead of becoming absorbed in her latest artistic project, she simply wanted to devote herself to her daughter. The studio was a tribute to her skill and industry. Paintings of locomotives, some yet to be completed, were everywhere. Those she'd rejected altogether stood in a pile in the corner. She walked across to her easel.

'This is where I used to spend my days,' she explained. 'Robert chose this bedroom for me because it gets the best of the light.'

'That must be very important for an artist.'

'It is, Lydia.'

'Do you want Helen to follow in her mother's footsteps?'

Madeleine laughed. 'It's far too early to make a decision like that.'

'But she may well have inherited your talent.'

'I wouldn't call it that. All that I had was a knack of drawing things. When Robert saw that, he encouraged me to develop it and paid for me to have proper instruction. I put my success down to a combination of hard work and some very good teachers. It was years before I was good enough to offer my work for sale.'

'You've shown such tenacity, Madeleine.'

'I love painting. That's my secret.'

After showing her friend some of the individual canvases, Madeleine took her downstairs to the drawing room. She was pleased with the obvious improvement in Lydia. There was no hint of dread about her now. Having been for two walks, and spent some time alone outdoors, Lydia looked and felt so much better. Fears of her stalker were receding gently to the back of her mind. Madeleine felt able to introduce the subject again without causing discomfort.

'Have you remembered who Daniel Vance was yet?' she asked.

'No, I haven't, but I know I've heard that name before.'

'Was it someone you met?'

'It could be. Then again, it could be someone of whom I only heard mention.'

'You have such a good memory as a rule, Lydia.'

'I like to think so. That's why I'm coming to think that Daniel Vance belongs in my past. If we ever met, it must have been years ago.'

'I suppose there's no chance that . . .' Madeleine let the words die. 'No, that's a silly thought. I apologise.'

Lydia read her mind. 'There's no need. I've thought the same thing. Perhaps that *is* his real name. Then I tell myself that he'd never give himself away like that so he'd hide behind an alias.'

'But why choose that particular one?'

'Who knows?'

'It's so mystifying.'

'The best thing I can do is to ignore him altogether. I'm safe here and I can walk out of that door without any worries. On the other

158

hand, I don't want to impose. This is my problem, not yours.'

'We're friends, Lydia. We share problems.'

'But you don't have any. Your life is perfect.'

'Is that what you think?' said Madeleine, amused. 'I spend every waking hour worrying about my daughter, I miss my husband terribly and I'm afraid that my days as an artist are well and truly over. Is that what you call a perfect life?'

'No,' admitted Lydia, 'it isn't.'

'As for you being an imposition, that's absurd. You help to take my mind off Helen and to forget that Robert is so far away. And when you were praising my work up in the studio just now, you kindled an urge in me to paint once again. You may not need me,' she said, embracing Lydia, 'but I certainly need you.'

The journey seemed interminable and became progressively more tedious. As a man who liked physical action, Victor Leeming hated being cooped up in the compartment of a train with companions who chattered continuously. When he changed trains in Carlisle, he was relieved that he was at last setting off on the last leg of his trek. He just wished that there were not so many intermediate stops on the way. As the train pulled out of Haydon Bridge, he consoled himself with the thought that he would soon see the circus encampment beside the line. Light was starting to fall but he nevertheless expected to get a good view of it. He was therefore amazed when all that was left of it was the huge patch of grass on which the camp had been set up.

Arriving at Fourstones Station, he jumped out of the compartment and ran for the exit. When he reached the Station Inn, he dashed straight upstairs and knocked on the door of the room occupied by Colbeck. Since there was no response, he opened the door and saw that the inspector's luggage had disappeared.

No circus, no Colbeck and no explanation – Leeming began to wonder if he was hallucinating.

'Where *is* everybody?' he cried.

'My wife and I would be delighted to act as your hosts, Inspector.'

'That's a very kind offer, sir, but I have to decline it.'

'You'd be far more comfortable in our home,' said Tapper Darlow. 'You'd have better food than this place could ever provide and I'd put a carriage at your disposal to drive you back and forth from the city.'

'There'll be no need,' Colbeck assured him. 'We'll stay here.'

'May I remind you that I was the person who summoned you here? We're dealing with a crime that caused great inconvenience to my railway. I insist on being at the centre of this investigation.'

'You'll be informed of any development, sir.'

'I don't want to rely on a string of messages,' said the other, peevishly. 'I want to be able to discuss the case at length across the dining table.'

'There'll be little time for that, Mr Darlow. Detection is far more important than discussion. While we're dining with you, we're being diverted from our primary purpose. Moreover, as I've reminded you before, we're handling *two* cases. Now that we know the name of the murder victim, that investigation will take more of my time.'

Darlow slapped his knee. 'I protest strongly against that.'

'Your protest is noted, sir,' said Colbeck, suavely.

They were seated in the lounge of the hotel in Newcastle he'd chosen as the base from which to operate. Close to Central Station, it lacked the superior facilities of the Grand Hotel but it was ideal for the detectives. As on previous occasions, those who'd actually summoned them expected Colbeck and Leeming to move in with them during the time they were there. It was the last thing they wished to do.

They'd be hampered and deprived of privacy. Having to face someone as fussily inquisitive as Darlow over the breakfast table every morning was a prospect that filled Colbeck with horror. He and Leeming could only function at their best if given complete freedom to do so.

'I repeat,' said Darlow, raising his voice as if speaking to a deaf person, 'that my telegraph brought you here from London.'

'That's partly true, sir, but it was the second telegram that had more impact on me.'

'Who sent it?'

'It was an old colleague of ours, Brendan Mulryne. He works for the circus. Mulryne was actually on the train when it came off the rails. That's why his testimony is so much more important than yours.'

Darlow reddened. 'I have the authority to speak for the NCR.'

'Mulryne speaks for the people and animals that survived the ordeal.'

'You can be very exasperating, Inspector.'

'Then I apologise. It's not intentional.'

'How much time might we expect you to devote to the derailment?'

'That's in the lap of the gods, sir.'

'Damn it, man! Do you have to be so evasive?'

Colbeck fixed him with a stare. 'We won't let you down, Mr Darlow.'

After fulminating for a few minutes, the older man accepted that he couldn't browbeat the inspector and backed off. Telling Colbeck that he could be contacted at his office the next day, he stamped off. No sooner had he disappeared than he was replaced by Victor Leeming, who came into the lounge with a valise in his hand. Seeing Colbeck, he came across to him.

'What did you do to Mr Darlow?'

'I told him the truth.'

'I could almost see the steam rising from him.'

'That was probably the most appropriate response to our conversation,' said Colbeck. 'You look tired, Victor. Sit down.'

'Thank you,' said the other, flopping into an armchair. 'I'm exhausted. I came all the way from Bristol to find that the circus had vanished and that you were no longer at the Station Inn. It was weird.'

'I left you a letter explaining where you'd find me.'

'Yes, I read it. Why did Mr Moscardi decide to move?'

'When you've had a chance to recover,' promised Colbeck, 'I'll give you all the details. Before we do that, I suggest that we order a drink and look at the dinner menu. There's a lot to discuss, Victor, and it's best done on a full stomach.'

Having finally got on the move again, the circus had made good time. It camped for the night in a field within five miles of Newcastle. Moscardi chose a site that had a supply of water nearby, grazing for the horses and some rising ground forming the perimeter. Gianni immediately commandeered that for his sentries. With armed men defending them on every side, everyone felt reassured. The derailment and the fire still lingered in their minds without dominating them. Once fed, the animals were much calmer. Some of the artistes even started singing. Mulryne was delighted.

'They're getting back something of their old spirit,' he said, grinning. 'It's good to hear them.'

'I won't start singing until we reach Newcastle,' said Moscardi.

'We'll be very safe there, sir.'

'I hope so,' said Anne. 'Everyone is so tired and unsettled. They won't be happy until they see our marquee up again and can rehearse properly in it.'

'I'll enjoy helping to put it up tomorrow,' said Mulryne. 'I love pulling on those ropes. It's a good way to build up a thirst.'

'Don't get too thirsty. You know our rules.'

'We'll have no drunkenness in this circus,' decreed Moscardi.

162

'People are entitled to a drink as long as they have it in moderation. If anyone finishes up in a drunken stupor, I'll throw them out straight away.'

They were sitting outside the Moscardi caravan and enjoying the warm evening air. Fires had been lit for cooking and lamps burnt all round the camp. From the sound of playful banter, they could hear that a sense of camaraderie had returned. Mulryne had just come back from a tour of the whole area.

'What do you have to report?' asked Moscardi.

'I have nothing but good news, sir. The danger is over.'

'It doesn't *feel* over,' complained Anne.

'The rest of us think so, Mrs Moscardi. Your brother-in-law will make sure that we have an uninterrupted night. All is well.'

'I thought that when we came through that copse,' recalled Moscardi.

'We let our defences down and we learnt from our mistake. But wasn't it wonderful to get such a welcome in the villages we passed through? They treated the Moscardi's Magnificent Circus like conquering heroes.'

'In a sense, that's what we are.'

'It lifted everybody,' said Anne. 'Applause like that is our lifeblood.'

'We'll have plenty of that when we get to Newcastle, my love.'

'Right,' said Mulryne, 'I'll be on my way. I know you'll want to have a meal in private.' About to move away, he paused. 'Oh, there was one thing.'

'What's that?' asked Moscardi.

'I was talking to Karl Liebermann earlier on. When we came through that last village, he thought he recognised a face in the crowd. He'd worked with the man, he said. I wondered if you'd heard of him.'

'What was his name?'

'Bev Rogers.'

Moscardi started. 'Say that again.'

'Karl thought he saw this Bev Rogers but he couldn't be sure. You've obviously heard the name before. Who is he?'

'Rogers was the Strong Man with Greenwood's circus. He's stopped performing now but he was kept on because he was useful. Now I see just how useful he can be,' said Moscardi, scowling. 'Rogers is a big man. He'd stick out in a crowd. That's why Karl spotted him.'

'I thought I should mention it to you, sir.'

'Thank goodness you did. It proves I was right all along.'

'What do you mean?'

'Rogers is not here to watch us performing. He's a spy, and it's more than likely that he was responsible for the attacks on us. I knew that Sam Greenwood was behind it. He's set his Strong Man on to us.'

'We've got plenty of strong men of our own.'

'I know that, Mulryne. I'll be sending some of them out in search of Rogers tomorrow. Their orders will be simple. Beat him to a pulp until he confesses.'

'Inspector Colbeck should be told about this.'

'He won't take it seriously,' said Anne, sadly.

'That's right,' added her husband. 'He refuses to believe that we're under attack from one of our rivals. According to the inspector, the person who's been hounding us has a connection with the railways. Well, I've got news for him,' he continued, eyes blazing. 'We know who's been sent to destroy us now. It's definitely one of Sam Greenwood's men.'

The tankard of beer had revived him and the imminent prospect of food reminded him how hungry he was. Leeming was already starting to forget the boredom and discomfort of the train journey. His first task was to hand over the letter from Madeleine. Dying to open it, Colbeck nevertheless kept it in his pocket until the sergeant had delivered his report. He was interested to hear about the visit to Bristol and explained why he now thought Greenwood was innocent of the accusations hurled at him by Mauro Moscardi. Having had plenty of time to reflect on what he'd learnt, Leeming agreed with him wholeheartedly.

'Moscardi and Greenwood are two of a kind,' he said. 'They're like wild dogs barking at each other from a distance.'

'And that's all they do, Victor. They bark but never bite.'

'Superintendent Tallis can do both simultaneously.'

'Yes,' said Colbeck, laughing. 'He's a circus act in himself.'

'There's something else I must tell you, sir. I daresay it will be mentioned in your wife's letter but you ought to hear my version first.'

He went on to describe the trouble that Lydia Quayle had been having with a stalker and how the man had actually booked into her hotel. The news that he'd also stolen a dress of hers alarmed Colbeck.

'This is rather more than unwanted attention,' he said.

'Miss Quayle was really frightened.'

'I'm glad that Madeleine invited her to move into our house. Your action was very prompt, Victor. It was good of you to help her in that way.'

'Unfortunately, I wasn't able to catch the man.'

'Somebody ought to do so.'

'Well, it's no use turning to the superintendent for permission to institute a search for him. He'd claim that no crime had actually been committed.'

'A dress was stolen.'

'That wouldn't justify assigning a detective to the case in his eyes. You know what he's like. I did all I could do in asking the constables on the beat in your area to look out for the stalker.'

'That will help but the problem will remain until this individual is stopped.'

A waiter came into the lounge to tell them that their table was ready. Leeming took the opportunity to slip up to the room reserved for him, partly to get rid of his luggage but mainly in order to give Colbeck the chance to read Madeleine's letter. When he eventually rejoined him, the inspector had a contented smile. Over the first course, Leeming heard what had been happening while he was away. He was abashed.

'A positive identification of the murder victim and another attack on the circus,' he said, morosely. 'I always miss the excitement.'

'I should have thought a visit to the superintendent provided enough of that.'

Leeming gave a hollow laugh. 'Tell me more about this Mr Underhill.'

'He's a curious fellow,' said Colbeck. 'I ought to be grateful for all the information he supplied but he troubles me. The truth is that he's given me far too much information about Mrs Pulver. I was swamped with unnecessary detail. It was almost as if he was planning to write her biography.'

'At least, we now know who she is, sir.'

'Quite so – in that sense, Underhill has been a godsend. The parents will have to be told, of course, and that's best done by the police on Guernsey. I've set that in motion. Underhill has volunteered to help with funeral arrangements because he thinks that the parents will be too frail to cope.'

'That's very kind of him.'

'Is he being kind or simply intrusive?'

'I don't follow.'

'Well, he asked me to inform him of the date of the inquest so that he can be here. Why should he do that? At one point, he even asked me if I could take him to the place where the body was discovered. That borders on the ghoulish.'

'The death of someone you know can have strange effects.'

'Mrs Pulver is not someone he *knows*, Victor. She's a woman he loved.'

'Was it that obvious?'

'You can see for yourself,' said Colbeck. 'I've sent word to his hotel that I'd like to speak to him tomorrow morning. You'll come with me. I'd appreciate your opinion of him.' After adding some pepper to his soup, he stirred it with his spoon before tasting a first mouthful. 'We've met someone like Mr Underhill before.'

'That's what I was just thinking.'

'Someone who is so desperate to know what's happening at every stage of an investigation could have an ulterior motive. He's keen to save his skin.'

'Should we add him to the list of suspects?'

'Judge for yourself when you meet him,' advised Colbeck. 'I trust your instincts. Now eat your soup before it goes cold. It's delicious.'

For the first time since she'd moved into the house, Lydia Quayle woke up without even the most vestigial anxieties. The time spent with Madeleine had been both enjoyable and restorative but she felt that she should move back to a hotel to regain her independence. To work up an appetite for breakfast, she decided to take a brisk walk. Madeleine intervened.

'Wait until we've eaten,' she suggested. 'When the baby's been fed, she soon goes off to sleep. We can both go for a walk then.'

'I can manage on my own, Madeleine. I did so yesterday.'

'That's true.'

'What harm can come to me if I have a ten-minute stroll?'

'None at all, I suppose,' said Madeleine.

'Then we must talk about my leaving.'

'But there's no need to do that yet. Look upon this house as your home.'

'That's very sweet of you but I can't hide away for ever. That's what I've been doing. When I got up today, my first thought was that I ought to start looking for a hotel, somewhere discreet in the suburbs. Then I had another idea,' she said. 'Why don't I take advantage of the situation to have a holiday?'

'Where would you go?'

'I'm not sure yet. I just think it might be wise if I get well away from London for a while. If he is still trying to pursue me, his enthusiasm might wane if I go off to Devon or somewhere like that.'

'There's some truth in that, Lydia.'

'It's not that I'm running away,' said the other. 'I adore being here and fulfilling my role as an unofficial aunt. I just can't see enough of Helen. For my own sake, I need to drag myself away. It's ages since I had a holiday of any kind.'

'You used to go to Italy a lot at one time, didn't you?'

'That phase of my life is over.'

'I understand.'

'Italy has no appeal for me now, Madeleine.'

It had been on a visit to Italy that Lydia had first met Beatrice Myler, the older woman with whom she'd later lived for a while. Drawn together by a mutual love of art and Italian history, they'd discovered many other things they had in common. After her decisive break with her, Lydia didn't wish to be reminded of the country where they first encountered each other.

Sad as she was to let her friend go, Madeleine could see the virtue of a holiday. A change of scene would be restful for her. Crucially, it would get her away from the man who had been stalking her so relentlessly. She tried to sound a positive note.

'You're right, Lydia. A holiday would be the making of you. We'll miss you, of course, but your niece will still be here when you come back. We expect you to have lots of wonderful adventures to tell us about.'

A new day brought all of the old zest back to the circus. They were within striking distance of a major city where they always enjoyed a rapturous welcome. The dazzling sunshine was a good omen. Putting their setbacks behind them, they set off early with smiles on their faces. Moscardi knew how to catch the eye. Ever the showman, he unfurled banners, passed out flags and dressed the horses in their prettiest harness. Rosie the elephant was brought to the front of the cavalcade with a young female acrobat astride her in a glistening costume. Close behind was the band that would play them into the city and let the whole of Newcastle know that the long-awaited visit of their favourite entertainment had at last arrived.

Clowns put on their full make-up and their outrageous wigs. Tumblers, jugglers, acrobats and tightrope walkers donned their costumes. Dressed in her finery, Anne Moscardi sat beside her husband as he drove the caravan. He was wearing the red coat and black top hat he used as the ringmaster. At the first village, they were mobbed by excited children who ran alongside them and revelled in the antics of the clowns. The lions attracted great attention but one mighty roar could disperse a crowd in seconds. While the artistes were on display, Gianni Moscardi and his men rode ahead to check that there were no obstacles to the safe passage of the circus. From time to time, he galloped back to report to his brother.

'Everything is clear ahead,' he shouted.

'Thank you, Gianni. Is there any sign of that Strong Man?'

'No, we haven't seen hide nor hair of Bev Rogers. He's a difficult man to miss. Karl must have made a mistake.'

'You don't make mistakes about a man you worked with for years.'

'I suppose not.'

'Keep your eyes peeled, Gianni.'

A train thundered past to their left. 'That's the best way to get there.'

'We can't drum up business if we arrive by rail.'

'We don't need to do so,' Anne interjected. 'They know us and value us in Newcastle. Lots of the people there live a hard life. Coming to the circus is one of the biggest treats they ever get.'

'Coming to *our* circus, that is,' corrected her husband. 'I wouldn't give a fig for any other one.'

'Neither would I, Mauro.'

'I'll get back to the others,' said Gianni.

'Spread the word about Bev Rogers,' warned Moscardi. 'I want him caught.'

'What if he puts up a fight?'

'You've got a gun, haven't you?'

Gianni nodded. Wheeling his horse, he kicked it into life and raced off.

Leeming disliked the man on sight. Coming from a humble background, he'd always had a latent fear of those from the higher ranks in society. Even though Colbeck had told him many times that he had no cause to feel inferior, the residual unease remained. Donald Underhill was the sort of man who induced both disquiet and anger in him. At a glance, the sergeant found him too patrician, too vain and too disdainful of those, like Leeming, from the lower orders. When they were introduced, Underhill gave him an almost scornful smile whereas Colbeck merited obvious respect. The three men sat down together in the hotel lounge.

'We're sorry to delay your departure, sir,' Colbeck began.

'That's the advantage of being the senior partner,' said Underhill, airily. 'I'm not tied down to regular hours. I come and go as I please.'

'I wish we could,' said Leeming under his breath.

'What did you wish to see me about, Inspector?'

'There's something I forgot to ask you,' said Colbeck. 'Have you ever been to this corner of the country before?'

'As a matter of fact, I have – though it was years ago. I came by invitation. I spoke to a roomful of lawyers on aspects of the Criminal Law. It was only for a weekend.'

'What was your impression?'

'I liked the place and I found the countryside around here quite enchanting.'

'We feel the same.'

'But there's a big difference between us. I only came to *talk* about the law. You and the sergeant are here to enforce it.'

'We have to find the killer first, sir,' said Leeming, 'and he's very elusive.'

'Why do you assume that it must be a man?' asked Colbeck. 'Women can administer poison just as well. We've dealt with cases of three husbands who died at their wife's hands that way.'

Underhill was surprised. 'Are you serious, Inspector?'

'We must look at every option.'

'But the body was found in a remote location, according to you. How could a woman carry the corpse there?'

'It would have been possible to get reasonably close with a trap. Mrs Pulver was not heavy. Another woman could have carried her – or dragged her along.'

'Why would any woman even think of poisoning her? Mrs Pulver had no enemies. All the women in her village worshipped her.'

'Perhaps they only pretended to,' suggested Leeming. 'The question we have to ask is why someone who lives in Shropshire should end her life so far away? Who or what brought her here? It would be interesting to visit Mrs Pulver's village to find out if anyone was absent during the time that she was.'

'That's precisely what I intend to do,' said Colbeck.

'Couldn't I do it on your behalf?' asked Underhill, keen to be of assistance. 'It would save you time and trouble.'

'There's no trouble when we have a railway system at our disposal. Thank you for your offer, sir, but there are some things we must do ourselves. To be frank, I'd rather like to see the place where Mrs Pulver seems to have become an icon.'

'I look forward to showing you around.'

Colbeck made a mental note to resist being shown only what Underhill decided to show him. When he asked about the area, he was given what amounted to a gazetteer of the county. Leeming had to butt in to end the recital.

'That's very helpful, Mr Underhill,' he said, 'but you have your work to do, albeit at hours of your own choosing. If one or both of us come to Shropshire, I'm sure we'll manage to find our way around.'

'But I could introduce you to the people who count, Sergeant.'

'All people count to me, sir. I make no distinctions.'

'No,' said Underhill in a lordly tone. 'I can see that you don't.' He turned to Colbeck. 'I suppose you have no idea how long the investigation will go on?'

'It will take some time, that's all I can say.'

'You can always reach me by telegraph.'

'That's a comfort to know, sir.'

'Needless to say, the local newspapers will want to write about the case. Have I your permission to reveal that I was the person who identified Mrs Pulver?'

'Go ahead and do so. The more publicity this case gets, the more likelihood of jogging someone's memory. I've already been in touch with the national press. Mrs Pulver's name will soon be known all over the country.'

The detectives had come to ask the questions but it was Underhill who now took charge of the interrogation. He tried to wrest every last detail of the case from them and was irritated when they remained circumspect. Eventually, realising that he was making no headway, he gave up.

'Right,' he said, fussily, 'if there's nothing else, I ought to be on my way.'

'Thank you again for coming, sir.'

'It was my duty, Inspector.'

After a respectful nod to Colbeck, he ignored Leeming entirely and went out through the main door. A porter was standing by with his luggage. The detectives looked after the departing solicitor.

'Well,' said Colbeck, 'what did you think?'

'I didn't like him one bit, sir.'

'I was asking about his character.'

'As to that, I'd say that he was proud, arrogant and too fond of himself. I'm sure he's well educated but nobody has taught him good manners.'

'I want to see him on his home territory.'

'I'd be happy if I never see him again, sir.'

'Could he be a potential suspect?'

'Oh, yes,' said Leeming. 'I'd have no trouble believing that.'

'We've established that he's been to the county before. That could turn out to be significant. On the other hand, he doesn't *look* like a man who'd actually kill someone. He'd delegate anything as distasteful as that to an accomplice.'

'If that were the case, he'd surely be the last person to come forward to identify the victim. He'd hide away in Shropshire, wouldn't he?'

'Maybe, maybe not. I just don't think he has a credible motive for murder.'

'I agree, sir.'

Getting to their feet, they were about to leave when Cyrus Lill came bustling over. Colbeck had left details with him of their whereabouts at the start of the day. Lill was patently relieved to catch them.

'There's a problem with the circus,' he announced.

Leeming winced. 'Was it another attack?'

'No, it's nothing like that. One of the acrobats thought he recognised someone in a crowd yesterday who used to be the Strong Man with Greenwood's Circus.'

'Yes, that's right. His name is Bevis Rogers.'

'Mr Moscardi is convinced that he's come to destroy them.'

'That's nonsense,' said Colbeck, 'and I explained exactly why to him. This is not a plot hatched by a rival circus.'

'You won't ever convince Mr Moscardi or his brother, come to that. Gianni is out on patrol with a loaded gun and we've seen how hot-headed he is. If he gets a glimpse of this man, Rogers, he'll kill him on the spot.'

174

CHAPTER THIRTEEN

As the circus came to another village, they were greeted yet again by cheers and applause. The elephant was the most popular attraction but the clowns were by far the most active. Leaping off their wagons and caravans, they went into the crowd to play tricks on them and kept them laughing uncontrollably for minutes. Mauro Moscardi was pleased with the reaction they were getting. He could afford to breathe more easily. Their problems seemed to be over.

Half a mile ahead, however, his brother was getting a more frosty reception. As he cantered along in advance of the circus, he came upon a group of men blocking the track. They were led by a burly farmer with a sheepdog beside his feet and a shotgun in his hands. His companions were armed with staves and hay forks. One had a sledgehammer over his shoulder.

Gianni tugged on the reins and brought his mount to a halt in front of them.

'Are you from the circus?' demanded the farmer.

'Yes, I am.'

'Well, you're not crossing my land till I have compensation.'

Gianni was nonplussed. 'What are you talking about?'

'Don't pretend you don't know.'

'I'm not pretending anything,' said Gianni, reasonably. 'My elder brother runs the circus. Since we left Carlisle, we've been attacked twice. I'm riding ahead as a scout to make sure that the coast is clear.'

'Then you can tell your brother that it's not. We're in the way.'

'And we'll stay in the way,' said the man with the sledgehammer, 'until we get our money. Those sheep were ours. You stole them.'

'We did nothing of the kind,' asserted Gianni.

'Yes, you did. People from your circus were seen rustling.'

'That's a lie.'

'We've got a witness,' said the farmer. 'He watched the sheep being taken early this morning and warned us about it. The circus stole them to feed the lions. You won't get past this spot until you admit the truth and pay up.'

'We'll do neither,' said Gianni, temper rising. 'We always carry enough meat for the lions and provisions for the other animals as well. We don't *need* to steal any sheep. Where's the man who accused us? I want to speak to him.'

'You can't do that. He's gone now.'

'What was his name? Where does he live?'

'Forget about him. He gave us his word that he saw people from the circus rounding up the sheep and carrying them off. They've probably had their throats cut by now and are being butchered.'

'Give us compensation!' shouted the man with the sledgehammer.

'Pay the full cost or we'll call in the police.'

'Go ahead and do that,' urged Gianni, 'because it's the only way we can sort this out. Moscardi's Circus has *never* stolen any livestock. We always respect the owners of any private land we have to cross. If anyone dared to rustle a sheep, we'd not only throw him out of the circus, we'd make sure that he finished up in gaol.'

'Don't try to fool us, Moscardi.'

'He's just another greasy Italian,' said someone.

'They're all the same – liars and thieves.'

'I say they should be sent back where they came from.'

'Don't you dare insult us!' yelled Gianni. 'I'm proud to have Italian blood. I won't listen to these hateful comments.'

'Then pay up and get off our land as quickly as you can,' said the farmer.

'Listen, you idiot, I swear to you that we've done nothing wrong.'

'Three of our sheep are missing. Some of your men took them.'

'The lions are fed with meat we bought in Carlisle. If you don't believe us, we can show you the receipts.'

'And we can show you the field where the flock was grazing. A shepherd always knows when some of his sheep have gone astray. He knew that something was amiss this morning. When he counted them, he found that three were missing. We know who took them.'

'Are you in charge here?'

'Yes,' said the man. 'My name is Seth Pearce. I own this farm.'

'Then I'm sorry you've lost some animals, Mr Pearce. I hate rustlers as much as you do,' said Gianni. 'I'd string them up from the nearest tree.'

'Hand over the man who stole from us and that's what we'll do to him.'

'Nobody from the circus is to blame.'

'I don't trust you.'

'We keep a strict control over the people we employ. In fact . . .'

His voice died away as he saw the farmer's shotgun pointing at him. Pearce was adamant that the circus was responsible. Unless he got an apology and full compensation, he would not allow them to traverse his land. As a result, Gianni feared, they'd be forced to make a wide detour. He resented being associated with a crime neither he nor anyone in the circus had committed. Further argument, however, would be unproductive. That was clear. Pearce looked as if he was getting very close to the point where he wanted to pull the trigger. As he rode away, Gianni was sent off with a chorus of expletives.

Now that she'd alighted on the idea of a holiday, Lydia Quayle became more and more convinced that that was what she most needed. It would get her away from any threat from the stalker and enable her to gather her strength before moving into her house. Since money was no object, she was able to look far and wide for a suitable resort. Madeleine supplied a steady stream of suggestions.

'What about Cornwall?'

'It would certainly be on my list.'

'I've always had an urge to visit Scotland. The nearest I got to it was Wylam in Northumberland when Robert took me to see Puffing Billy.'

'You've got a painting of that in your studio.'

'I used the sketches I took while I was there. It's part of locomotive history, Lydia. That's why I wanted to see it.'

'I love your work, Madeleine, but I could never hang a painting like that on my wall. I'd prefer a landscape or a seascape that reminded me of an idyllic holiday.'

'Yorkshire?'

'Possibly.'

'The Lake District?'

'That's always appealed to me.'

'You could always go abroad, of course.'

'No, I think I'll confine myself to England for the time being.'

'Don't leave Wales out. I'm told there's some wonderful scenery.'

Having set out together after breakfast, they'd already walked much farther than they intended. Madeleine was glad to see how poised and self-assured her friend had become. It was as if her problems with the stalker had never existed. If either of them was uneasy, it was Madeleine. When she was away from the baby for any length of time, she began to worry about her even though she knew she had no cause to do so. Sensing her eagerness to return to the house, Lydia agreed to go back to it and they opened another discussion of where she could best go for a holiday. It took them all the way to their destination. They were so preoccupied that neither of them noticed the cab on the other side of the road or saw the man peering out of it.

When the two women went into the house, he used his cane to tap the roof of the vehicle. It drew away from the pavement and vanished around the corner. Sitting back in the cab, the passenger had the triumphant smile of someone who had just found a lost treasure.

The task of speaking to the three potential suspects had been allotted to Victor Leeming. Having decided to start with Jake Goodhart, he first had to find him in a warren of streets. The former porter lived in a tenement so shabby and dilapidated that it reminded him of the ones he'd once visited in the Gorbals during investigations in Glasgow. There was the same desolate air about the place and the same filth in the gutters. After knocking on Goodhart's door, he was startled when it swung open almost immediately. Goodhart's glum face came into view. He wore grubby clothing and had a glove on one hand.

'Are you Mr Goodhart?'

'Aye, man.'

'How are you, sir?'

'Ah'm in reet bad fettle.'

'I'm Detective Sergeant Leeming from Scotland Yard,' said the other, 'and I'm making enquiries relating to the derailment of a train.'

'Ah heerd of that.'

'I believe you spoke to Inspector Lill.'

'Aye, man.'

'I have a few additional questions. Might I come in, please?'

'There's nee need.'

'Then we'll talk here, if you insist.'

'Wheer's Lill?'

'The inspector is escorting the circus into town.'

'We 'ad a street barney or two in t'old days.'

'What does that mean?' Goodhart put up both fists. 'Ah, you had a fight or two. Yes, I was told about that. You had a reputation for it.' Goodhart jerked his thumb over his shoulder. 'I understand. You have a wife and family now. You're a good boy. I'd like to find out just how good you are.'

Leeming asked him about his days on the railway and, by dint of guesswork, he managed to translate most of the dialect words that came out of the other man. He heard that Goodhart had been employed by the NCR for some time. Though he'd finished up as a porter, he'd had other jobs during his years with the company. One of them made Leeming's eyebrows lift.

'You were part of a maintenance crew, were you?'

'Aye, man.'

'What exactly did that entail?'

Goodhart was bewildered. 'Spake English, will ya?'

'What did you *do*?'

Goodhart talked fondly and freely about what had obviously been the most enjoyable period of his time on the railway. Most of his job consisted of repairing deficiencies on the track. That often meant replacing a section of line, fixing it firmly into new sleepers and bedding it in with ballast. Manual work had suited Goodhart. It took him up and down the NCR. When Leeming asked him how well he knew the route, Goodhart reeled off the names of all the stations between Newcastle and Carlisle. He was certainly strong enough to manhandle a couple of sleepers on his own.

'Do you own a telescope, Mr Goodhart?' The other man shook his head. 'Have you borrowed one from a friend recently?' There was a more guarded reaction this time. Goodhart looked away. 'What happened to your hand?'

'Ah cut it wi' a knife.'

'Do you mind if I have a look at it?'

'Why d'ya want to do that, man?'

'I'm interested, that's all.'

Inclined to refuse, Goodhart was conscious of his visitor's rank. He'd long tried to avoid confrontations with policemen. He removed his glove with a tenderness that surprised Leeming. What emerged was a bloodstained bandage. He thrust his hand under the sergeant's nose then drew it back quickly.

'Ah've to go,' he said.

Without another word, he retreated behind the door and slammed it shut.

Cyrus Lill caught up with the circus just in time. Mauro Moscardi had been incensed by what his brother had told him. Being accused of a crime was more upsetting to him than being denied access to someone's land. He was also enraged when Gianni recalled the racial insults hurled at him. Gathering half a dozen sturdy men around him, Moscardi was just about to confront the farmer when Lill arrived in a trap. The inspector listened to what had happened then insisted on going along with them as a peacemaker. Gianni was sceptical.

'They're not interested in peace,' he said. 'They want a fight and we'll give it to them. They can't block our way.'

'Technically, that track is a public right of way that runs

over private land. They don't have the authority to stop you.'

'We'll tell them that,' growled Moscardi.

He climbed into the trap with Lill and they set off. The others followed on horseback, all of them carrying weapons of some sort. Moscardi believed that a show of strength would be enough to defuse the situation. As soon as he saw Pearce and his men, he realised that that was a vain hope. The farmer would not back down. The two sides squared up against each other. The inspector leapt from the trap and interposed himself between them.

'I'm Inspector Lill of the Newcastle Constabulary,' he said. 'If a crime has been committed, the perpetrator will answer to us.'

'The bastard is right behind you,' claimed Pearce, pointing at Moscardi. 'He's obviously the owner of the circus so he gave the order to rustle our sheep.'

'We never touched your sheep!' roared the Italian.

'Before hot words lead to violent blows,' said Lill, holding up both hands, 'let me tell you something, Mr Pearce. That is your name, isn't it?'

'What if it is?' retorted the other.

'Clearly, you don't read the newspapers.'

'We never have time.'

'Then let me tell you about two stories you missed. A train carrying the circus was derailed not far from Fourstones, causing untold suffering among the passengers and forcing Mr Moscardi to shoot an Arab horse whose legs had been broken. As someone experienced in animal husbandry, you'll know how painful that was to him.'

'It's not as painful as having your sheep stolen.'

'The second item you missed concerned an attack on the circus when it went through a copse. Bushes were set on fire to cause a stampede. Mr Moscardi was lucky not to lose more of his horses, remarkable animals that are vital to the circus.'

'Why are you telling us this?'

'It's because, in the wake of the two attacks, I arranged for constables to accompany the circus in order to protect it. They've been there day and night. If someone had rolled up with three dead sheep, my men would have noticed at once and arrested the people who did the rustling.'

'I'd have arrested them myself,' affirmed Moscardi, banging his chest, 'and fed them to the lions bit by bit. There are no criminals in my circus.'

'I can vouch for that,' said Lill. 'When we knew that the circus was coming to us, we asked for a report from the Carlisle Constabulary. They told us that there had been no trouble whatsoever and that Mr Moscardi's employees were above reproach. They're all decent people,' he continued with a glance over his shoulder, 'and they must be thinking that Northumberland folk like you offer poor hospitality.' He stepped forward and directed his question at Pearce. 'Why don't you gather evidence before you make wild accusations?'

'We had evidence,' replied Pearce. 'A man actually saw people from the circus stealing our sheep. He swore by it.'

'I'd like to meet this man.'

'He was a stranger to the area. He's moved on.'

'I'm sure he has.'

'He couldn't have seen my men rustling,' said Moscardi, 'because none of them would dare to do such a thing. My guess is that he knows exactly what happened to those sheep because he stole them himself in order to put the blame on us. I think he's the same man who attacked us twice before. His name is Bev Rogers.'

'You're right, Mauro,' agreed his brother. 'He'll do anything to stop us.'

'There is another explanation,' Lill reminded them, 'and Mr

Pearce ought to be mindful of this. We've had Gypsies in the area. For the last couple of weeks, we've had reports of stolen chickens, stolen ducks and even a missing milk churn. They wouldn't baulk at rustling a few sheep.'

Mauro stepped forward until he was inches away from Seth Pearce.

'I give you my word that we're not rustlers,' he said, seriously. 'I'm sorry you've lost your sheep, Mr Pearce, but they were stolen by someone who hates our circus. That's my belief, anyway. The inspector's given you another possibility but I think I'm right. The man you met was Bev Rogers. I feel it in my bones.'

Pearce looked into his eyes and saw a blazing sincerity. He turned to the people who'd come with him. To a man, they were signalling that they didn't think the circus was in any way responsible.

'I owe you an apology, Mr Moscardi,' said Pearce, reluctantly.

'Does that mean we can use the road?'

'Yes, it does.'

'We'll help you,' volunteered Gianni. 'I'll forget about the insults you flung at me and I'll search the area thoroughly with some of my men. We'll find those sheep of yours. My brother told you who the rustler was. It's the man who's been lying in wait for us since we left Carlisle.'

'Wait a moment,' said Lill. 'We're forgetting something. There's one way to test your theory, Mr Moscardi.' He turned to Pearce. 'You spoke to this so-called witness, did you?'

'Yes, I did,' replied Pearce.

'Before I ask you for a full description of him, let me suggest that he might have had one hand bandaged. Am I right?'

Hiring a trap for the purpose, Colbeck drove to the place where the dead body had actually been discovered. Leeming had given him explicit instructions how to reach it and marked the location on the map. It did not take Colbeck long to find it. Since he was able to get the trap within twenty yards of the spot, he could see that the murder victim would not have had to be carried far. As he looked down at the grave, he wondered why someone had travelled all the way from Shropshire to such a secluded spot. Margaret Pulver had been known to visit London in the past. Why had she come to Northumberland? Did she go there of her own volition or had compulsion of some sort been involved? Was the killer a local person who'd invited her there in the guise of a friend? Why was someone as well versed in the woman's movements as Donald Underhill be unable to account for her presence in the north or – Colbeck could not dismiss the possibility – had he actually taken her there himself?

There were too many imponderables. He couldn't even decide if he was looking for a man or a woman. All that Leeming had done was to examine the grave and the immediate area. Colbeck was more systematic. He widened the search considerably and used a stick to poke about in the bushes. Someone had taken care to remove labels from the victim's clothing so that they could not help to identify her. Margaret Pulver's shoes had also been missing. What had the killer done with them?

The area had been searched before but without success. He therefore went further afield, using a stick to poke every bush apart. It took well over an hour of painstaking work before he got his reward. In the course of it, he got mud on his shoes, dirt on his hands and had his hat knocked off by a low branch. Colbeck's main fear was that his frock coat might be snagged on a twig and torn. His vanity made him move with care. He eventually came upon a rabbit hole stuffed with earth and his interest was immediate. Scraping the earth away with his stick, he found what he'd hoped to chance upon. The treasure trove comprised a coat, a hat, a pair of shoes and a small silver crucifix. He held it up to the light to examine it.

'Perhaps she was a saint, after all,' he said.

Leeming was given short shrift by the second of the people on whom he called. Geoffrey Enticott was as brusque with him as he had been with Colbeck. He repeated that he was leaving the NCR to work for the NER because he'd been offered a promotion. With a family to support, he found the increase in salary irresistible. It would mean that they had to move south but they were more than willing to do so. No matter how much he pressed the man, Leeming could get nothing out of him that raised the slightest suspicion. The sergeant retreated and shifted his interest to Owen Probert, the other man who'd left a managerial position with the NCR.

'Do I offer congratulations or sympathy, sir?' asked Leeming.

'I don't know what you mean.'

'Inspector Colbeck told me that you were attending an interview.'

'Yes,' said Probert, 'and I was offered the post.'

'Good for you, sir.'

'Thank you.'

'After all those years on the railway, the coal trade will be a big change.'

'I'm looking forward to it.'

They were in Probert's cottage in Hexham and the Welshman was less than welcoming. He was sour and laconic. Leeming smiled at him.

'You don't like policemen, do you, sir?'

'I like them well enough if they keep out of my way.'

'Have you been in trouble with the law at any time?'

'I find that question insulting,' said Probert. 'It's just as insulting as the ones the inspector put to me. I resent the fact that you're both treating me as a suspect in an inquiry for the simple reason that I resigned from the NCR. Why are you still pestering me? I gave honest answers to your superior so I'd be grateful if you could leave me alone.'

'One of your answers was not exactly honest,' said Leeming. 'When Mr Enticott's name was mentioned, you denied knowing him.'

'So?'

'I've just come from the gentleman. I asked him about you and he said that you'd worked in adjoining offices for a while. Is that true or false?'

'It's . . . true to some extent,' confessed Probert.

'Then why say you didn't know him?'

'What I meant was that I didn't know him as a *friend*. To be frank, I didn't like the man so I kept out of his way. Lots of people worked in the same offices. I saw dozens of faces every day.'

'You'd have recognised Mr Enticott's – it's very distinctive.'

'That's a matter of opinion.'

'Why didn't you like him?'

'If you've met him, you should be able to work out why.'

'Yes,' said Leeming, 'he was a bit short with me.'

'I'd prefer the word "abrasive",' returned Probert.

'Then you haven't met our superintendent. Compared to him, Mr Enticott was quite amiable. Talking to the superintendent is like being caught in a roll of barbed wire. It hurts.'

'I'll take your word for it.'

'Where do you come from, Mr Probert?'

'Isn't that rather obvious?'

'Oh, I know that you're a Welshman but your accent is very different from the ones I've heard. When I was in uniform, I walked the beat with Denzil Davies from the Rhondda Valley. He sounded like all the other Welshmen I've met.'

'Your friend was from the south. I come from North Wales.'

'Which part?'

'I was born and brought up in Bangor.'

'What sort of place is it?'

'It can get very windy indeed, Sergeant.'

'Why is that, sir?'

'It's close to the Menai Straits. The prevailing winds there are especially strong. That why so many people like to sail there.'

'Do you ever go back to that part of Wales?'

'I take my family there every year,' said Probert. 'We stay in my old home. My father has a small boat. If the weather is fine, I take my children out in it.'

Leeming suddenly remembered something that Colbeck had told him.

The circus reached the point where Pearce and the others had been standing and continued on its way. There was no resistance now. The farmer had accepted Moscardi's assurance that nobody in the circus would dream of trying to rustle sheep. But it was Cyrus Lill's intervention that had been critical. The fact that some of his men were escorting the circus had weighed heavily with Pearce. They wouldn't have countenanced theft of any kind. When Moscardi and the farmer had parted company, there had been a handshake. Lill had looked on with approval.

With only a mile to go to the city, the circus paused for a rest. Climbing down from his caravan, Moscardi went in search of Lill. He found him talking to one of the uniformed constables, who, to their disgust, had been mistakenly viewed as clowns by some of the children they passed along the way. The Italian took Lill aside.

'I've been thinking, Inspector,' he said.

'That's always a wise thing to do, sir.'

'I believe that the man who said we rustled those sheep was Bev Rogers.'

'But he didn't fit the description we were given.'

'He *could* have,' said Moscardi. 'I haven't seen Rogers for the best part of ten years and a man can change a lot in that time.'

'Mr Pearce said that he was tall, middle-aged and had a beard. He wore a good suit and rode a horse. That doesn't sound like your Strong Man to me.'

'If he'd been ill, Rogers could have lost a lot of weight.'

'Pearce said that he had an educated voice.'

'That is a snag, I admit.'

'It's not him, Mr Moscardi.'

'Then it's someone hired by Rogers with money from Sam Greenwood.'

'The only certainty is that the witness was the same man who was watching the circus through a telescope. As he fled, he was shot in the hand. Pearce confirmed that the man he spoke to did have a bandage around his wrist. He'd been wounded.'

'He'll be more than wounded when I get hold of him.'

'Do you want to finish up in the cell next to him?'

'No, of course not.'

'Then you'll have to curb your anger.'

'That's easier said than done, Inspector. I love these people,' he went on, indicating the whole circus. 'I feel responsible for the ordeal they went through on the train. Some of them still have horrible gashes and bruises. I'll wager that they have nightmares about what happened – I know that I do. My blood boils when I think that someone is trying to harm us.'

'Remain calm, sir. You need all your concentration.'

'Inspector Colbeck gave me the same advice.'

'I agree with him. It's clear from what happened this morning that your attacker has not run out of ideas to disable you. If the local newspaper had run an article saying that you were accused of rustling, it would have had an adverse effect on your ticket sales. Thanks to the truce with Mr Pearce,' said Lill, 'that won't happen. As one trick fails, however, your enemy will think of another.'

'Our enemy is Sam Greenwood.'

'So you keep saying.'

'We know for a fact that Rogers is tailing us on his behalf.'

'But that's *all* you know, sir.'

'It's more than you and Inspector Colbeck found out. Where is he, anyway?'

'He's patiently gathering evidence.'

'Evidence of what?' asked Moscardi. 'Is he trying to catch someone who wants to put my circus out of business? Or is he more concerned about that woman who was found? She is dead but we are alive and we need to know that we have a future. He should put us first.'

Victor Leeming arrived in the nick of time. He got back to their hotel as Colbeck was coming down the stairs with his valise in his hand. The sergeant rushed across to intercept him.

'Where are you going, sir?'

'I'm going to sample the air in Shropshire.'

'Why – has something happened?'

'Walk to the station with me and I'll tell you on the way.'

They left the hotel and walked side by side. Colbeck explained about his discovery of Margaret Pulver's clothing and why he felt it necessary to visit her home. Leeming then recounted details of the three interviews he'd conducted.

'Did you think that any of them could be culpable?' asked Colbeck.

'Enticott and Probert certainly could,' said the other. 'Goodhart is not clever enough to organise anything but he'd be ready to obey orders from someone else.'

'What grudge would any of them hold against a circus?'

'I couldn't find one, sir.'

'Nor could I,' admitted Colbeck.

'What I did find was a strange coincidence and it could link both crimes.'

'Go on.'

Leeming told him about the conversation with Owen Probert and how the Welshman had talked about sailing in the Menai Straits. The murder victim and her husband had been part of the sailing community in that area. It was not impossible, Leeming contended, that Margaret Pulver had met Probert at some point and become attracted to him.

'I didn't like him one bit, sir, but he's a handsome devil.'

'He's also somewhat younger than Mrs Pulver.'

'Wouldn't that be part of his appeal?'

'I think you may be stretching coincidence too far, Victor.'

'Hear me out, sir. When I asked Probert about his work for the NCR, he boasted about his importance to the company. The NCR sent him down to London from time to time, he said, on some kind of business.' He lowered his voice. 'Or is that what Probert used to tell his wife?'

'I see your point.'

'I stumbled on a possible way to link Mrs Pulver with Northumberland. We knew that she used to go to London. Is that where she met Probert?'

Colbeck was not convinced. 'It's an interesting suggestion,' he said. 'You extracted rather more out of Probert than I contrived to do. As for his ever becoming the secret lover of Mrs Pulver, I doubt it. But nothing is impossible. Thank you for telling me, Victor.

When I get to her home, I'll find out if she and the Welshman met in the sailing community.'

'What will I be doing while you're away?'

'Join forces with Inspector Lill and keep a close eye on the circus.'

'Mr Moscardi will be angry that you're deserting him altogether.'

'He doesn't need to know that I'm giving priority to the other investigation.'

'That's true.'

'Tell him that I've gone to Bristol to take a look at Greenwood for myself,' said Colbeck with a conspiratorial smile. 'That ought to pacify him for a while.'

When they'd split up to search the area, Brendan Mulryne had ridden off with Gianni Moscardi. Maintaining a steady canter, they'd gone several miles in a wide sweep before pulling up for a rest. Mulryne rubbed his buttocks.

'I say that we give up,' he argued.

'We must keep going.'

'But we've been at it for the best part of two hours, Gianni, and my arse is on fire. That farmer *knows* we didn't steal his bleeding sheep. It's not our job to find them for him.'

'He's in the saddle himself, Brendan. While he covers the eastern side, I said that we'd search westwards.'

'Well, we have done and we failed.'

'Let's ride on.'

'The circus will be in Newcastle by now. We're needed there.'

'We'll go in that direction very soon.'

Gianni led the way, making sure that they covered new ground. Mulryne was a moaning companion but he knew that what they were doing was in their interests as much as those of Seth Pearce. If they found the sheep, the circus would be exonerated in the most demonstrative way. For that reason, he stopped complaining and ignored the discomfort. They were trotting across a field when Gianni heard something. He raised a hand. They came to a halt. Mulryne was mystified.

'Why have we stopped?'

'Be quiet!' snapped the other. 'And *listen*.'

Mulryne did as he was told. His hearing was less sensitive than Gianni's so he took time to pick up the plaintive sound. It was filled with pathos. The Italian heard it again and looked around. It was difficult to see from where it was coming. A long, twisting drystone wall ran up the hillside ahead of them. When they trotted across to it, they realised that there was a ditch on the other side of it. Huddled in the ditch were three forlorn sheep tied to a stake.

Mulryne grinned. 'That farmer is going to be very pleased with us.'

He walked along paths he'd known since childhood. Alarmed that his victim had been discovered, he wanted to inspect the grave where he'd placed her so carefully. On his way there, he passed the rabbit hole where he'd hidden her clothing in the belief that it could never be found. Yet it had been. When he saw that the hole was now empty, his blood curdled. Having committed what he thought was a perfect crime, he realised that he was now the object of a manhunt. Biting his lip, he resolved to hold his nerve.

CHAPTER FOURTEEN

Getting from Newcastle-on-Tyne to Shrewsbury was problematical but it was the kind of challenge that Colbeck enjoyed. With the aid of his Bradshaw, he planned his route and marvelled afresh at the labyrinthine character of the railway system. Having evolved at random with no master plan, tracks went everywhere, varying in width and often linking the same towns that rival companies did. Negotiating the fastest route between two different points on the map was an art. As he thought about the many railway companies with which he'd been associated, Colbeck realised that every one of them had someone like Tapper Darlow in a dominant position – a busy, assertive, single-minded, ruthless man who revelled in the exercise of power. Such qualities were essential in a railway magnate. Colbeck was the first to acknowledge that. He just wished that power had not been allowed to develop unchecked in so many cases. There were chairmen he admired and general managers he was ready to applaud but, almost to a man, they were forced into aggressively acquisitive tactics against their smaller competitors. Metaphorically, most railway lines were dripping with blood.

Whereas a long journey was anathema to Victor Leeming, it was a sheer delight to Colbeck. He loved the idea of adding new stations to his already extensive collection and of catching glimpses into the lives of people in different counties of England. Never having been to Shrewsbury before, he didn't quite know what to expect.

When he finally arrived in the county town, he was struck by the weathered beauty of its buildings. Set on a peninsula in the River Severn, it was unspoilt by the effects of heavy industry and gave the impression of a sleepy and picturesque haven. Many of the houses were half-timbered Tudor dwellings, leaning at odd angles like inebriated revellers trying to support each other. One of the largest of them had been converted into the offices of Underhill and Bridger, Solicitors. The senior partner was startled by the arrival of Colbeck.

'Why on earth didn't you tell me you were coming to our little backwater?' he asked. 'We could have travelled here together.'

'I had things to do in Northumberland before I could leave.'

'I'd have waited for you, Inspector.'

'There was no point, sir. You had commitments here. The sooner you got back, the more time you'd have had to deal with them.'

'That's true.'

Underhill went on to list the various people he'd informed of Margaret Pulver's death, beginning with the editor of the local newspaper. The solicitor obviously expected to gain kudos from being the person to identify the anonymous murder victim. It would be front-page news. Having spread the word in the town, he went out to the village where the woman had lived and first spoke to her servants.

'The next person I called on was the vicar. He was distraught. Like me, he had no idea why Mrs Pulver should have been in that part of the country.'

'I'd like to speak to him myself,' said Colbeck, 'and to Mrs Pulver's servants, of course. I called in here to get her address and to ask for directions.'

'You won't need any, Inspector. I'll drive you there.'

'I couldn't put you to that trouble, sir.'

'It will be a pleasure.'

Colbeck quailed inwardly. His earlier vow to go to the village alone had been broken. Glad that he'd escaped a train journey in the man's company, he'd now have Underhill looking over his shoulder and regaling him with more anecdotes about the dead woman. On the other hand, he told himself, the solicitor would be able to give him a detailed report of his earlier visit, saving Colbeck the trouble of asking the same questions of stunned villagers. Unable to refuse the offer, therefore, he soon found himself sitting beside Underhill in a gig. He remembered enough about medieval history to know that Shrewsbury had been an important frontier town in the reign of William the Conqueror and he noted plenty of remnants of its fortifications. What he couldn't see was any evidence of manufacturing industry.

'What is the town's claim to fame?'

'It has many,' replied Underhill. 'Would you like me to list them?'

'I was really asking what you make here.'

'There's nothing of any great significance. If anything, Shrewsbury is famed for its cakes and brawn, jellied loaves that always sell out on market days. For the rest, we have a mixture of trades. There's a population of over twenty thousand and most of us are engaged in some useful activity.'

'I see. Incidentally, has the vicar known Mrs Pulver for long?'

'They've been close friends ever since she came to live in the county. Apart from the servants, nobody in the village knows her better than Mr Berry. He's very old, by the way,' warned Underhill, 'and not in the best of health. I'm afraid that the shock of losing her will shorten the limited time he still has on earth.'

Newcastle could not have given them a more resounding welcome. The circus entered the city to be greeted by cheering crowds at every turn. Its journey through the streets was nothing short of a triumphal procession. For the time being, their worries faded into oblivion. News of the discovery of the three sheep had given everyone a fillip. At a stroke, it removed the stigma of accusation from them. Instead of being seen as rustlers, they were hailed as supreme entertainers. Reaching the park where they were due to perform, they were pleased to see that their marquee and their equipment were already there, and that construction work was under way.

After their success in finding the missing sheep, Mulryne and Gianni Moscardi were viewed as heroes, rescuing the circus's reputation by appeasing an angry farmer. The Irishman had little time to enjoy the adulation. Erecting the marquee was a task that called for every pair of strong hands available and he was quick to join the others. He only broke off when the bulk of the work was done. Running with sweat, he dipped a tin mug into one of the buckets of water provided. Once he'd drunk that, he poured a second cupful down his throat.

'It's thirsty work, by the look of it,' said Leeming, coming over to him.

'Yes, it's worse than hoisting a mainsail on a galleon.'

'The whole city came alight when you arrived.'

'That's not because of me,' said Mulryne. 'It's because of all the performers, not to mention the animals. Rosie the elephant draws crowds wherever she goes and no circus has so many wonderful horses as we do.'

'Inspector Lill has just told me about your trouble with a sheep farmer.'

'That's all in the past. The sheep were rustled and the blame put on us. Gianni and I found them still alive. They're back with the shepherd now.'

'What about the man who stole them in the first place?'

'He's still out there somewhere.'

They both knew that he was likely to launch yet another attack on the circus before long. Leeming was told of the security arrangements put in place for their time in Newcastle. They were very thorough. Mulryne was to be in charge of the night patrols and extra guards would be put on all the animals. Inspector Lill would be providing a certain amount of police protection. The sergeant was thrilled by the news that they now had a description of the man believed to be their tormentor.

'That eliminates Jake Goodhart, anyway,' he said.

'Who's he?'

'One of our suspects – they kicked him out of the railway company so he has a reason to plot against it. Also, his right hand has been wounded.'

'You should have arrested him.'

'It did cross my mind but I'm glad that I didn't now. If the man who spoke to the sheep farmer was well dressed and educated, it couldn't have been Goodhart. He looks like a vagrant and speaks in a language all his own.'

'But he might have been an accomplice,' said Mulryne.

'It's not impossible, I suppose, but highly unlikely. According to Lill, the man was a nuisance in his younger days but he's behaved himself since he got married. It changes you – having a wife, I mean.'

The Irishman chuckled. 'I know. I've met a lot of wives in my time.'

'I'm talking about holy matrimony.'

'It never reached that stage in my case.'

Leeming was stern. 'I thought you were a Roman Catholic.'

'Oh, I am in most ways.'

Before the sergeant could chastise him for his lapse in faith, he was joined by Mauro Moscardi. The Italian was grinning from ear to ear. In spite of the attacks, his circus had got to Newcastle in the end. It had been feted on arrival and most tickets had already been sold for the opening performance, which would be attended by the Lord Mayor and his family. Other local worthies would also be in the audience.

'Where is Inspector Colbeck?' he asked.

'He decided to go to Bristol,' replied Leeming.

Moscardi was elated. 'He's going to arrest Sam Greenwood?'

'He's going to find out if there are any grounds for doing so.'

'I can tell you one,' said Mulryne. 'Greenwood runs the worst circus in the country. He should be prosecuted for lowering the standards of the profession.'

'He's guilty of far worse crimes than that,' claimed Moscardi.

'What we need is cast-iron proof,' said Leeming.

'If the inspector has disappeared, does that mean you'll be spending all your time looking for the killer of that woman?'

'No, sir, I'll be staying with the circus.'

'That's a relief. We need you.'

'I have to ask you a favour, however.'

'What is it, Sergeant?'

'Well, let's be honest, nobody would take me for a circus artiste.'

'I don't know,' teased Mulryne. 'You could pass for a clown any day.'

'With your permission, Mr Moscardi, I'd like to disguise myself and mingle with your employees. If I worked alongside Brendan, for instance, I'd be taken as part of his team. That would make me virtually invisible.'

'I'm happy to agree to that,' said Moscardi.

'Thank you, sir.'

'And so am I,' added Mulryne, 'but you're going to need instruction.'

'I know how to look like a labourer.'

'Yes, but you don't know how to handle Jacko. When he's not performing in the ring, he sits on my shoulder and keeps me company.'

Leeming was irritated. 'When he did that to me, he knocked my hat off.'

'That's why you must learn his language and become his friend. Believe me,' said Mulryne, 'your time with us will be an ordeal if you don't do that. It's not Mr Moscardi who runs this circus – it's that little monkey.'

Descending from the nursery, Madeleine Colbeck went along the corridor to the library. She expected to find Lydia Quayle reading in there. When she entered the room, however, she saw that her friend was gazing straight in front of her. Lydia was quite unaware of her presence. Madeleine didn't know whether to speak to her or to withdraw quietly. In the event, she simply stood there and waited. After a while, Lydia came out of her trance.

'Good heavens!' she exclaimed. 'How long have you been there?'

'An hour or two, that's all,' teased the other.

Lydia laughed. 'Don't exaggerate.'

'To be truthful, it was a little while.'

'That was unforgivably rude of me.'

'There's no need to apologise, Lydia. Your mind was obviously on something important.' She looked around the bookshelves. 'I used to love reading when I first moved in here. Robert is so proud of his library. Since the baby was born, however, I've hardly been in here, let alone actually read a book.'

'It *was* something important, Madeleine.'

'Was it?'

'Yes, it came to me while I was sitting in here. Daniel Vance was something to do with my younger brother. I can't remember exactly who he was but I think he was at school with Lucas.'

'That must have been years ago.'

'All of fifteen years or more, at least,' said Lydia. 'That's why I couldn't place him. I still can't tell you who Daniel was but I know how to find out now.'

'You can ask your brother.'

'I'll write to Lucas immediately. He loved his schooldays so he'll remember everything about them.' She got up to hug Madeleine. 'I do apologise.'

'It was all in a good cause.'

'If you mean that we've solved a problem, you're right. But the question still remains – why did someone claiming to be Daniel Vance follow me everywhere, then steal a dress of mine?' she bit her lip. 'It's baffling.'

Throughout the journey, Colbeck had been wondering how he could detach himself from Underhill so that he could speak to people on his own. Unexpectedly, the vicar came to his rescue. Hearing that the inspector was investigating the murder, he asked to see him alone and took him into his study. Underhill was left in the drawing room with the vicar's wife, a bosomy woman in her seventies with heavy jowls and an eyelid that kept winking inappropriately. Colbeck, meanwhile, was lowering himself into a chair and appraising his host. The Reverend Walter Berry was a white-haired old man with a scholarly hunch and a battered dignity. Colbeck noticed that his hands trembled constantly.

'I understand that you were a close friend of Mrs Pulver,' he said.

It was all that was needed to set the vicar off into a eulogy of a woman he'd admired deeply as a friend and respected as a true Christian. Much of what he said duplicated Underhill's description of her but many new elements were added. Berry had been in charge of the funerals of her husband and two children. He spoke of the long hours he'd spent offering condolence and guidance. Her contribution to the village church was unmatched by anybody. Financially and spiritually, she'd devoted herself to it. Colbeck probed gently.

'Did Mrs Pulver ever talk about her visits to London?'

'She said nothing to me, Inspector, but she usually had a few words with my wife about the shopping she'd done. She always came back with something new.'

'New clothing must have stood out in a village like this.'

'It was always smart but very subdued.'

'Did she ever speak of meeting someone in London?'

'No, but she always returned in a buoyant mood. That's more than I could have done. I hate trains and abhor railways. They're the work of the devil.'

'We must agree to differ on that subject,' said Colbeck, 'because they've been invaluable to me in the course of my work. Since you knew Mrs Pulver so well, I wonder if you could describe a typical week in her life?'

'Yes, of course.'

The details he gave were largely those already gleaned from Underhill, though there were some useful additions. Colbeck learnt that she had been racked by guilt after the loss of her husband and children. Ordinarily, she'd have been in the boat with them but had been busy elsewhere on that fateful day. Having been born and brought up on a tiny island, she'd learnt to sail from a young age. It was a passion shared with her husband. In the wake of the calamity, she'd never gone back to the family cottage on the Welsh coast and had lost her love of sailing.

'Did she have any reason to visit Northumberland?' asked Colbeck.

'None at all, as far as I'm aware,' replied Berry.

'It's a remarkable part of the country.'

'The north-east is a closed book to me, Inspector, but I've heard many people praise its scenic beauty – Mr Underhill is one of them.'

'Oh?'

'He has a cousin who lives in Durham and visits him occasionally. In their young days, they used to go on walking holidays in Northumberland.'

Colbeck was astounded. 'Are you certain of this, sir?'

'I'm only repeating what he told me.'

'How much do you see of the gentleman?'

'In the last couple of months,' said the vicar, failing to keep a faint note of disapproval out his voice, 'we've seen rather more of him because he's started to attend services at our church. Since his dear wife became disabled, she's more or less housebound. They always used to go to the abbey church in Shrewsbury and there is no way that we can compete with something of that size. Yet Mr Underhill seems to prefer us. He told me that it was because he admires my sermons but I'm not so egotistical as to believe that.'

* * *

When he'd changed into coarse garb, Victor Leeming looked like a typical labourer. He blended easily with the team of men under the control of Brendan Mulryne. It meant that he had privileged access to the circus encampment and he enjoyed it to the full. One of his main jobs was to patrol the perimeter and keep interlopers out. Armed with a description of the wanted man, he scrutinised every male face that came near him but he saw nobody who bore any resemblance to him. At one point, he heard Mulryne's voice berating someone. He picked his way between the caravans and arrived in time to see his friend grabbing someone by the scruff of his neck and helping him on his way. The man turned to unleash a mouthful of vile abuse then took to his heels as the Irishman threatened to punch him.

'What was he doing?' asked Leeming.

'He was doing what they all try to do – peep at the pretty girls in their pink tights. He just wanted to leer.'

'I wish you hadn't got rid of him like that, Brendan.'

'Why?'

'I'd have valued a word with him.'

'Who is he?'

'Jake Goodhart – we've been questioning him.' He moved away. 'I'll see if I can catch up with him.'

But he went no further than a few yards. Something landed on his shoulder and brought him to a halt. The next moment, his hat went spinning in the air and the animal moved to his head. Jacko the monkey had arrived.

Mulryne shook with mirth. 'He likes you.'

Writing to her younger brother gave Lydia Quayle an opportunity to review her situation. In becoming estranged from her family, she had really cut herself adrift. Her decision to move in with Beatrice

Myler had been prompted by loneliness as much as affection. Looking back, she could see how carefully the older woman had prevented her from trying to repair the rift with her parents. Her father's murder had forced her to reacquaint herself with the family but there was no happy reunion. The only person who gave her a welcome was Lucas. Her old brother Stanley had not wanted her anywhere near the family estate. Because of her friendship with Madeleine Colbeck, her status as an orphan had not troubled Lydia. She had simply exchanged one family for another. Then the stalker had entered her life and she realised how unprotected she was if she chose to live alone.

Who was Daniel Vance? That was the question that sent her to the writing table. Lydia could not remember meeting anyone of that name. Lucas Quayle was the only person who could help her. Yet even as she blotted her letter, she knew that her brother could only provide limited assistance. Daniel Vance was a pseudonym used by the man who tried to stay under the same roof as her and, she feared, might have come into her room at night. Lucas might be able to tell her who the real Daniel Vance was. Was he the stalker or simply a person hiding behind the name? And how could she get rid of him for good?

Speaking to the servants in the Pulver house, Colbeck was hampered by the presence of Donald Underhill but he nevertheless pressed on. The solicitor did have the grace to remain silent. From the looks that the domestic staff shot at his companion, Colbeck could see that he was not entirely popular. In view of what the vicar had told him, he wondered if the man attended the same church as Margaret Pulver in order to be invited back to the house after the service. From Underhill's evident familiarity with the place, it was clear that he was a regular visitor. The solicitor's earlier claim to have only seen Mrs Pulver occasionally was exposed as a glaring lie.

The most coherent of the servants was the housekeeper, Mrs Lanning. Apart from the fact that she'd been at the house from the moment when it had been bought by Richard Pulver and his wife, she had coped best with the news of the murder of her employer. Because the others were prone to burst into tears, Colbeck addressed most of his questions to the housekeeper, a short, tubby, watchful widow in her fifties.

'How often did she go to London?' he asked.

'Oh, it was never more than once a month or so, sir.'

'And did she always go alone?'

'Yes, she did.'

'I believe she usually came back with some shopping?'

'Mrs Pulver was very particular about her clothes.'

'So I understand.'

Colbeck had come to Shropshire with his valise. Out of it, he slowly took the coat and hat he'd found. They produced a gasp of horror from Mrs Lanning, who brought both hands to her face.

'They belonged to Mrs Pulver,' she said.

'Are you sure?'

'I'd know them anywhere, Inspector.'

'What about these,' he asked, taking out the shoes.

'Yes, I recognise them as well. They were her Sunday best shoes.'

Underhill stepped forward. 'Where did you get them?'

'They were hidden close to the murder scene,' said Colbeck. 'You must have seen these shoes before as well, Mr Underhill. If Mrs Pulver wore them to church, you'd have seen them every Sunday when you attended a service there.'

'Yes,' admitted the other, uneasily, 'I suppose that I did.'

After questioning the housekeeper at length about daily life in the house, he switched back to the period of time when the husband and children were still alive. Not surprisingly, Mrs Lanning had gone to the Welsh coast at weekends to look after them. She spoke of their regular trips with affection.

'Did they get to know others in the sailing community?'

'Oh, yes, Inspector. Mr Pulver was a very sociable man. He used to invite people back for drinks.'

'Can you remember any of them?'

'I'm not sure. It was over five years ago now.'

'Does the name Owen Probert mean anything to you?'

'Let me think . . .'

To jog her memory, Colbeck described the man to her and she remembered that someone of that name had come to the cottage with his family a few times.

'Was he ever invited here?'

'No,' she said, 'he left Wales shortly before that terrible accident at sea. I don't think Mrs Pulver ever saw him again.'

Colbeck was less certain about that. Having established a possible link between the woman and one of his suspects, he was determined to look more closely into it when he returned north. He was very conscious that he was standing next to someone who also provided a link between Margaret Pulver and Northumberland but he decided not to tackle Underhill about his claim to have been in the county only once before. It was better, he felt, that the solicitor didn't know that his statement had been contradicted by the vicar.

Mrs Lanning's eyes were fixed almost covetously on the clothing.

'Will you be leaving those things here, Inspector?' she asked.

'I'm afraid not.'

'Why is that?'

'Strictly speaking, they represent evidence that should be available at the inquest. I brought them to get confirmation that they belonged to Mrs Pulver.'

'But I've already identified the body for you,' said Underhill, peevishly.

'Corroboration is always valuable, sir.'

After plying the housekeeper with more questions, Colbeck thanked her for her help then crossed to the fireplace to look at a painting above the mantelpiece. It showed a stretch of railway line against a rural background and seemed out of place beside mementoes of Richard Pulver and the two children. Studying it, Colbeck guessed what he was looking at.

'This is the line that runs through your land.'

'That's right, sir,' said the housekeeper. 'Mrs Pulver had it painted by a local artist. There's a framed plan of the whole line in the study. Because she showed such an interest in the work, the engineer gave her a copy. He was invited in for a drink sometimes and they talked endlessly about the branch line. Building it took ages and there was a lot of noise and disruption but Mrs Pulver didn't mind that at all. She used to walk down to the site almost every day to see what was happening.'

'There you are, Inspector,' said Underhill, butting in. 'You've discovered something you've never seen before – a woman with an abiding interest in railways.'

'They are rare creatures, I admit,' said Colbeck with a smile, 'but I have met one of them before. In fact, I had the good sense to marry her.'

Having been startled by the monkey, Leeming made an effort to befriend him with gifts of food. If he tried to get rid of the animal, Jacko would only torment him even more. It was easier to allow him to sit on his shoulder as he walked through the camp. At one point, Jacko leapt to the ground, took Leeming's hand and walked beside him like a small child. When someone stepped out to block their way, the monkey leapt back into the sergeant's arms. Tapper Darlow was not impressed.

'So this is how you spend your time, is it?' he said. 'Instead of hunting for the man who tried to cripple my railway, you play games with a monkey. And why are you dressed like that, anyway? I didn't recognise you at first.'

'I'm part of the circus now, sir. Your railway suffered only one attack. The circus has already had to cope with three. I'm here to prevent a fourth.'

'Where's the inspector?'

'He's making enquiries elsewhere, Mr Darlow.'

'Do they relate to the NCR?'

'Of course, they do,' said the other, the lie coming easily to his tongue.

'What has he found out?'

'I'm sure you'll get a full report eventually.'

'I want confirmation that you're actually working on the case.'

'Then I can tell you I've spoken to all three suspects you kindly picked out for us, sir. Enticott tried to shoo me away but I stood my ground. Since he's going to work for another railway company, he said some disparaging things about the NCR.'

'Don't believe a word of them.'

'Probert didn't like being questioned either. He was very evasive.'

'What about Jake Goodhart?'

'I couldn't make much sense of what he said.'

'The Tyneside dialect can be confusing to an outsider.'

'Of the three of them,' said Leeming, 'I thought that Enticott was the most likely person to want to harm the NCR. He seemed to have a grudge. As for Goodhart, I was ready to rule him out at first because he doesn't have the brains to plan a series of attacks like the ones we've seen. But I've changed my mind now.'

'Why is that?'

'First of all, he has an injury that he keeps hidden and we know that a man caught watching the circus was shot in the hand. The other thing is that Goodhart was actually here not long ago, trespassing inside the camp. Why would he do that if he wasn't intending to cause more harm?'

'Stop going on about the damned circus!' complained Darlow.

'But this is where the man who derailed one of your trains will strike again, sir, and I'm starting to believe that his name might be Jake Goodhart. He's only an accomplice taking orders from that man with the beard.'

'I disagree. I can tell you who's behind the derailment.'

'Can you, sir?'

'Yes, I've been doing your job for you, Sergeant. I looked at the employment records of the three men whose names I gave you and I chanced on an interesting piece of information.'

'What is it?'

'Jake Goodhart had a cousin who worked for the NCR.'

'Go on.'

'His name is Geoffrey Enticott.'

Having dined with them, Caleb Andrews had stayed well into the evening. While Lydia Quayle had retired for an early night, he and his daughter were now in the drawing room. Andrews was worried.

'A young woman of her age shouldn't be tired, Maddy.'

'She isn't tired.'

'Then why did she say that she was?'

'It was a polite way of leaving us alone together. Lydia feels that she takes up too much of my time and that you appreciate being with me and the baby.'

'Well, I do.'

'Also, she's excited at the idea of taking a holiday.'

'Is that wise?'

'I think it's very sensible. A change of scene will act as a tonic and she'll be far away from whoever is making her life such a misery.'

'Have there been any sightings of him?'

'No, Father. He may have lost interest.'

'Oh, I doubt that, Maddy. Men of that kind don't give up easily. If he goes to the trouble of staying at the same hotel as Lydia, he'll keep looking until he finds her again. I didn't want to say that to Lydia,' he went on. 'I thought she seemed a lot less nervous this evening.'

'Staying here has revived her.'

'Ever since I took her for that walk, she's started to improve.'

'Lydia goes out alone now.'

'That's good,' said Andrews. 'My only complaint is that Victor Leeming wasn't able to do more to put her mind at rest.'

'He did what he could. The real problem is Superintendent Tallis. If this was reported to him, he wouldn't take it seriously.'

'He would if Robert tackled him.'

'Pretty young women are followed by men every day. It's not a crime.'

'It ought to be. And don't forget that he stole her dress. That's very upsetting.'

'Very. I know how I'd feel if it happened to me.'

'Well, it won't, Maddy. You're a respectable married woman.'

'That's no defence. A man with an obsession will take no notice of that. It's not only single women who arouse unwanted attentions.'

Andrews grimaced. 'Yes, it happened to me once.'

'That's not the same thing, Father.'

'It felt like it at the time. I was terrified.'

The memory had been burnt into his mind. When he'd befriended a woman to whom he was attracted, her unscrupulous sister had intervened in the hope of wresting a marriage proposal out of him. He'd been lucky to escape.

He got up. 'Anyway, it's time I went back home,' he said, wearily. 'Lydia may not be tired but I am. These old bones of mine are starting to creak.'

'I'll see you to the door.'

They went into the hall and she took his hat from the peg to hand it to him. Before he put it on, he gave her a farewell kiss.

'I know I've said it before, Maddy,' he told her, 'but having a detective inspector as a husband isn't as useful as it ought to be. Robert is never here when you really want him.'

'That's because he's sorting out a crisis somewhere else.'

'His family should come first – every time.'

Opening the door, he was about to step out when a figure walked towards him. Andrews was astounded. Hand to his heart, he stepped back sharply. Madeleine was equally amazed. Emerging out of the gloom was her husband.

'Good evening,' he said, raising his top hat in greeting. 'How did you know I was coming?'

CHAPTER FIFTEEN

Victor Leeming was beginning to entertain doubts that the kinship between the two men was anything more than coincidence. Darlow, however, was convinced that he'd unmasked the villains behind the derailment. He wanted them taken into custody at once. Before he went off to confront the suspects, the sergeant first changed into his normal apparel, then he recruited Cyrus Lill.

'I couldn't arrest them as a labourer,' he explained. 'They wouldn't take me seriously.'

Lill issued a quiet warning. 'We may not have to arrest them at all.'

'That's my feeling, Inspector, but Mr Darlow insisted. He thinks that he's solved the case and wants to take all the credit for doing so.'

'What he really wants is to see his name in the newspapers.'

'Well, I fancy that he'll be disappointed this time.'

They were sharing a cab that was taking them to the home of Geoffrey Enticott. Since the circus now had its security guards in place alongside some uniformed policemen, they felt they were leaving it in safe hands. Leeming had been at first delighted when a close link between two of the suspects had been established. On reflection, however, he was less than persuaded that Darlow had reached the right conclusion.

'I can see why Goodhart might want to cause trouble for the NCR,' he said, 'and it's possible that Enticott did so as well. What I can't see is why either of them would want to stop the circus from getting to Newcastle.'

'I agree. All that Mr Darlow thinks about is his railway company. He simply won't understand that the real target was not the NCR but Moscardi's Magnificent Circus.'

'Inspector Colbeck has told him that a dozen times.'

'What was Goodhart doing at the camp?'

'I've no idea.'

'Was he searching for something?'

'Whatever it was, he stood no chance of getting it. Brendan Mulryne threw him out on his ear.'

'Years ago, Goodhart would have fought back.'

'Only a moron would try to fight Brendan.'

'Goodhart *is* a moron,' said Lill. 'Well, you've met him, haven't you?'

'Yes, I have. I'm still trying to work out what he said to me in that foreign language of his.'

'We've cleared up one mystery, anyway. I always wondered how he managed to hold on to a job with the NCR when he was so unreliable. The answer is obvious now. His cousin spoke up for him.'

'I didn't like Enticott at all,' said Leeming. 'He looked down on me and nobody gets away with that. I'm hoping that he resists arrest so that I can clap a pair of handcuffs onto him.'

When the cab reached the house, Lill asked the driver to wait until they came out. As it happened, they never even got inside the house.

The servant who answered the door explained that Enticott and his wife were over fifty miles away, inspecting their new home before spending the night there. Since one of the suspects was beyond their reach, they concentrated on the other one and told the cab driver to take them on to another address. Eventually, they drew up outside the tenement where Goodhart lived. He, too, was not at home. There was no need to use the knocker this time. Mrs Goodhart stood outside the front door with her arms folded and her nostrils flared. She was a tall, stringy woman, her once appealing features hardened into stone. She had a rasping voice. She told them that Goodhart had dared to return to the bosom of his family with the smell of beer on his breath. It was enough to get him ejected by his wife with the warning that he wouldn't be allowed back in again until he was sober.

The two men felt sorry for him. He'd obviously committed what was, to his wife, a heinous domestic crime. Dire retribution would follow. Since her husband was unlikely to be back for hours, the detectives postponed the arrest until the following day and climbed into their cab once more.

'Mr Darlow is going to be very upset,' said Lill.

'That's his problem.'

'With respect, Sergeant, I reckon that it's yours.'

Leeming stiffened in protest. '*Mine?*'

'You were the one to whom he gave the order,' reasoned the other, 'so you're duty-bound to report back to him. When he gets angry, by the way, he can be quite caustic. My advice is that you stand well away from him.'

Colbeck's unheralded return had transformed the atmosphere in the house. Madeleine was overjoyed. When she met him the following morning, Lydia was at once startled and reassured. For his part, Colbeck had the delight of seeing his child again and of lying with

215

his wife in his arms after what seemed too long a time. Everybody was happy. The general excitement, however, was short-lived. As soon as breakfast was over, he set off for Scotland Yard.

Taken aback by his sudden arrival, Edward Tallis quickly recovered and castigated him for sending few accounts of his progress in Northumberland. Colbeck stepped forward to place a detailed report on the superintendent's desk, then he supplemented it with an account of what he'd learnt in Shropshire and what Leeming was now doing. Tallis was appalled.

'The sergeant has joined the *circus*?'

'It's a necessary disguise, sir.'

'In what capacity will he appear in front of the public? Is Leeming to fly daringly on a trapeze or will he continue to draw his pay from the Metropolitan Police while walking a tightrope in Newcastle?'

'The sergeant is not a performer. He's there solely as a guard.'

Tallis read the report with a practised eye and kept Colbeck waiting until he'd finished it. He gave a grudging snort of approval.

'You seem to have made some advances.'

'We've made several, sir. After my visit to Mrs Pulver's home, I have a clearer idea of how she came to be so far away from home when she was killed.'

'But you still don't know who murdered her.'

'It's not impossible that I may already have met the man.'

'Is it this solicitor – Mr Underhill?'

'He must remain a suspect and so must Mr Probert.'

'Which one snuffed out the poor woman's life?'

'I can't be certain,' confessed Colbeck. 'Neither of them may be guilty. The killer may be someone else altogether.'

'At least I've been spared one of your famous theories,' said Tallis, gratefully. 'You're amassing evidence properly before making your usual wild guess.'

'My theories are neither wild nor based on guesswork, sir.'

They traded verbal blows for a few minutes before Colbeck recalled that he had a train to catch north. Before he left, however, he was determined to honour his promise to Lydia Quayle.

'I wish to bring another crime to your attention, sir.'

'What does it concern?'

'It concerns the theft of a woman's dress from a hotel.'

Tallis was apoplectic. 'A woman's *dress* . . . ?'

To the relief of all involved in it, the circus had passed an uneventful night. The animals had settled in quickly and there were no reports of interlopers. Mauro Moscardi toured the camp to speak to all his artistes in turn in an attempt to raise their spirits. Their first performance was that evening. He wanted everything to be perfect. When he entered the marquee, he saw that several people were rehearsing in there. In one part of the ring, his brother had set up the board he used during his performance as a knife-thrower. Unable to perform any longer as an acrobat, Gianni had trained himself to hurl knives at a board against which a young woman bravely stood. As he practised, he was using a dummy instead of a human being.

Brendan Mulryne watched the rehearsal. Moscardi joined him.

'You did a good job last night, Mulryne.'

'Thank you, sir.'

'We had no trouble at all.'

'My men saw to that – Sergeant Leeming among them.' He looked at Gianni. 'Those knives are getting closer and closer to the body. Is his assistant safe?'

'My brother knows what he's doing.'

'He's talking about using hatchets as well.'

Overhearing them, Gianni threw a gleaming hatchet that stuck in the board only inches above the head. Pulling it out again, he walked over to the two men.

'What's happening?' he asked.

'*Nothing* is happening,' replied Moscardi, 'and it's the reason we are so relieved. It's a beautiful day outside and we're being allowed to get on with our work. That hasn't happened for days.'

'He'll be back,' warned Mulryne.

'Then he's all mine,' said Gianni.

'We'll have to devise a plan to keep him at bay.'

'No, I want him to come into the marquee when I'm performing. Then I can do this to him.' Swinging around, he flung the hatchet at the board with great force and it split the head of the dummy in two. 'That's all he deserves.'

'You'd end up being hanged for murder, Gianni.'

'It would be worth it.'

Sauntering back to the board, he pulled out the hatchet and tossed it into the sawdust. Moscardi watched him with an affection tempered by concern.

'My brother is aching to get revenge,' he said.

'We all are, Mr Moscardi, but we have to be careful. I'm hoping that the man who's been dogging us will be caught very soon.'

'Do they know who he is?'

'They have the name of a man I caught trespassing in the camp yesterday. He looked dangerous. Sergeant Leeming said that they know who his accomplice was. He's working with his cousin.'

'Then why doesn't he arrest both men?'

'That's exactly what he and Inspector Lill have just gone off to do, sir. With luck, your brother won't need to keep that hatchet of his sharpened. The villains will soon be in custody and your circus will be safe.'

* * *

On their second visit to the tenement, the detectives didn't need to knock on the door in order to ask if Goodhart was at home because he was curled up in the passageway. Cyrus Lill brought him awake with a gentle kick. Goodhart opened a pair of bleary eyes and squinted at him.

'Get up, Jake,' said Lill. 'We need to speak to you.'

'Ah'm tired, man.'

'We don't care about that.'

By way of reply, Goodhart first yawned then broke wind. He closed his eyes and settled into a sleeping position again. After a stinging rebuke from Darlow the previous night, Leeming was in no mood for delay. Irritated by Goodhart's response, he grabbed hold of him and pulled him upright.

'You heard the inspector,' he said. 'We need to ask some questions.'

'Haad yer rotten tongue or I'll borst yer gob,' yelled Goodhart.

Leeming blinked. 'What's he saying?'

'Let me do the talking,' suggested Lill. 'I understand him.'

Now fully awake, Goodhart wallowed in self-pity. He claimed that he'd had a first alcoholic drink in years and been thrown out of the house by his wife. Even when he came back sober, she refused to let him in. Sleeping outside the door was his punishment. No husband, he wailed, had ever been treated so badly.

'We might have to treat you far worse,' said Lill. 'You're under arrest.'

'Why?'

'We believe you might be involved in a conspiracy to attack the circus.'

'It started when you helped to derail that train,' said Leeming. 'You were working with Geoffrey Enticott, weren't you?' Goodhart was befuddled. 'He is your cousin, isn't he?'

'Yer deed reet, man.'

'The two of you were working hand in glove.'

'Eh?'

'Talking of hands,' said Lill, 'we think you got that injury when someone fired a shotgun at you and made you drop a telescope.'

Goodhart was such a picture of injured innocence that both detectives began to wonder if they were not making a big mistake. Their doubts increased when Goodhart pulled off the glove he was still wearing and tore off the bloodstained bandage to reveal a long gash on his hand. It was clearly no gunshot wound. As for his cousin, Goodhart explained, he was no friend. Sacked from his job with the NCR, he'd gone to see Enticott and pleaded for him to use his influence to get him work for the NER. His cousin refused. He gave him a small amount of money and told him never to come back. Goodhart was embittered.

Leeming had no difficulty believing the account of Enticott's behaviour. It was characteristic of him. Instead of working with his cousin to disable the NCR, Enticott had treated him shamefully. The only thing of which Goodhart was guilty was drinking beer in defiance of his wife's orders. One mystery remained.

'What were you doing at the circus yesterday?' asked Leeming.

He found Goodhart's answer so garbled that he had to turn to Lill for a translation. The explanation had a simple honesty about it. Short of money, Goodhart could not afford to take his children to the circus. Almost all of their friends would be going and they would be left out. Goodhart had gone to the camp to see if he could scrounge some tickets off someone. Before he had the chance to approach anyone, he was chased away by a big Irishman.

It was left to Leeming to mumble an apology for the mistake. There would be no arrest, after all. As soon as he heard that, Goodhart curled up on the floor again.

'What about Mr Enticott?' asked Lill.

'We ought to speak to him, I suppose.'

'But he and his cousin were obviously not in league with each other.'

'Enticott might have had another accomplice.'

'Is that likely?'

'No,' admitted Leeming, 'but I don't want to tell Mr Darlow that we didn't even bother to question him. He was quite fierce when I reported to him last night. I'm not going to give him another chance to blame us for not doing our job.'

The train journey gave Colbeck the thinking time he always found invaluable in an investigation and, having been away from Northumberland, he was able to see it in a slightly different perspective. What had possessed Margaret Pulver to go there? Why had she exchanged the relative calm and cleanliness of Shrewsbury for the grime and industrial hubbub of Newcastle? Had she gone there willingly or under duress? It was conceivable that Donald Underhill had taken her there with a promise to show her the beautiful countryside not far from the city. It had now transpired that he knew the whole area much better than he'd cared to admit. But what motive could have compelled him to kill a woman on whom he obviously doted?

Colbeck thought that the man was a bundle of contradictions, helpful yet obstructive, honest yet deceitful, married yet paying attention to another woman. The Reverend Berry had distrusted him and Mrs Pulver's servants had disliked him. Yet he had many qualities that would appeal to a lonely widow. If there had been a close friendship between her and the solicitor, where had it developed into a more intimate relationship? Both were too well known in the locality to risk being seen together but each of them visited London on occasion. Had that been where trysts took place?

Before he committed himself too early to the notion that Underhill was the killer, Colbeck reminded himself that it was the solicitor who had moved the case on significantly by identifying the murder victim. Had he not done so, she might have remained nameless for some time. When she failed to return home from her latest trip, Mrs Pulver would have been declared a missing person and attempts would have been made to find her but nobody would have suspected that she'd ended her life so far north. When she took the train to London, everyone who knew her believed that that was her destination. The search for her would be concentrated in the south. If he'd actually poisoned the woman, Underhill could have remained silent and joined in the search. That was how most men would behave in the circumstances. But, Colbeck decided, the solicitor was a complex character who might do the thing least expected of him. For that reason, he had to remain a suspect.

The same applied to Owen Probert. He was younger than Underhill and had the kind of brooding intensity that some women might find attractive. He'd boasted about regular visits to London and might have arranged them to coincide with those of Mrs Pulver. Yet all that Colbeck had established was that Probert had befriended the family years before when they were members of a sailing club on the Welsh coast. Had he kept in touch with her after the death of her husband? It was possible but by no means certain. One way of finding out would have been to examine Mrs Pulver's private correspondence but Colbeck had no warrant to do so and, in any case, he began to have doubts that he'd unearth anything that would point in the direction of the killer. Her status had to be borne in mind. By common consent, Margaret Pulver was a saint. Such divine beings, Colbeck knew, did not leave compromising billets-doux behind them.

They were on the point of going out for a walk when the doorbell rang. Since they were in the hall at the time, Madeleine stepped forward to open the door. A fresh-faced man in his late twenties stood on the threshold.

'Miss Quayle?' he asked.

'No,' she replied, 'I'm Mrs Colbeck.'

He became deferential, 'Oh, I do apologise. I didn't realise that . . .'

'I'm Miss Quayle,' said Lydia, stepping forward cautiously.

'I'm Detective Constable Hinton. I've been asked to help you.'

Lydia turned to her friend with a look of utter amazement.

'I did tell you that Robert could move mountains,' said Madeleine.

Geoffrey Enticott was annoyed when he found two detectives on his doorstep this time. They increased his ire by insisting that they were invited inside the house. Having let them in, he rounded on them.

'What is it *now*?'

'We have a few questions to ask you, sir,' said Lill.

'I've answered them already.'

'These are slightly different.'

'That's right,' said Leeming. 'Do you have a cousin by the name of Jake Goodhart?' Enticott refused to answer. 'It's no use denying it, sir. We have proof.'

'Then why bother to ask me?'

'We wanted to see your reaction.'

'Have you ever met Jake?'

'Yes, I have.'

'And I've had the privilege of arresting him more than once for disturbing the peace,' said Lill. 'We both know him.'

'Would either of you want a boneheaded idler like that in your family?' demanded Enticott.

'Blood is thicker than water,' said Leeming.

'He's an embarrassment.'

'Yet you got him a job on the NCR.'

'That's true – but only because his wife begged me to do it.'

'He told us that he asked you for help recently.'

'Yes,' said Enticott, 'he had the brass neck to think that I should bail him out yet again. But I'm not taking him with me to my new company. In fact, I'm glad to be moving well away from him. Jake is a liability. I gave him some money and sent him on his way.'

'He needs all the assistance he can get, sir.'

'Then he can look elsewhere for it.'

'Do you have any children?'

'Yes, of course. I have twin boys. They're fourteen.'

'I daresay they've been asking you to take them to the circus, then,' said Leeming. 'I have two sons as well. When there's a circus in town, they snap at my heels until I agree to take them.'

'Yes,' said Enticott, smiling for the first time, 'we do have tickets.'

'Then we have no more questions, sir.'

'Wait a moment,' said Lill. 'We haven't covered all the ground we need to.'

'Mr Enticott has saved us the trouble of doing that, Inspector.'

Leeming looked his companion in the eye and transmitted a message. Lill understood it at once and followed him to the front door. When the detectives left the house, the sergeant had a final word for Enticott.

'Goodhart has children as well, sir,' he said. 'It's not their fault that their father is a boneheaded idler.'

'Goodbye,' said the other, closing the door.

'I shouldn't have needed to be prodded like that,' said Lill, apologetically. 'You made the right decision, Sergeant. Why would a man who is taking his children to the circus do his best to prevent it reaching Newcastle?'

'Mr Darlow is going to be very unhappy when I tell him that both men had nothing whatsoever to do with the derailment.'

'If Goodhart and his cousin are in the clear, it only leaves one suspect.'

'Yes,' said Leeming. 'Owen Probert.'

Colbeck changed trains at Carlisle and travelled on the NCR to Hexham. He shared a compartment with an assortment of companions. The one who stood out was a barrel-chested man in his late forties with a beard that made him look like a minor prophet. With a high forehead and gleaming eyes, he seemed to exude intelligence. Colbeck wondered why he wore gloves on such a warm day. Other people chatted to each other but the bearded man remained resolutely silent and virtually motionless. It was only when they sped past the site of the derailment that he looked out of the window with interest. Colbeck did the same, pleased to see that everything had now been cleared away and that the only mementoes of the event were the deep channels gouged into the grass verge.

When they reached Hexham, the inspector was the only person who alighted from the compartment. He walked from the station to Probert's house. Over the garden wall, he could hear sounds of young children playing with their father. The Welshman was about to move to a new, more important managerial position in the coal industry. It seemed unlikely that he'd risk losing his wife and family because of an entanglement with a widow somewhat older than himself, but Colbeck had met husbands before who'd allowed themselves to get trapped in such a predicament. As a result, he made no hasty assumptions.

When Probert's wife let the inspector into the house, he had a few moments with her and established that she was a local girl from Bangor who'd been a near neighbour of Probert's. Strikingly pretty and with long dark hair, she had the same pleasing accent as her husband. She was distressed that Colbeck had called again and went to fetch her husband. Probert confronted his visitor in a truculent mood.

'What sort of game are you involved in?' he asked.

'It's not a game, sir.'

'First of all, you come here and treat me like a criminal. Then your sergeant turns up to do the same and now you're back to carry on the sport. Have you nothing better to do with your time than to harass innocent people?'

'We have not yet eliminated you from our enquiries.'

'Look,' said Probert, palm to his chest, 'I swear to you, hand on heart, that I had nothing to do with the derailment of the circus.'

'I know that, sir.'

'How?'

'You're a family man. You'd never dream of robbing the children of the fun of going to the circus.'

'Then why are you here?'

'I wanted to ask you about Mrs Margaret Pulver.'

Probert's immediate response was to move to the open door to close it tight.

'Why did you mention *her*, Inspector?' he asked.

'I should have thought you could have guessed that, sir.'

'Her name has been in the newspapers, I know that, and I'm desperately sorry for what happened to her. Beyond that, I have nothing to add.'

'You seem curiously uninvolved, Mr Probert.'

'What do you mean?'

'I visited Mrs Pulver's home in Shropshire yesterday. During the time when she and her late husband were staying on the Welsh coast, I was told, they became acquainted with you.'

'They met lots of people. Richard Pulver was a generous host.'

'Since you enjoyed his hospitality, I'm surprised that you aren't more upset to hear of his wife's murder.'

'I said that I was desperately sorry, Inspector.'

'You didn't say it in a way that made me believe you,' said Colbeck. 'When did you last see the lady?'

'It must have been . . . years ago.'

'Have you never visited her in Shropshire?'

Probert was offended. 'What call would I have to do that?'

'It's in the nature of friendship, sir. When we hear of the untimely death of someone, we often have the impulse to offer sympathy to their nearest and dearest.'

'I wasn't really a *friend*, Inspector.'

'I'm beginning to see that.'

'Look, why exactly are you here?' asked Probert.

'I was intrigued by the way that things turned out. Years ago, you meet a woman on the Welsh coast, then, you imply, you lose touch with her completely.'

'That's the truth!'

'Out of the blue, Mrs Pulver then turns up dead only a relatively short distance away from where we're standing. Did someone entice her here, I wonder?'

'It was not me, Inspector. I'd take my oath on the Bible.'

'Are you a man of faith, sir?'

'Yes, I am.'

'Mrs Pulver was very religious as well, so you had that in common.'

'We lost touch ages ago,' said Probert, regaining his composure. 'That's all I can tell you.'

'What about your wife, sir? Would Mrs Probert confirm that?'

'There's no need to speak to her.'

'If you're telling me the truth, you have nothing to worry about.'

'Can't you take my word for it?'

227

'No, sir,' said Colbeck, 'I can't, Bible or no Bible.'

He tried to move to the door but Probert stepped sideways to block his path.

'I've just remembered something, Inspector.'

'What's that, sir?'

'Since her husband's death, I did bump into Mrs Pulver once.'

'And where did this encounter take place?'

'It was at the sailing club in Bangor.'

'Can you remember the date?'

'Oh, it must have been three or four years ago,' said the other, expansively. 'To be candid, I didn't recognise her at first. If she hadn't stopped me, I'd have walked straight past her.'

'Was Mrs Probert with you at the time?'

'No, no, she wasn't, as it happens.'

'That's a pity,' said Colbeck. 'If she had been there, she could have told me that such a meeting did take place. Since you claim to have been alone, I'm bound to tell you that your story is a complete fabrication. I have it on good authority that, after the tragedy, Mrs Pulver never went back to the Welsh coast and why should she when it held such sad memories? I warned you about telling lies before, Mr Probert. Do you wish the rest of this conversation to take place in a police station?'

The colour drained instantly from the Welshman's face.

Lydia Quayle was simultaneously pleased and discomfited by the fact that a detective had been assigned to her case. Glad that it was being taken seriously, she was self-conscious when forced to reveal certain details to a complete stranger. Hinton was polite and efficient, jotting down everything in his pad before promising to pay a visit to the hotel where the theft had occurred. By the time that he left, Lydia had overcome her embarrassment. She went in search of Madeleine and found her in the studio, looking wistfully at her paintings. Her friend told her what had happened.

'You're so lucky to have a detective looking after your case. When my father reported a stolen bag some years ago, he made a statement at the police station and heard nothing more. The police simply don't have the resources to solve every case of theft.'

'This was more than a case of theft, Madeleine.'

'Yes, of course. It's far worse.'

'Constable Hinton said that it will be so much easier to catch him once we know his name. My brother would have got my letter today. With luck, I should have an answer from Lucas tomorrow.'

'I can't wait to ask Robert how he did it. Ordinarily, the superintendent would never look into a case like this. He'd dismiss it as being too petty.'

'It doesn't feel petty to me, Madeleine,' said Lydia.

'I'm sure that Robert made that point to him.'

'Perhaps he appealed to the superintendent's finer feelings.'

Madeleine laughed. 'He doesn't have any.'

'Let's go for that walk, shall we?'

They let themselves out of the house and strolled along the pavement. Madeleine was grateful to be out in the fresh air. Because her plight had been taken seriously by the police, Lydia felt liberated.

He was given the use of Mulryne's tent to change his clothes. When he emerged, Leeming could pass for a labourer once more.

'I'm sorry I can only offer you a tent,' said the Irishman.

'I've got no complaints, Brendan.'

'One day, I'd like to own one of those pretty, brightly painted caravans but I'll have to save up for a long time before I can do that.'

'You're going to stay with the circus, then?'

'Yes, it's the best job I've ever had.' He broke off to catch Jacko as the monkey jumped down from the edge of the marquee. 'Did you make any arrests?'

'No,' said Leeming, 'we didn't.'

'I thought you went off to nab two suspects.'

'They were both innocent. We were badly misled by Mr Darlow.'

'Is he the man who runs that railway company?'

'Yes, Brendan, he's been cracking the whip over us ever since we got here. He had the cheek to blame me for going after Enticott and Goodhart when he was the one who put us up to it in the first place. Honestly, you don't get much in the way of gratitude when you become a policeman.'

'That's why I joined the circus instead.'

'You all seem to get on so well together.'

'Mr Moscardi insists on that. He likes everyone to be happy.'

'I wish our superintendent had that attitude,' said Leeming, gloomily.

The next moment, there was an explosion of noise. Dozens of voices were raised and people started running past them. The commotion quickly grew in volume. As one of the clowns charged towards them, Mulryne put a hand out to stop him.

'What's happened?' he asked.

'Someone has just seen Bev Rogers.'

'Then we have to catch him at once. Come on, Sergeant,' said Mulryne, breaking into a run. 'We're chasing the Strong Man who's been trying to close this circus down.'

Leeming joined the pack at once and raced through the camp.

CHAPTER SIXTEEN

Bevis Rogers was a big, hefty, rugged man in his fifties with broad shoulders and well-developed muscles in his arms and legs. Given his bulk, he could run remarkably well. But the very things that had qualified him to become a circus Strong Man now began to work against him. Moving so much weight at speed took its toll on him and he was soon panting. Since he'd retired from performing, he'd acquired a paunch and a slight stoop. Ageing legs, burning lungs and the increasing burden of his own body combined to slow him down. He managed to get as far as the trees but there was no way he could outrun the dozens of angry people now haring after him and creating such a hullabaloo. Forcing himself on and ignoring the intense pain, he reached a clearing at the very moment when they caught up with him. Someone flung himself on to Rogers' back and brought him crashing down to earth.

It only served to enrage him. Throwing the man off as easily as he might discard a coat, the Strong Man struggled to his feet and faced his enemies like a wounded bear at bay. Anyone who got too close was beaten back by a huge fist or kicked by a vicious foot. Forming a circle around him, the crowd jeered and threatened but nobody could bring him down. It was left to Mulryne to capture him. Light on his feet, he swayed in front of Rogers and dodged every blow that was thrown, getting in some counter punches each time. One of them landed on the other man's nose. Little by little, he took all the energy out of his opponent and made him stagger. Mulryne then chose his moment, stepped in and felled him with an uppercut.

Half a dozen men dived on Rogers. Someone held up a rope.

'Let's string him up right here!' he cried.

'No!' shouted Leeming above the clamour. 'Stand back.'

Though he was almost out of breath, he still had the strength to drag people off Rogers one by one. Cyrus Lill joined him.

'Yes,' said Leeming, looking around the faces, 'I know how you feel. You think this man tried to kill some of you and you may be right. But that doesn't mean you can behave like an unruly mob. He's our prisoner.'

He turned Rogers over so that Lill could handcuff him from behind.

'Listen to the sergeant,' said Mulryne. 'I want to tear this bastard limb from limb just like the rest of you. But that would mean the hangman would make me dance and I've no taste for that kind of jig, if you don't mind.'

'After what he did to us,' yelled Gianni, waving a hatchet, 'he deserves to be cut up into slices and fed to the animals.'

'They'd only get indigestion from his rotten carcass.'

The laughter at the Irishman's comment helped to ease the situation. People with murder on their minds now drew back. Leeming helped Rogers to his feet. Blood was streaming from the Strong Man's nose. Mulryne pointed at him.

'That ugly face of his looks better since I tapped his claret.'

There was more laughter. Gianni raised the hatchet as if to strike but Leeming stood between him and his target. After a long exchange of glares, the Italian backed away. Cyrus Lill explained the situation to him.

'This man will be taken to the police station and interrogated,' he said. 'If he is guilty of the crimes you blame on him, he'll feel the full weight of the law. As for you, I suggest that you remember why you're here. You're circus folk, come to entertain the people of Newcastle. What will they think if they hear that you're nothing but a bloodthirsty gang of ruffians? Who will pay to see you perform then?'

'Off you go,' added Leeming. 'We'll take care of him now.'

'You heard,' said Mulryne, reinforcing the order with a wave of his arm. 'Go back to what you do best. That marquee will be full this evening. Give them all a performance that they'll remember.'

The crowd began slowly to disperse. Gianni was the last to go, albeit reluctantly. The detectives were relieved that the danger was over and they praised Mulryne's intervention.

'Ah, it was nothing,' he said, chuckling. 'I need a good fight now and again. It reminds me that I'm an Irishman.'

Probert was an enigma. He appeared to live a contented and law-abiding life yet had an irrational dislike of the police. Colbeck and Leeming had both discovered that. The man's only interest was in getting rid of them as soon as possible. He had not been able to do so on this occasion. Colbeck was far too tenacious. Having given the Welshman a fright, he put him under greater pressure.

'Have you ever been in court, Mr Probert?'

'Of course, I haven't.'

'Then let me introduce you to the concept of perjury. It

means lying under oath. If a witness is found guilty of it, the punishment can be severe. Most of what you've told me so far would be considered as perjury in a court of law, so I'd suggest you'd confine your answers from now on to the plain, unvarnished truth.' Colbeck wrinkled his brow. 'Do you agree?'

'Yes, Inspector,' murmured the other.

'You did not have a chance meeting in Bangor with Mrs Pulver, did you?'

'No, I didn't.'

'To begin with, it was not a chance meeting.'

'I suppose not,' said the other after a long pause.

'Was it in London?'

'Yes.'

'Was it prearranged?'

'To some extent, it was.'

'Do you stand by your claim that it only happened once?'

'Of course I stand by it,' said Probert, earnestly.

'When was this?' asked Colbeck. 'I don't want an approximate time. I want to know the exact date. My feeling is that it was a meeting of some significance so you'll remember it well.'

'I do.'

'When was it?'

'It was some months after the . . . accident.'

'Mrs Pulver would have been in mourning.'

'We both were, Inspector.'

'So soon after the tragedy, she'd have been in a highly emotional state.'

'That's why she asked for the meeting.'

'Oh?' Colbeck was surprised. 'It was not at your instigation, then?'

'No – after what happened, I never expected to see her again.'

'Why was that?'

'I thought that the friendship had come to a natural end.'

'Ah, so it's a friendship now, is it?' said Colbeck. 'Earlier on you said that you were no more than an acquaintance of the Pulvers. I can't see you going all the way to London for a mere acquaintance.'

'Make of it what you wish,' said Probert, sparked into life again. 'I have insufficient facts, sir.'

'Mrs Pulver and I met once in London and that was that. From that day forward, I never set eyes on her or had any communication with her.'

'Did you want the friendship to continue?'

'That's irrelevant.'

'Then I can only assume that you did, sir.' Probert said nothing. 'Do you know what I think? I believe that you're still unable to cope with the guilt.'

'You're quite wrong. The past is the past. I never look back.'

'But you've been talking about what must have been a harrowing experience.'

'It's faded into obscurity.'

'I refuse to accept that, Mr Probert.'

'I'm a different person now.'

Colbeck held his gaze for a full minute before asking his question. 'Does that mean you're now being faithful to your wife?'

Too shaken to reply, Probert shrunk away. After glancing at the door again, he chewed his lip and lowered his head. Colbeck pressed on.

'That's why you met in London, wasn't it?' he said. 'Both of you were overwhelmed with guilt. Margaret Pulver should have been in the boat that day but I suspect that she had a prior engagement with you.' He saw the Welshman twitch. 'While you were together, she lost her entire family. Given her religious conviction, she must have seen it as some kind of divine retribution. It's no wonder she dedicated herself to the Church by way of a penance.'

'We both made vows to live a better life, Inspector.'

Colbeck asked the final question like an assassin quietly sliding a knife between the ribs of his victim.

'How long did you keep them?'

At the time when Bevis Rogers had been caught, Mauro Moscardi was being interviewed in an office in the city by reporters from the *Evening Chronicle* and the *Newcastle Courant*. It was only when he returned to the circus that he heard that Rogers had been seen, chased and caught. The news sent him hurrying to the police station to demand access to the Strong Man. The duty sergeant explained that the prisoner was being questioned and was therefore unavailable. Moscardi protested in vain. When he finally stopped shouting, he folded his arms defiantly.

'I'll wait.'

Seated behind a table in a bare, featureless room, Bevis Rogers looked better now that his nose had stopped bleeding and his face had been cleaned but he was still in pain. Cyrus Lill and Victor Leeming sat opposite him. The sergeant led the interrogation.

'You were sent to cause trouble for the circus, weren't you?'

'No, I wasn't,' replied Rogers.

'I went to Bristol to meet Mr Greenwood. Some of the performers told me that you'd been ordered to come here.'

'That bit is true.'

'Were you told to derail the circus train?'

'No!' howled the prisoner. 'I'd never do a thing like that.'

'Did you arrange for someone else to do it on your behalf?' asked Lill.

Rogers was insulted. 'It would never cross my mind,' he said.

'I was born and brought up in a circus. It's been my whole life. I respect people like Mr Moscardi.'

'So why did you spy on him?'

'That's all that Mr Greenwood asked me to do. I was to watch and send back reports. He's always looking for new artistes. If there was someone who stood out, I was to see if I could interest him in joining us instead.'

'Did you approach anyone?' asked Leeming.

'I couldn't get near enough,' complained Rogers. 'After the train came off the line, everyone was on guard. All I could do was to watch from a distance.'

'You were seen in the crowd at one point.'

'That was stupid of me. I stayed out of sight after that.'

'What about that fire among the trees?'

Rogers looked blank. 'What fire?'

'Then there were those sheep that were stolen. I suppose you know nothing about those either?' Rogers shook his head. 'Why did Mr Greenwood pick you?'

'He needs someone to do odd jobs.'

'You were a bad choice in this case,' said Lill. 'You stand out too much.'

Rogers was offended. 'I can't help that.'

After taking it in turns to aim questions at him for another ten minutes, the detectives came to the same conclusion. The Strong Man was telling the truth. He had not been sent to damage the circus in any way. He was simply there to gather intelligence for a rival. By straying too close that day, he'd been recognised, chased and beaten. Sitting up, he flexed his muscles.

'He'd never have knocked me down in the old days,' he bragged. 'You'd have needed a sledgehammer to stop me.'

'I believe you,' said Leeming.

'What happens now?'

'That's an interesting question.'

'It's not as if I committed any crime.'

'You were spying. Mr Moscardi would call that a crime, though he does the same thing himself.'

'What about those people who jumped on me when I was knocked to the ground? I was assaulted, Sergeant. I was wounded. They're the ones who should be prosecuted.'

'They were provoked,' said Lill.

'All I did was to wander round the edge of the camp.'

They sympathised with him. Mistakenly thought to be at the root of the circus's woes, he'd been hounded by a mob in the grip of hysteria. If the detectives had not arrived when they did, Rogers could have suffered serious injuries. As it was, his face was bruised and his clothing was covered in grass stains.

'Thank you for saving me,' he said, 'but you have to let me go.'

'That may not be advisable at the moment,' said Leeming. 'I thought I heard Mr Moscardi's voice a while ago. He sounded angry. Holding you here might be the best way of keeping you alive.'

The process of recovery was almost complete. When she first moved into the Colbeck residence, Lydia Quayle had been in a state of terror because she was victimised by a stranger. It was impossible for her to step outside the house. Days later, she not only went through the front door without trepidation, she went for long walks on her own. The surprise visit home by Colbeck had injected even more confidence into her because his advice had been so sound. Keeping his promise, he'd somehow persuaded the superintendent to send a detective to speak to her. As a result of the man's visit, Lydia felt like skipping along the pavement. She was not only being given police protection, there was an active search for her stalker. When she received a letter from her younger brother, she hoped, she would be able to provide a name. The man would then be arrested and the persecution would cease.

Her walk took her as far as the river. Late afternoon sunshine was turning the water to silver. Craft of all sizes glided to and fro and she enjoyed the simple pleasure of taking in the familiar scene. People went past her in both directions and she caught snatches of their conversations. She was still watching the birds skim over the water when she felt someone brush gently against her shoulder. When she turned round, all she could see was the back of the man's frock coat as he walked away. Under his arm was a flat box, which he put on a coping stone before strolling on. Lydia wondered what the box contained and why it had been left behind. She was just about to pick it up and run after the man when a warning bell rang inside her head.

Moving forward tentatively, she reached the box and lifted it up carefully. It felt very light. Lydia couldn't resist opening it. When she saw what was inside, she felt all of her new-found confidence being stripped away in a flash.

The man had returned her dress. And he'd touched her.

Robert Colbeck arrived at the police station in Newcastle and walked into the middle of a violent argument. Moscardi had grown tired of waiting. Gesticulating madly, he was demanding to be allowed to see the prisoner. The duty sergeant was refusing to allow him anywhere near Rogers and threatened to lock him up if he kept on causing such a scene. The noise had brought a couple of uniformed constables out to see what was going on. Colbeck put a restraining hand on Moscardi's shoulder.

'There's no need to shout, sir. The duty sergeant has excellent hearing.'

'Then why won't the idiot listen to me?' said the Italian.

'What exactly is your complaint, sir?'

'They've got Sam Greenwood's spy locked up in there and they won't let me see him. He's the man who derailed our train.'

'That's simply not true,' said Colbeck, patiently. 'And even if it were, you're not entitled to act as judge and jury.' He looked at the clock on the wall. 'You've clearly forgotten what time it is. By my calculation, the performance in your marquee will start in just over an hour. I hope they have another ringmaster standing by.'

Moscardi was stunned. 'Is that the time?' he gasped. He turned on the duty sergeant. 'This is *your* fault.'

'I think you should go, sir,' advised Colbeck.

'What about Rogers?'

'He'll still be behind bars when the performance is over.'

'Then I'll be back.'

After snarling at the duty sergeant once more, Moscardi rushed out. Colbeck apologised on the man's behalf, describing the intense pressure he'd been under to get his circus safely to the city. The duty sergeant was simply glad to get rid of him. He gave the inspector more detail about the arrest of Bevis Rogers. A few moments later, a door opened and Leeming stepped out. Colbeck didn't at first recognise him in his disguise.

'You look more like the prisoner than the man who arrested him.'

'We did that to rescue him, Inspector.'

'Has he been charged?'

'There are no grounds for doing so.'

'Then he has to be released.'

'We're not doing that until the circus is under way,' said Leeming. 'If Mr Moscardi or his brother gets their hands on him, they could easily end up facing a charge of murder. We need to get Rogers away from here altogether.'

'I'd like a word with him first,' said Colbeck. 'Where is he?'

Leeming opened the door. 'Follow me, sir . . .'

Madeleine had never seen her in such a state before. Sobbing on her friend's shoulder, Lydia was trembling all over. It was minutes before she had enough control to be able to speak coherently.

'There's no rush,' said Madeleine. 'Speak when you feel ready.'

'I never thought that I'd get back here. My legs almost gave way.'

'But you *did* get back and you brought that dress with you. Where did you get it and who does it belong to?'

'It's *mine*, Madeleine. It's the one he stole.'

The memory of his touch set Lydia off into another bout of sobbing. When she'd dried her eyes, she apologised and gave Madeleine a brief account of what had happened. Her friend was appalled.

'He knew where you were all the time.'

'I felt him brush against my shoulder. It was horrible, Madeleine. I was defenceless. Just think what he might have done to me.'

'You mustn't go out alone again, Lydia.'

'I'm not going out of this house with *anybody*,' cried the other. 'I'm staying here until someone finally catches that monster.'

Mauro Moscardi was in a towering rage when he got back to the circus. It took all of his wife's skill and patience to calm him down and make him see that he had an important job to do that evening. His most urgent duty, she said, was to instil some self-belief into the artistes. In order to reach the city, they'd endured some terrible setbacks and there was bound to be fear at the back of their minds. Her husband had to expel it completely.

'Tell them that our worries are over. Rogers is in custody so there's nothing more that he can do. Rouse them, Mauro.

Remind them that they belong to the finest circus in England.'

'It's the finest in the whole of Europe,' he asserted.

'Only when we are at our best,' she emphasised.

'I'll keep them up to scratch.'

'People have been queuing for hours. The marquee will burst at the seams.'

'I told the newspaper reporters to expect something very special.'

'That's exactly what they'll get,' said Anne.

They were in their caravan, surrounded by all their trophies and lucky charms. She reached for his costume and passed the coat hanger to him. Moscardi began to take off his clothes.

'I'm not worried about any of the performers,' he said. 'They can overcome everything. With animals, it's a different matter. You never know how they'll react to something out of the ordinary like a derailment.'

'The horses are the real problem. They've been skittish ever since they were stampeded by that fire. We were lucky to get them all back unharmed.'

'It was Rogers who started that fire.'

'I know, Mauro.'

'He ought to be burnt alive.'

'Get dressed or we'll be short of time.'

Anne knew better than to argue with her husband when his mind was set on something. Unlike Moscardi, she was not convinced that the Strong Man had indeed engineered all the attacks. Pretending to agree made for a quieter life. Her main aim was to get him into the costume and character of the ringmaster. When he was strutting around in his red coat and top hat, he was at his happiest. Once the performance began, he'd forget all about Bevis Rogers.

* * *

It took only a minute of conversation with Rogers to be convinced that he had nothing to do with any attempts to stop or disable the circus. The Strong Man was indignant that anyone should even suspect him of such a vile crime. After a discussion with Superintendent Finlan, it was decided that he would be released without charge in due course and accompanied to the railway station by someone who made sure that he caught a train that would carry him well away from the circus. Colbeck and Leeming, meanwhile, summoned a cab to take them to the park where the performance was due to take place. The sergeant was keen to learn what Colbeck had discovered during his absence. He was fascinated to hear the inspector's description of the visit to Shropshire and flabbergasted that Edward Tallis had actually been talked into releasing one of his detectives in order to help Lydia Quayle. Of all the information he was given in abbreviated form, however, nothing intrigued him so much as Colbeck's account of the interview with Owen Probert.

'Why didn't you arrest him, sir?'

'I was tempted, Victor.'

'He admitted committing adultery with Mrs Pulver. Disgraceful.'

'What I don't know is if the relationship continued or if he was being honest when he told me that it had decisively finished years ago.'

'It sounds to me as if he was lying,' said Leeming. 'The connection between Probert and the murder victim accounts for everything. It explains why she ended up in Northumberland and why her killer laid her so carefully in that grave. Part of him still loved her.'

'But what was his motive?'

'She might have been making demands on him.'

'That's possible,' said Colbeck. 'Mistresses who make excessive demands are always playing with fire. And if she'd threatened to tell his wife what was going on . . .'

'That's the obvious explanation. Probert is a family man with a new job that will give him more power and, I daresay, more money. If someone threatens that, what is he likely to do? Will he put his wife and children first or will he side with a woman he's been seeing in secret for all those years?'

'We don't *know* for certain that he's been seeing her.'

'Think of that tragedy in the storm off the Welsh coast. While that was happening, he was betraying his wife and Mrs Pulver was betraying her husband. That gave them a bond.'

'Probert described it as an albatross around his neck.'

Leeming started. 'What does that mean?'

'It's a literary reference from *The Ancient Mariner*.'

'Who was he?'

'It's a poem, Victor. The albatross is a badge of shame.'

'If he's prepared to deceive his wife like that, Probert *has* no shame.'

'Oh, I think he does,' said Colbeck. 'I just wonder if it's strong enough to stop him from doing the same thing over and over again.'

'Arresting him might loosen his tongue.'

'And what if he's innocent? All that we'll have done is to imperil his marriage and make his new employers look at him with a jaundiced eye. Besides,' he went on, 'Probert is not the only person who provides a link between two contrasting counties. We must never forget Underhill.'

'He was too smarmy for my liking.'

'That's not the word I'd use.'

'How would you describe him?'

'Machiavellian.'

* * *

Having manufactured a plausible excuse to get into the house again, Donald Underhill sat at the writing desk and looked around the room. It reflected all of Margaret Pulver's interests. Her favourite books lined the shelves, landscapes of the home county she loved so much hung on three walls and every surface had a collection of prized silver objects. On the wall directly in front of him was the framed copy of the plan for the railway line that ran through her property. In a room so tastefully furnished and decorated, it seemed incongruous but it had obviously been cherished.

He basked for a few minutes in fond memories of the dead woman, recalling how they'd first met and how their friendship had developed to the point where she'd placed great trust in him. His reminiscences were then cut short by the housekeeper, who opened the door without knocking and stepped into the room.

'Have you finished yet, sir?' she asked, pointedly.

The whole of Newcastle seemed to have turned up for the first performance by Moscardi's Magnificent Circus and there was an anticipatory excitement that was almost tangible. Colbeck and Leeming arrived and had to pick their way through the bustling throng before they could find a quiet spot away from the entrance.

'You're not going to be very popular with that hat,' said Leeming.

'I'll take it off before someone knocks it off and I'll make sure I sit towards the rear. Children take precedence at a circus. I don't want to get in their way.'

'I wish that I could watch the performance as well.'

'You have to stay behind the scenes, Victor.'

'I'll miss all the fun.'

'That's not true,' said Colbeck. 'I'm only a spectator; you're actually a *part* of the circus. I'll see the artistes from a distance;

you'll mingle with them. Best of all, you'll be cheek by jowl with the animals.'

'I could do without being so close to Jacko. He must have fleas. He's always scratching himself.'

'Cheer up and think of all the tales you'll be able to tell to your children. They'll be so impressed to hear that their father joined a circus and made friends with a monkey.'

'Yes,' said the other, brightening, 'I suppose they will.'

'Right,' said Colbeck, 'I'll try to have a word with Mr Moscardi before the performance starts. You'd better find Mulryne and get your orders. It's ironic, isn't it? He was once dismissed from the police force yet he's now giving orders to a detective sergeant.'

'I don't mind that at all, sir. He knows what he's doing. Having seen him knock that Strong Man to the ground, I take my hat off to him. I wouldn't have liked to tackle Rogers.' He looked around. 'This crowd is massive. I'm glad that they'll make a profit this evening but these hordes will cause us problems.'

'Yes, you can't keep a close eye on all these people.'

'If someone really wants to harm the circus,' said Leeming, worriedly, 'this would be the ideal time to strike.'

The man bided his time. There was no hurry. He waited until the audience had been thrilled by the acrobats and reduced to helpless laughter by the clowns. Rosie the elephant trotted into the ring to thunderous applause. It would not be long now. He'd deliberately watched the last performance in Carlisle so that he knew the programme. When the elephant had finished her act, there would be some jugglers to entertain the crowd. As their act finished, the ringmaster would announce that the lion tamer would risk his life by playing with three wild creatures from the heart of Africa. The animals would then be released from their cages and sent down a steel tunnel to the sawdust ring. There they would perform a series of well-rehearsed tricks.

Tonight, however, it would be different. After the elephant had left the ring to an ovation, the jugglers went sprinting into the marquee to be introduced. The man then kept to the shadows and made for the cages. They were already in position along with the tunnel that would guide them into the ring. Standing beside the cages was the keeper whose job was to release the animals but he was suddenly replaced. The interloper stepped out from his hiding place and used a cosh to knock the keeper senseless and send him to the ground. He then pushed back the bolt on the first of the cages and opened the door before running away. It all happened so quickly that the group of people standing nearby were taken by surprise.

The lion took full advantage of the offer of liberty. Bounding forward, he leapt down from the cage, entered the tunnel and scampered along it until he emerged in the ring. When he bared his teeth and emitted a first roar, the crowd screamed in fear and drew back. The jugglers, meanwhile, abandoned their clubs and retired to the other side of the ring. One of the clowns ran bravely forward and tried to calm the lion but a flailing paw forced him to jump back out of the way. Parents were throwing protective arms around their children and some were looking for a way out. Others, however, thought that they were watching an act and they started to urge the lion on. It responded by running around the perimeter of the ring and roaring in anger.

Two people then appeared at speed. One of them was the lion tamer, holding a whip in one hand and a chair in the other. Lending his support was Mulryne, armed with nothing more than a hay fork. The animal turned its attention to them. As the lion tamer tried to coax it towards the exit, it responded with the loudest roar yet and looked as if it was about to jump on him. He used the chair to keep it at bay and cracked the whip to direct it. Mulryne took his orders from the other man. He simply showed the lion the two sharp prongs of the fork from time to time and it moved back. Slowly and steadily, they took control and manoeuvred the animal towards the opening of the tunnel. A final crack of the whip sent it scurrying back to its cage.

The deafening applause was a mixture of relief and delight. Terrified by the lion's dramatic entrance, most people thought that they could be torn apart by the animal. They now believed that there was no real danger because the lion tamer and his assistant had been going through one of their usual routines.

Mauro Moscardi had been horrified that the animal had got loose but he recovered his wits with great speed. Stepping into the middle of the ring, he acknowledged the applause with a bow and spread his arms wide.

'That act was called the Hunting of the Beast,' he yelled, 'and it featured our courageous lion tamer, Otto. Please show your appreciation for his feat of bravery.'

The applause was even louder and Otto ran out to enjoy it.

Mulryne never appeared. With Leeming at his heels, he was too busy searching the encampment for the man who'd unlocked the cage and come close to creating a disaster. The Irishman was still brandishing his hay fork.

'If we catch up with him,' he warned, 'he's all mine. I'll flay him alive.'

CHAPTER SEVENTEEN

The first time that Colbeck was able to have a proper discussion with Leeming was when they had breakfast together next morning at the hotel. After the performance, the inspector had spent hours with Moscardi, offering him advice about how he could boost security around the circus. The sergeant, by contrast, had been involved in a long and fruitless search for the interloper. Lack of sleep made him jaded and listless. There were dark pouches under his eyes.

'One good thing came out of last night,' said Colbeck.

'Well, I'm not aware of it, sir. We came very close to a calamity.'

'The lion tamer saved the day – with the help of Mulryne, of course.'

'It could so easily have been far worse,' said Leeming. 'Think what would have happened if the lion had started mauling some of the spectators. Anyway,' he went on, eating the remains of a sausage, 'what's this good thing you talk about?'

'I finally convinced Mr Moscardi that he's not being attacked by a rival circus. At the time when someone unlocked that lion, Rogers was on a train that was taking him to Bristol. How could he do Mr Greenwood's bidding if he wasn't even here?'

'That lets the Strong Man off the hook.'

'But where does it leave *us*, Victor? All four suspects have vanished.'

'No, they haven't, sir. We still have Mr Probert.'

'Yes, but he's a suspect for the murder not for hounding the circus.'

'Does it matter? As long as we arrest him for *something*, we can get the superintendent off our backs.'

'When you're properly awake, you'll regret saying anything so cavalier.'

Leeming stifled a yawn. 'I'd like to sleep for a week.'

'Let me tell you what I've been mulling over.'

Colbeck shared his thoughts. The man they were after, he believed, may not have had a specific grudge against Moscardi, after all. He might simply be impelled by a deep hatred of that particular form of entertainment. Because of its pre-eminence in the field, Moscardi's Magnificent Circus had come to symbolise the art. To bring it crashing down would give its enemy far more satisfaction than if he'd assailed a much smaller touring company.

'Why would a man harbour such bitterness and detestation, Victor?'

Leeming shrugged. 'It could be a case of overpowering envy, sir. What if this man felt that he had some special talents but was rejected by every circus in the land? That would leave a sour taste in anyone's mouth.'

'It wouldn't be enough to drive him to such extremes.'

'Then suppose he wanted revenge,' said Leeming. 'We've seen the mess that a camp of that size can leave behind. This man could be a disgruntled landowner. A circus may have camped illegally on his territory and left it in a frightful state.'

'We're looking for someone who's driven by a twisted passion.'

'Then we know where he must've come from, sir.'

'Where's that?'

'The lunatic asylum.'

Letting himself into the empty church, he walked down the nave and on into the chancel before kneeling in front of the altar. He offered up a long prayer of supplication before getting up and walking back to the pulpit. After adjusting his surplice, he climbed up the steps and looked around the pews at the imaginary congregation he saw clustered there, waiting for him to justify the Word of God. There was no need for any notes. He knew the sermon off by heart. There was no call for an apology for what he had done. It was in the nature of a sacred mission. Taking a deep breath, he launched into his homily.

'Circus is an abomination. It appeals to the very worst elements of human nature. It sullies, it corrupts, it misleads, it destroys the soul. Someone must resist its evil encroachment on all the virtues we cherish and I thank the Lord above that he has chosen me to lead the fight . . .'

'What have you decided to do about Probert?' asked Leeming.

'I think we should watch and wait.'

'That would give him time to escape, sir.'

'Where is he going to go? He has a wife, a family and a career. He's not going to throw all three aside at once, is he? Besides, flight would be a confession of guilt. Probert won't give himself away like that – if he is the killer, that is.'

'Yesterday, you were not sure.'

'I feel much the same today, Victor.'

'They're a strange pair, aren't they?' said Leeming. 'I wonder what it was about Mrs Pulver that made her attract two such different men.'

'I'd rather concentrate on their similarities.'

'Do they *have* any?'

'Oh, yes,' replied Colbeck. 'I think so. Both men are clever, intelligent and unsatisfied in their respective marriages. Each of them yearns for something they don't possess – a rich, beautiful, cultured lady who has shaped a new life for herself after a tragedy. Underhill's wife is disabled and Probert married someone from the same street in which they grew up.'

'There's nothing wrong with that,' said Leeming, defensively. 'Estelle and I lived only three doors away from each other and, after all this time, we're still very happy together.'

'It's always a joy to be with your family, Victor.'

'Thank you, sir.'

'But your situation is not the one in which both Underhill and Probert find themselves. You've had the sense to know when you've found something rather magical and I've been lucky enough to share that experience myself. It's one that neither of our suspects has known. They did find someone magical eventually,' said Colbeck. 'Her name was Margaret Pulver.'

'She must have been a very special person.'

'Without question – had I known the lady, I'd certainly have been an admirer.'

Leeming was almost shocked. 'You don't mean that, sir.'

'I'm talking of admiration, Victor, not of anything stronger. There's an aspect of her character that I've only discerned once before in a woman. She adores railways. Mrs Pulver not only had a drawing of a nearby railway line in her drawing room, she also has a copy of the engineer's original specifications for it. That's something that even Madeleine wouldn't have on display and she's a railwayman's daughter.'

'You know my feelings about railways,' grumbled Leeming.

But his comment went unheard. Colbeck had clasped his hands together and gone off into a reverie. When he came out of it, he apologised for being so rude.

'You're entitled to think when you want to, sir, and so am I, for that matter.'

'Meditation is part of our stock-in-trade.'

'I remember something you said early on.'

'What was that?'

'You reminded me that poison was often the choice of weapon for a woman,' Leeming said. 'Instead of looking at Mr Underhill and Mr Probert, should we be talking to their wives? Yes,' he added quickly before Colbeck could interrupt, 'I know that Mrs Underhill is disabled but that wouldn't stop her paying someone to act for her. Mrs Probert would also resent the fact that another woman came between her and her husband. Could she be a possible suspect?'

'Having met her briefly, I'd dismiss the idea. Mrs Probert would indeed have reason to hate her husband's mistress but only if she was aware of her existence, and I doubt that she was. What struck me about Mrs Pulver's corpse was how apparently unharmed it was. When someone kills out of passion,' said Colbeck, 'they usually like to cause pain as well as death.'

'It was just an idea, sir.'

'It was a valid one.'

'All this talk of wives has made me think of mine. I know that Underhill thinks that Mrs Pulver was a saint but he hasn't met Estelle. She does everything for me,' said Leeming with a smile. 'No woman alive could put up with me the same way that my wife does. Being apart from her is always a wrench. You must feel the same about your wife.'

'Oh,' said Colbeck, 'I certainly do.'

* * *

Lydia had been in a state of suspense all morning. Every time she heard a noise in the hall, she thought that the postman had called, even though she'd been warned that he rarely arrived with the mail before noon. Madeleine was bending over the crib, shaking a rattle at the baby and laughing at her delighted reaction when the front door was heard opening. Lydia was on her feet at once. She rushed hopefully into the hall then stopped when she saw one of the servants leaving the house. Lydia went swiftly back to her friend.

'It may not even come today,' Madeleine pointed out.

'I know that.'

'It may be that Lucas is not at home at the moment so he won't even have got the letter you sent to him.'

'That's more than possible.'

'Even if he did get it yesterday, he may not have decided to reply yet.'

'Oh, I think he would, Madeleine. I know my brother. If he was made aware of what was going on, he'd write back immediately.'

'Then let's hope he does.'

Lydia sank down on the sofa. 'In some ways, I don't *want* him to write.'

'That's ridiculous. You said he'd recognise the name Daniel Vance.'

'I'm not sure that I want to know who he is.'

Madeleine was livid. 'Lydia, for goodness' sake, what's got into you? Do you want this torture to go on?'

'No, of course I don't.'

'Then you should be praying that Lucas can identify the man who has been stalking you? Have you forgotten what happened yesterday? He brushed against you then left your dress. When you got back here, you collapsed into my arms.' She sat beside Lydia and took her hands. 'This has got to end.'

'As ever, you're right. I'm being cowardly again. I must stand up to him.'

Madeleine looked at her, hunched up on the sofa and stricken by fear. In the time leading up to the birth of her daughter, she'd received unwavering love and support from Lydia who'd helped to repair the absence of Madeleine's mother. During the early weeks of the baby's life, Lydia was always there to help, growing into a role for which she had no experience and, at the same time, coping with a major problem in her private life. Madeleine now treated her as one of the family. It grieved her to see the way that she was suffering.

'Can I ask you a favour?' said Lydia.

'Yes, of course.'

'If my brother does write, could you read the letter out to me, please?'

'Why?'

'I desperately want the truth but I need you to help me confront what I'm afraid is going to be a dark and disturbing secret.'

Everyone in the circus was still thoroughly jangled by what had happened during their first performance in the city. They knew how close they'd come to destruction. If a member of the audience had been mauled by the lion, their stay in Newcastle would have come to an abrupt end. Nobody would have wanted to see them and there'd be a collective demand for refunds. Since an animal in their care had attacked someone, it would have to be shot and Moscardi would be liable to prosecution. Bad publicity would ruin the remaining part of their tour. If they couldn't guarantee the safety of the spectators, people would stay away in droves.

That fear stoked Mauro Moscardi's anger. When he held a

discussion in his caravan with his brother and Mulryne, he was quick to allot the blame.

'This is your fault,' he said, jabbing a finger at the Irishman. 'You're supposed to be in charge of security and you've let us down badly.'

'No, I haven't,' said Mulryne.

'How could you let someone release that lion?'

'I can't be everywhere, Mr Moscardi. We've had lots of flares and torches but they only create light in small patches. There are always lots of shadows. That's why he was able to creep up to the cage.'

'I don't want excuses. I just want you to leave my circus.'

'That's unfair,' said Gianni. 'You can't get rid of Brendan.'

'I can do as I wish.'

'But he's been a Trojan. Think back to all the things he's done for us since he joined the circus. It was only yesterday that he caught Rogers for us. Nobody else could have knocked him unconscious but Brendan did.'

'It was a good punch,' said Mulryne.

'And when that lion was on the loose, who went into the ring after it? You didn't, Mauro. You were cringing in a corner. It was Brendan who risked his life to help Otto. Between them, they saved us.'

'That's true,' admitted Moscardi.

'You can't make him take all the blame.'

'It isn't just because of what happened last night, Gianni. First, there was the derailment, then the stampede and then all that trouble with the sheep farmer.'

'I didn't hire the train to take us to Newcastle,' argued Mulryne. 'That was your doing, Mr Moscardi. I not only helped to get everyone safely out of their carriages, I found

Jacko for us. That monkey is an important part of this circus.'

'But Jacko wasn't all you found, was he?' asked Moscardi. 'In searching for him, you stumbled on a dead body. As a result, Inspector Colbeck has shown far more interest in that than he has in us.'

'The woman was *murdered*,' said Mulryne. 'That's a heinous crime.'

'So is trying to kill off my circus.'

The row escalated until both men were yelling at once. For a change, it was Gianni, the established firebrand, who appealed for calm. Moscardi and Mulryne fell silent and eyed each other warily.

'This will get us nowhere,' said Gianni. 'We have to work together, Mauro, and, when I say "we", I'm including Brendan. He belongs here.'

'Not if he keeps making mistakes,' said Moscardi.

'You've obviously forgotten that he helped me find those sheep. If he hadn't done that, we'd still have been arguing with that farmer. Get rid of Brendan and he won't be the only person to go. He recruited some of the people we've taken on in our maintenance team,' said Gianni. 'They're very loyal to him. If he goes, they do.'

'They're all good men,' added Mulryne, 'and they've worked hard for you. Most of them have stayed up all night on guard duty – and so have I, for that matter.' He looked at Moscardi. 'Well? Do I still work here or don't I?'

'You still do,' said Gianni, clapping him on the shoulder.

'It's your brother's decision.'

There was a lengthy pause. 'You still do,' said Moscardi at length.

'Thank you, sir. The next performance is this afternoon. He won't come near us in daylight. And I'll promise you that he won't get anywhere near our animals after dark. Put your trust in me and Sergeant Leeming. As for Inspector Colbeck,' he went on, 'he isn't neglecting you. He was in the audience last night so he knows the danger you face. He told me that he'll be speaking on your behalf to the chairman of the railway company today. The inspector will find out somehow who put those sleepers on the line.'

Tapper Darlow had inherited the office from his predecessor and it mirrored that man's commitment to railway travel. Any available space on the walls was covered with charts or drawings of locomotives in service on the NCR. Colbeck was especially interested in the plan pinned to a board and occupying pride of position by the desk. Darlow looked over the detective's shoulder.

'That's the branch line to Alston. It's the only one we built, unfortunately.'

'Isn't there a Border Counties line under construction?'

'Yes,' said Darlow, sourly. 'That belongs to the North British.'

'You seem to be beset by rivals, sir.'

'We'll survive somehow.'

'I'd like to be able to report that we've caught the man who derailed one of your trains,' said Colbeck, 'but that's not possible yet. However, I do get the feeling that we're getting closer.'

'I don't want to hear about your feelings, Inspector. I want an arrest.'

'So do we – and so, of course, does Mr Moscardi.'

'You can't compare the problems of a circus with those of a railway company. Until that train came off the line, we had a very good safety record.'

'So did the circus until last night.'

'Why – what happened then?'

'Let me just say that one of the lions decided to give the audience a fright. If he'd leapt out of the ring, the whole performance would have been derailed.'

When he'd sworn Darlow to silence, he told him the truth about what had happened. Unaware of the activities of the interloper, the morning newspapers had reported how convincing the new routine with a snarling lion had been. Darlow learnt the truth and it made him gasp. He was relieved to hear that the lion would not appear in the ring again. When he performed his act, the lion tamer would only work with the other two beasts.

'It must have been a frightening moment, Inspector.'

'It was, sir.'

'Thank heaven my grandchildren weren't there.'

'Luckily, everyone accepted that it was a well-rehearsed act and there was a round of applause. Something in our natures means that we like being scared and then released from that fear. It may be the reason we have so many melodramas onstage.'

'I'm starting to feel sympathy for Mr Moscardi.'

'You might also feel gratitude, sir.'

'In what way?'

'Most passengers in a train that left the line would think about suing your company for compensation.'

'It wasn't our fault that those sleepers were on the line.'

'Nevertheless, you must bear some responsibility. Mr Moscardi was hopping mad at first and was determined to drag the NCR through the courts. He's calmed down a bit since then.'

'We can't afford compensation,' said Darlow. 'As it is, we already have some heavy costs. Every carriage was badly damaged and the locomotive will be out of service for some time.'

'All I'm suggesting to you is this, sir. When you think of what happened that day, don't view it entirely from the point of view of the NCR. The circus was the real victim. Apart from the driver, fireman and guard, none of your employees was in the train at the time – and neither were you.'

'I accept that.'

Colbeck studied the plan again. 'Your predecessor must have been very proud of the branch line. It follows an interesting route.'

'Yes, it was one of his better initiatives. Some of the others were . . . well, let me say that I'd never have sanctioned them.'

'Why not, sir?'

'Let me give you one example,' said Darlow. 'Mr Nicholls, the former chairman, was a deeply religious man. He decided to appoint an NCR chaplain.'

'What function did the man have?'

'As far as I can see, he didn't have any particular duties. He was allowed free travel on our line, presumably so that he could spread an air of sanctity. Oh, and he did take the occasional service for employees who were minded to attend.'

'Who was this chaplain, sir?'

'He's a parish priest from somewhere in Carlisle, I believe. I'm glad to say that I've never had the misfortune to meet him. As for some of the other decisions that Nicholls made, one or two of them were even stranger. The first thing I did when I took over was to reverse them.'

'I thought you wanted to carry on the traditions of the NCR.'

'Traditions are something I respect. It's the eccentricities I can't tolerate. But you came here to talk about the circus train,' he went on. 'Now that you've discounted the three people I suggested, have you found any other suspects?'

'We have a much clearer picture of the man we're after, sir.'

'But you don't have a name.'

'Not as yet, I fear.'

'When do you expect to get one?'

'Well . . .'

Colbeck's attention wandered once again to the plan on the

wall. Neatly drawn and annotated, it had been signed by the engineer. It had been based on a surveyor's report of the area through which the line passed and took account of its contours. The plan was mesmerising. It made Colbeck remember something that Underhill had told him during his visit to Shropshire.

Forced to wait so long, Darlow became petulant.

'This conversation has its own branch line,' he complained.

Conscious that she was irritating her friend by constantly darting into the hall, Lydia Quayle withdrew to her bedroom and watched for the postman from behind the curtain in her bedroom. She remained out of sight because she feared her stalker might be watching. The dress that he'd returned to her had been thrown away. In view of where it had been and with whom, Lydia couldn't bear to touch it.

Downstairs in the drawing room, Madeleine was chatting with her father. Andrews was saddened to hear the latest turn of events. He could imagine the shock that Lydia must have felt when the man appeared out of nowhere.

'She must only go out with someone else, Maddy.'

'I offered to go but she insisted on walking alone.'

'It's not your company she needs. She should have a man to escort her.'

'None was available, Father.'

'All you had to do was to send word with me. If I'd been walking with her, this man would have realised that she was being protected. That would have helped to scare him off.'

'You've just given me an idea,' said Madeleine. 'Perhaps she *does* need a man to accompany her each time she goes out. It would send a signal.'

'I'm standing by, Maddy.'

'This is a job for somebody else. If Lydia is seen with you, the man will assume you're an older relative. What we need is a much younger man, one who could be taken for a suitor. If it looks as if she's spoken for, that might work in her favour.'

'In that case, what you want is someone young and handsome and I don't think we know anyone like that.'

'Yes, we do, Father.'

'Who is it?'

'Detective Constable Hinton.'

'I haven't met him yet.'

'If he can be persuaded, he'd be ideal.'

The doorbell rang and it was followed by the sound of Lydia's footsteps descending the stairs at speed. Madeleine and her father looked into the hall. Lydia appeared as one of the servants opened the front door and accepted some mail from the postman. When she'd closed the door, the servant offered the letters to Madeleine, who handed them over to Lydia at once. They watched as she went through the batch of correspondence, searching for the letter that she wanted. At length, she gave up.

'There's nothing for me, Madeleine,' she said in despair.

'I'm so sorry,' said Madeleine.

'But there is one for you. It looks like your husband's writing.' She handed over the letters. 'Do excuse me.'

Shoulders sagging, she trudged off back upstairs.

There were still hours to go before the performance that afternoon but people had already started to gather outside the marquee. Everyone had heard about the act featuring the lion and wondered if they would be lucky enough to watch it. The buzz of excitement was constant. Mulryne had deployed his men carefully and all the animals now had additional guards.

Back in his labourer's garb, Leeming came across to his friend.

'I'm so glad to see you, Brendan,' he said. 'I heard a rumour that Mr Moscardi was going to get rid of you.'

'He had the sense to see how much I do for this circus.'

'You're part and parcel of it. They'd be mad to let you leave.'

'I'd be very sorry to go, I can tell you. There's one consolation, though.'

'What's that?'

'Jacko will have a good home. If I disappear, *you'll* look after him.'

Leeming was petrified. '*Me?*'

Right on cue, the monkey jumped from a wagon onto his shoulder.

'You're his friend,' said Mulryne, laughing. 'He can't keep away from you. It could be worse. If Rosie had taken a shine to you, you'd have her trunk wrapped around your neck all day.'

'Working for a circus is too dangerous for me.'

Mulryne became serious and told him about the way he'd placed sentries at strategic points around the camp. No trespasser could get in without being seen. Leeming was impressed by the thoroughness of the arrangements. He himself was deputed to walk among the crowd and – to his delight – actually get to watch the afternoon performance. When he saw Colbeck walking briskly towards him through the crowd, he handed Jacko back to his friend and went to meet the inspector.

'You look as if you're in a rush, sir.'

'I am, Victor. I just came to tell you that I have to leave.'

'Where are you going?'

'I've got to pay a second visit to Shropshire.'

'Does that mean you're going to arrest Mr Underhill?'

'No, it doesn't. This is nothing to do with him.'

'Then why are you going?'

'I need to take a second look at a photograph of a branch line.'

'It's a long way to go just for that, sir.'

'I have a feeling that it will be worth it. What will you be doing here?'

Leeming beamed. 'At long last, I'll be watching the circus.'

'Don't sit in the front row,' warned Colbeck. 'If the lion gets out again today, you might offer him too much temptation. Just think – those teeth, that jaw . . .'

'I wouldn't stand a chance.'

'It will only be a flying visit. If the trains are on time, I anticipate being back in Newcastle this evening.'

'Will you be watching the evening performance?'

'No, Victor, I'll be trying to solve some atrocious crimes.'

'What are you going to do about Mr Underhill?'

'Avoid him.'

As soon as her father left, Madeleine tore open the letter from her husband and read it avidly. Hoping to hear that the investigation was near completion, she was disappointed to learn that he might be away from home for some time yet. He sent his love to her and to the baby and asked her to pass on his best wishes to Lydia. There were scant but tantalising details about his progress so far and she could see that trying to solve two crimes simultaneously was presenting special problems for him. One comment puzzled her. Colbeck had written that she had something in common with Margaret Pulver but he didn't explain what it was. Madeleine was worried about being compared in any way to a murder victim. Trying to understand what he meant kept her preoccupied for minutes. She didn't even hear Lydia Quayle enter the room. When she finally noticed her, she apologised.

'Have I come at the wrong time?' asked Lydia.

'No, no, you're very welcome.'

'I can see that you've been reading Robert's letter. Is there any news?'

'He won't be back for a while,' said Madeleine, folding the pages up.

Lydia sat beside her. 'I owe you an apology for the way I behaved earlier on,' she said. 'When my brother's letter didn't arrive, I was like a child who didn't get the toy she was expecting on Christmas Day.'

'You were disappointed. That was only natural.'

'Yet I also felt strangely relieved and I don't know why. It's almost as if . . . as if I'm afraid to learn the truth.'

'But until you know it, you'll be kept in suspense. Do you really want to carry on in that state?'

'No, I don't.'

'Then you must brace yourself, Lydia. And you must stop hiding away in here. You can't let this man take away your right to go anywhere you wish. As long as you have company, you're safe.'

'I won't feel it, Madeleine.'

The doorbell rang again and she sat up sharply, putting a hand to her throat. Lydia then made an effort to relax. She heard the door open and the sound of a man's voice. When she realised that it belonged to Constable Hinton, she stood up. Shown into the room by the servant, he exchanged greetings with the two women.

'Thank you for contacting me at Scotland Yard,' he said. 'I'm so sorry to hear about the latest incident.'

'It was terrifying.'

'I'm sorry about that, Miss Quayle. You're sure it was the same man?'

'Oh, yes. How else could he have got my dress?'

Hinton was hesitant. 'Did he . . . do anything to the dress?'

'I don't understand what you mean, Constable.'

'Was it in the same state as when it was stolen?'

'I didn't examine it in any detail,' she explained. 'To be honest, I just wanted to get rid of it. As far as I'm concerned, it's been soiled. I'll never wear it again.'

'That's not an unusual reaction.'

Madeleine looked at him carefully. He was polite, diligent and eager to help a victim. But for the fact that there was a slightly rougher edge to him, he might have reminded her of her husband. She was acutely aware of being in the way.

'The baby will be waking up soon,' she said. 'I'd better go.'

'We don't want to drive you away,' said Lydia.

'You and Constable Hinton have a lot to talk about. I daresay that you'd like a cup of tea, wouldn't you, Constable?'

'Yes, please. Thank you, Mrs Colbeck.'

'You know how to order it, Lydia.'

She took her leave, walked into the hall and paused to listen to them for a while. It was the first time they'd ever been left alone together and their voices softened perceptibly. Madeleine was pleased. The best antidote to the harassment of one man, she felt, was to spend some time with a man who respected her. The bell tinkled to summon the maid. Madeleine made her way happily upstairs.

CHAPTER EIGHTEEN

The afternoon performance was superb. Determined not to be cowed by any threat of attack, everybody put extra commitment into their individual routines. An audience that, for the most part, was accustomed to seeing only carthorses toiling away in the streets, marvelled at the speed, grace and sheer beauty of the equestrian acts. Arab horses with sleek coats cantered around the ring as young female acrobats jumped on and off their backs. It was scintillating entertainment. Rosie garnered her usual ovation, as did the clowns, the tumblers, the tightrope walkers and the trapeze artistes. It was, however, the lions that gathered most applause and this time there was no unscheduled appearance by any of them.

When they adjourned to their caravan to toast their success, Moscardi and his wife were ecstatic. Surpassing their earlier performance, they'd sent a delirious crowd out into the city to publicise their work at no extra cost.

'We never achieved that level during our time in Carlisle,' he said.

'No,' agreed Anne, 'but we were not fighting for our lives there.'

'I just hope that devil doesn't come back tonight.'

'I'm hoping that he does, Mauro. Everyone is ready for him now. Since you had the sense to keep Mulryne, the security has been tightened more than ever.'

'I was wrong to threaten him with dismissal.'

'You're *often* wrong. Always discuss things with me first.'

He drained his glass of wine. 'I could do with another one.'

'Then you'll have to wait for it,' she told him. 'You've got work to do. Without exception, everybody gave of their best in that marquee. I think they deserve congratulations, don't you?'

'Yes, my love.'

Still in his costume, he left the caravan and went around the encampment to let his employees know how grateful he was. He shook hands, patted backs and stole a number of kisses from the female performers. It was important that everyone, high and low, felt that they were appreciated. Moscardi gave Mulryne a friendly hug then noticed someone carrying two large wooden buckets of water. When the man put them down beside the marquee, the Italian recognised him as Leeming.

'What are you doing, Sergeant?'

'We're covering every eventuality.'

'I don't understand.'

'It was Brendan Mulryne's idea, sir. We have so many people on guard that it's impossible for an interloper to get near enough to cause trouble in the camp. That's what we thought, anyway. Then we spoke to Gianni.'

'And what did my brother say?'

'He told us about a circus he saw in Arizona,' said Leeming. 'They staged a fight between cowboys and Indians. They dragged a fake log cabin into the ring and the cowboys got inside. When the Indians galloped round in circles and whooped, they were shot through the windows but they got their revenge.'

'How did they do that?'

'One of them fired a flaming arrow onto the thatched roof and set it on fire. The cowboys had to fight their way out and shoot all the Indians, knocking them off their horses and into the sawdust.'

'It sounds like a dangerous stunt to me.'

'No,' said Leeming, 'they had buckets of water all ready and doused the fire in no time at all. Just in case our interloper thinks of trying to set light to our marquee, we've got supplies of water everywhere.'

'That's very wise.'

'Your brother is the one to thank, sir.'

'Gianni's experiences in America have come in very useful to us.'

'So he keeps telling me.'

'By the way,' said Moscardi, 'you told me earlier that Inspector Colbeck was going to see the chairman of the railway company.'

'That's right, sir.'

'Do you know how he got on?'

'I only saw him briefly,' said Leeming, 'but I noticed that gleam in his eye. It's a good sign. He's picked up a vital clue somewhere. I can always tell.'

It was a paradox. The person who was making him return to Shrewsbury was the one he least wanted to see. It was not only because he found Underhill objectionable, it was because Colbeck didn't want to alert him to the fact that he was under suspicion. All too aware that it was a long way to go on a simple errand, he nevertheless believed that there would be a substantial reward for his efforts. He whiled away the journey by trying to see Margaret Pulver through the eyes of her two admirers. What did Donald

Underhill and Owen Probert hope to gain from her? She had clearly made a profound impression on both men but how much influence had they had over *her* life? The solicitor had claimed to have seen her only occasionally, a lie already disproved. When had she and the Welshman last been in touch? If she'd suddenly begun to make intemperate demands on them how would each of the men have reacted? These were the questions that engaged his mind as he sat in stuffy carriages or stood on draughty platforms awaiting a change of trains.

Arriving in due course in Shrewsbury, he took a cab from the station to the village where Margaret Pulver had lived. The housekeeper opened the door to him then stood back in surprise.

'Inspector Colbeck! What are *you* doing here?'

He smiled disarmingly. 'I was hoping to be invited in, Mrs Lanning.'

'Yes, yes, of course,' she said, standing back so that he could step into the house. 'You're most welcome.'

'Thank you.'

He was already savouring an experience that differed from his earlier visit. On that occasion he'd been shackled to Underhill and therefore unable to ask certain questions he deemed important. Alone with the housekeeper, it was as if he was now seeing the place properly for the first time. He began by trying to put her at ease, complimenting her on the way that she kept the property in such an obvious state of order and cleanliness and asking if she would show him around. She was happy to do so, taking him from room to room with a sense of pride that was edged with sorrow. Having worked so hard over the years, the widowed Mrs Lanning now had to face the prospect of leaving a house and a position in which she'd been very happy.

'I need to ask you a favour,' he told her. 'This is very much a private visit. I'd be grateful if Mr Underhill doesn't get to hear of it.'

'I'll make sure that he doesn't,' she said with feeling.

'I know that he brought the dreadful news about Mrs Pulver and I was grateful that he volunteered to do so. Has he been here since? And I don't mean the time that he kindly drove me out here.'

'He called yesterday, Inspector.'

'Did he come for any special reason?'

'Mr Underhill said that he needed the addresses of Mrs Pulver's relatives so that he could . . . write to tell them what had happened. He sat at the desk for a long time and made a list from the address book.'

'Contacting everyone who needs to know is a task he took upon himself and I'm very grateful to him. He's also offered to help with the funeral arrangements when the body is finally released.'

'I daren't even think about that,' she confessed. 'It's something I could never do. It's not my place, in any case, and I wouldn't know where to start.'

'Mr Underhill mentioned a plan of the branch line that runs through your land. I'd like to see it, if I may.'

'Then come with me, Inspector. It's kept in the library.'

She led the way down the corridor and into the room. Mrs Lanning said how much time her former employer spent there.

'Mrs Pulver would read for hours in here,' she recalled. 'It's enough for me to read a laundry list. Getting through a whole book . . . well, I just couldn't do it.' She indicated the desk. 'You'll find the address book in the right-hand drawer. Stay as long as you like, sir. I won't disturb you.'

After a respectful bob, she backed out and closed the door behind her. Left alone, Colbeck first ran his eye along some of the titles on the shelves. Poetry was well represented and so were novels. There were also some histories of the county and a book about birds. Since she travelled by train so much, he expected to find the well-thumbed copy of Bradshaw but the volume about railway engineering took him by surprise. He reasoned that it might have been bought by her husband but, when he looked inside for the publication date, he saw that it was two years after Richard Pulver had died. The book had therefore belonged to the wife. Crossing to the desk, he took out the address book and leafed through it. As the names were in alphabetical order, he soon found the one for which he was looking. Owen Probert's address was recorded in looping calligraphy.

When he searched the other drawers, he found nothing out of the ordinary. His gaze then lifted to the framed plan on the wall. It was like the many others he'd seen over the years, replete with a mass of detail. Pulver land was clearly marked. As he recalled what the housekeeper had told him, Colbeck wondered why Underhill had spent so much time seated at the desk. The addresses the solicitor was after could have been copied down in little over five minutes. Had he simply luxuriated in the pleasure of being in what was the inner sanctum of the woman he adored? Or had he come there specifically to search for something? The length of time he spent there suggested that he might not have found it.

Colbeck had an advantage over him. He came from a family of successful cabinetmakers and, at an early age, had watched his father and grandfather create the most exquisite desks for aristocratic clients. Almost invariably, they had one or more secret drawers and the young Colbeck was often challenged to find them. As a result, he knew all the most likely places to look. In spite of a thorough search, he found only one hidden secret drawer and it contained only two items. The first was an expensive diamond ring in a little box but it was the second item that interested him far more. It was a list.

Hereford, Ross and Gloucester 30
Harleston and Beccles 13
Crewe and Shrewsbury 32
Worcester and Hereford 26
Severn Valley 42

After copying the list, he put it back in the secret drawer with the ring then pressed the hidden device that enabled it to slide out of sight. He added a few other things to his notebook, incuding the name of the engineer responsible for the plan that Mrs Pulver had framed. When he came out the room, he saw the housekeeper waiting for him at the other end of the corridor.

'Are you leaving already, Inspector?' she asked, coming towards him.

'I found all that I need to know, Mrs Lanning.'

'Can't we offer you some refreshment?'

'That's very kind of you,' he said, 'but I'm in something of a hurry.'

She was incredulous. 'You came all this way to spend five minutes in the library?'

'It was enough, I assure you,' said Colbeck.

They traded farewells then he left the house. When he climbed into the waiting cab, he was suffused with a warm glow of excitement.

Madeleine did not have to make the suggestion herself because they'd reached the decision on their own behalf. When she heard them in the hall below, she came downstairs to find that Lydia and Hinton were about to depart. The detective had asked her to retrace her steps to the place where she'd had the fleeting encounter with the man who'd stolen her dress.

'I feel that it's important for Miss Quayle to be able to go out again,' he explained. 'She's been telling me that she'd rather batten down the hatches and remain here.'

'I would,' said Lydia. 'The thought of going out makes me feel queasy.'

'You must go,' urged Madeleine. 'If he's out there, you must show him that you have the courage to do exactly what you want.'

'But I'm not sure that I do have that courage.'

'Draw strength from the fact that Detective Constable Hinton will be with you. And if you get the slightest glimpse of the man, point him out at once.'

'Yes,' said Hinton, 'but do it discreetly, please. If it's obvious that you've spotted him, he'll vanish at once. Just tell me where to look.'

'I will, I promise,' said Lydia.

'Goodbye, Mrs Colbeck.'

Madeleine bade them farewell and opened the front door. Lydia hesitated.

'I'm not sure that I can do this, Madeleine.'

'You can do anything, Lydia. I can't believe you've forgotten the situation you were in when we first met. You were facing very serious problems then and you did so with commendable spirit.'

'That's not entirely true.'

Lydia was right. While she had coped well with the news of her father's murder, she had lost some of her confidence when she had to return to the family home for the first time in years. She'd turned to Madeleine for help and their friendship had really begun from that moment. Once again, she was getting encouragement from Madeleine and she responded to it. Holding her head high, she stepped out of the house with Hinton and walked off down the street. Madeleine watched them go and wished that Lydia was holding the arm of her escort to give the impression that their relationship was closer than it really was. She soon saw that it would have been a mistake to advise such a move. The couple were still strangers to each other. With arms linked, they'd be too self-conscious. Lydia had ventured out of the house again and that was a real achievement. Madeleine felt that it was a small but telling sign of progress.

It was early evening. When the first members of the audience began to arrive outside the marquee, Cyrus Lill was standing near the entrance with Mulryne. The detective was surprised to see Jake Goodhart coming towards him. Accompanied by his wife and children, the man had made an effort to smarten himself up. He was wearing an old, faded suit and a hat two sizes too large for him. The children were in their best attire with well-scrubbed faces and clean hands. Goodhart's wife looked as if she might have been going to church. Evidently, such an outing was a real treat for them and they had all made an effort to look their best.

'Good evening, Jake,' said Lill. 'I never thought to see you here.'

'Nor did ah, man.'

'I hope you all enjoy the circus.'

'We will,' promised Goodhart, taking something from his pocket. 'Mah cousin gie us these free tickets. Geoff's a rotten miser most of the time. Ah dunno what gor into 'm.'

'Maybe someone had a word with him,' said Lill, recalling the conversation that he and Leeming had had with the man. 'Mr Enticott may not be as hard-hearted as you thought.'

'Yes, he is,' said the wife, grimly.

'Aye,' added Goodhart, 'Geoff's as tight as a bloody drum.'

She nudged him hard. 'Jake!'

'Sorry, mah love.'

'Mind ya language.'

'Ah will.'

Since they were not allowed in yet, the family broke away and lingered near the marquee. Lill was pleased to see them there.

'Yesterday, he couldn't afford to come here,' he pointed out. 'Today, he can.'

'What made the difference?' asked Mulryne.

'I like to think that Sergeant Leeming and I did.'

'Oh?'

'We interviewed him and his cousin, Mr Enticott, as suspects. Goodhart was right about him. He's a very mean man.'

'I've met lots of people like that. They're as mean as hell and as tight as a froggy's arse – and that's watertight.'

'That's not quite how I'd put it,' said Lill, grinning. 'Anyway, we told him that his cousin would suffer badly with no money coming in and – lo and behold – the tickets pop up.'

'Well done, Inspector. You made him feel guilty.'

'We did our best.' Looking around, he became serious. 'What do you think will happen this evening?'

'The audience will have a wonderful time and they'll go home happy.'

'That will only happen if he leaves us alone.'

'He'd better. I've got men on the lookout everywhere.'

'But we don't know what he looks like.'

'We've got a vague idea and, of course, there's that injured hand.'

'Goodhart had an injured hand as well. Newcastle is full of manual labourers, doing jobs that sometimes result in damage to their hands. He won't be the only one, Mulryne.'

'I'll know him if I see him.'

'What makes you say that?'

'It's a sixth sense I've got, Inspector.'

'How did you develop that?'

'It was probably through walking the beat as a policeman,' said the Irishman. 'There's always someone who's ready to sneak up behind you in the dark with a brick or an empty beer bottle. I arrested a lot of men who tried that.'

'The one we're after is far more dangerous. He's derailed a train and let one of the circus lions loose. You won't hear him creeping up behind you.'

'We'll get him. You watch.'

'If we don't, Inspector Colbeck will. He's nothing short of a genius.'

Mulryne inflated his chest. 'I taught him all he knew.'

'Then we've nothing to worry about,' said the other, laughing. 'Well, I'm off. I'd love to watch the performance but my eyes are needed out here. I'll patrol the park and make sure all my constables are in position. This man is wily but even he won't get through our cordon.'

Watching from a safe distance, the man counted the number of uniforms and realised that there were even more than on the previous evening. The whole area was filled with the sound of happy children. They'd come to see a rare event. It might be years before Moscardi's Magnificent Circus came to their city again. That fact weighed with him. In addition to the policemen, he noticed the number of armed men protecting the camp. It might be time to reconsider his plan.

They reached the point where Lydia had stopped before and simply kept on walking. She was enjoying the pleasure of his company so much that all her fears slowly evaporated. Lydia had met several young men in the past and a couple of them had tried to become her suitor. Neither, however, had impressed her enough to be allowed too close. When she did find someone she could love, she was cruelly separated from him by her father and the man in question was dismissed from the estate. It was the reason that she'd largely withdrawn from male company.

Hinton was different. He was easy to talk to and reassuring to stand beside. Proud to be part of the Detective Department, he talked about his ambitions to emulate some of Colbeck's achievements though he accepted that it might take him many years before he could do so. Lydia could see that he was astute, alert and modest yet not without ambition. When she got him talking about his life, she forgot all about the reason they were out walking together.

'It's time to go back,' he said, eventually.

'Yes, I suppose it is.'

'Did you have the feeling that you were being watched?'

'Funnily enough,' she said, 'I didn't.'

'But then you weren't aware of it when he *was* following you.'

'I couldn't understand that.'

'It means that you were off guard or that he's becoming cleverer.'

'I fancy that both of those things were to blame. I was convinced he didn't know where I was and he kept his distance a bit more. Today,' she went on, looking round, 'I've kept my eyes peeled but I haven't seen anybody watching or trailing us.'

'You told me that you plan to go on holiday, Miss Quayle.'

'That's true.'

'Might I suggest that you delay the decision as to where you go until we've caught and dealt with this man?'

'Yes, I will. I thought I could shake him off by going away but the chances are that he'd simply follow me.' They walked on in silence for a few more minutes. Lydia then became inquisitive. 'Have you dealt with a case like this before?'

'As a matter of fact, I have.'

'What happened?'

'The person was being harassed in much the same way as you are, Miss Quayle. In that case, however, the victim was a man at the mercy of a woman who took incredible pains to hound and frighten him. If we hadn't caught her in time, he might have been seriously injured. She threatened violence throughout.'

'That hasn't happened to me.'

'No,' he said, 'you're lucky in that respect. But there's no reason to be complacent. We don't know this person's state of mind. In some cases, rejection by a woman can turn the mildest of men into killers.'

The performance that evening was another riotous success and the acclaim was even longer and louder than it had been in the afternoon. Jake Goodhart and his family were part of the multitude that streamed out of the marquee in a mood of delight. Sitting on Mulryne's shoulder, Jacko was there to wave them off. When the numbers had thinned considerably, Victor Leeming drifted across to his friend.

'I need to take some time off, Brendan.'

'Sure, you can take as much as you wish. We can manage here. We frightened him off at last.'

'I'd like to come back – just in case.'

'That's up to you.'

'Right,' said Leeming, 'I'll use your tent to get changed, if I may, then I'll go back to the hotel. I arranged to meet Inspector Colbeck there. If I go into the dining room looking like this, they'll probably throw me out.'

'You can take Jacko with you, if you like. He'd liven things up.'

Right on cue, the monkey jumped excitedly on to Leeming's shoulder.

After handing him back, the sergeant went off to change then made his way back to the hotel. Colbeck was waiting for him in the lounge. He ordered drinks for both of them then took out his notebook. When he found the page on which the list had been copied, he showed it to Leeming.

'What do you make of that, Victor?'

The other man gaped. 'I can't make anything of it.'

'Look at the numbers. What could they represent?'

'I haven't a clue, sir.'

'They're the number of miles of track being built on each of the lines.'

'Is that what these names are?'

'Yes,' said Colbeck, 'they're railways that have been built – or are still in the process of construction. The Act authorising the building of the Severn Valley railway, for instance, was passed in 1853 yet it won't be completed for a year or more. But, then, as you see, it's over forty miles long.'

'This is all very interesting, sir, but what's it got to do with either of our investigations?'

'It's a light in the darkness, Victor.'

'We could certainly do with one of those.'

'I found these details in a secret drawer in Mrs Pulver's desk.'

'Why should she bother about the railway system?'

'I went back to Shropshire to find out that very thing.' Retrieving his notebook, he sat back in his chair. 'What do men do when they fall in love?'

'They do the most stupid things, sir. I know that I did when I met Estelle.'

'It's a serious question.'

'Then my answer would be that they try to endear themselves to the woman in question by giving her a bunch of flowers or some other gift.'

'They also try to impress the object of their affection.' He patted his notebook. 'What you saw was an example of that.'

'Was it?'

The conversation was stopped by the arrival of the drinks. Leeming seized his tankard of beer gratefully and sunk half of it in a series of gulps. Colbeck sipped his whisky then put the glass on the table.

'Because you didn't burst in here with the latest tales of terror,' he said, 'I assume that the performances today went off without interruption?'

'We had no problems at all, luckily.'

'That's good.'

'Let's go back to the list. Who could possibly be impressed by that?'

'Mrs Pulver certainly was. They were all projects on which her admirer had worked as an engineer. He was the person who must have given her the plan of the branch line on her land. It hangs above her desk.'

'Who'd want to look at the plan of a railway line?'

'I would, Victor.'

'That goes without saying, sir.'

'To Mrs Pulver, it wasn't just an example of engineering skill, it was a treasured reminder of someone. I suppose that I should thank Mr Darlow for setting me on the right road at last – or the right railway line, I should say.'

Colbeck went on to explain that the sight of a similar plan in Darlow's office had reminded him of something that the housekeeper had told him on his first visit to the house in Shropshire. Mrs Pulver had taken a close interest in the building of the branch line, befriending the engineer and even inviting him into the house. It was the beginning of a friendship that developed, in the wake of her husband's death, into something far deeper.

She'd become so interested in the man and his work that she'd even bought a book on railway engineering.

'His name is Nathan Furnish.'

'How do you know that?'

'It was written on the framed plan that she looked at every time she sat down at her desk. He'd signed it for her then written out that list of names.'

'If I'd done anything like that, Estelle would never have married me.'

'That would have been her loss, Victor.'

'Thank you, sir.'

'Something about that list struck me at once.'

'What was it?'

'An old friend of ours was involved as a contractor in each case.'

'The only contractor we've had dealings with is Mr Brassey.'

'That's exactly who it is,' said Colbeck. 'These are all small-scale when compared to some of the huge projects he's taken on in this country and in several foreign ones. Since his men built all the railways in my list, he'd know where Nathan Furnish could be found. That's why I've tried to contact him by telegraph.'

'What if he's working abroad?'

'I'll have to get the information by other means.'

'And do you think this man might really be the killer?'

'I'd say that he got a lot closer to Mrs Pulver than either Underhill or Probert. Their names were in her address book but the secret drawer was reserved for the man who gave her a ring and who told her about the other projects he'd undertaken. There were no love tokens from our other suspects.'

'I thought she was supposed to be a saint.'

'That was the image she cultivated, Victor. And there's no doubting the sincerity of her religious commitment. But there was another side to her and the only person who can tell us about it is Nathan Furnish.'

Hinton stayed longer than he needed to but Madeleine didn't mind that in the least. He didn't wish to go and Lydia was clearly enjoying his company. When he was invited to stay to dinner, however, the detective got to his feet and issued a stream of apologies for staying so late. Lydia went to the front door to see him off before returning to the drawing room.

'He's such a gentleman,' she said.

'You actually seem to have enjoyed your walk.'

'I did, Madeleine.'

'Then I'm glad that we talked you into it.'

'So am I.'

'They have such a diverse group of people in the Detective Department. At one end, you have someone like Victor Leeming and at the other you have Robert. I suspect that Detective Constable Hinton is closer to my husband than he is to Victor, but you may disagree.'

'I think that he's his own man, Madeleine.'

'Did he say anything about the superintendent?'

'No, he was very discreet.'

'I'll be writing to Robert later on. I'll ask him what he knows about your bodyguard.'

'He's not my bodyguard,' said Lydia. 'He's just trying to solve a mystery.'

'Is he optimistic?'

'Oh, yes. It's only a matter of time, he says.'

'That's good to know.'

The doorbell rang and Lydia looked in the direction of the hall as if hoping that the detective had come back for some reason. In fact, it was a courier who'd come to deliver a letter. The servant brought it into the drawing room and held it out.

'It's for you, Miss Quayle,' she said, handing it over.

'Thank you.' She saw the calligraphy. 'It's from my brother.'

'Open it and see what he says.'

Lydia tore it open and unfolded the missive, reading it with her heart pumping.

'Lucas didn't see my letter until today,' she explained. 'Because I was so anxious for a reply, he sent it by courier.'

'God bless him!'

Madeleine watched her carefully as she read the letter. Lydia was tense and nervous. Her hands were shaking. She was totally bemused.

'Well,' said Madeleine. 'Does he tell you who Daniel Vance is?'

'Yes, he does,'

'So there really *is* such a person?'

'There was, Madeleine. He died over forty years ago.'

CHAPTER NINETEEN

Victor Leeming felt that being so far away from home had its compensations. He was enjoying the thrill of working with the circus and was delighted to be spending time with his old friend, Brendan Mulryne. The two cases in which they were involved fascinated him because they were so complex and unusual. Though he was on duty at the camp for most of the night, he was staying in a comfortable hotel and eating some excellent food. As he now had dinner with Colbeck, he savoured each mouthful.

'It was the last thing I expected, sir,' he said. 'When we first came here, I thought the two investigations were completely separate.'

'So did I, Victor.'

'But you found a link between them. Both started with a railway.'

'I'm not complaining about that,' said Colbeck. 'It adds a kind of symmetry to our work here. On the other hand, we're looking for two very different malefactors. One is ready to derail a train while the other makes a living by building railways. If they ever met, I suspect that they'd have some lively arguments.'

'What if we can't find Nathan Furnish?'

'I'm keeping my fingers crossed that we will.'

'Mr Brassey may be thousands of miles away. Didn't you tell me that he's taken on projects in places like India and Canada?'

'Yes, I did, but that doesn't mean he's somewhere like that now. I imagine that his wife is not happy for him to be so far away for any length of time and he still has many projects in this country. As a contractor, he's very much in demand.'

Leeming sighed. 'So are we, unfortunately.'

'Success may have its disadvantages, Victor, but who wishes to be known for his failures?'

'Nobody, I suppose.'

'Frankly, since we came north, we haven't achieved much success but I feel that the tide turned today. I'm fairly certain that we've identified the killer.'

'But he's a railway engineer. Like Mr Brassey, he could be working on a project overseas somewhere.'

'If that's the case, we go after him.'

'What if he happens to be thousands of miles away?'

'That won't stop us.'

Leeming groaned. 'I hate sailing even more than travelling by rail.'

'Then you'll be glad to know that it's unlikely we'll have to board a ship. Ask yourself one question. Where did the murder take place?'

'It was not all that far from here.'

'And it was in a secluded spot,' Colbeck reminded him. 'That means Furnish knows this area well. In other words, it's more than likely that his home is somewhere in Northumberland.'

'How will we get his address?'

'With luck, Thomas Brassey will be able to provide it. There was a telegraph station in Shrewsbury so I made use of that. I asked him if he could send his reply to Newcastle. When we've finished this splendid meal, we'll go along to Central Station to see if there's anything waiting for me.'

'I promised to go back to the circus.'

'Do you want to miss the opportunity of arresting a killer?'

'No, I don't.'

'Then you can send word to Mulryne that something important has come up. He'll understand. He used to be a policeman.'

Leeming chuckled. 'Something *always* came up when Brendan was around.'

'You'll get back to the camp at some point,' said Colbeck, 'and you may be in a position to pass on some good news.'

'Yes – we've solved a murder.'

'Mulryne will be more interested in the consequence. With one investigation closed, we'll be able to give all our time to the circus. He'll enjoy passing on that message. It will be music to Mr Moscardi's ears.'

Until she read the letter herself, Madeleine Colbeck didn't understand what her friend meant. Lydia Quayle had put so much faith in her younger brother being able to help her by revealing the identity of Daniel Vance that she felt let down. Madeleine now realised why. The man who'd been tormenting Lydia had used a pseudonym that would only be recognised by former pupils of the exclusive public school to which both of her brothers had been sent. The establishment had a strange tradition, named after the eccentric and light-hearted man who had founded the school and been its first headmaster. On the last day of the summer term, one of the senior boys was appointed as Daniel Vance, Lord of

Misrule, a free spirit who was given licence to devise hoaxes, play tricks, cause a rumpus and generally run riot for the amusement of the other pupils. There were limits on what was allowed and there was a strict rule that no damage would come to school property. Within those limits, however, Daniel Vance had great scope.

Madeleine drew more comfort from the letter than her friend had done.

'But he's given you a name, Lydia.'

'It's only a suggestion. During his time at the school, Lucas would have seen over ten Lords of Misrule and there have been many others since. All that we really know is the school where this man was educated.'

'It's also where he enjoyed playing practical jokes.'

'What's happening to me is *not* a practical joke,' said Lydia, sharply.

'I still think you should take this name seriously.'

'Why?'

'To start with,' said Madeleine, 'look at the reason why Lucas suggested this Bernard Courtney. Of all the Daniel Vances that your brother saw, Courtney was the most memorable because he went completely wild. He broke windows, hid furniture in the coal cellar and stole a gown from one of the housemasters before throwing it into the fountain. Your brother says that he was completely out of control.'

'That doesn't mean he'd take an interest in me. I never met him.'

'Are you certain?'

'I remember all the school friends of Lucas's who came to stay with us and Bernard Courtney – or Daniel Vance – wasn't one of them.'

'Does the name mean nothing at all to you?'

'Actually, it means a great deal, Madeleine.'

'Really?'

'Everyone in Nottinghamshire is aware of the Courtney family.

They own lacemaking and other factories in the county. Philip Courtney, the head of the family, is a man of real substance.'

'Then your father must have known him.'

'They belonged to the same club.'

'There's your answer, then,' said Madeleine, handing the letter back. 'You said that you'd never met Bernard Courtney but he may well have met – or seen – you.'

'What are you talking about?'

'Think back to your father's funeral. Every major businessman in the county must have been there. Philip Courtney certainly was and, since his son will be part of the family empire, he'd have been likely to attend. The Courtneys would have been invited back to the house afterwards.'

'I never spoke to the son.'

'You didn't need to, Lydia. Can't you see what might have happened?'

'No, I can't.'

'Bernard Courtney will have *seen* you. Even in a crowd, you'd always stand out. Isn't it possible that this is how it all started? He took an interest and found out where you were living.'

'But my father was killed over a year ago, Madeleine.'

'Obsessions can take a long time to build up.'

Lydia read the letter again, slowly moving from profound dissatisfaction to a measure of hope. She thought back to the events surrounding the funeral when so many people had been milling around the family home.

'Do you know what your problem is?' asked Madeleine, gently.

'What?'

'You don't look in a mirror, Lydia. If you did, you'd see what an attractive woman you are. In any gathering, you're bound to turn heads.'

'I don't do it deliberately.'

'You just can't help it. Bernard Courtney noticed you. Remember what your brother says about him. As a boy at school, he always went too far. He probably used the name of Daniel Vance because it reminded him of a time when, for one day, he could do almost anything he wanted. He obviously hates rules.'

Madeleine's argument was persuasive. Lydia eventually accepted it.

'What shall I do?' she asked.

'Show that letter to Detective Constable Hinton as soon as you can.'

Having changed out of his ringmaster costume, Moscardi had supper with his wife then went for a walk through the camp. He was relieved that there'd been no attack on the circus during the day but feared it might come at night. The first person he sought was Mulryne and he found him near the lion cages.

'Have you ever thought of becoming a lion tamer?' he asked.

'I don't have the skills for it, Mr Moscardi.'

'Yes, you do. You proved that yesterday. You imposed your authority.'

'Otto was the one who did that. I just backed him up. But I must admit that it was very exciting.'

'We can do without that kind of excitement.'

'It won't happen again. There are padlocks on all the cages now. He won't be able to open one of them again. Besides, he'll never get this close.'

'It's all very well to keep him out but I want him caught.'

'We all do.'

'Then why hasn't Inspector Colbeck done his job and arrested him?'

'It's because he's up against a very clever man,' said Mulryne. 'There have been lots of those in the past and the inspector always gets the better of them in the end. He was slowed down this time by people who had different theories.'

'I was one of them,' admitted Moscardi. 'I'd have bet my life savings that Sam Greenwood was at the back of it all.'

'Then you'd have lost your money. Inspector Colbeck rescued you from doing that. But you weren't the only person demanding attention. There was Mr Darlow, the chairman of the railway company. He provided the names of three possible suspects and insisted that one of them derailed the train. According to Sergeant Leeming, he made a real nuisance of himself.'

'So did I, Mulryne.'

'The inspector will forgive you.'

'Where is he now?'

'I had a note from the sergeant to say that something's afoot. That sounds very promising to me,' said Mulryne. 'They've obviously picked up a scent. We might get some good news before morning.'

The house was near Wylam, a small village some ten miles west of Newcastle. It was disfigured to some extent by the colliery, which brought noise, coal dust and industrial ugliness to an otherwise tranquil location. Nathan Furnish lived in a large detached house with outbuildings. Darkness had fallen by the time that the detectives got there in their hired trap, so they could only see it in outline at first.

'I told you that Mr Brassey would help us,' said Colbeck. 'After what we did in France for him, he owes us a favour or two.'

'Suppose that Furnish is not at home?'

'There are lights in the downstairs windows so someone is

there. At the very least, we'll be told where we can find him.'

'It looks as if there's a stable at the rear, sir.'

'That's exactly where I'd like you to go, Victor. If he's there and does try to bolt, he'll come hurtling out of the back door to saddle his horse.'

Leeming grinned. 'I'll introduce myself.' He looked at the silhouette in front of them. 'It's a big place. Railway engineers are obviously well paid.'

'This particular one is about to retire.'

Colbeck sent the sergeant off, allowing him plenty of time to take up his position at the back of the property. He then walked down the track to the front door of the house. Since there was no bell, he rapped on the timber with his knuckles. A curtain was drawn back from a window and someone looked out quizzically. He withdrew immediately. When the door opened, a tall, slender man of Colbeck's own age was standing there.

'Can I help you?' he asked.

'Are you Mr Nathan Furnish?'

'Yes, I am. Who might you be?'

'I'm Inspector Colbeck from Scotland Yard and I'd appreciate some of your time, sir. May I come in?'

Furnish was phlegmatic. 'Yes, of course,' he said, calmly.

After showing Colbeck into a study, he went off to speak to his wife. During the time he was alone, the inspector was able to look around the room. It was filled with books, drawings and photographs relating to railways. In one of the photographs, Colbeck recognised Furnish standing next to Thomas Brassey. Turning his gaze on the books, he saw a copy of the volume on railway engineering that he'd noticed in Margaret Pulver's library. Beside it, however, was a book that seemed strangely incongruous among the rest of the collection.

It was only when Furnish came back into the room that he was able to appraise him properly in good light. The man had interesting rather than handsome features and there was a keen intelligence in his eyes. Well dressed and clean-shaven, he had remarkable self-possession. He indicated a chair and Colbeck sat down. Furnish sat opposite him in the chair nearest the door. He looked relaxed and confident.

'Do I need to explain why I'm here, Mr Furnish?'

'No, Inspector, your fame preceded you. I saw your name mentioned in the newspapers and hope that your visit has a successful outcome.'

'This conversation is about you, sir, not about me.'

Furnish was blank. 'I don't see what interest I can have for you.'

'Did you know a Mrs Margaret Pulver?'

'Yes, I did – and I was grieved to hear of her death.'

'When did you last see the lady?'

'It was some years ago – four, at least. I was the engineer on a branch line that ran through her property. Mrs Pulver and her husband took pity on me, standing out in the pouring rain while we took measurements. They invited me into the house.'

'That was when the husband was alive.'

'Yes, Inspector.'

'Did you go into the house *afterwards*?'

'I'd moved on to another project by then, Inspector. It's in the nature of my job. I tend to travel around.'

'I see that you worked with Mr Brassey.'

'That was a stroke of fortune. His name is a recommendation in itself.'

'I agree, sir. I had the pleasure of meeting him in France when he was involved with the line between Mantes and Caen. He was a model employer.'

Furnish eyed him shrewdly. 'Why are you telling me this?'

'I'd like you to know that Mr Brassey is a good friend of mine. It's the reason I've always kept abreast of his activities. The only reason that I found you is that he provided me with your address.'

'Yes,' said the other, warily, 'but why did you need it in the first place?'

'Do you *really* need to ask me that?'

'As a matter of fact, I do.'

'Then it's because I saw the framed copy of the plan that you gave to Mrs Pulver. It's on the wall by her desk and bears your signature.'

'There's nothing questionable about that, is there?' said Furnish, smoothly. 'Mrs Pulver took an unusually close interest in the building of that line. When she requested a copy of the plan, I was glad to oblige.'

'Is that all you gave her, sir?'

'What are you suggesting?'

'I fancy that you might have given her a diamond ring.' The other man's facial muscles tightened. 'You also gave her a list of your accomplishments. There are very few women who could be wooed with a record of engineering projects.'

Furnish regained his poise. 'Mrs Pulver was kind enough to ask about my work. I jotted down some of the lines I worked on. There's nothing wrong in that, is there?'

'What about the diamond ring?'

'The only diamond ring I ever bought is the one that my dear wife wears.'

'That's only right and proper, sir – if it happens to be true.'

'Are you saying that I'm a liar, Inspector?'

'I'm saying that, when I open a secret drawer in a woman's desk

294

and find something you've written nestling beside a diamond ring, there's only one conclusion I can reach.'

'I can think of an alternative.'

'And what's that, sir?'

'The ring was an unwanted present from a solicitor in Shrewsbury. Mrs Pulver told me that he'd been bothering her.'

'But that was well after her husband's death and you claimed that you didn't see her once your work in the area had been done.'

'I did have to go back once, as it happens,' said the other, recovering instantly. 'There was a project near Wenlock that I was offered but I turned it down because the line was only four miles long. As I was travelling back, I paid a courtesy call on Mrs Pulver.'

'Did you ask her if she was still wearing your ring from time to time?'

'I gave her no ring,' snapped Furnish. 'How many times must I say it?'

'Oh, I think you'll go on telling lies as long as anyone will listen. Let me give you another opportunity to do so,' said Colbeck. 'Acccording to Mr Brassey, you've been working on a line in Epping. When did you come back here?'

'I returned three days ago.'

'Is that the truth?'

'You can ask my wife and I can produce other witnesses.'

'I've no doubt that you can, sir. We both know that you were here days earlier to take your victim to the place where you buried her. Once that was done, you fled the area and stayed away long enough to give yourself an alibi.'

'You've no proof of that.'

'There's no such thing as a kind murder but you sought to minimise the pain of your victim by administering a poison.' He reached a book off the shelf and held it up. 'This is rather out of place among all these engineering manuals. If Mrs Pulver had realised that you were reading an encyclopaedia of toxicology, she might have been less willing to visit you in Northumberland.'

Furnish was unmoved. 'We have a problem with vermin out here,' he said, coolly. 'That book gives good advice on how to kill them.'

'Are you telling me that you regarded the lady as vermin?'

'I'm merely telling you the truth.'

Colbeck looked him up and down. There was an annoying confidence about the man, a trait he'd seen in other killers who felt that they'd left no trail of evidence to link them with their victim. He changed tack.

'You must be away from home a lot, sir.'

'As I told you, it's in the nature of my work.'

'Then we're two of a kind. I, too, have to travel a great deal. My wife always records my absences in her diary. I daresay that Mrs Furnish does the same thing with regard to you.'

'She certainly does,' said Furnish, seizing on the comment, 'and you're welcome to see it. You'll find confirmation of the day when I got back here.'

'What about the days you spent in London with Mrs Pulver? Are they all listed in your wife's diary?'

'That's a very insulting question, Inspector.'

'It was meant to be, sir. See it as a justifiable riposte. When someone insults my intelligence by telling me a farrago of lies, I feel duty-bound to respond. I've been to Shropshire and spoken to the housekeeper. She told me how regularly Mrs Pulver went to London. If I look at your wife's diary, I'm sure that they'll correspond with days when you were absent from home. In short,' he went on, 'you had a series of assignations with another woman in the nation's capital. I know that's where you bought her that ring because the jeweller's name was inside the box. Am I right?'

Furnish was stung. 'No, you're not.'

'Perhaps you've forgotten when it was. A glance at that diary would help us.'

'I deny all these spurious accusations.'

'Would you prefer to have your wife and her diary in here with us?'

'There's no need for that,' said the other, quickly.

'Does that mean you'd appreciate a moment alone with her so that you can explain why I'm going to arrest you on a charge of murder and take you off to Newcastle with me?'

Furnish leapt up. 'You have no reason to do that.'

'Circumstantial evidence is very strong, sir.'

'I have not set eyes on Mrs Pulver for years,' claimed the other.

'Would you swear to that in court?'

'Yes, I would.'

'Then you'd be committing perjury.'

'I'm stating a simple fact, Inspector.'

'Before I became a policeman,' said Colbeck, 'I was a barrister. As a result, I became very familiar with the way that murder trials are conducted. I know when a guilty verdict is more or less inevitable and it certainly is in this case. Killers like you always make mistakes, you see.'

'I am not a killer,' insisted Furnish, stamping a foot. 'Why should I murder a woman I *liked*?'

'It was because she grew to like *you* far too much, sir. And I can see why. You have obvious appeal for her and belonged to a profession that she greatly admires. When a woman is caught up in the throes of passion, she can make awkward demands on a man. Is that what Mrs Pulver did, sir?' asked Colbeck. 'Were you being forced to choose between her and your family?' He stood up to confront the man.

'Did the saint of Shropshire threaten you with exposure?'

'Don't talk about her like that!' snarled Furnish. 'You never knew Margaret.'

'I know how revered she was by everyone around her.'

'She was an amazing woman.'

'One of her other admirers would agree with that, sir. By an odd coincidence, he lives in Hexham and used to work for the NCR.' Furnish was shocked. 'You can't expect such a beautiful woman to reserve her favours entirely for you. He actually confessed that he met her in London on one occasion.'

'You're only trying to provoke me.'

'His name is in her address book. I checked.'

'There *was* nobody else, I tell you! She swore to me.'

As he yelled out, he realised that he'd given himself away and collapsed onto the chair. He cut a sorry figure. All the bravado had seeped away. Though he had no sympathy for the man, Colbeck did have sympathy for his wife.

'Do you have children, sir?' Furnish nodded. 'They'll have to know in time. Your wife must be told first. At this stage, you might simply wish to inform her that you're coming back to Newcastle with me. That's up to you.'

'She deserves the truth.'

'Then I'll wait here while you speak to her.'

Colbeck moved to open the door. After lapsing into remorse, Furnish stood up and straightened his coat. He stared at the detective with a blend of hatred and gratitude, resenting the fact that he'd been caught but thankful that he was not being hustled away in handcuffs. That would have been mortifying. It was time for him to speak to his wife. Before going out, he ran his tongue over dry lips then took a deep breath. Colbeck left the door wide open and waited.

* * *

Leeming, meanwhile, was standing beside the stables and shivering in the strong breeze that had suddenly blown up. Minutes fled by. The long wait gave him time to compare himself with the inspector. They operated in totally different ways. The sergeant saw only what was directly in front of him whereas Colbeck could envisage what wasn't actually there. If he'd seen a plan on the wall of Darlow's office, it would never have occurred to Leeming to connect it with the one in Mrs Pulver's house. And since he would have been unable to open the secret drawer in her desk, the ring and the telltale list would have gone undiscovered. Even if he had seen them, he knew, they would not have sent him after an engineer called Nathan Furnish. Leeming contented himself with the thought that, while he could never compete with Colbeck, he nevertheless had qualities that made him a good detective. Some of those qualities now came into play.

He heard the soft tap of feet and knew that someone was running towards him on tiptoe. Standing behind the stable, he waited until a figure came out of the gloom and started to unbolt the door. Leeming stepped out to grab him by the collar.

'Good evening, Mr Furnish,' he said. 'I'm Sergeant Leeming. The inspector had a feeling that you might try to escape.'

'Let me go!' cried the other, struggling.

'I'm afraid that I can't do that, sir.'

'Get off me!'

Desperate to escape, Furnish stamped his foot hard on Leeming's toe, causing him to cry out in pain and loosen his grip. The engineer was off at once, running across the yard and out through a gate that led to a field. Although he could barely see the man, the sergeant gave chase and winced every time his injured foot hit the ground. Furnish was faster than his pursuer but he had none of Leeming's tenacity and desire for revenge. When the engineer began to tire, the gap between the two men closed inexorably. The closer he got, the clearer Leeming was able to see his quarry. It gave him fresh energy. Squeezing a final spurt out of his aching legs, he got within reach of Furnish and dived onto the man's back, causing him to lose his balance and stumble. The two of them came crashing down on the grass.

Leeming was the first to recover from the impact. He turned the other man over and pummelled him with both fists to take away all resistance. Furnish finished up with his hands over his face, begging for mercy. He was hauled unceremoniously to his feet before being handcuffed. They headed back towards the house.

'Thank you, sir,' said Leeming, gasping for breath. 'I needed the exercise.'

Having heard so much about Scotland Yard, she had always wondered what went on inside it. Lydia Quayle now had her opportunity to find out. She arrived outside by cab and looked up at it. At first sight, it was rather forbidding but she reminded herself that it was where Colbeck and Hinton both worked and, as such, should hold no demons for her. Entering the building, she asked to see the detective constable and was dismayed to be told that he was now off duty. She would have to leave a message for him. Lydia was trying to write it when Superintendent Tallis came out of his room and noticed her. When he heard what had brought her there, he invited her into his room and offered her a seat. He returned to his chair behind the desk.

Lydia was intimidated by his rank and by his looming presence. For his part, Tallis was always uncomfortable when talking to women so the conversation was very uneasy at first. She thanked him for assigning someone to her case.

'I have a good memory, Miss Quayle,' he told her. 'I

remembered that we investigated the murder of your father. That would have robbed you of the person to whom you could naturally turn for help in this situation. Because of that, I felt that we had a duty to assist you.'

It was untrue but Lydia didn't contradict him. Had her father still been alive, he'd have been the last person on whom she could rely for protection. Tallis already had details of her case so she handed over her brother's letter to him and explained why she felt that Courtney was the man harassing her. Tallis was sympathetic. Since she'd befriended Madeleine, she'd heard a lot of criticism of the superintendent and his disdain for women. Yet he was now showing an almost paternal interest in her predicament.

'The question we must ask is this,' he said, returning the letter. 'What is Mr Courtney doing in London?'

'He's come in pursuit of me, of course.'

'I don't think so, Miss Quayle. If that was the impulse that brought him here, he'd have arrived several months ago. My feeling is that he had a reason for being in the city and, once here, discovered where you were living. You tell me that he works in the family business.'

'That's right, Superintendent.'

'Is it confined to this country or does it export its products abroad?'

'Oh, they sell things all over Europe.'

'Then it might well have a London office that liaises with foreign buyers. If I was a French or Italian businessman, I'd much rather come here than have to tramp all the way up to Nottinghamshire. Do you follow my reasoning?'

'Yes, I do.'

'If Philip Courtney has an office in London, the chances are that his son might run it. That's why he's here and how we'll find

301

him. Detective Constable Hinton will begin the search for him first thing tomorrow morning.'

'Thank you,' said Lydia, effusively. 'Thank you so much.'

'Meanwhile,' said Tallis, 'I believe that you're staying with Mrs Colbeck.'

'That's right. Madeleine has been very supportive.'

'Then perhaps you can pass on some news that will interest her. Within the last hour, I had a telegraph from her husband. The murder he was investigating has now been satisfactorily solved and a man is in custody. When the inspector has dealt with the other crime that sent him there,' he added, stroking his moustache, 'he will be on his way home.'

Lydia left the building in a state approaching euphoria.

It was Cyrus Lill who broke the news of the arrest. Though it was late evening, he returned to the circus and found both Moscardi and his wife still very much awake.

'I was in the police station when the killer was brought in,' he said.

'That's wonderful,' said Anne.

'It would be even more wonderful if he'd arrested the man *we're* after,' said Moscardi. 'The inspector seems to have forgotten us.'

'That's not true, Mauro. We've had Sergeant Leeming almost living with us.'

'He's back here again,' said Lill. 'We left the police station together. The sergeant is using Mulryne's tent to change into something more appropriate. He was keen to take off his frock coat. Because he had a tussle with the killer, it got torn and covered in grass stains.'

'I'll make a point of congratulating him,' said Anne.

Her husband tapped his chest. 'And I'll make a point of asking when he's going to rid us of *our* problem.'

'But we've had no trouble today, Mauro.'

'He'll be lurking out there somewhere.'

'I'm not so sure, Mr Moscardi,' said Lill. 'When he let the lion out of the cage, I feel that he shot his bolt. There's nothing worse he could have done. My feeling is that he's admitted defeat and gone.'

'I agree,' said Anne.

'The man is not stupid. He must have seen the patrols you put in place. That scared him off. We can at last sleep soundly in our beds.'

Wearing his old clothes again, Leeming was seated on a log as he told Mulryne about the capture of Nathan Furnish. He was honest about his failings.

'When I chased him across the field, my top hat was blown off and I had the most terrible job to find it in the dark.' The Irishman shook with laughter. 'It's not funny, Brendan. I trod on it by mistake.'

'I've had my share of losing things in a fight – teeth, mostly.'

'Inspector Colbeck knew he'd make a run for it. That's why I was in the right place to stop him.'

'The inspector always thinks ahead. Did the killer confess?'

'He did more than that,' said Leeming. 'He spent the journey back to Newcastle trying to justify what he'd done. His mistress got fed up with seeing so little of him that she began to make demands. Furnish said that the only way he could resolve the situation was by killing her. His family came first, he insisted. He had to protect his wife and children.'

'Having a mistress is hardly the best way to do that.'

'I told him that, Brendan. But he's so convinced that what he did was the right thing that he wouldn't listen to reason. He's one of those men who will simply never accept blame for their actions.'

'There are too many of them about.'

It was close to midnight and the moon was obscured by low cloud. Braziers had been lit and some torches burnt to shed light. Apart from the occasional noises from the animals, everything was peaceful. The camp was largely asleep. It was soon jerked out of its slumber. The gunshot reverberated throughout the whole park and set off a tumult in the animal enclosures. Leeming and Mulryne ran in the direction from which the noise had come and eventually reached Gianni Moscardi. He was standing at the edge of the camp with the shotgun in his hands.

'I saw him,' he said. 'I saw someone creeping towards the horses and trying to cut through the ropes to get at them. When I fired at him, he ran away.'

'Did you hit him?' asked Mulryne.

'I couldn't see in the dark. I ran towards him but he had a horse nearby and got away. It's infuriating,' he went on. 'I thought we'd seen the last of him.'

'No,' said Leeming. 'I'm afraid not. He won't give up.'

'It's the truth,' said Mulryne. 'He'll be back again and again.'

'Why is he picking on us?' cried Gianni. 'It's so unfair. What does he have against our circus?'

Leeming put a consoling hand on his shoulder. 'That's the first question I'll ask when we arrest him.'

Courtney and Son Ltd had an office in central London that handled the distribution of their products in the south of England as well as the company's exports. As the man who ran the office, Bernard Courtney felt able to come and go as he pleased, leaving the bulk of the work to his clerks. When he finally arrived that morning, he gave a nonchalant wave to his minions then stepped into his office.

Someone was waiting for him. The visitor got to his feet.

'Mr Courtney?'

'That's right.'

'I'm Detective Constable Hinton from Scotland Yard. I need to ask you some questions regarding Miss Lydia Quayle.'

'Oh, I see. Ask what you wish.'

There was no hint in his voice that he'd done anything wrong. The description given of him by the hotel manager had prepared the detective to meet a good-looking man but he hadn't expected him to exude so much charm. Courtney was relaxed, amiable and engaging. At his invitation, Hinton sat down and Courtney followed suit. His manner was familiar, as if he were sitting in his club with an old friend.

'Now then, what seems to be the trouble?'

'You have been following the lady,' said Hinton.

'Yes, I have – now and then.'

'You also stole a dress of hers from a hotel.'

'I must correct you,' said Courtney, smiling. 'I didn't *steal* it, I merely borrowed it. I returned it undamaged.'

'Unfortunately, the lady herself was not undamaged. You caused her a lot of discomfort and anguish.'

'That certainly wasn't my intention.'

'Then what was, may I ask?'

Courtney grinned. 'I was simply having some fun.'

'That's not a credible defence, sir.'

'Well, it's the only one you're going to get,' said Courtney, tone hardening. 'Why are the police involved? This is a matter between me and Lucas's sister. We were at school together, you know, Lucas Quayle and I. For some reason, he never liked me. It might have been because I teased him a lot. Anyway, when I realised that he had such a pretty sister who lived in

London, I went in search of her when I was transferred here.'

'Then you began your campaign against her.'

'Don't make me sound so hostile. I'm quite the opposite, I promise you. I adore the woman. Any red-blooded man would. Lydia Quayle is a—'

'That's enough,' said Hinton, interrupting him and rising to his feet. 'I'm afraid that I must ask you to accompany me, sir.'

Courtney was astonished. 'Whatever for?'

'I'm placing you under arrest.'

'But I've done nothing wrong.'

'Stealing someone's property is a crime.'

'I meant no harm. Be reasonable, man. Haven't *you* ever taken an interest in a young woman and wanted to know more about her? It's what we chaps do. There's a primal urge inside us that takes over.'

'Then there's the small matter of registering at a hotel in a false name.'

'Well, I didn't want to give myself away, did I? Besides, I've always had a soft spot for Daniel Vance. He founded my old school, you see, and we had a tradition associated with him. The name brings back vivid memories.'

'We must go, Mr Courtney.'

'This is absurd,' protested the other, getting up. 'Do you know who I am? Do you know how important a position I hold? I'm not having some petty officer of the law pestering me like this. Be warned. I'll be speaking to your superior about this unwanted intrusion into my private life.' He waved an arm. 'Now get out!'

'You're coming with me, sir.'

'You have no grounds for an arrest.'

'I've already mentioned two.'

'Damn and blast you, man! Stop treating me as a criminal.'

'That's exactly what you are, sir.'

'I'll have you dismissed for this.'

'It all began – to use your own words – with an unwanted intrusion into a private life. Then it developed into persecution. You are no longer at school, sir. Your days of playing tricks on people are over.'

Courtney eyed him sullenly, like a child that has just had a favourite toy taken away from him. He pointed an accusatory finger.

'Who put you up to this?'

'Don't make this difficult for yourself.'

'It was Lucas Quayle, wasn't it? He was always a spoilsport.'

'Superintendent Tallis sent me. On the basis of information received, he authorised your immediate arrest.'

Courtney pouted and folded his arms. 'Well, I refuse to go with you.'

'Then I suggest that you look out of the window. Because you seem to be interested in nobody but yourself, you obviously haven't noticed the two uniformed policemen standing outside. They are here to help me if you resist arrest.'

'Look, I told you – it was all in fun.'

'Out we go, sir,' said Hinton, taking a firm grip on his arm. 'It's *our* turn to have some fun now.'

Colbeck's breakfast that morning consisted of sips of coffee and a great deal of writing. With sheets of paper in front of him, he jotted down the salient points about the man who was still at large. He had some connection with the NCR and was sturdy enough to move a couple of sleepers. Because he launched some of his attacks during the day, he must have a job that allowed him freedom of movement. Every time he struck, he caught the circus unawares. He knew exactly the right moment to release the lion into the ring. When they thought he'd given up, he'd returned the previous night in a bid to release the horses. Unless he was caught, he would continue to plague the circus. He was involved in a mission that he'd never abandon.

Every so often Colbeck reached out to drink some of his coffee. The rest of the meal was ignored. He still couldn't decide if the man was acting alone or if he had a confederate. On balance, he felt, they were dealing with one man, an individual with a manic fixation that nobody else could share. When Leeming finally joined him, Colbeck had pages of notes. The sergeant sat down heavily and reached for the menu.

'I'm sorry I'm so late, sir,' he said. 'I had very little sleep.'

'I'm afraid that you'll have very little breakfast as well, Victor. We're leaving at once.'

'Where are we going?'

'We're taking the train to Carlisle.'

'But I'm starving, sir.'

'Making an arrest is more important than your hunger pangs,' said Colbeck, getting up. 'You'll have plenty of time to eat later on.'

Leeming dragged himself to his feet. 'What's happened?'

'I've just realised that we've made a serious mistake.'

'Oh?'

'I'll tell you about it on the way.'

They returned to their rooms to collect their hats then left the hotel and walked the short distance to the station. Only when they were ensconced in an empty compartment did Leeming get an explanation.

'Do you remember the time we spent in Derby?' asked Colbeck.

'Yes,' said the other, disconsolately, 'I was allowed to eat my breakfast without interruption there.'

'We were looking at the case from the wrong angle. It was only when I helped to operate the turntable in the railway works that I saw there was another way of interpreting the facts. It's the same here.'

'I don't think so. Someone is bent on destroying the circus. There's only one way of interpreting that fact.'

'I disagree. He may have derailed the train but he made sure that the damage was limited. That was not simply because he had a kind heart, it was because he didn't want to harm the animals.'

'As a result of the accident, one of the horses had to be shot.'

'It was not part of his plan,' said Colbeck, 'and would have upset him. Look at the next incident. When he stampeded the horses in that copse, he wasn't trying to hurt them. His aim was to liberate them. He hates the idea of keeping animals in captivity when they should be roaming free.'

'Is that why he let the lion out of the cage – to roam free?'

'He was making a statement, Victor. He meant to frighten rather than to cause harm. He knew quite well that all the lions were hand-reared in captivity and trained to roar whenever they came into the ring. The one he released was unlikely to leap into the audience to maul a spectator.'

'I don't know about that, sir. Otto, the lion tamer, said his animals can be unpredictable sometimes.'

'What happened last night?'

'The bearded man came back. Gianni scared him away with his shotgun.'

'But where was he? According to the note you slipped under my door, he wanted to set the horses loose.'

'That's right, sir.'

'It fits the pattern,' insisted Colbeck. 'A man who resents the way that animals are caged, controlled and made to do tricks for the amusement of a baying crowd will have the urge to liberate them.'

'What he's doing is illegal and dangerous,' argued Leeming.

'He doesn't see it that way, Victor.'

'Who is he?'

'He's a man who knows this railway extremely well.'

'How are we going to find him?'

'Let's get to Carlisle first.'

Hinton had called at the house to describe what had happened. The two women were delighted to hear of the arrest. Lydia almost swooned with relief.

'How did Mr Courtney react?' asked Madeleine.

'It's odd,' said Hinton. 'He refuses to believe he did anything wrong.'

'That's wilful self-deception.'

'He seems to think that he's above the law.'

'What will happen to him?'

'He's going to have a very nasty shock when he appears in court. His time behind bars will be an ordeal for someone who's always been so carefree. From dawn to dusk, he'll be told what to do. He'll get only the most basic food. Prison is no place for a gentleman.'

'It's the ideal place for this one,' said Madeleine.

'I'm starting to feel sorry for him,' admitted Lydia.

'How can you say that?'

'I know how his father will react. He'll say that his son has brought shame on the whole family. He might even disown him.'

'It would be no more than he deserves,' said Hinton. 'He tortured you, Miss Quayle. He knew that he was upsetting you and took pleasure from doing so.'

Lydia nodded and expressed her thanks to him. While the news had come as a profound relief, her joy was fringed with disappointment. Since Courtney had been arrested, there was no chance of her seeing Hinton again and she was very sorry to part with him. Watching the two of them exchange glances, Madeleine felt that he was equally sad to be parting company with Lydia. He'd obviously enjoyed coming to the rescue of such an appealing young woman. Lydia had put her trust in the detective and he'd removed a threat from her life. Her smile was filled with gratitude. There was an awkward moment when she was tempted to embrace him and he wanted to offer his hand. In the event, neither of them had the confidence to make a move. But the seeds of a friendship had been sown. For a while, they were unaware that Madeleine was standing beside them. Their sole interest was in the other person.

'I must go,' he said at length.

'Thank you, Constable.'

'I was glad to be of help.'

'You've been my salvation,' said Lydia.

'It was my pleasure, Miss Quayle.'

He did offer his hand this time and she was quick to grasp it.

The stationmaster in Carlisle not only gave them the name they wanted, he told them exactly how to reach the man. The parish church of St Barnabas stood in the very heart of the city. It was a small, compact structure with a history that stretched back to medieval times. The vicarage was less than thirty yards away, a fairly modest house with a thatched roof and a garden at the rear. When the cab dropped them outside the building, Colbeck decided that there was no need to place Leeming at the rear to cut off any attempt at escape. This would be a very different arrest. He used the heavy knocker on the door and a servant came to open it. They were admitted into the hall and waited while she went to find the vicar. There was a pervasive smell of damp and they could see signs of neglect. Wallpaper was stained in places and a piece of the skirting board had come adrift.

When the maid returned, she conducted them to the study. Leeming had his first look at the Reverend Neville Anderson but Colbeck realised he'd met him before. Anderson was the bearded man with whom he'd once shared a compartment on a journey to Hexham. Unlike the vicar he'd met in Shropshire, thought Colbeck, this one was tall, imposing and altogether more robust. There was another difference between the two men. Anderson's right hand was bandaged. It explained why he'd been wearing gloves on the train.

After the detectives had introduced themselves, he congratulated them.

'How did you find me?'

'I was told that the NCR had a chaplain,' said Colbeck, 'with the privilege of free travel on the line. As you went to and fro, you'd have seen exactly where sleepers were stored. And over the years, you'd have developed friendships with people who worked for the company. It wouldn't have been difficult for you to discover when one of the circus trains was due to leave. Also, of course, you'd have control over your time. The only day when you're tied down is on a Sunday.'

'I'd never have believed a vicar was guilty,' said Leeming, staring at him.

'The real guilt lies with the circus,' declared Anderson.

'You're supposed to believe in peace and good fellowship.'

'That was a crucial factor in my thinking,' said Colbeck. 'As a Christian, you were mindful of the commandment Thou shalt not kill. If you'd really wanted to demolish the circus altogether, there were several points along the line where that could easily have been achieved – coming over a bridge, for instance, or running alongside a lake. Derailment there would have killed or wounded dozens of people. But you chose a location where,

312

you clearly hoped, nobody would die and no major destruction would take place.'

'There was a death,' said Leeming. 'A horse had to be put down.'

'I saw the report in the newspaper,' said Anderson, 'and it grieved me. The last thing I'd want to do is to harm an animal. My aim was to set them free.'

'That's what the inspector believed.'

'Lions are reputedly the kings of the jungle. They shouldn't be kept in cages and treated like slaves. That elephant belongs in India, running with a herd, not reduced to being a mere source of merriment for children. The way that animals are exploited in a circus is revolting. There ought to be a law against it.'

'There *is* a law against the sorts of things you've been doing,' said Colbeck.

'Someone has to stand up for the animals.'

'Oh, I think there's more to it than that. You've let your feelings get the better of you. It may have started as a protest but it became a mania you couldn't control. What would your bishop say if he knew of your ungodly behaviour? And what of the flock who look up to you? They'll be horrified.'

Anderson was rocked. The full meaning of what he'd been doing seemed to dawn on him at last. He finally realised that there would be dire consequences to face. Lost in thought, he plucked absent-mindedly at his beard. Then he looked at his visitors in turn before dredging up a painful memory.

'Do either of you gentlemen have children?'

'I have two boys,' replied Leeming.

'And I have a baby daughter,' said Colbeck. 'You've been keeping me from her, Mr Anderson. That was very inconsiderate of you.'

The vicar spoke quietly. 'I used to have three children – two girls and a boy,' he said. 'One of the girls died in childbirth and another was stricken with pneumonia. That left Harry. All our hopes were vested in him.'

'We can understand that, sir.'

'Did he want to follow his father into the church?' asked Leeming.

'No,' said the vicar, bitterly, 'he rejected everything that I represented. Harry dared to mock Christianity. I tried to beat it out of him but that only made him worse. Last year, he defied me. When the circus came here, he begged me to take him along to a performance because all his friends were going. I refused on principle. I didn't want my son defiled. And what did Harry do? He went behind my back.'

'I'd have done the same in his position,' muttered Leeming.

'My son preferred that low, disgusting, vulgar entertainment to what the Church had to offer. He betrayed me, Inspector. That was unforgivable. To punish him for his defiance, I gave him the thrashing of a lifetime. It was my duty.' He looked at them pleadingly. 'You must see that. A father is entitled to obedience.' He gave a shrug. 'The next day, he was gone and he never came back. From that day to this, I haven't set eyes on Harry – nor have I wished it. He's no longer my son.'

'How did Mrs Anderson feel about that?' asked Colbeck.

'It was too much for her to bear,' confessed the other. 'My wife was very frail. Losing two children had already depressed her. When we lost Harry as well, she had no will to live. You'll find her grave in the churchyard.'

Leeming was moved. 'So you lost your entire family.'

'Yes, I did.'

'We sympathise with you,' said Colbeck, 'and can imagine how you felt when your son ran away. But that didn't license you to wage war on Moscardi's circus.'

'I had to strike back somehow,' snarled Anderson, striking a pose. 'You must accept that. Sin should not go unpunished. It all started when my son sneaked off to that circus. It led him astray. It gave him cheap and meaningless thrills that could never compare with the inspiration of the Scriptures. Offered the sacred, Harry chose the profane. That's why the very sight of a circus is enough to set me on fire.'

'I can imagine how you felt when Mr Moscardi came to Carlisle.'

'It was intolerable. I had to listen to everyone telling me what a wonderful time they'd had in that marquee. Well,' said Anderson, 'it wasn't quite so wonderful the afternoon that I forced myself to see it. Horses were sent in endless circles and controlled with the crack of a whip. The elephant was turned into a pathetic clown and the lions were bullied into doing tricks that robbed them of all nobility. All God's creatures should be respected and not turned into machines for making money. It was painful to watch. And it was for *this*,' he concluded, 'that my son spurned his religion and disowned his family.'

'If you hated the circus so much,' said Colbeck, 'why not walk out?'

'I couldn't – I was fuelling my desire for revenge.'

Head on his chest, Anderson fell silent. Leeming was already fingering his handcuffs but Colbeck signalled to him to do nothing. They waited for several minutes before the vicar was ready to speak again. He was subdued.

'You were right to stop me, Inspector.'

'It was clear that you couldn't stop yourself,' said Colbeck.

'That's true, alas. I was helpless. Every child I saw going to that circus was my own. I could bear it no longer. The circus deprived me of my son and killed my dear wife. Surely I was entitled to register a protest.' He glanced towards the door. 'May I get a few things together before we leave, please?'

'Yes, of course.'

When the vicar left the room, Leeming tried to go after him.

'Stay here, Victor. He's not going to run away. He's grateful that we came,' said Colbeck. 'We've saved him from this dark obsession of his.'

'I don't trust him, sir. I think he might do something stupid.'

'He's a man of the cloth.'

'That hasn't stopped him creating merry hell.'

'Mr Anderson is a soul in torment, Victor. Bear with him.'

They didn't have long to wait. When the vicar reappeared, his mood had changed and he was now openly aggressive. Carrying a rifle, he pointed it at each man in turn then motioned for them to stand against the far wall. They shrank back cautiously and waited for a chance to wrestle the weapon off him. But there was no time for that to happen. Moving quickly in front of the large crucifix that stood on the mantelpiece, Anderson put the barrel of the rifle in his mouth and pulled the trigger.

Edward Tallis congratulated his detectives on their success in solving a murder and identifying the man who'd carried out such a persistent campaign against the circus. After all his years in the army, very few things shocked him but the report of the suicide disturbed him at a deep level.

'A vicar takes his own life?' he gasped. 'It's unimaginable. A man who's devoted his life to his parishioners has made it impossible for his remains to be buried in consecrated ground. Suicide is anathema to the Church of England. He'll lie in an unmarked grave.'

'He may prefer it that way, sir,' suggested Colbeck.

'It's against all tenets of Christianity.'

'And yet it happens again and again,' said Leeming, artlessly.

'There's a lot of killing in the Bible, sir. People led such terrible lives in those days that there must have been a lot of suicides as well.'

'We can do without the benefit of your opinion on the Good Book.'

'I'm sorry, sir.'

'Some will doubtless say that his death will save us the trouble of putting him on trial,' said Tallis, 'but I'm consumed with sympathy for the man. He must have been in such turmoil.'

'It's over now, sir,' said Colbeck.

They were in Tallis's office, delivering their report. There had been occasions when the superintendent was so pleased with their work that he'd produced his box of cigars by way of celebration. This was not one of them. Tallis was far too sombre.

'I'm glad to have you back where you belong,' he said, crisply. 'London is still overrun by criminal activity. You can help me to stem it again.'

'Yes, sir,' said Colbeck, 'we will. But, first of all, let me thank you for taking a personal interest in the case of Miss Quayle.'

'The matter has been resolved. Mr Bernard Courtney is in custody. He lived in a fantasy world. I had the pleasure of introducing him to the realm of reality.'

'In doing that, sir, you probably saved other young ladies from suffering the same fate at his hands.'

'I never saw you as a beacon of hope for oppressed women, sir,' said Leeming with a grin. 'It's a new side to your character.'

'I'm an upholder of the law, Sergeant,' boomed Tallis. 'I make no distinction between the genders of the victims. Well,' he added, regarding each in turn, 'you've been sorely missed here. I console myself with the thought that you've solved some terrible crimes while you've been in Northumberland. What is your abiding memory of your time away?'

'Mine was discovering a woman with a passionate interest in railways,' said Colbeck, sadly. 'I'm sorry that I didn't have the opportunity to meet her.'

Tallis arched an eyebrow. 'Leeming?'

'That's easy, sir,' said the other, taking something from his pocket and holding it up. 'These are free tickets for Moscardi's Magnificent Circus whenever it gets close enough for me to take my family along. After all the efforts I made on their behalf, I think I'm entitled to see them in action.'

'There is something else that must be recorded,' said Colbeck, 'and that's the role of Brendan Mulryne. Since he worked for the circus, he was well placed to give us invaluable help.' Tallis scowled. 'I know that you had your differences with him, sir, but he proved himself to be an able detective.'

'That's right,' said Leeming. 'And, by the way, he sends his regards to you.'

Tallis's eyes began to blaze with fury. It was time to leave.